AF265780

ONE NIGHT ONLY

Shelby Knudsen

Copyright © 2024 by SHELBY KNUDSEN ALL RIGHTS RESERVED.

No part of this publication may be reproduced, stored in a retrieval system, or transmitted, in any form or by any means, without prior written permission of the publisher, except by a reviewer who may quote brief passages in a review to be printed in a newspaper or magazine or broadcast on radio or television.

One Night Only is fiction. The characters and events that take place in this story were conjured up in the author's imagination, however, the locations, musical venues, and most of the artists mentioned are real. If your name appears in this book it is because the author respects and admires your music.

ISBN – 978-1-0688505-2-3

ISBN EPUB – 978-1-0688505-3-0

www.shelbyknudsenauthor.com

Published by: East Shore Books

P.O. Box 2284

Fernie, B.C.

@EastShoreBooks

Cover Design by Shelby Knudsen

Cover Photo – iStock – Order # 2097811829

Back Cover Photo – Christopher Edmonstone

ONE NIGHT ONLY
Shelby Knudsen

EAST SHORE BOOKS

FERNIE, BRITISH COLUMBIA, CANADA

A note for the reader:

The chapter titles in *One Night Only* are song titles. There is a complete playlist, including artists, at the back of the novel. Each song had a lyric or a vibe that resonated for me with what was going on in the chapter. This music has kept me company on the long days, inspiring both my life and my writing, as all art inspires more art. Thanks to all the artists who wrote, produced, and sang these songs.

Rock on,

Shelby

"I know, as an audience member, there's a certain thing that's going on for me during this ritual, anticipation, yes, but the instrument, the instrument being prepared, being perfected, being tuned, put into alignment, or allegiance and/or harmony with some kind of higher order in the world, a better order, somehow, with the wavelengths of all that is and all that can be good in the world… then, and this is my little brainstorm, so please forgive… in the build up of tension which has arisen during the tuning, then, in the guitar being donned, being "put on," between that and that first chord, the beginning of that first song, which is flight, which represents possibility and transcendence, in that gap, in that silence, oh I don't know Shelby, there is a kind of magic, the emergence of the possibilities which exist between instrument, player, and the audience member."

Mark Kusnir, when providing feedback for this novel.

For Mark

1. Find the Cost of Freedom

Sky stands beneath the rusting marquee of Vancouver's Imperial Theatre, staring up at the thick block letters that spell out SKY BLACK: ONE NIGHT ONLY. A heavy ache spreads across her chest.

The sun has come out after hours of dark March drizzle and steam rises from the drying sidewalk. The stench of soggy cigarette butts and stale beer floats heavy in the air. She left her apartment in a rush and her tangled hair is stuffed in the collar of her jacket, clinging to her neck like it might choke her. She rests her guitar case gingerly on the dirty street, gathering the long black strands with her fingers and flicking them loose. They fall heavy against her leather-clad back with a satisfying slap. She continues to squint at the sight of the hundred-year-old building wearing her name.

ONE NIGHT ONLY.

Sliding the phone from her back pocket, Sky enters her password. Her contract with the Imperial dictates she post at least three notifications about the gig. Most of the venues she plays have this clause, and she signs on the line but often doesn't fulfill the obligation. Tonight is different, so she holds her arm steady above her head, points her phone at the sign, and snaps a few shots, her brain working on autopilot, authoring a caption that lands somewhere between desperate and arrogant. A shout-out to the venue and a thank-you to her sister, Jani, who organised the whole thing. She'll add exclamation points, playing along and asking people to come to the show like she promised Jani she would, because she can't deny it'll all be worth it when she steps on stage. When she's in a groove and connecting with the crowd she's as close to heaven as she'll ever be. She exhales and smiles to herself, feeling a wave of anticipation dance across her skin. Her screen lights up with an onslaught of comments she was tagged in after her show last night, a small gig at a high-end bar she plays every Wednesday. She knows she shouldn't, but she scrolls through the posts, sliding past the compliments about her sound and her looks, pausing to study the creative ways people find to insult her.

Jake Small @RodeoKing: "Went to see @SkyBlack tonight with @WallHung. She sung the shit out of the place, but she's a bit too hippie for my taste. You think she shaves her pits?"

Jennifer Walters @Jennyfromhere: "@SkyBlack was playing @TENT in Yaletown tonight. She's good, but I think she knows it, you know? It was annoying. Like, she was way too IN to herself."

Wilma Knot @WilmasRoad: "@SkyBlack sucks. Couldn't find parking anywhere near the venue and we had to line up EVEN THOUGH we had a RESERVATION. Raining, of course. I had to sit the whole night in wet jeans."

Sky hears footsteps and looks up from the screen, then quickly steps aside as three teens wearing layers of torn denim and glossy faux-leather almost run her over. They look from her face to the guitar case she's placed at her feet and whisper to each other. A boy with reflective sunglasses and stripes shaved into the sides of his head stops.

"Hey, are you…," he glances at the sign over her head, "Sky Black?"

"Uh…yeah. That's me." Damn.

"Cool, can we take a picture with you?" His friends – girls with shiny teeth and too much makeup – erupt into giggles.

"Sure. Why not?"

Sky forces a smile as they gather around her, leaning in too close with their thick perfume and unfamiliar bodies touching hers. Their arms slide around her back, snagging pieces of her hair. She picks up her guitar and holds it firmly in front of her so she won't have to put her hands on them.

"What are you guys up to today?" Sky asks. She doesn't care, but she has to say something. The boy who requested the picture ignores her question, too busy setting the filters on his phone. The girls are fussing with their hair and Sky's not sure they even heard her and the whole thing is so uncomfortable she can't wait for it to be over. The boy leans in closer, juts out his chin, and raises his phone in front of their foursome.

"Ready? Look hot, you guys. I'm posting this on all my feeds."

Sky looks straight at the screen and curls the corners of her mouth into what is technically a smile, although her eyes are lifeless staring back at her. The girls twist and contort their bodies, asses and chests forced out at choreographed angles. No one dares to say cheese, at the risk of ruining perfectly pouted lips. Seconds stretch in a hollow silence. The boy studies the image, adjusts the angle, and finally presses the button.

Sky has learned not to bother asking more than simple, uninteresting questions in these types of interactions. Inquiring about where people are from or if they like her music, or any music, is pointless. Just smile and be present, because the posts bring bodies to her shows and win her followers, a currency almost as valuable as talent these days.

"Oh my God it's so cute! What's your handle? I'll tag you."

He keeps his head down, not looking at her, lost in the precious world he's clutching in his hands.

"Oh, thanks. It's just @SkyBlack."

"Cool. Bye!"

He still hasn't looked up. They all have their phones out now and the girls say nothing as they retreat down the sidewalk behind him, heads down, typing. Sky hears a loud rumble and spit. A bus accelerates as it approaches the intersection that the kids are about to stroll right through. She yells at their slouched backs.

"Hey! Watch out!"

A wild squealing of brakes and girls merges with honks from the bus and another car behind. The kids jump back to the safety of the sidewalk and huddle together, then turn to yell back at her.

"Holy shit! Thank you!"

"You're our hero!"

Sky smiles and gives a small wave. She feels heat rise in her cheeks when she notices people on the sidewalk have stopped to stare.

She picks up her guitar case and walks away from the sign. The pictures she took still live privately in her phone. The words ONE NIGHT ONLY feel ominous, like a threat, and if she had an empty bottle she'd heave it through the air and revel in the shattering explosion and deluge of broken glass.

The artist's entrance is around back and it's time for Sky to sound check. Jani and her husband, Dave, and even some of her old friends from home are coming to the show, driving the eight hours from Nelson. People she hasn't seen or talked to in years. She considers what she'll say when they ask why she's retiring. Jani and Dave know, but not the others. Why now, after she's devoted her entire life to music? She'll lie, tell them she's tired of the grind for no money and the toxic business music has become. The truth is Sky loves to perform. She'd die to keep playing.

2. Brother

There's an alley behind the Imperial where a scratched-up metal door is used by musicians to load in their gear. It's off East Hastings Street, a part of the city Sky knows well. She lives in a rundown apartment building a few blocks away, despite her sister's misgivings. It's not a great area of the city to call home and Jani hounds her about moving almost every time they talk, but it's affordable and walking distance to most of her regular gigs. The alley is a sanctuary for the destitute and addicted, and today several people are scattered along the narrow space, their places marked by tattered blankets and soggy pieces of cardboard. Sky chooses a careful path, lifting her guitar case high so she doesn't accidentally bump anyone. The acrid smell of urine is so strong she can taste it on her tongue. A teenage boy looks up from his four feet of claimed ground and catches her eye. He's relatively clean and seems out of place wearing a black rain jacket from a high-end brand, the zipper gaping open to reveal a Blind Melon T-shirt. Lanky like an athlete, his legs stretch out in front of him. He has the shaggy remnants of a good haircut and possibly a home and parents who still give a shit.

Sky hesitates, then turns away before the kid can ask her for money.

"You playin' tonight?" he asks, his voice soft.

Too late.

"Yeah. Big night." She pauses, considers rifling through her bag for some cash, but it's a disaster, jammed with makeup and a wardrobe change and random pieces of paper scrawled with lyrics. To find her wallet in that mess she'd have to put both the bag and her guitar case down in the filth. She looks the kid in the eye, something she rarely does with strangers, unless it's from the stage. He speaks before she can find the words that will let her walk away.

"Cool. I play guitar, too. Music is the source. There's nothing without it. Truly."

Sky almost laughs. This boy's too young to be so wise. She tries to ignore the strong urge to help him, to give him some money for a warm meal. The longer she studies his face, the more she suspects that cash will end up in his dealer's pocket within the hour.

"Where'd you hear that?"

"Kurt Cobain." He raises his chin as he speaks the name. A sign of respect for his fallen idol. This kid is a piece of work. She can't resist engaging him.

"Sometimes music's not enough, though. Sometimes you have to wake the fuck up and move on."

"Kurt didn't think so."

"No. I guess not."

Sky's feet stick to the soggy ground. This kid. This conversation. There's a buzz in her head as he looks up at her, challenges her while spouting rock-and-roll prophecy. He reminds Sky of herself at that age, when she believed in the dream. Write the perfect song at the perfect time and let the fame machine do the rest. Sky flashes back to her youth, on the road with her old band. They were young and wild and had no responsibilities, other than to get into the van and roll on to the next city and the next stage. It was the best time of her life, before it went so wrong, and maybe he's right, and music is the thing, the why that makes all the struggling worth it.

The promises Sky made at AA storm her consciousness. She can see the passage from *The Big Book,* AA's version of the Bible, word for word:

"I am responsible. When anyone, anywhere, reaches out for help, I want the hand of AA always to be there. And for that: I am responsible."

Someone helped her, once. She was a disaster, but she got clean and promised that if she was ever in the same situation, she would help, too. This kid is reaching, and if Sky doesn't do something to help him then she's a broken cog in the machine. A machine that saved her from herself. It's her turn and she knows if she turns her back on this kid, she could be this kid again.

"Look, sorry buddy, but I gotta go; I'm already late for sound check." She says the words but doesn't move, takes a deep breath, and looks around her. Junkie quicksand. This boy could sink below the surface so easily. Sky reminds herself: she does have something to offer. Tonight, she has centre stage. She's on the sign out front, and when you're the headliner it's expected that you have *people.*

"You wanna come with me backstage and hit the green room? It should be stocked by now. Come grab something to eat."

She hears the words come out of her mouth and can't believe she actually said them. The boy jumps to his feet.

Wobbles slightly. His collar bones protrude sharply from the exposed skin at the base of his neck. His checkered sneakers squish when he stands. He looks down at his rumpled clothing and attempts to smooth his jeans with rough strokes of his hands, then lifts his arms and gives himself a quick whiff. Defeat drags his shoulders down.

"I'd love to, but I smell like garbage. I don't want to embarrass you. Thanks, though, for the offer. For real." He bends over to sit back down on the dirty street.

Sky considers what he said. She's not sure what the manager will think of her bringing in this kid as her entourage, but she can't leave him here in the alley. Fuck it. They can't exactly fire her.

"Don't worry about it. There's a shower in there. You can get cleaned up. I'm sure I can find you a fresh T-shirt. What's your name?"

The boy's face breaks into a huge smile. His still-white teeth beam.

"I'm Sam." He reaches out his hand.

The filth of this place makes Sky hesitate for a second, but the boy's hand looks clean enough, and who the hell is she to judge anyone. She extends her own and they shake firmly.

"Hey, Sam. I'm Sky. Come on, we're late." She starts to walk and Sam reaches out for her case.

"Can I carry your guitar for you?"

She doesn't like anyone touching her guitar. She's been hauling it around most of her life and feels awkward when she's not carrying it, like a vital appendage is missing. She especially hates it when men think carrying her guitar is some kind of chivalry, but she knows that's not what this is. She can see how much Sam wants to be a part of what's happening.

"Uh…sure. Thanks."

She reluctantly hands the black case to the kid and hikes the worn strap of her leather bag higher on her shoulder. They climb up the few steps to the Imperial's back door. A sign advises to Press the Button Hard and another says No Money on Premises. Sky jams her thumb onto the red button and hears a buzz echo throughout the building. After a few seconds the door opens and a weathered-looking man wearing a denim vest and a headset greets them.

"Hi, you must be Sky. I'm Wyatt. Stage manager. We're all set up on stage and sound is ready for you. Right this way." He glances at Sam but doesn't say anything.

They weave through large amps and discarded equipment. Sam follows directly behind Sky. She isn't sure why she's chosen this moment to scoop someone off the street, but maybe it's a small distraction from this night. Maybe she needs a wingman to shoulder some of the energy that's about to come at her, or maybe she's blatantly trying to piss off her sister, who pressured her into a *final show*. That option seems the most likely, and Sky smiles, imagining Jani's face when she asks who the hell Sam is. Totally worth it.

They walk behind Wyatt, down a dark hallway that smells of mouldy towels and leather, then pop out onto the back of the stage. Sky stops to look out into the empty theatre and Sam runs into the back of her.

"Shit. Sorry."

She doesn't respond, distracted by what's in front of her. There's a large open floor below the stage, able to accommodate a few hundred rowdy concert-goers. Without a band behind her it won't be that kind of show, and she wishes the space was full of chairs. Past the floor is a single step up to the bar area and a rail that runs the width of the building. Skinny tables and chairs fill this upper level. In the back left corner is the sound booth. Sky can see two men standing behind the large board of buttons and knobs, watching her. She gives her head a small shake and clears her throat. It's coated in acid and burns right up to the back of her tongue.

"Hey, guys. I'm Sky. I'll be ready in a minute. This is Sam." Both men raise a single arm and give a thumbs-up. Sound-guy sign language.

The shiny black stage reaches out on both sides of her, spanning sixty feet across. Much larger than the stages Sky's used to playing. There's a single black stool placed in the middle, one step back from a microphone stand holding an SM58. When this is all over, she'll miss the feeling of thin metal mesh against her lips, of pre-show butterflies and the anticipation of what might happen. It's always unknown, no matter how good you are or how experienced. The crowd comes with an energy of their own. Sometimes you click and groove together. Sometimes you don't.

She puts her bag down and turns for her guitar, forgetting to ask Sam for it, but he seems to know. He lays the beat-up case on the stage, unbuckles the latches, and gently pulls the vintage Martin D-18 from its burgundy velvet bed. He looks up to Sky as he hands her the guitar, wearing the same expression he had in the alley. Eager and out of place. Sky grips the neck like it's a familiar hand reaching out to her.

"She's a beauty," Sam says.

Sky smiles, appreciating that Sam referred to the guitar as a her. Just like she does.

"Thanks. I've had her for a long time. She was my dad's. Can you hand me the strap from the compartment?"

Sam lifts the small flap in the case and retrieves the coiled leather strap, hesitating before handing it to her. Sky takes it and attaches both ends to the buttons on her guitar, slinging the instrument over her head, and adjusting it on her body until it fits like skin. She begins to tune it, plucking each string while turning the metal peg it's twisted around to adjust the tension until each note rings true. A routine she's performed countless times, like sharpening a sword before battle.

The strap was custom made for her by a musician she used to play with. Honey brown leather with dark stitches meticulously sewn by hand. Over the years it's become worn and soft, like a cat's ear. The letters engraved on it were burned into the supple hide with a torch while Sky got high with a spastic drummer who was cooking something on a spoon. She woke up in the backseat of a car with the drummer and the strap and another blacked-out night she's grateful she can't remember. Only This, it reads.

The plucking of strings transports her back to the stage. Her skin is clammy and her hands tremble from the memory of whatever she'd been fixing that night. It sneaks up on her like that. She feels like she's good, like she's got a handle on it, and then she looks at a fucking guitar strap and her body starts craving.

She finishes with the low E string, then looks up to see Sam watching her. Excitement colours his face. He's so young. Even with his blond hair sticking up at weird angles and dirt darkening one cheek, he has a boyish charm the girls his age would find adorable. His eyes are a translucent green and framed with impossibly long black lashes. Sky doesn't know where this urge to help him is coming from. She turned thirty this year and until this moment she's never had a motherly bone in her body. Her sister can attest to that. She looks after herself, a task that's proven more than she can handle at times. Now here's this kid, crouched at her feet, looking to her for instruction or maybe inspiration and she has no idea what the fuck she's doing.

Her fingers move unconsciously on the taught metal strings and she strums a G chord. The instrument rings perfectly. She steps to the mic stand, taking the guitar cable that's dangling from the adjustment knob and plugging it into the hole at the bottom of her guitar. It's connected to a tuning pedal at her feet and the screen lights up with red letters. Sky stomps the pad on the pedal, un-muting her guitar and sending the signal through a DI box and out to the sound board where the techs are waiting. She calls out to the back of the room.

"All set!"

Even with the PA still cold, her gravelly voice booms through the empty theatre, off the walls and the ceiling. One of the sound guys starts bringing the system to life; the other comes up closer to her so they can communicate more clearly. He holds an iPad in his hand where he can make all the monitor adjustments. Sky starts to play her guitar in a steady rhythm, letting the guys go to work. They make tweaks to the levels and the sound starts to even out. She waits until the one with the iPad looks to her for input.

"Can I have more guitar in the centre monitor, and I'm getting some buzz on the right."

Sky glances over and finds Sam side stage. She recognizes the look on his face. The appreciation of being present as it all comes together, and wishing it were him up there.

She's been doing a version of this dance for fifteen years. First in a horrible punk band with some high school friends who had a little talent and a lot of desire to make noise. They wore chains dangling from their pockets and black eyeliner thick under their eyes and smeared across their lips. They were soon banned from every music venue in Nelson. A reinvention was necessary. Sky and her two best friends – Joe on guitar and Marley on drums – moved on to alternative rock, leaving the others behind. They played for ten years together and were aptly named: Broken Yellow Line. Continuously on the road, touring and partying with no consideration for their families, their bodies, or the people they used and left in their wake. It was an absolute blast. In their fantasies, fame was waiting just around the corner. They spent most of their earnings on drugs and travel, but saved a little to make recordings, then sent them to every label or agent they could find an address for. Sky can barely stomach listening to those songs now. Mumbled words with no meaning, written and performed in a drug-induced haze. Now that she's sober, she feels the music deep inside. The connection with the audience, when it happens, races through her veins and tingles her skin, like something that came from a needle. She left the band when she stopped caring if she woke up in a stranger's bed, or if she woke up at all. She left because she broke Joe's heart, betraying him callously when he might've been the only person who understood her fucked-up mind. The only person who knew her damaged past and had enough patience to tolerate her icy heart. The only man who ever loved her.

"Okay, Sky, if you're happy with the guitar levels, try the vocal."

The mic turns hot and Sky gives them a series of "check mic," "hey hey," and when they give her what she needs in the monitors she starts a song. She didn't know what she was going to play until she started strumming. It's one she wrote a few weeks ago.

You said it would burn, but not like that

You said I'd be fine, but I never came back

Take my hand, I'll go where you lead

Light my cigarette and let the ink bleed

You're all that I need

You're all that I need

The vampires are coming, just let them feed

Her voice is full and pleading and it hurts like hell to push through the chorus, but she does it anyway, closing her eyes as an image of scorched earth fills her mind, black and crumbling. The burn rises up from inside. It rakes her throat raw, then leaches out on her haunting tone, saturating the empty theatre.

The guys in the sound booth put their heads together and mumble to each other. They give a thumbs-up and she stops abruptly. She needs to save every ounce of her voice for tonight. She thanks them and stomps the pedal to mute her guitar, then rests it on the stand behind her. The pain in her throat makes her nauseous and she has the urge to curl up in a ball, right there on the stage. She forces herself to keep moving.

"Let's find you some food and a shower, Sam."

"Holy shit! Sky! That was incredible! You're amazing! I can't believe I've never heard of you before."

Sky can't help but laugh at his honesty. Getting people to hear of you is the hardest part.

"Yeah, well this is my last show, so don't worry about it. You haven't missed anything." She picks up her bag, walks past him, and descends the steps. Down the hall she finds a piece of paper taped to a black door that says Artist: Sky Black. Sam scurries behind her, banging the empty guitar case against his legs.

"Your last show? No way! You're too talented. You could be huge!"

Sky laughs again. This kid sure is good for the ego.

The room is laid out with the items Sky put on her rider. A bucket of KFC. Six bottles of water, and a bag of Sour Patch Kids. She added the candy to see if she'd get it. Luckily, they also gave her a platter of cheese and meat, crackers, and some fruit.

"I have to head out to the lobby. Go for it, help yourself. I think the bathroom is in the back. Just save me a few waters and some chicken."

Sky leaves Sam alone. He's still holding her guitar case and staring at the food with his mouth slightly open. She walks out the door and turns right towards the front of house, feeling good about her decision to help him. Before she opens the door to the foyer, she can hear her little sister's excited voice. She pushes through and almost slams into the back of Jani's curly head.

"Hey, loser. Can you keep it down? I heard you from the back alley."

"Sky!"

Jani jumps at her, seizing Sky's body in a custom Jani hug. Considering how tiny Jani is, it's quite a feat. Sky lets her cling on for a few seconds, forcing herself not to hold Jani at arms length and scrutinize the lack of meat on her bones. Jani's doctor – an eating-disorder specialist – has warned Sky that commenting on her weight can be detrimental to her progress, so she tries not to mention it anymore, something she finds incredibly difficult.

"Okay, okay, Jani. Chill. You're making a scene."

She removes her sister's vice grip from around her back and pulls pieces of Jani's wild golden hair from her mouth. It's pinned up for the big event, but strands have already begun escaping, springing out in tight coils from Jani's scalp. She's wearing lip gloss and sparkly gold powder around her eyes, highlighting her pale skin and wash of dark freckles. The only distinctive feature that reveals the girls are sisters is their eyes, chocolate brown and oval shaped with thick, black lashes. Sky's looks reflect her heritage – her parents had Greek and Italian roots – so all three had olive skin and dark hair, but not Jani. Her bright looks and brighter personality have always reminded Sky of a woodland sprite, dropped in from some mystical place, oozing sunshine and the benefit of the doubt.

"Sky, I've been calling you. I'm not on your list, and this guy doesn't believe I'm your sister." The guy in the ticket booth looks uninterested in who Jani is, only relieved she's not his problem anymore.

"Sorry, I forgot to do the list thing," Sky says to him, as she shifts her focus to another woman standing by the door. Her long brown hair is laced with silver strands. Dozens of colourful string bracelets wrap around her wrists. Flowy red cloth enrobes her small body. Sky can't tear her eyes away. Her fingers flinch as she remembers gently outlining the tattoo of a hummingbird that hovers just beside the woman's throat. It's strange to see her in the real world. In Sky's mind she's a character from a childhood book she once adored. Standing on the stained lobby carpet, she looks tragically out of place. Sky's eyes meet hers in a look impossible to translate, layers of opposing emotions bleed into one another. Sky loves her and hates her, completely. The woman steps forward and opens her arms slightly, like she's hopeful Sky might rush in. Her lips are turned up in a sweet smile. Vomit rises in Sky's scorched throat.

"Mom. What the hell are you doing here?"

3. Blow at High Dough

Sam can't believe his luck. He stares at the spread of food in front of him, trying to remember the last time he ate. His mind digs up the foggy image of a homeless shelter volunteer handing him something – a sandwich, maybe? – but he was flying too high to see it clearly now and he can't remember if it was yesterday or the day before. Who cares? He laughs out loud, drops his coat on the couch and rubs his hands together, lowering his head and grooving from side to side. A patented victory dance he hasn't performed since the dramatic exit he made from high school. *Yeah, baby.* Just when he started to fear he might not land on his feet this time, along came salvation cloaked in black leather and carrying a guitar. Sam knew, from the moment he saw Sky Black, something good was about to happen.

He walks to the back of the room to use the washroom. After wetting down his unruly hair and washing his face, he rinses his mouth, then scrubs his hands for several minutes with the lemony soap and gloriously hot water. He stares at his reflection, thinking that he looks pretty good, all things considered. He has a bit of stubble building up. It makes him look older and tougher. He straightens his shoulders and puffs out his chest to accentuate the look, then gives his armpits another smell check, the result instantly deflating him. He stinks. The one thing Sam can't stand about his free-living situation is that he stinks. People react differently to you when you smell bad. It's embarrassing, and Sam hates it when people who get near him scrunch up their noses in disgust. He manages to keep himself clean-ish thanks to the few public washrooms that he has access to, but there's not much he can do about the smell. One night on the street is all it takes for a stench to set in and linger.

Sam's stomach roars with anticipation as he closes the door behind him and walks over to the food table. He selects a few crackers and slices of cheese, then moves the ones that remain to cover the gaps. His mom always hounded him not to impose on people. He might be free range at the moment, but he has his pride. He will always be polite. He's biting into the salty goodness when a rough knock at the door interrupts him.

"Come in!" he mumbles through the crumbs, spinning around while wiping his lips with the back of his hand. The door swings open and the guy wearing the denim vest leans in, bracing his large body against the door jamb.

"Hey, man. Sorry, I didn't catch your name."

"Sam. It's Sam." Too good to be true, Sam thinks as he looks back down at the tray of food and considers grabbing a handful of crackers before this guy punts his ass back to the alley.

"Sam. Cool. Everything okay in here? Can I get you two anything else? Sky didn't specify anything to drink besides water on the rider. I could grab you some beers?"

Sam almost gags on the ball of soggy cracker he's forgotten to keep chewing. He's tempted to say "Why, yes please, sir," and let the man bring him a six-pack, which might help take the edge off his growing need to use. But he doesn't want to be greedy, or push this fabulous run of luck any farther than he already has.

"Oh, no. Thanks. This all looks amazing. If you want to check with Sky, she just went to talk to somebody. She should be right back."

"Sure. Let me know if you need anything. Sky killed in sound check. Should be a great show."

"Yeah, I agree. She's insanely talented. Thanks."

The door closes and Sam is blissfully alone again. He carefully assembles another multi-layered cheese and cracker stack, then looks around the room, taking in the view like he's been allowed access to the Batcave, and the privilege could be revoked at any minute. A ratty orange couch is the centrepiece, flanked by the table of food and a smaller table strewn with music magazines. In the back next to the washroom is an empty metal coat rack on wheels, wedged into the corner. Sam picks up his coat and goes to hang it on the rack, studying the walls that are plastered with posters from shows of the past, the vintage ones framed and the newer ones pinned up with tacks. He scans the images, wishing he had been front row at every single show. He steps closer to the wall, drawn to the artists his mom loved. He remembers sitting in the back seat as the songs blasted from the car radio at top volume, his mom singing along. She was the one who inspired his love of music. She bought him his first guitar when he was only eight and always encouraged him to play, clapping along to his inconsistent strumming. She wouldn't believe where he is right now. Maybe he'll tell her all about it, one of these days.

He lifts the tattered corner of the Blue Rodeo poster. Jim Cuddy stares back at him, his transcendent coolness obvious. Bryan Adams. Spirit of the West. Sarah McLachlan. Ruby Waters. Beck. Jann Arden. Futurebirds. The New Pornographers. City and Colour. The Tragically Hip. Old and new, all plastered together like wallpaper. Sam lays his hand on

Gord Downie's face, hoping to absorb an ounce of his greatness.

He turns back to the room and considers which delicious morsel he will shove in his mouth next, when his gaze comes to rest on Sky's empty guitar case. She took her bag with her, but the case is there and Sam freezes, staring at it, considering what's stashed inside. He noticed a bottle of Advil and a small leather pouch earlier, when he lifted the compartment flap to retrieve her strap for her.

Was it actually Advil in that container? And what's in the pouch?

He's craving – which manifests a hateful voice in his head he calls Nag. A voice that never hides too deep and always responds to opportunity. Nag suggests he open the case and help himself. Even if there are no drugs, there might be some cash in that pouch.

No. NO.

He won't let Nag wreck this. That voice tries to destroy everything good, but he won't let it have this moment. This is sacred. Sam's still in control, and he's damn well gonna act like it.

Fuck off, Nag.

He picks a small bunch of grapes off the platter and lifts his chin, popping them into his mouth one by one, like a king. His teeth pierce the flesh and sweet juice explodes onto his tongue. He wishes someone he knows could see him. His buddies from school or his bitchy ex-girlfriend. His mom, who told him a few months ago he wasn't welcome in her house anymore. The truth is her dick-face husband Andy doesn't want Sam around. Andy's running things now, a point made clear to Sam when they were left alone. Then made crystal clear when Andy smashed Sam's beloved Telecaster, stomping the neck clean off, so Sam couldn't "pawn it for drug money." The sadistic bastard smiled as the maple cracked and splintered.

But Sam doesn't let that shit get him down and he sure the hell won't think about it right now. He's backstage before a show at the Imperial, popping grapes into his mouth. Living the goddamn dream. The smell of warm chicken wafting through the air is intoxicating, daring him to eat it. He reaches into the paper bucket and takes the smallest piece he can find. Merely a scrap, he tells himself in a plucky British accent – like Renton in *Trainspotting* – as he sucks the greasy meat clean off the bone. There's a garbage can behind the couch. Sam plants a shoe on the orange velour, then launches himself over the back, and while spinning in the air, expertly fires the tiny bone into the can. When he lands back on the ground, he holds his hands above his head, locking in the follow-through and celebrating the two points. Applause roars in his head. An hour ago he was hungry and cold in an alley. Now he's friends with a rock star and has his own personal gofer. Gordie starts to sing in Sam's mind and he resumes his dance, performing for the audience of legends on the wall who stood here, just like him, sucking out the marrow of life.

4. The Cave

Sky doesn't wait to hear her mom's explanation for what she's doing here. She hasn't seen her in years and now is not the time to start rehashing why. Without another word, Sky spins on her heel and walks back through the door and out of the lobby. Her ears ring with a high frequency that breaks in and out like lost radio waves. It's a condition called tinnitus and she's had it since her experimental punk days, when she thought ear protection wasn't cool. Now she pays the price for the arrogance of youth. Stress amplifies this problem and seeing her mom's face makes Sky's ears go off like they haven't in a while. The sound is unbearable, like horrid screeching from inside.

Her hands clench into fists as she enters the dressing room. Sam is sitting on the couch, feet crossed on the wooden table, beaming a giant smile like he's sharing a joke with someone. He jumps up when Sky walks in.

"Hey! I saved you all the chicken, except one tiny wing, but it barely had any meat on it. Are you okay?"

She can't respond, unable to speak above the piercing ring in her head, so she nods, then spots her guitar case beside the couch. She walks over, lays the case flat on the ground, and unlatches the buckles to retrieve her Advil from inside. Sky pictures the blackness again. Spreading. Blackness at the base of her tongue. She wants to reach inside her mouth and tear the poison free. She stares down at her hands, imagining bloody pulp on them. She needs help and there's no one here who can help her. She needs a fix. She should call her sponsor, Gary, to talk her down. She starts to wonder what the point of staying sober really is. The Advil taste bitter on her tongue and she turns for a water, then remembers Sam, watching her from the couch, and realizes she's too far inside her head. She wonders what Sam was smiling about, and wishes she could smile, too. Sky swallows the pills dry, willing herself to come back. To step through the screaming in her ears and the death in her throat. She looks at Sam.

"Sorry, what did you say?"

"Just wondered if you were okay. You don't look so good."

"I'm fine. Throat hurts a bit. Thanks. Shit, I forgot to get a shirt for you. Do you want to go out to the lobby and ask the guy in the ticket booth if he can find you something?"

Sam gets up, eager to do anything.

"Yes. If you're sure it's no trouble?"

"I'm sure. Hey, Sam, how old are you?"

"Uh…seventeen. Why? Is that okay?"

"Do you still talk to your parents?"

He seems taken aback by the question. His eyes widen like he got caught doing something wrong.

"No, not really. My dad lives in Calgary. Mom's remarried, and unfortunately the guy's a real asshole. I have a sweet baby sister, though. She's four. Her name's Poppy. I'm not exactly welcome at the house, anymore. I stop by every few days when my stepdad's at work to shower and get new clothes, but I can't sleep there. He went nuts on me a few months ago and purposely snapped my Telecaster: 1963, Ocean Turquoise."

"What a prick. Sorry to hear that."

"Yeah. I'm gonna get a new one as soon as I can. A better one." He pauses for a few seconds, seemingly imagining the new guitar in his mind.

"How about you? Do you talk to your parents?"

Sky's surprised by the flip of the question. She prickles at the intrusiveness, then realizes she asked the exact same one. What did she expect?

"Uh…no, although, strangely enough, my mom was out in the lobby, just now. She came with my little sister. I haven't seen her in – like – seven years, I think? It was a shock, to say the least. My dad's gone. He's dead."

"Shit. I'm sorry – about your dad."

"No worries. He was a jerk."

"Oh. But he did give you that sweet guitar."

Sky laughs, the fact that she's capable of it right now surprising herself. She plunks down on the couch next to Sam.

"Yeah, he didn't exactly give it to me. When I was a kid I was obsessed with playing that guitar. My dad said if I touched it he'd beat my ass, so of course that only strengthened my desperation to play it. Every time he was gone on a bender, I was playing."

"Ha! That's awesome. Did he eventually teach you how?"

"Hell no. I'd watch him play, which he did on rare occasions, and try to memorize where his fingers went. Mostly I taught myself. Eventually I joined a band, and I learned a lot from them. My dad always had music playing in the house. Lots of Zeppelin. Stones. Lynyrd Skynyrd. He even named my sister after Janis Joplin. My mom got to name me, unfortunately. She's a hippie to the core, so I got stuck with Sky."

"I think Sky is a rad name."

She smiles at him, struck by how this sweet kid ended up on the street.

"Thanks. I guess it's not so bad. Why don't you go grab that shirt. I better start getting ready."

She stands up and walks to the bathroom, locking the door behind her. She hasn't spoken to anyone about her childhood in years, and dragging her thoughts back there has left her shaky. She doesn't know who else Jani has invited from home, but suddenly this all feels wrong. Before she can stop herself, she wonders if Joe will be here. If she finds his face in the crowd, she's not sure she'll be able to stay focused. She clutches the counter top to stop the vibration in her hands. It's not her style to make such a big deal out of a gig and she regrets agreeing to this. Jani was the one who insisted Sky play one last show before she bows out. Now she's realizing it was a bad idea and she wants to run. To disappear. One hour until show time. She leans over the toilet and pukes.

***

Sky forgets the name of the stage manager in the denim vest. Wylie? Wyatt? He yells from the dressing room door that she has fifteen minutes. She should change her shirt and put on some mascara, at least. Sam has showered and is wearing a Leeroy Stagger & the Rebeltone Sound T-shirt, left behind from a show last week. The shirt's too big and makes him look even more childlike, but he smells better. Since their conversation he's been quiet and unassuming and Sky's surprised by how quickly she's grown to like him. She'll figure out a way to help, but first she has to survive this night and not act on all the tempting options her mind is throwing at her.

She's replaced the Advil that ended up in the toilet and has managed to keep it down. The ringing in her ears has subsided and her throat feels temporarily manageable, even though the acid that coats it is thick and tastes like death. She's been spitting it into the sink for the last twenty minutes as she warms up her voice, hoping Sam can't hear her through the door. She expects the crap to look like ash, but it doesn't. It's pink. Tinged with blood.

Sky's last few years have been a journey of soul-searching and honing her sound. Music always came naturally, so she was able to get by without any real effort. Just float. She took this talent for granted most of her life, but rehab taught her that doing things that are hard, things that make you uncomfortable, are worth more than anything that comes easy. After rehab Sky quickly realized that everyone she knew drank and most of them used drugs. To stay sober she had to stay away from that scene, so she was suddenly friendless, with lots of time on her hands. She practised. She wrote. She was desperately lonely. But now she's done the work, and it shows. Her voice and her playing and her songs are better. People come up after her shows, bursting to tell her how good she is. Sky thought she was on the verge of making it, that she was about to be discovered, at the next show, or the next. She inquired about recording some demos, then booked more shows, sometimes two a night, and saved the thousands she'd need to have her songs professionally recorded and produced. The more she played the more her throat started to ache, which isn't an uncommon affliction for a solo musician holding down the gig herself. But this was different. Raw. Throbbing when she swallowed. It wouldn't go away until the next morning, then the next night. Then it never went away.

Sky was in agony, but on the mic, her voice had changed. It became bolder, deeper and from her gut, because it hurt her throat less when she pushed from way down there. Her singing stopped bar patrons halfway through stories they were yelling to their friends. They'd turn. Look at her with wide-eyed expressions: holy shit, this girl is good. After months of using only Tylenol or Advil to soothe it, Sky's pain became too much to manage.

The doctor she eventually went to see gave her a referral to a throat specialist, along with a prescription for Tylenol with codeine. Sky stared at the scrawled writing. Should've thrown it out immediately, because she's in recovery, but she's an addict. Still and always and even though she's three years sober, one slip and she could tumble right back down the rabbit hole. She walked around with that prescription scrunched in the bottom of her bag until the paper became so thin she could see through it. The throat guy was backed up for six months so Sky made do. Getting her voice ready for shows became something that took hours, not minutes. She put off recording the demos until her pain could be more manageable.

By the time the appointment with the throat specialist came up, Sky was used to seeing blood in the sink. She swallowed pain relievers like candy and longed to fill that prescription. The doctor put on glasses with huge lenses like telescopes and looked inside. Swabbed and prodded and used a tool that cut little chunks of her throat out. To test, he said. He had her make all kinds of sounds. Sing scales. Then he told her to come back in a week for a follow-up appointment. Sky waited it out in a strange place of denial. She went back to the office a week later hoping for a date for some kind of simple surgery and a warning not to push it until everything healed. The doctor brought her into the little consultation room and asked her to sit. He looked different without the funny glasses. Younger and more human. Concerned. That's the first time Sky heard the word cancer. Even after the doctor said it, she was still waiting for the shrug off, but that wasn't what happened. He said cancer. Cancer on your vocal cords. Serious and aggressive.

Biopsy.

Surgery.

Chemotherapy.

Radiation.

Cancer.

Words you never think will be directed at you, all delivered in one long monologue, pulling the walls in around her until they crumbled on her lap.

After her diagnosis, when she wasn't gigging, Sky was walking. For days that turned into weeks, when the daylight shone through her grimy window, she would force herself to get up, get dressed, grab a coffee from the convenience store on the corner, and walk the streets. The isolation of her apartment was now too much to bear. Too many questions to ponder. What's the point of staying sober? What's the point in trying to write anything new? What's the point to anything? She let all the emotions run though her like dirty water down the drain. What would she do with her life if she couldn't perform? Music makes her special. It's her guts. Her insides. So, Sky kept walking, searching for an answer that wasn't the end – of her career or her life or her sobriety.

Now she comes out of the bathroom and picks up her bag from where she discarded it on the floor. Her mind is racing like the clock, counting down to the unknown, and on a whim she decides to add a song to her performance. She plunks down next to Sam on the couch and rifles through her bag, removing the folded set list she made that morning. She finds a pen on the small side table, noticing with amusement that at some point Sam has tidied it, organizing the magazines into two neat, almost equal piles. Sky scribbles "Caged Bird" above "Going Down," then throws the paper on the table. Sam looks over, but says nothing.

"Thanks for hanging out, Sam. I'm glad you're here," she says impulsively.

"Oh, it's cool. I mean…thanks for bringing me along! It's been the best day I've had in a long time. I can't wait to see your show."

She smiles but can't respond. Feels the slow burn of tears welling in her eyes. But Sky doesn't cry. Ever. She has to stay focused. She mumbles something about getting changed and collects her bag off the table, walks back into the bathroom, closes the door behind her, and looks in the mirror. She's almost as skinny as when she was using. The doctor warned her to gain weight, but eating hurts, and she quickly loses her appetite. At least now she has some muscle clinging to her bones. The years of walking and carrying her guitar from gig to gig have produced a lean layer, leading people to think she's fit, not sick. She's wearing tight black jeans, chunky boots that take her everywhere, and a cut off T-shirt from a northern BC band she saw last week called Dead Horse Hill. She strips the T-shirt from her body, averting her eyes from her protruding ribcage and the stripes of bone showing between her breasts. Her necklaces rattle and fall back to her skin. A collection of artifacts from flea markets and thrift stores. A jade guitar pick with a hole through it. A brass butterfly wing. A piece of driftwood carved into a circle the size of a quarter, framing a tiny pink stone from the shore of Kootenay Lake. Joe made it for her.

Rifling through her bag, she finds deodorant and a black tank top rolled up together. She slinks the tiny swath of material over her head. It sits two inches above her thick leather belt, showcasing her toned stomach and a silver and turquoise belt buckle engraved with the name Steve Earle in curly script. She bought the buckle on the road years ago, when they were touring dive bars in the States. She takes out a hairbrush and runs it through her tangled hair, which rests almost at her waist now. Pieces get stuck in her mouth when she plays so she gathers the sections near her temples and twists a few small braids, securing them to the loose parts with black elastic bands. She thickens her dark lashes with a coat of mascara. Her face is already flushed and she hates getting lipstick on the mic, so that's it. She's ready. Rolling her shoulders back, Sky stares at her image. People tell her she's striking. Sexy. Never pretty. The scars on her arms and pain in her eyes stop anyone from using that description.

You've got this, she convinces herself, leaning in closer to blur everything but what's inside. You've got this. You've fucking GOT this.

She starts to hum "Caged Bird," running through the lyrics. She hasn't performed that song in years but after seeing her mom's face, she has to.

The stage manager yells from the green room. Show time. She backs away from the glass, gathers her things off the counter, and stuffs them back in her bag, then draws in a long breath, reminding herself to savour this moment. Her mind will drift back here in the months to come, and she'll wish like hell she could re-live it. Her stomach churns and sweat drips down her back. There's a gentle knock on the bathroom door and Sam's voice comes through the cheap wood.

"Hey, Sky, sorry to interrupt. The big guy says it's time."

"I'll be right out."

She clears her throat one more time, feeling like there might be holes tearing away every time she does, then takes a gulp from the water bottle on the counter.

When she leaves the bathroom, Jani is sliding into the room through a small opening in the door, ducking her head like she might get caught.

"Hey, Jani. Show's starting. Get the hell out of here."

She jumps at Sky's voice, her hands clutching her chest.

"Jesus, don't do that! I don't have a backstage pass and I had to sneak in here. Thanks for forgetting, by the way. You could be a little more grateful. Do you know how much work I did to set this thing up?" As she's berating Sky, her eyes move to Sam, who's standing beside the couch.

"This is Sam." Sky says with a grin.

Jani looks from Sky to Sam with a *what the fuck?* expression wrinkling the skin on her forehead.

"Sam, this is my annoying sister, Jani. Janis, like Joplin. But she totally isn't. Has anyone ever been less like their namesake than you, Jani?"

"Very funny, jerk." She looks at Sam. "Hi, Sam. Nice to meet you. Sky never has any friends, so this is a shock."

Sky laughs, but sadly, she's right.

"I just wanted to say good luck. Have fun out there. And I'm sorry to spring Mom on you like that. I honestly didn't think she'd get in the car this morning, and I didn't want to stress you out for no reason."

Sky wants to be mad at her sister, but it's impossible. It always has been. She shakes her head and throws an arm around Jani, leaning down to touch her forehead to Jani's cheek.

"Any more surprises I should know about? Did you dig Dad out of his grave and bring him along, too?"

"Ha, ha. No."

"Good, then we'll talk about Mom later." Sky releases Jani and walks towards the door, then stops, turning back.

"Hey, can you take Sam with you? It's always a better show from the audience than from side stage. That cool with you, Sam?"

"Uh…yeah. Of course."

Sky notices Sam's looking a little shaky. It's been a couple of hours since they first met, and he'll be coming down from whatever he took last. She knows this feeling well. It's not a time you want to be around strangers, unless they're going to hook you up.

"Actually, I changed my mind. Why don't you hang side stage, in case I break a string or need something."

"Sure." Sam's shoulders soften with relief.

Jani is watching the exchange with curiosity. Sky's not about to explain Sam now.

"I gotta get out there, guys. I'll see you after the show. Unless it sucks. Then I'm making a run for it." She turns to leave and Jani steps closer, putting a hand on her arm to stop her.

"I have to tell you one more thing. I didn't invite him, but I saw him last week at home and he had all these questions about how you were doing. I tried not to say too much, but I kinda let it slip that you were taking a break. For health reasons. I'm sorry, Sky. Joe's here."

Joe's here.

Her heart speeds up immediately and she can feel it pound against her ribs. She can't say anything so she doesn't, just walks out the door, leaving Jani's hand floating in the air.

In the narrow hallway Sky can hear the rumble of the crowd. People talking and laughing, moving around each other. It sounds like the room is full of bodies, but she can only think of one.

The sound tech is waiting side stage, chatting with the house manager who will introduce her when she's ready. She can see a small slice of the crowd from where she stands. The faces all look the same and none are familiar. The lights will drop when she goes out and she won't be able to see him because he'll be near the back. Joe would never watch a show from up front. He hates getting shoved by strangers and he knows the sound isn't as good up there. Sky needs to focus on what she's doing and forget about Joe. This is her last show. It has to be the best music she's ever played. She wants to experience the magic one more time. In front of her sister and her friends and even her mom. Then she'll go to her doctor's appointment scheduled for tomorrow, postponed more times than Sky can count, and she'll start treatment. Like a good patient. Like someone who wants to get better.

There's a tap on her shoulder and she turns to see Sam handing her the set list. She'd left it on the table and without it, especially right now, she might completely blank on what she was going to play.

"Thanks, Sam. I need this."

Sam smiles. The house manager, some guy named Allan, looks to Sky and she nods. The sound tech speaks into his headset. The lights drop and the house music cuts out. The crowd cheers. Without an opener they're probably drunk and bored and ravenous for action. A single spotlight shines down from the ceiling and onto Sky's guitar, the black stool, and the lone mic stand. Allan walks out into the cheers and gets to the mic, handling it roughly and adjusting it higher. Sky hates that. Allan starts his spiel about the venue and tipping the staff, about keeping phones in pockets, no recording, even though they won't listen.

"And now, here she is, Sky Black!"

Jani's social media onslaught obviously worked. The Imperial's capacity is five hundred and it's jammed. Sky shakes her shoulders and stands up straighter. Dries her sweaty hands on her thighs. Looks at her set list. "Caged Bird."

She puts on her stage smile and steps forward, crossing the empty space between her and her guitar, lifting her arm to give a wave. The crowd screams, the energy electric. Allan's teeth are nasty and Sky wonders if he uses meth. He brings her in for a fake hug, his hands spread wide across her narrow back. She lets him pretend they're friends. That's show business. The screams continue and she can hear her sister screeching the loudest. She grabs the neck of her guitar, picks it up, and slides into the strap. *Only this.* What will she have without it? She shuts that thought down immediately, reaches out and readjusts her mic, moving it back to where she had it, then plucks through each string to make sure her tuning has held up. She watches the notes dance across the tiny screen. E, A, D, G, B, E.

"How's everybody doing?" Her voice is so deep and gravelly it surprises her. She shifts backwards to clear her throat. Swallows. The faces in the front row are mostly female and she doesn't focus on any of them. They hold out their contraband phones and look up like they want to eat her alive. She scans past the tops of their heads. Joe is several inches over six feet and usually stands out in a crowd. Sky surveys the taller guys near the back, searching for his familiar face. The room gets blurry and starts to tilt off axis.

"Thanks for coming out tonight. I know some of you travelled a long way, from my hometown of Nelson." She stops talking while people cheer even louder. Some because they're from Nelson, or they've heard of it. Some scream because it's the weed capital of the country and everyone knows it.

"I want to thank my sister, Jani, for organizing this show. It'll be my last."

Sky stomps her pedal and starts picking the melody for "Caged Bird" as people react to what she's said. Whoops and boos and everything in between. She lets her guitar take over the moment, while the crowd quiets down. Her thumb slides off the low E too quickly and she loses the rhythm for a split second. Panic creeps across her skin. Her breath quickens. There's no one to lean into. No bass player to even her out. No drummer. It's just her holding everything down and if she screws up, if she were to stop playing – simply stop moving her fingers between the tiny gaps in the strings – the show would stop. The thought starts to mess with her mind. The sneaky, evil voice that tells people to get closer to the ledge, or to step into traffic, tempts her. She steps away from the mic and turns her back to the crowd so they can't see the bead of sweat drip from her forehead. Her ears start a slow wail. Maybe she can't do this.

Fuck.

Calm down.

Breathe.

Feel it.

Breathe.

Sky circles back on the intro chords as she exhales and taps her foot, lulling herself into the rhythm: 1. 2. 3. 4. She bends her knee slightly with each tap, letting the beat flow into the rest of her body. Softening her. Most people won't notice what just happened, but musicians will. Joe will.

She channels all her practice, her sacrifice, and the love she has for making music. She has the groove back now and it starts to feel good. She stops focusing on her guitar and her foot and the timing. She lets her body take over, then looks into the dark nothing above all those heads, and sings.

You left before I was ready

Ran off into the night

You told me I was fine, but I was barely getting by

I had nothing to cling to

No reason not to lie

Pretend my heart beat steady then jump into the sky

The glass looks like a promise, if the sun shines through it right

It might've seemed like freedom 'til it almost took your life

Caged birds can't be trusted, living behind the wire

If they had their way, they'd light the whole damn house on fire

If you could only break your wing, you'd have a reason

The door is open wide, but the cage still holds your mind

You don't dream of flying, cause you're too busy dying

Look me in the eye, caged bird, just try

Birds are born to fly

And when you feel like talking, we'll hide your cage from sight

So hush, little bird, don't you know it's quiet time.

No one wants to hear your lullaby

The crowd is silent. Barely moving. A girl in the front row cries. Sky closes her eyes to free herself from distractions. She was only twelve when her mom left. Just a lost kid, scared of being alone with her drunk, criminal father. Terrified for her baby sister. Emotions almost choke her, but Sky pours them into the lyrics. She comes to the end of the song and plays the final few notes. Silence. And then an eruption of applause and cheers and the crying girl bursts into hard sobs. The reaction feels like a physical punch and Sky struggles to stay on her feet. There's a silver bucket beside her guitar stand with several bottles of chilled water. She bends to grab one, then walks around her mic stand and leans down to pass it to the girl. The girl's friends reach frantically for their phones and start recording. Their young faces all look up at Sky like she's important and they want to be her or touch her or have her in some way, and it feels so fucking good. To be special. Powerful. Why the hell would she ever give this up?

5. Creep

Rod Birk loves young thighs. Thighs that have tone and a line of muscle bisecting them. Thighs without cellulite squishing out from the back. They can't be Botoxed or faked, so they're the first to go. The telltale sign of fading beauty. He'd love to run his hand up a firm, young thigh right now.

Birk needs to find some new talent, and it better be soon, or he'll be looking for a new career. The label he works for, Space Monkey Records, is one of the largest in the country, and they're hungry to even out their client list by signing more female acts. Without any new prospects, Birk's had to revisit a few "artists" he's already deemed not good enough. His producer, Vince, won't even schedule the studio time now without a sound sample, so Birk has to sit and listen to them bleat out songs about how lonely they are because their boyfriend fucked another chick, or wanted his sweater back, or some other dumbass cliché he can barely stand.

Every day he has the office assistant, Miko, bring him a list of all the performers playing in the city that night. Most of them are familiar. He's already heard them, hates them, or they're property of another label. Today he picks up the list and scans it for female names at venues he likes, where the drinks are strong and the food edible. He circles the name of a girl called Vender playing at a bar on Granville. He's never heard of her, so she's either new in town or she's trying to rebrand herself. Her photo is blurry but promising, although photos can be misleading. Sometimes taken a dozen years and pounds ago. He'll have to see her for himself. He circles the name Sky Black, playing at the Imperial. He recognizes the name, but can't place her, so he picks up his phone and dials "0."

"Yes?" Miko's chilly voice greets him.

"How do I know Sky Black?"

"Hold." He can hear her long, sculpted fingernails tapping on her keyboard. Miko keeps a detailed spreadsheet of every musician she's ever seen, heard of, or who's booking dates in Vancouver. Birk likes to mock her about it, but secretly he loves it because it makes him look good to his boss.

"Sky Black. She used to front a three-piece indie/alt band from Nelson, Broken Yellow Line. I saw them at Edgefest in 2018. The band was average, but according to my notes she was great. She's got chops on the guitar. Smooth vocal, Serena Ryder-ish. She went solo three years ago. According to last year's gig data she's playing a lot, but only small venues. Fifty to a hundred people, tops."

"She's at the Imperial tonight. That's not exactly small. Should I check her out?"

"Yes, but don't be a creep about it. Behave yourself. If you think she's good, don't drool all over her."

"I don't drool on chicks. They drool on me." Birk hangs up before Miko can come back with a smartass quip. She's good at that.

The fact that Miko – who rarely gives compliments – says the girl's got chops helps a lot. Birk hates the manager at the

Imperial, but he'll have to deal with him. He grabs his jacket off the back of his chair and runs his hand through his hair. It's starting to thin up top and the coloured tonic he gets smeared into it weekly doesn't seem to be working as well as it used to. He's considering getting plugs, and wonders if he can expense them as part of his job. His image is an important part of his role and his expense account reflects it.

As per his regular routine, before he closes his computer, he checks his personal email one last time. No new mail. He's already done the math today, but he finds himself doing it again. Forty-two days since he sent his son, Charlie, an invitation to join him for a Harry Styles show in May. Front-row seats and backstage passes. Birk even told him he could bring a couple of his buddies. What kid would turn that down? Birk scrolls back through their thread of emails, reading the ones he'd sent before the one titled: Harry Styles.

Dec. 27 – "Hey, Charlie – so, did you get the phone? It's the most up-to-date iPhone you can get. Your friends will be so jealous! If your mom didn't give it to you, let me know. I wouldn't be surprised if she took it and sold it. Email or text me to let me know."

Dec. 23 – "Sorry, kid, can't make it. Work got crazy again. I have a Christmas gift for you; it'll blow your mind! I'll have Miko courier it over tomorrow. Merry Christmas."

Dec. 4 – "Hi, Charlie. I was hoping to get to your hockey game last week, but I got so busy at the office. I'll make it up to you. Let's get dinner soon."

A heaviness creeps into Birk's gut as he reads each unanswered message. He slams his computer closed and kicks himself away from the desk on his fancy leather chair. It's Italian and expensive so the wheels really track well and he bumps into the wooden shelf behind him. He's doing the best he can. He's busy, for fuck's sake, and how does Charlie expect him to pay for his fancy school and hockey fees and new skates? That shit's expensive. His ex has started taking Charlie to shrinks and getting him diagnosed with stuff, and Birk thinks it's really gotten in the kid's head. She's all worried that he's *anxious* and *emotionally unavailable*. In Birk's opinion, he's just a regular thirteen-year-old boy dealing with the crap life throws at you. Birk knows he hasn't exactly been the best father, but his ex is such a stone-cold bitch that Birk feels his rage start boiling up anytime he sees her name on his phone, usually telling him he owes her more money. The risk of seeing her in person makes it a struggle to spend time with Charlie, but he genuinely digs the kid, and he's afraid he might've really fucked it up this time.

Miko is sliding her thin arms into a black trench coat and getting ready to leave when Birk walks into the spacious lobby. She's off limits and has made that perfectly clear to him on numerous occasions, although he's pretty sure his boss has tapped that. Lucky bastard. Birk's noticed Miko dates women, too, which makes her even more of a catch, in his mind. She runs the office and assists the five A&R reps. She knows almost as much about music as he does, although he can't say their tastes line up. She's obsessed with seventies metal and compares every band Birk likes to Led Zeppelin. It's impossible to win an argument with her.

"Miko, come hit a few gigs with me. Let's get a drink. Bond."

"You know the answer, Birk. Why do you keep trying? Besides, I'll cramp your style, don't 'cha think?"

"Impossible. I don't have any style; isn't that what you keep telling me?"

"True. I do say that. Don't make my day miserable tomorrow. No strays. No promises. Got it?"

"Yeah, yeah. Don't worry about it. Besides, I have a good feeling about tonight. I might just find some magic."

"I've heard that before. Have fun. Check her ID. Use a condom."

Miko walks out before Birk has a chance to respond, heels clicking on the glossy concrete, and a large black leather bag slung over her shoulder.

Birk turns out the lights and locks the door. It's just before seven and the last glow of sunlight is fading in the spaces between the buildings. The air is thick with moisture and the smell of fried food. He hails a cab and directs it to the bar on Granville where Vender is playing. One name. For no apparent reason he hates her already, but he's thirsty. Hungry. Ready to throw his credit card around and get some attention. His suit is a size too small and the crotch pinches off the blood flow to his balls. He thinks Leon – the company stylist – did this on purpose. A restrictive reminder that Birk should lose some weight. He leans to one side and attempts to gain room for the boys by pulling on one of his pant legs. Leon tells him this slim-fitting style is all the rage, but Birk misses the wide-legged pants of the nineties. Pants where you could comfortably walk around with a partial, letting your mind wander, and your blood pump.

He pays the cabbie and steps out onto the dirty sidewalk, coloured with chewed gum and spit and God knows what else. There's a small lineup, about ten people, waiting outside. The bouncer knows him and moves to let him in. Ah. Respect. That's more like it. Birk nods and hands the guy a pre-folded twenty. Old school. Classy. It's dark inside and smells like weed. He moves through the crowd, angling towards the long wooden bar at the back. It's early for it to be so crowded and he feels a pang of excitement. Maybe there's some promise here. Maybe she'll be incredible and he can make the phone call he's wanted to make to John Westlake, his boss, for more than a year. Tell him he's found a star. Execs who sign the big names are given all the perks. A bigger office and a healthy bonus and most importantly, some goddamn respect.

The bartender is cute and has perky tits. He wonders for a minute if he's slept with her before. Most of the thirty-something girls have the same loopy blond hair, fake eyelashes, and foreheads shot so full of Botox it's hard to tell them apart anymore. Originality is dead. He decides to start a tab. Manoeuvres his wallet out of his ill-fitting pants and hands her his black Visa with Space Monkey Records written in gold lettering. She looks at the card and back at him with a smile that shows she knows exactly how this will go. She will stop looking at him like he's a gross old man. He'll tip her excessively. She'll tell him she plays a guitar or needs Coldplay tickets or has a friend who can sing. Promises will be made. At the moment all of this is unsaid, but he's heard the same shit so many times he could write the script. For now, he ignores her smile and pretends he didn't see her roll her eyes when he struggled to pry his fat wallet from his pocket. She slides him the stiff Johnnie Walker Red he asked for and lets his hand linger on her fingers.

"All right, you shitheads, welcome to the show! Don't be dicks, don't piss in the sink, tip your bartenders. And for Christ's sake, don't smoke weed in here or you'll get us shut down. Go the fuck outside. Okay, here's Vender!"

Birk looks up to the stage. The asshole on the mic needs to get turfed to the curb. Who decided that guy should MC a gig? He must own the place or something. The stage fills with a few musicians taking their spots. Birk recognizes the drummer from somewhere inconsequential. The guitar players start to tune and Birk signals for another drink, returning to his original fear that he's going to be disappointed and will need several stiff ones to get through this performance. Finally, a tall redhead in red leather pants and a lacey black bra walks out on stage. The crowd comes to life and starts to cheer.

"Show us your tits!" a classic jeer, is called from somewhere up front. Birk wishes she would, but tries not to smile. He's a professional, after all. She grabs the mic and addresses the waiting fans.

"Shut the fuck up, asshole. Hey, everybody! Thanks for coming out. I'm Vender."

Birk hates her name. He'll have to change it if she's any good. She looks older on the stage than she did in the promo pic. Rougher. The boys on the guitars finally get tuned and start to play. The sound is familiar. Rock-pop trying to be hardcore but failing. She gets on the mic and starts to sing. Her voice isn't bad. A shade of Florence + the Machine. Birk downs his second drink and turns back for a third. The tarty bartender has moved to the far end to whisper with one of her friends. They look over at him with their heads together. Plotting. He raises his hand to signal one more and she jumps to attention. Vender slides into the chorus and Birk waits for her to open up the vocal. Give it more. She does and it's a little shaky. Not pitchy, but it doesn't have anything that special. Not yet. The booze does what it's supposed to and he's feeling smooth and loose and a little less edgy.

"Thanks, sweetheart. What's your name?"

"Stacey."

"Of course it is. What's your friend's name?" He nods toward the girl who's watching them closely. She's brunette and a little more rounded than Birk prefers.

"That's Jade. I was going to introduce you to her, if you don't mind. She's an amazing musician. She has an EP out and she's looking for representation. You'll love her, I promise."

Stacey's practically promising sex. It's too easy and he's not ready. Not yet. He doesn't want to waste his time on the likes of Stacey and Jade if there's something better in store for him.

"Look, I have a really busy night. But I might come back later. What time do you get off?"

"Three. Will you be here?"

"Maybe." He avoids glancing at the friend again. Doesn't feel like giving her an opening to approach him and drone on about all her big dreams. He turns back to Vender. She's started another song and it's better. She's actually pretty good. Her band sucks. But her vocal is interesting and the writing is decent. She struts around the stage and connects with the audience. Her lips need to be closer to the mic, raking the metal cage, but he can fix that. It's the overall stage presence that seems impossible to change. If an artist is awkward up there, they're fucked. Nothing worse than watching someone stand on a stage and be uncomfortable. It's painful. Doesn't matter if they sing like an angel. Some just can't take all the eyes watching. He listens to two more songs while he finishes his third drink. Word has spread through the venue that there's a "label guy" in the house. He knows because heads start to turn. He'll have losers approaching him soon and he's seen enough. He'll ask Miko to stalk her on social media tomorrow and see how horrendous her pages are. Birk can't figure out why people feel like they have to post every stupid drunk moment that should never be seen by anyone. It's been the ruin of many an artist's career. The label won't touch somebody who comes across as a loser before their first single is even out. If their image is already in the shitter, it isn't worth it.

Birk's phone is vibrating in his pocket. He has to lean to the side to squeeze it out. It's too loud to take a call but he checks the number. The Imperial. He's known Allan, the manager, for years. They have a mutual dislike of each other, but unfortunately, they are spokes on the same wheel. Both trying to make money. A call might mean Allan's got something on stage worth seeing. Maybe this Sky Black is worth the trip down.

Birk pays the bill and doubles the amount. He's hoping he can do better than a bartender and her plump sidekick, but the pickings might be slim. He tells her he'll be back and walks outside. It's dark now and the street is busier. He could've called the company car to drive him, but he worries about what gets reported back to the bosses. He'd rather be incognito. He waits five minutes for a cab, the cool air and irritation starting to sober him. For a split second Birk considers going home, but there's nothing for him there except an empty inbox, and every night he passes on attention from young, eager woman is one less night he'll get it. Clock's ticking. He can feel it all the way down to his pinched balls.

He scrolls aimlessly through his phone so he won't have to talk as the cab weaves through traffic and eventually pulls up at the Imperial. It's lined up down the block, surprising for a barely known solo artist with no backing band, playing on a Thursday. Birk has to show his label card and have the idiot in the ticket booth bring out Allan before he can get in. Allan thinks Birk is a sleazebag who uses artists like currency, then discards them the second they stop making him money. Birk thinks Allan is a hypocritical hippie who's against the commercialization of music until he needs to pay for his expensive drug habit, then he comes crying to Birk for a cut. Bottom line is they need each other and they both know it. Everyone is supposed to scratch each other's backs, but eventually someone brings out the claws. Happens every time. Tonight, Allan doesn't waste any time with pleasantries, just jumps right into the ugly.

"Birk, it's about time one of you assholes showed up. I called your competitors, too. You're the only one here, so far. This might be your lucky night. I heard you've been on a cold streak lately, that maybe you're on your way out?"

He smirks, and Birk wants to drive his fist right through Allan's smoke-stained teeth, but he says nothing.

"I want fifteen per cent of the signing, Birk. This girl is incredible. She's absolutely slaying it in there. Fifteen per cent. It's only fair."

Allan reaches out his hand and Birk stares at it. He hears a muffled voice booming from inside the double doors. He's wasting time.

"Whoa. Allan, slow down a minute." He takes Allan's waiting hand and shakes it. Thinks, no deal, buddy. Smiles.

"Look, I don't even know if I like her yet. I've never seen her play. Even if I do like her, you know there's way more to it than that. Background check, outstanding deals, outstanding warrants. I have no idea what I'm walking into here, and I'm not making a deal on fifteen per cent of nothing. Let me go see what she's got, do my due diligence, and then we can talk."

They stand. A face off. Birk holds his gaze steady and Allan doesn't step aside to let him in. A song ends and the crowd goes completely nuts.

"I don't know, Birk. It's pretty packed in here. I might be over capacity. I'm gonna have to have my staff do a head count before I can let you in. Safety first, and all that."

He's got him by the balls and Birk knows it. It's late in the night. He's gotta get in there.

"Allan, calm down. If I end up signing her, we'll negotiate a payment, okay? You have my word." Birk gives his best look of sincerity. Keeps talking. Stroking Allan's ego.

"Obviously I need your venue. If I screw you, I'm out. I get it, I'm not an idiot. Thank you for the tip; now get the fuck outta my way before I miss the whole show."

Allan's shoulders slump slightly and his jaw clenches, teeth grinding together. He steps aside. Birk walks past him and pushes through the doors.

The room is crammed with bodies. Shoulder to shoulder. If the fire marshal does show up, Allan is fucked. Birk doesn't have a view of the stage and has to manoeuvre through the crowd, reeking of sweat and patchouli. He still can't see her but

Sky's vocal is strong and clear and full of conviction. The crowd stares up at her. Mouths closed. Listening. This is what tips Birk off. He could plug his ears and tell how talented a musician is by the reaction they evoke. It takes a lot to get people to shut the fuck up and listen. It has to be everything. The music and the presence and the sincerity. It has to connect. Make them feel like the words are just for them or exactly what they'd write a song about. If only they could. Birk finds an opening behind a group of girls so he can see over their heads. Sky Black is centre stage and she looks like an absolute fucking rock star up there, lost in her own sound, and taking everyone in that room with her. The lighting is perfect. It illuminates the muscles in her shoulders and bare arms as she moves. Her limbs are long and thin and she reminds Birk of a sleek panther, an intimidating creature that commands attention. When she turns and struts to the other side of the stage her shroud of black hair slides forward, exposing her back, wet with sweat. The straps of her top reveal part of a large tattoo. A tree. Branches stretching their jagged fingers to scrape across her shoulders. Birk's eyes are locked on her. She plays her guitar like she wants to speak to the crowd through it, confidently and without much consideration. When she sings it's raspy and full, breaking at times with emotion, like her body is fighting with the words and doesn't want to let them out. Birk's never seen anything like her and he knows. She's it. Finally. This girl will make him a fucking hero.

6. Yellow

Joe glances around at the mash of people stuffed into the large room, hoping someone stops letting them in because it's already too full. He keeps reminding himself that he's not the one playing tonight. He's just a fan like everyone else pushing into him, but he can't seem to stop the waves of nerves from turning his stomach. He shouldn't be here. Even though he's deep in the crowd, at the back near the sound guys, he's still too close to her. When she looks up from her guitar her eyes go to the back wall where he's standing. He knows she can't see his face, but his chest tightens.

She looks strong. That was his first thought, when she walked on stage. He ran into Jani last week and she told him that Sky was going to retire from music because of a health problem. That this would be her last show. She wouldn't tell Joe the specifics, but the thought that something might be wrong with Sky woke him the fuck up, made him realize he's been wasting precious time. He had to see her and he needs to talk to her, but watching her now, he can't imagine anything is wrong with her health. It must be something else.

Her name and then the sight of her hit him like a glass of cold water thrown at his face. She held her head high, flashing a smile, and raising a hand to the crowd. It's been three years. Longer since he's seen her smile. When she left she was strung out and broken. He can see she's different now. A stranger, yet every move and sound she makes is familiar. He wants to breathe her and hold her and never let her go.

Tonight, in this crowded room full of strangers, Sky's finally telling her story. About how badly she was hurt, about the pain she's endured, and the pain she's caused. It's raw and real and she's not offering apologies or excuses. Only truth. Joe lets her words land on him, lets them soak into his skin where they fill the gaping holes that have haunted him for years, pieces of the puzzle of Sky he could never solve.

It's just her up there and now it's obvious that the rest of their band was just a noisy distraction from her talent. She's been practising, working on all the parts of her performance, and it shows. Her voice is better. It's still raspy, but she's nailing the big notes and when she takes the energy down her words are clear and intimate. Sexy as hell. Her guitar skills are other level and Joe wants to tell her so badly. He saw a flash of nerves at the start, but now she's flowing, leaning in and creating a tempo with muted strings and raps on the guitar's body with her knuckles. The people in the room are witnessing something rare and they know it, looking to each other for confirmation that what they're hearing is as special as they think it is. Nodding to the stranger beside them, wide eyed, validating. 'Yes, this girl is fucking incredible. Are you hearing this? Can you believe it?" Lights blaze throughout the crowd as they sneak their phones up, attempting to capture what they're experiencing. When Sky is between songs, drinking water and tuning her guitar, Joe can't help but slide the phone from his back pocket. He flicks his finger across the icon and @SkyBlack comes up immediately. She's the reason he has the stupid app and she's the only person he follows.

Mike Benjoy: @Mikeylikesit – "You all should be @theImperial for the @SkyBlack show tonight. This chick is going LEGEND. I googled her, and the music industry is so fucked. How the hell does she not have a record out?"

SueRogers: @sue_rog – "Oh my GAWD you guys. Have you heard of @SkyBlack? Right? Me neither, but @LucyLou had an extra ticket and I didn't even want to go but I'm here and she's incredible! And so gorgeous it's crazy! I swear every person in here wants to fuck her."

MarcyDay: @Marc-Mellow – "@SkyBlack is the absolute bomb. Go see her, guys, if you still can. She says she's quitting or some shit. Let's start a petition."

Sky steps back to the mic and asks, "you guys having fun out there?"

They whistle and scream and raise their forbidden phones higher. Joe puts his away. They love her. They're pouring their energy at her and she's beaming. He's so proud of her, regardless of everything, all the horrible shit she did, all the ways she hurt him. He has an urge to push through them all and climb on to the stage, grab her hand, and take her away from here, so he can have her all to himself.

A guy from Nelson that Joe's known since he was a kid pushes into the space beside him, greeting him with a sloppy high five and slurring loudly into his face.

"Hey, man! Good to see you! Sky's awesome! And she's lookin' hot! You should be up there playin' with her, a Broken Yellow Line reunion!"

Joe steps sideways, making some room between them.

"I think she's amazing all by herself."

"Yeah, yeah, of course! Totally. How's the new band doing? You guys touring?"

"Heading back out in a few weeks."

"Cool. I heard you signed a record deal! What are you guys called again?"

"The Dirt Junkies." Joe doesn't try to hide his irritation; the guy is too close and too loud for his liking. Thankfully he seems to get the message, patting Joe on the back awkwardly, and disappearing into the fluid crowd.

When a space opens again Joe sees Marley making her way towards him with two plastic cups raised above her head. She spent more time than usual on her appearance, applying mascara and some other gunk to her eyes as they drove into the city, cursing at Joe like it was his fault when the car bounced through potholes. Her long blond hair is down, not in her customary messy knot. She's pretty and guys check her out as she pushes past them. She leans over to yell in Joe's overwhelmed ear, something about the craziness of the people or the cost or the wait. Joe can't hear her and he doesn't really care what she's saying or what's in the cup. He takes it with a smile and a shrug that he hopes will convey "thanks" and "I can't hear a fucking thing you're saying so please stop talking to me," then pours a long drink down his throat. Vodka and soda. He hates vodka and prefers gin, something Marley knows well, but he'll drink it anyway. When the three of them were in a band together it was Marley who spoke with the event organizers and stage managers while he'd wait in the van, enjoying the peace and quiet, Sky asleep on his chest. What Marley lacked in musical talent she made up for in keeping them organized, paid, and getting their assess to the next show on time.

Sky starts strumming a song, slower than the last few.

"I wrote this for an old friend."

Marley looks up at Joe but he pretends he doesn't notice. The crowd goes crazy for no apparent reason. Sky pauses, turns her lips from the mic, and looks side stage at someone standing in the shadows. Joe can't read her expression, diluted by the distance between them. Anticipation for what she might reveal causes his heart to thump loudly in his ears. He tilts the cup back and drinks until the ice crashes into his teeth, desperate for the alcohol to numb him.

You left your heart, in a letter by the bed

Now your words go round and round inside my head

The stove won't light and this house has a chill

I didn't leave you then so I guess I never will

I couldn't find the words to change your mind

So I stayed beside you, laid with you all night

It must be cold, when you're the only one who knows

Train's coming just for you, but you don't have to go

Let it roll, let it roll, that track won't take you where you need to go

Let it roll, let it roll, the sun will rise and time will heal your soul

I can't tell you, how you lost your way

Broken hearts are lost and found every day

You can hide inside your head, they can't tell

But running away will never make you well

Let it roll, let it roll, close your eyes, let that whistle blow

Let it roll, let it roll, the sun will rise, time can heal your soul

The song is him. His words. How he tried to save her and stop her from destroying what they had. From destroying herself. How she didn't listen. Marley's hands are clenched tightly around his waist. She pulls Joe into her and kisses his neck and leans up to tuck her head under his chin. Her body is too close and her hands too grabby. He knew it wasn't love, but just being in Sky's presence has turned Marley's overzealous petting into a sickening display of ownership he won't be able to shake off later. She's like milk that's curdled before his eyes, and he'll have to break up with her. Soon. He had an instinct this would happen, if he came here and saw Sky again. But he did it anyway and now it's going to blow up his life, and Marley's, too. She tilts her head up to kiss him, her lips lingering on his. Joe doesn't kiss her back. Physically, emotionally, he can't. He knows he's being cruel. She leans away from him and looks in his eyes, mouthing the words, *you okay?*

He has to tell her, and she's going to hate him for it. He thinks they both knew this was inevitable, but still, it will fucking crush her. He still loves Sky. It's so clear to him now. It's always been Sky and it doesn't matter anymore how much she hurt him. They are connected, like the twisted trees inked into her back. Even when they're apart, they're joined by something bigger.

7. Orange Bottles

They brought her back for two encores. They wouldn't stop clapping and screaming and Sky didn't know what to do with that kind of energy. It was overwhelming and she was in so much pain and wanted to end the show while she could still make sounds through the fire in her throat. She didn't take an intermission because she was afraid if she stopped playing, even for a few minutes, she'd lose her voice, then the crowd. And she had them, *fuck*, she had them and it felt so good.

Now she gives a final wave and leaves it behind her. Walks back to the dressing room, past Sam, who is still standing side stage and clapping enthusiastically, his eyes wide and a big goofy smile on his face. Sky can't stop moving and she can't talk to anyone. Not yet. She retreats behind the door and goes straight to the back, locking herself in the bathroom. The taps creak as she turns them both to full blast. She needs the white noise to surround her. The adrenalin pumping through her veins makes her hands shake. She gathers her hair in her hand and tilts her head under the tap, letting the water fill her mouth, then swirls it around and spits it back bloody.

Now they'll come. They'll want to chat loudly at her and drink the beer she can't and demand more from her. But she has nothing left and, aside from giving her sister a quick hug, she wants to get the fuck out of here. She's starving. She never did eat the chicken – or anything else all day, now that she thinks about it – and the delicious salty skin she loves will be cold and congealed in the bucket. She's craving warm, gooey pizza, and there's a place a few blocks from here that makes it soft enough to slide smoothly down her constricted throat. Her stomach rumbles at the image of the melting cheese and greasy pepperoni. She could grab a pizza and get back to her apartment and sleep. Not think. Not see Joe or her mom and have awkward conversations that will leave her gutted and nauseous with guilt. Just sleep. She's tempted and craving and very close to the line between sobriety and using. When she's feeling like this the only person she should be talking to is her sponsor, Gary, with the big hands and curly hair and gracious heart. Gary, who doesn't let her feel sorry for herself, who listens for as long as it takes but doesn't run his mouth with empty answers. He understands. Sky cups her hands under the tap and leans over to splash water on her face. When she leaves the bathroom Sam is sitting on the couch. He has her guitar case at his feet, as if he's guarding it. He stands when she comes into the room.

"Holy shit, Sky. That was incredible. The best show I've ever seen! Not that I've seen that many, but still. I just…I can't believe…anyway, I got your guitar from the stage; it's in the case now." He's pale and stumbling over his words, cheeks sunken where rosy young flesh should be.

"Thanks, Sam. I appreciate that. Listen, before people start coming in here, we need to talk." She comes around the couch to face him, her voice a shredded whisper. Sam takes a step backward, like he's afraid of what's coming.

"Obviously I don't know you very well, but trust me, I've been where you are. I'm assuming you use. I can't think of any other reason a cool kid like you would be in that alley. Am I right?" She waits for him to answer, but he seems a little stunned, and stays silent. A definite yes, in Sky's mind. She continues.

"I'm an addict too, Sam. Or I was, I guess, I've been sober for about three years now. I know how it feels, and I want to help you get clean. I had to do it, too. It sucks. It's fucking hard. But I promise you, you won't make it if you stay on this road." Sam doesn't have time to react before there's a knock on the door and then it opens. Jani comes in, drying tears, and throws herself at Sky.

"You're amazing! Everyone's freaking out. I can't believe…some of those songs…" She doesn't finish before tears overtake her again.

Sky hugs her back, watching over Jani's shoulder as Sam picks up the guitar case and puts it safely in the back of the room by the wall. He's going to disappear. Sky knows it and she's not sure what she can do to make him stay.

"Thanks, Jani. Get a hold of yourself, for Christ's sake. You're getting me all wet."

Jani punches her on the back, then reaches up to dry her face with her sleeve before pulling away.

"Oh, shut up. People are waiting in the lobby to talk to you. I told them I wasn't sure you'd come out. I know you hate this part, and your throat sounds really sore, but some of them drove hours to see you, Sky. And there's Mom, of course."

Jani hops from one foot to the other like a little kid who has to pee. Sky can tell she's been drinking and this isn't the time to explain that she might bail. She'll apologize tomorrow instead.

"I have to go to the bathroom. I've been holding it all night. I'll see you out there, yes?"

"Go before you piss your pants. Jesus, Jani, are you three years old? Why did you wait this long?"

"The line-ups were massive, and I didn't want to miss anything. Ever think about taking an intermission, idiot?" She's backing up as she says it, and with the last insult she vanishes through the door she came in. Sky can hear her apologizing to someone, and before she can get back to Sam the door opens again and the stage manager sticks his head in.

"Hey, Sky. Congratulations, that was a wicked show. The crowd loved it. Sorry to bother you, but there's someone who wants to see you: Rod Birk from Space Monkey Records. He's been here before; he's legit. You wanna talk to him?"

The room shifts. *Did I hear him right? Space Monkey is a huge label – that can't be right; should I ask for the sentence to be repeated? What did he say the guy's name was? Birk?* Sky's feet feel numb, like they might not be contacting the ground. She wants to say something but in her head there's laughing. *Am I laughing?* She can't be sure. Her mind is processing and then she realizes it's been too long without a response and denim-vest dude is looking at her with a strange expression. Sky tries to smile at him. *Of course there's a label guy interested in me. At my last show. When my throat is fucking collapsing and I'm infested with cancer. Where was this guy a few years ago? Speak. Now.*

"Sure. Why not…," the words stumble out, barely audible. She clears her throat roughly. Winces.

Rod Birk pushes past the large body blocking his way and steps into the room, clearly listening for Sky's response, and not needing any more of an invitation. He's wearing a grey suit, sweat marking the pits. His pants are all lumpy and gathered, and the whole look is way too young for his fifty-plus age. His hairline is dotted and strange, like he might have hair plugs, or hair dye has lodged itself into the empty craters. He's slightly shorter than her and she has no choice but to stare straight at it.

"Hi, Sky. Rod Birk. Space Monkey Records. You killed it out there tonight! Fucking awesome show."

He steps forward and shakes Sky's hand. Too hard.

"Thanks, Mr. Birk. It was fun." She finds some shreds of voice and pushes to make it as clear as she can. Her mouth fills with the coppery taste of blood. "Can I do something for you?"

"Yeah, you can. I heard you were retiring?! That's bullshit. You were levitating up there, and you took the rest of us with you. Your lyrics are raw. Authentic. Good guitar skills. But it's your voice. Your voice is magic. The tone is clear and the vibrato was perfect, even in the low ranges. Very rare for a woman. With the right management and exposure, you could be something."

She stands speechless and her mouth might be hanging open and it's all she can do to stay upright. *How can this be happening?* But it's too late. It's too goddamn late.

"Look, Mr. Birk. Like I said on stage, I'm done. I've been at this, solo, for three years, and a decade before that with my band. I've been working at this most of my life, and I can barely pay my rent in a shitty apartment, and my voice, well, I'm having some pain…"

"Call me Rod. And all the greats have pain, Sky. You were pushing too hard from the wrong places. We'll get you a coach for that. This is what all the hard work's been for. Right now. Don't give up when you finally get where you were trying to go. I know you're not with a label. Are you currently being represented by anyone?"

"Uh, represented? Like an agent? No."

"Management team?"

"No."

"Great. Perfect. Come to my office tomorrow. Let's talk future opportunities. Just hear me out, let me tell you what we can do for you. What do you have to lose?"

What do I have to lose? It's a question Sky has asked herself way too many times. A question that she hates the answer to. Nothing, except her music. The one thing she's giving up. She's stuck again in her mind. In time. He steps forward and jams the card he's been holding into her hand. She looks down at the small piece of paper, runs her thumb over the glossy writing like it's a key to an alternate universe. She has another, less shiny card sitting on her counter at home. It's from the oncologist's office and it has tomorrow's date scribbled on it in blue ink, the four previous appointments cancelled and crossed out. She can't reschedule it again. They warned her. She has an appointment at ten-thirty to discuss her treatment plan. Rod Birk's staring at her and she needs to be alone to think, but she has to get this guy out of her face first. She mumbles the answer he's looking for.

"Sure, I'll come by tomorrow." Sky stuffs the card in her back pocket, not sure what the hell she's saying.

"Fantastic. You're making the right call. I can make you fucking famous. You can sing, obviously, but beyond that, you've got the look. The energy. It's rare to find the whole package. You have it. We can set you up with the most skilled backup players and a marketing strategy that reaches the fans of your genre. You just keep singing like your heart's been shredded. I'll do the rest."

He winks at her and pats her on the shoulder. Classically condescending. *You just sing and look pretty; leave the rest to me.* It's not shocking, but it rubs her wrong every time. He wouldn't talk to a guy like this and she knows it. He'd compliment him on his technical skills. His writing style. Birk turns and walks out the door. Sky stands in the middle of the room. *Like her heart's been shredded.* As if it hasn't. As if it isn't so painful to be her that sometimes all she wants to do is close her eyes and make it all stop.

"Congratulations, Sky! You deserve it. I told you. You're amazing. Now everyone's going to know who you are."

She forgot Sam was still there, leaning against the back wall near her guitar. The sound from the lobby, loud voices and drunk laughter, is filtering in under the door.

"Come on, Sam. Grab my guitar. The pizza's on me. Let's get outta here."

Sam raises his eyebrows but says nothing. He picks up the guitar case and stumbles. Sky pretends not to notice. Jani will go apeshit when she finds out Sky's gone, but it's not the first time. She has to leave before she does something she can't come back from, even though part of her would love to walk into the lobby with a big smile and start shaking hands. Accept the love and compliments, because she's proud of what she did tonight. When it really mattered, in front of everyone, she killed it.

"You sure you want to leave? Everyone out there will go crazy when they see you. You had them in the palm of your hand all night. You didn't miss a lick, after that first little bobble, but I don't think anyone even noticed."

Sky stops walking and stares at Sam. This kid gets it. She laughs, and the smile on her face feels good.

"You noticed that, hey?"

"Yeah, but no big deal. Just a tempo slip. They were so loud I don't think they could even hear it."

Sweat beads on Sam's pale forehead. Sky knows he needs to get out of here, too, but she can't help but hesitate. Will she regret this? She imagines Joe. His blue eyes and big smile. The way he looks at her with that sexy grin, like he's picturing every inch of her body. What would she say to him, after so long and after the way she left him? She can't do it. Not tonight. And besides, Sam needs her. She has to help Sam.

"Let's go. My throat's killing me, and I need to eat."

8. Learning To Fly

The wooden chair in the doctor's office is wobbly and hard. Sky doesn't know where to rest her arms. She holds a small leather-bound journal in her lap, a gift from Jani. It's old and she's had it for years. The line on the top of the first page reads:

I'm Sky Black. I'm an addict and an alcoholic.

It's the opening line to everything at AA. Own your shit, then try to fix it. But you're never really fixed. Sky knows this. She can feel it just beneath her skin. She felt it last night as she and Sam escaped out the back door of the theatre and through the alley, where the discarded syringes littering the ground made her sweat. Sam disappeared with a greasy piece of pizza and Sky's address and phone number, written on a napkin and folded neatly into his pocket because he claimed to have a phone but wasn't sure where he left it. He promised he'd get in touch, but Sky's made many of the same promises, and kept very few. She had to let him go with nothing more than some advice. Go home. It can't be worse than living on the street. Now she stares at the scrawled writing in her book, a declaration of what she is. She puts the tip of her pen to the paper and adds:

And cancer. I have cancer now, too. Fuck.

She's still exhausted from her show, her adrenalin-saturated brain refusing to stop replaying the sounds and the faces and all the what-ifs. She couldn't sleep so she laid on the couch, staring at Rod Birk's card. *How can this be happening now?* Her phone has been turned off since she and Sam walked out the door of the Imperial. Jani will be pissed and stalking her. She'd be here trying to hold Sky's hand if she'd been offered an invitation.

Steps squeak in the hall. Sky stops writing, closes the book, and slides it back into her bag. There's a brief knock and then the door opens and the doctor walks in carrying an iPad.

"Hi, Miss Wysack. Thanks for your patience. I had to track down all your labs and scans, but I think we have everything now." He moves to the large desk in the corner of the room as he speaks. Sits and flips open a laptop.

"It's Sky. Black. I don't go by Wysack anymore. Haven't for years."

"Oh, I apologize. Miss Black, then?"

"Sky is fine."

"Great. Sky it is. Well, by the look of your CT, and the biopsy results, I'm very sorry to say that we have confirmed Dr. White's original suspicion. The pain and symptoms you're suffering are caused by laryngeal cancer."

He speaks like he's reading a script. *Tell the patient it's cancer. Stop. Wait for reaction.* Sky doesn't react. Instead, she thinks of her book and the words she starts every entry with. *I am an alcoholic.* Step one. Over and over again. Because you're never not an alcoholic after you are one. She wonders if she'll ever not be a cancer patient, now that she is one.

She lets her mind return to last night. The rush. The crowd screaming and chanting her name. Wanting more, of her and her music. The smile drifts back to her lips. If she'd gone out to the lobby after the show, what would they have said?

Her sweaty hand slips from the arm of the chair and she remembers she's still with the doctor, who's looking at Sky with concern. The small of her back is damp and chilled. She wants to take out her book and keep writing. She could make something up that wouldn't be this. She looks at the doctor. Can't remember his name. Nods.

"I know this is difficult to hear, especially considering your profession, but there is good news. From what we can determine from your results, the cancer is stage two. It's in the glottis – the area that contains your vocal cords – and has also affected the tissue near the base of your tongue. Surgery to remove the affected tissue, followed by chemotherapy and radiation, may be able to preserve your voice. You're young, and I see in your chart that you've quit drinking and smoking. It's possible to make a full recovery, but I recommend acting quickly. This type of cancer can be very aggressive."

He's talking so much and Sky lost him at vocal cords. She knows the cancer is in her vocal cords. The burning and the blood are a pretty clear sign. But she's never sounded better than she did last night and now she has a card from a record-label guy and a meeting in a few hours to discuss *future opportunities*. She feels like she's been going uphill her whole life and maybe this might be the one time she actually caught a break. She thinks of all the people she passed on the way in, overflowing the chemo lounge and the waiting room. Faces hollow and eyes distant. Tubes full of poison pumping from metal stands down the plastic pathways that lead straight into their veins. Killing. Destroying. The cancer, but other things, too. Maybe everything it touches.

"Sky, I know this is a lot to take in. Is there anyone you could call? It can be comforting to have a support person when coordinating a treatment plan. I'll have my assistant, Margie, find out when the next spot is available at the Cancer Agency. Their cancer care team is world class."

Sky thinks if she hears that "C" word one more time today she's going to tear something to pieces. She stands up. Hadn't planned to, but her body switched to autopilot. She can't shake the faces with the tubes and she needs to get out of here before she's chained to her own pole and pumped full of weed killer. Now she's standing and she has to say something.

"Well, thanks, doc. I have to go, I have a meeting to go to. I'll be in touch when I decide. I'll call the secretary." She reaches for the door.

"Sky, you can't just go. This is serious. You understand we can't waste time with this, right? It's not really a decision, if you want to live. I don't want to scare you, but I need to be honest. If we're going to save your vocal cords, we have to treat you soon. I'd like you to leave here with an appointment for your first treatment session, and we still have to schedule a full CT and more labs to rule out metastasis."

The doctor has stood up now, too.

"Sorry, but I can't be late. I'll call, come back next week. I promise."

She's out the door and walking. Down the bright white hall and past the reception lady, Margie, who's speaking into a headset while her fingers speed across her keyboard. Past the waiting room and the lounge and the places Sky can't fathom belonging to. The doctor is calling to her, but she's already thinking of a song. Something about breaking chains and running so fast your feet are silent. She has to get outside before she suffocates.

***

The air is heavy. Vancouver is usually wet in the winter. It's not that cold by the numbers, but when the wind blows off the ocean it moves right through you. The people who pass her are layered in oversized puffy coats and wool toques and don't make eye contact. Sky wears her leather jacket and refuses to buy something more practical, so she stays cold. She had a truck, when she first came here. An old F150 that broke down on the regular so she had to sell it. She couldn't afford the parking, anyway. Now she walks. Her hands calloused from carrying her guitar case. It's fine in the summer, enjoyable, even, but not in the winter. Not when the mist lays against your flesh, lingering like a bad decision.

She pauses to power up her phone, desperate for a distraction, a connection, something to steal her thoughts, even if it's just more trouble. Now it vibrates incessantly. Texts from friends and alerts from social media pour onto the screen, then a call from Jani. She'll just keep calling, so Sky takes a deep breath and answers. The word cancer sits on her lips and she wants to swallow it. Spit it.

"Where the hell have you been, Sky?! Everyone was waiting last night, wanting to tell you how *awesome* you were. You couldn't just come say hi?" Jani's voice berates her at a higher pitch than normal, her words barely decipherable through her panting breath.

"Good morning, lovely sister. Thank you for calling to check in. I'm fine, thanks. You?"

"Oh, shut up. You have no idea what I do for you. Where did you go?"

Sky assumes she's out for a run, Jani's go-to outlet for releasing stress since they were kids. "Stop moving for a minute, would ya? I can't hear you, and anyway, Dr. Garner said you're not supposed to be running until your weight is up to your goal range, right?"

"Fuck you, Sky. You'd be running too if you had to share a hotel room with Mom. She got up at four this morning and started doing some chanting thing. It was creepy. I think she was putting a spell on you. Now she's meditating and I had to be *silent* and Dave went to a movie – that's what he said, but I don't think theatres are even open yet – and obviously, I'm losing my mind. Don't twist this around on me like you always do."

Jani continues breathing like she's hyperventilating.

"Well, at least walk for second. I'm sorry I left last night, but I was exhausted and my throat was killing me. I knew you could handle it. I knew I couldn't. I was triggering pretty hard. Okay?"

Jani exhales and Sky can tell she's stopped moving. She hates throwing her *I'm in recovery* bullshit at anyone, but in this case, it's true. And she knows it'll stop any further inquisition. She has bigger problems right now.

"I'm sorry, Sky. I didn't think…where are you? I went by your creepy building. I swear you're going to get murdered in that neighbourhood."

"How many times do I have to explain this to you? It's the only place I can afford that's walking distance to all the places I gig. It's not as bad as it seems. It keeps me honest."

"Yeah, whatever that means. Seriously, where the hell are you because I know you're not there. There's no way you could sleep through that door buzzer. I rang it for twenty minutes."

"Oh great. My neighbours will be thrilled." Sky veers to the right and takes the cement path for pedestrians, away from the noise and smell of the traffic.

"I just met with the oncologist."

Silence. Breathing.

"And?"

"And he confirmed what we already knew. Just like the throat guy said. Cancer. Stage two. Laryngeal. He wants me to book a surgery date, then chemo and radiation."

"Fuck. Sky, I'm so sorry. I'm…" Jani covers the phone with her hand or shirt and Sky can hear her letting out long, shuddering breaths. She sticks the toe of her boot in a muddy rut beside the cement path. It oozes in and she pushes harder and finds she left a satisfying hole when she lifts it up.

"Hey, Jani, it's not surprising, right? I knew it was coming. At least I got to play the show last night. I wouldn't have done that without your help, without you being so pushy and bossy. So, thanks for being such a pain in my ass."

Jani sniffs loudly. Sky's made another, larger hole in the wet earth beside the first one. Didn't even realize she was doing it. Thick mud coats the toe of her boot.

"Ha. Ha. Fine, Sky. Don't take it seriously."

She exhales, probably straightening her shoulders and switching into her "take on the world" mode, then continues.

"Did he say anything about your voice? Will it…be affected?"

"Hard to say. Pun intended."

"Sky!"

She can picture Jani stomping her feet like she used to do when she was a kid. Even though she's four years younger, she's had to be the mature one, the one who takes care of the details, most of their life. After their mom left, Sky was so wrapped up in her own shit that she had no time for her little sister. The girls lived with their dad, and most mornings they were hungry and Jani's crazy hair was dirty and never brushed. Sky used to tell her it was the hair that got them all busted. After years of pretending everything was fine when child services stopped by, the school reported signs of neglect, and when the police investigated further, they found an absent father and a garage full of illegal guns. He went to jail, and Jani and Sky, at the ages of twelve and sixteen, were put into foster care. That's when Sky, Marley, and Joe formed the band, dropped out of school, and got the hell out of town. Marley's uncle had a place in Merritt that needed house-sitting, so they used that as their home base when they weren't touring. They got jobs, Joe helping out at a mechanic's shop and the girls waitressing, saving up until they could afford to put gas in the van, then they'd book gigs and hit the road. A year passed before Sky came home. During those months, Jani had starved herself so thin she looked skeletal. Sky raged at the foster mother who hadn't noticed, and begged Jani to start eating. It was only in the last few years that Jani would even admit she had a problem. Dave, as boring as he could sometimes be, was a good influence on her. They met at the forestry office, where they both had administrative jobs. Dave in the environmental division and Jani coordinating logging trucks. They only dated for six months before they got married, a small ceremony at a park by the river. Sky was so high she barely remembers it, but there's a great picture of her and Jani, cheeks squeezed together and arms wrapped around each other like ropes. Jani and Dave like to watch movies and go fishing. They have a brown dog they rescued from the SPCA, named Pineapple. They want to have kids, but the doctor says Jani won't be able to conceive until her health improves.

Sky lets Jani process what she's told her about the diagnosis. When Jani speaks again, she's clear. Confidant.

"I know you'll be okay. You're going to fight this and you're going to be perfect. Better than ever. Hey, remember Willa Phillips? She was a year younger than you, her parents owned that big place with the wraparound porch at the top of West Richards Street?"

"I don't know, Jani, maybe? Why do I care; was she at the show or something?"

"No, she's a naturopath now. There was a big article about her online last month. She's designed a holistic therapy program for cancer patients, and she's having tons of success with it. She has a fancy clinic up the lake, close to the ferry terminal. I think you should come home when you have a break from your chemo. Come and see her."

Sky exhales loudly. Jani always has a million fixes for everyone but herself. Right now she's still reeling from what the real doctor told her, never mind some woo-woo dandelion doctor.

"Honestly, Jani, I think I'm going to focus on what the medical doctor prescribes. Didn't Willa used to pierce people's eyebrows in the bathroom at lunch?"

"Well, yeah, but so what? She's curing people, Sky! And I think you need a trip home. It's been three years. People miss you. You forget that you have people who care about you. You don't have to keep punishing yourself. I know Joe forgives you. Come home."

"Jani, stop. Okay? One thing at a time."

"Fine, but I'm going to send you the article and a link to Willa's website. Just read about what's she's doing. Read the testimonials from people. What have you got to lose?"

The dreaded question. Sky stays quiet.

"Listen to me, Sky. What you did last night, I've never been present for anything like that before. By anyone. I swear. It was incredible."

Sky wants to make a smart-ass comment but her mouth has suddenly gone dry. Jani keeps talking.

"Your voice has changed. I've heard you singing since…forever. It's all I can remember. You belting out songs from your room. The garage. The freaking bathroom. To be honest, I never thought you were that great."

Sky laughs out loud. It feels good.

"Thanks a lot."

"No, listen. I mean, you guys were fun to watch and everything, but it was a lot of noise. I never really knew what you were saying, the lyrics were just words without meaning. It didn't feel like it was really you up there. It felt like you were pretending to be someone, like you were faking it, you know?"

"Where are you going with this, Jani? You're not exactly helping me feel better."

"I'm saying you've changed. Your voice, it was so different. Big and gritty and it had so much emotion. And the songs! The songs made me cry. They made everybody cry! It was really you up there. I don't know how many people have ever seen the real you, like that, before. Joe and Marley were speechless."

Sky freezes, her foot still in the newest hole.

"Joe and Marley? They were there together? Like, as a couple?"

"Yeah. Sorry, Sky, I thought you would've seen that on social media. They've been together for about six months, I think."

Sky swallows hard.

"If it helps, Joe looked bored with her. They were in the lobby after the show and she was pawing at him and I saw him step away from her on multiple occasions. He asked me where you lived. I told him."

"Jesus, Jani! Seriously?"

"I had to. You should've seen the look on his face. He still loves you, Sky. Who cares what happened. That was years ago and you were stoned out of your mind. You're sober now.

You're different. Joe knows that. You guys were so good together. You were your best self with him."

Sky knows she's right, and if Jani were here, she'd pull her into one of those sister headlock hugs and that would be enough. On the phone she needs words to express all the emotion tied up in one of those hugs. It's not possible, so she gets squirmy and starts moving again.

"Yeah, well that was a long time ago. Hey, I'm tired, so I'm heading home. I'll call you later. Good chat."

It's a tagline they've used since they were kids, trying to navigate adult conversations. A way to break the ice after they'd discuss their dad's prison sentence, or his death, or the fact that their mom completely lost her mind and should probably be kept in an institution. Jani's eating disorder. Sky's addiction. Joe. They've had no shortage of tough conversations. Sky hears her laugh on the other end of the line and wants to hang up before she says anything else. She can't tell her about Rod Birk. Not until she's sure. Maybe it's not even real.

"You better call me, Sky. You know I won't stop calling until you answer. We're only here for a couple of days. Mom would really love to see you. I know it's hard, and you don't have to forgive her, but maybe just listen? Can you please try, for me?"

That's all she needs right now, her mom deciding she finally cares and might show up for her, now that she's sick.

"I don't know, Jani. That's all I can say. Bye."

She doesn't go home. She doesn't go towards the meeting at Rod Birk's office. She walks. Follows the path along the seawall, letting the runners dodge her, bouncing past in their high-tech clothing and brightly coloured shoes, their earbuds plunged deep enough that they can't hear themselves breathing like savages. She thinks of her life and all the ways she's tried to ruin it. She's come so far from where she was three years ago. She thinks about what Jani said about her voice, and how good it felt up there last night, to know she was doing something exceptional, and to see it reflected back to her on the faces in the crowd. She pictures herself getting a job at a store or restaurant. At the calendar kiosk in the mall, where she worked for a few months last year when she was desperate for money. It's not a life she has any interest in. Her feet hit the ground, one after another, and without being conscious of when it actually happened, she's changed direction. Away from the ocean and its peaceful promise and back towards the city. A guy in black spandex and a stupid-looking headband runs past and yells at her for being on the wrong side of the sidewalk. Even with all the luxuries this guy enjoys, he's still a miserable asshole. Immediately, Sky knows. Fuck it. What's the point of living an unhappy life? She'd rather go out in a blaze of goddamn glory.

9. Fast Car

Sam opens his eyes cautiously, peering into the dim light, his gaze landing gratefully on the sea-blue beauty of Kurt Cobain's piercing stare. He's home. In his bedroom with his posters and his clean clothes and breakfast. *Sweet.* All the sensations of comfort and familiarity come flooding into his brain. He's warm, dry, and safely wrapped in his checkered duvet. His mom must've washed it recently, the tinge of Tide burns so good in his nose. He snuggles in deeper, pulling the softness around him like a cocoon. Maybe if he stays here long enough, it'll transform him back into something good.

He can hear female voices and a tiny pair of bare feet running up and down the hallway, slapping the shiny maple floors. Claws scurrying behind. Scents of coffee and something sweet – waffles or toaster strudel – waft under his door. His thoughts drift back to the night before, Sky's show and the rush of the stage and the screaming crowd. Being *with the band.* He loved the feeling of being important. He wished he wasn't just standing side stage, but actually walking out there with Sky. Sam's played his guitar on stage before, at his school talent show and in a few community centres where no one gives a shit what you're playing, but nothing like the Imperial. If he could do that, if he could be up there playing like Sky, he could show everyone – especially Andy the Asshole – that he's worth something. Sam knows he's given Andy enough reasons to hate him, but still, aren't adults supposed to give kids a break? Maybe Andy had a shitty childhood or he hates his job, Sam doesn't care. He sees the way Andy watches him – when he's joking with his mom or playing with Poppy – his eyes fill with venom and his face scrunches up, like he's jealous or something. It's creepy.

The handle of his door turns slowly. Through the widening crack of light, a crown of blond curls creeps inside.

"Sammy, are you wake yet? It's after lunch already, but we made waffies!" Her hoarse whisper grows louder as she gets closer to him, inches from his face.

"Hey, Poppy. It's super early; is the sun even up yet?"

She scoffs at this, crunching her eyebrows together and blowing air out of her pursed lips, then climbs up onto his bed, her little mouth twisting in concentration.

"I watched *Paw Patrol* and *Magic Bus*. I had two snacks and Mom says it's past noon. It's eatin' time! Get up, would ya? I want to play with you before you go. Mommy says you won't stay long."

She lays the tiny weight of herself on top of his body. He gets one arm loose and pats her curly mop, feeling the soft blow of her naïve words like a punch to his gut. He has an expiration date here and the clock is ticking. She looks up into his face with her vibrant green eyes. They percolate with questions and he usually has to set a limit or she'll never stop inquiring. Her four-year-old brain is ravenous for all the *whys* of his unpredictable life. In this soft light with clean-smelling comforts all around him she seems surreal, like a creature too perfect and innocent to exist in the same world he does. He worries that if he stays around her too long he might damage her in some way. It's something Andy reminds him of constantly, including last night, when Sam knocked on the door and, according to Andy – "woke the whole fucking neighbourhood." Luckily, his mom intervened with promises of only one night and the fact that it was too cold and dangerous to turn Sam away at that hour. She grabbed Sam's hand and pulled him into his room, a flash of fear in her eyes as she closed the door on his slurred gratitude.

The crack of light coming through his open door explodes as Chester hurdles through it, his honey-coloured fur releasing from his coat like exhaust and hanging in the air behind him. He launches himself off the floor but doesn't quite make it on to the bed, so his front legs cling desperately to the blanket and their bodies. It's a symphony of slipping claws and panting breath and high-pitched squeals from Poppy. Chester's wet tongue laps at everything in its radius. Sam tucks his head back under the blanket to escape the madness.

"Oh my goodness, what's going on in here? Chester, get out! Go! Poppy, you spilled your Cheerios all over the floor in the living room. Go pick them up, please, before Chester gets to them first. And not after a while. Right now."

His mom's voice is stern, but soft. Andy will be at his office, manipulating people to invest money in some stock that only makes rich people get richer. But at least he's gone, so his mom can be herself, not tiptoeing around on a knife edge. Poppy slowly untangles herself from Sam's arm.

"Okay, Mommy. But you guys come out of here. No yelling. You promised, 'member?"

"Yes, Poppy. I promised. Go."

"See you soon, Sammy Salamander."

"Later, Poppy-gator."

She chuckles, then slides off his body and scampers away, leaving a cold void where she had been lying. Sam takes a deep breath and pulls the blanket off his face, ready for his mom's look of disappointment. The one that's worse than rage. She smooths out a flat spot at the foot of his bed and gently sits, waiting for him to start, this time.

"Thanks for letting me crash last night, Mom. Breakfast smells amazing. I'm starving." She sits. Watching him. They've had this conversation countless times and it never changes. She doesn't want him home, or around Poppy, unless he's clean. He can't get clean. He tries, but his good intentions are so quickly abandoned, even though when he's promising – when he's begging and pleading for another chance – the words feel so much like the truth.

"Do you remember coming here last night? You made a huge scene, as usual. Just about knocked the door right down. Andy's furious. He wanted to call the cops. I had to beg him not to. I just, Sam, you know we can't do this anymore. You know our rules, and you continue to defy them. You have no idea the position you're putting me in, as a mother, and as a wife, and…"

Her shoulders are slumped low, back bent, like someone who's been broken. She sounds worn out, way past sad.

"Mom, I know. I know I broke the rules, but something happened to me last night. Something so cool. I met this musician, Sky Black. She was playing at the Imperial and we started talking outside and she asked me to help her out! I carried her guitar and helped her get ready. I even got to watch the show from side stage! She gave me her number, and she said I could hang with her anytime."

"That's great, Sam. It sounds fun. But the state you were in when you showed up here was not acceptable. You know you're not welcome at our house, or near your sister, in that condition."

"I'd never hurt Poppy. Ever."

"Sam, I know you wouldn't *want* to hurt Poppy, but you don't understand what you're like when you're using. It's not even you! It's some spooky-eyed stranger I can't stand, and I'm guessing this Sky woman is no better off than you, am I right?"

"No, Mom. That's just it, she's sober and she wants to help me get there, too. I just need to buy another guitar and show her I can play. I want this, Mom. I want to be a musician, just like Sky." He sits up, the words coming faster as he taps into the rush of last night. The plan is forming as he speaks. He's used to saying whatever he can to placate his mom, always spinning her a colourful story so she won't judge him so harshly. But this time he means it. He wants to get sober. He wants to be a musician.

"Sam, it's wonderful to see you so excited, but I'm missing something. If she's sober, then how did you show up here wasted out of your mind? What happened?"

Sam tries to piece together the sequence of events from last night. They ducked out the back door of the gig, and Sky took him to a pizza shop a few blocks away. They talked, about music and gigging and…it's hard to remember the details. Nag's voice was impossible to ignore at that point, insisting he find a way to score a hit. His hands started to shake and his skin itched like he was covered in ants. When he gets like that, stillness is excruciating. He doesn't like being in public or around anyone sober – he just needs to fix. Fast. They parted ways on the corner, and he promised Sky he was going home. He didn't mention he was going to get high first, but he's sure it wouldn't come as a shock. Sky knows what addiction is like. Sam went to an alley he frequents and found a tweaker who was holding. He had twenty bucks, money Sky had given him for a cab, but he promised to pay the difference later. The guy put the dirty needle into his arm and Sam stopped shaking. It wasn't enough to get him flying, but the pain stopped. Then he took a bus home, because he didn't want to start their new friendship off by lying, even though he knew he was breaking his mom's rules.

"Mom, I mean it. I want to get clean. I want to try rehab again. I'll commit. I promise."

He sits up and looks her straight in the eye, so she'll believe him. She's spent thousands of dollars and way too many tears on his failures and broken promises.

"Oh, Sam. How can I believe you? You know Andy will go crazy if he finds out I even let you stay for the day. I promised him you'd be gone first thing. I can't ruin my relationship with him, Sam. You know what he said about custody of Poppy. I can't lose her, too…"

"He's such a controlling asshole, Mom. Can't you see that?"

"That's enough, Sam! Enough."

She stands up abruptly, her shiny blond hair swinging behind her. He's sure she knows what kind of guy Andy really is – she has to – but she's gotten herself so deep into this life and now she has no way out. When it was just her and Sam, for most of Sam's life, she didn't care about all the material crap that surrounds her now. She was only seventeen when she had him. The same age Sam is now. Her friends called her Cake, but now she goes by her real name, Catherine. Her hair was long and wild and she didn't care if the string of daisies tattooed around her bicep showed beneath her shirt. She's still beautiful, but now she's smoothed out and covered up and never misses a Pilates class. She cooks fancy food and pairs it with expensive red wine, dresses up and eats late, when Andy gets home and after he's had a few stiff drinks. She's just how Andy likes her to be.

"Come have breakfast. Poppy's been waiting for hours. She's driving me crazy asking about you. That little girl is obsessed with you, Sam. She asks where you are and when you're coming home every day. Let's make this fun for her, okay? She deserves that. After we eat you can shower and change, but then you have to go."

"Go where, Mom? I have nowhere to go except back to the alley with all the meth-heads! Please, let me stay. I'll talk to Andy tonight. I'll apologize, make him see that I mean it. I want to go to rehab. I want to be a musician, Mom. You know how much I love playing. You know how good I am. Please, let me try to fix my life. Sky said she'd help me. She's been right where I am, and look where she is now. Please." Sam knows his mom wants to believe him. She wants this just as bad as he does.

She bends down and picks up his discarded jeans, tossing them on the foot of the bed. His room has been kept how he left it when they kicked him out three months ago, after he failed at rehab and then lied about it so he could come home for Christmas. It's neat and dust-less and his desk has been cleared of his papers, scribbles, and lyrics and bullshit job applications he never got around to submitting. The part that hurts the most is the skeleton sitting in the corner, an empty black guitar stand, painfully void of his beautiful Telecaster. He can't even look at it. Panic tears him out of bed. The thought of walking out of here and going nowhere makes him feel desperate. He stands and faces his mom, ready to beg. Plead. Anything it takes.

"Guy-yi-yi's!! Come on out now. Cheerios are cleaned and I set up my pony pen and Sam has to be Sebastian because he's a boy, and Mom you're Robin 'cause she's old, and I'll be Juniper Jones the Princess Pony. Come on!"

"Alright, we were just coming. Let Sam have some coffee first, okay?"

His mom brushes past him and scoops up Poppy. They leave him in his room and retreat down the hall, Poppy firing questions as they go. Sam puts on his jeans and grabs a black Element hoodie hanging on a hook on the back of the door.

It's brand new and he thinks he got it at Christmas but can't be sure. Those days are a blur of yelling and threats and lies, ending with the snapping of his guitar. Sliding on the hoodie hides the bruises on his arms from Poppy's prying eyes.

The house is bright and clean with huge windows displaying the North Shore mountains, because Andy has a shitload of cash, and he wants people to know it. The coffee pot is full and Sam detours through the modern kitchen to pour a cup, stopping to look at Poppy's collection of artwork, laid out on the granite island for him to peruse. Most of the pictures are of him, or horses, and say "To Sam Love Poppy" or "Brother" in big wavy letters. There's a large, red stick-boy with something like a bird over his head. It's titled "Sam and Angel."

"That's your guardian angel. She protects you when you're not here. Poppy prays to her every night, to keep you safe." His mom has come up behind him. She lays a gentle hand on the middle of his back. "Okay, Sam. Let's try it again. I believe in you."

"Really? Thanks, Mom! I can do it. Sky did it, so I can do it, too." He wraps her in a bear hug, feeling her bones protruding beneath her soft sweater.

"I'm waiting!! Are you guys coming or what?"

"Keep your pants on, Poppy. We're coming!"

"Ha! Sam, you're so silly!" She crumbles to the floor, releasing peals of joyous laughter. Sam finds his favourite mug at the back of the cupboard. It's white with a chip on the rim, big painted letters spelling out SEATTLE in green. He fills it with hot coffee and glugs of cream, then walks over to where the plastic horses are meticulously displayed in a row on the floor. The radio is playing softly through the speakers wired into the ceiling, Barney Bentall and his Legendary Hearts promising there is, in fact, something to live for. He can't help but groove a little on his way by.

10. Crash Hard

Space Monkey Records is housed inside a revitalized brick warehouse in Yaletown, one of the artsy districts in downtown Vancouver where rows of craft breweries and trendy pubs pop up and then disappear unceremoniously. Sky gigs in this area whenever she can book a show. Most of the male patrons are trying to impress her or whomever else might be watching, so they fill her tip jar with twenties, making a show of depositing the bill in between songs so everyone takes notice. Playing the role of a *generous music lover* helps them get chicks. They nod at Sky as they drop in the money, hoping for some sign of appreciation that might lead to more later. That rarely happens. The university girls flock to the area in large groups, wearing cropped T-shirts and loose-fitting jeans and cheering loudly between songs, which she deeply appreciates. The manager takes notice of happy patrons – especially female ones – and deems the night a success.

Sky finds the address on Rod Birk's card and pauses to exhale, summoning up the courage she had when she made the decision to come here, then pushes open the giant weathered wooden door. A beautiful Asian woman in a black dress looks up from her red metal desk. It's placed exactly in the middle of the sparse room. The ceilings are twenty feet high and Sky's steps echo.

"Welcome to Space Monkey Records. Do you have an appointment?"

Her tone is bored with edges of irritation. She's so beautiful Sky can't speak. Stares. She feels scruffy and unclean in her jeans and mud-crusted boots, her toes soaked from the wet ground and long walk.

"Hi. Yeah, sort of. I got a card last night from Rod Birk. He told me to come by this afternoon?" She's not sure why she posed it like a question.

"Rod and his fucking cards," she murmurs as she picks up her phone, pressing the buttons harder than necessary.

Sky feels like a very un-special idiot. Does this Birk guy give his cards to everyone? *Shit.* She knew this was too good to be true.

"Rod, there's a…" she pauses, looks up at Sky and raises a perfectly manicured eyebrow in expectation.

"Sky Black," she stumbles out. A hint of recognition crosses the woman's face.

"Sky Black is here to see you."

Sky wants to run. She feels like she's selling something unwanted. The assistant hangs up the phone and directs her gaze behind Sky. She turns to see a row of chairs.

"Have a seat. He's coming out."

Sky steps back to go sit, or maybe leave – she's still not sure.

"Hey," the woman says, a little more softly, "sorry for the attitude. Rod tends to get drunk and drop cards to musicians – mostly female ones – and then he won't come out and I have to deal with the tears and disappointment. Not my favourite part of the job."

Sky lowers herself into a modern-looking chair that's so uncomfortable she flinches.

"Don't worry about it," she says into the large gap between them. "I'm not entirely sure why I'm here, either."

"I'm Miko, by the way. I didn't recognize you at first, but I've seen you play. With Broken Yellow Line at Edgefest. You were good. And if it helps, Rod sounded excited that you came. He doesn't get excited very often."

Sky doesn't know what to say. This roller coaster of emotions has left her spinning.

"Oh, cool. And that does help. Thanks."

She pulls her phone out of her bag so she isn't staring into the empty space, and starts scrolling the list of texts from last night. She skips all the ones from Jani, already knowing what they'll say and unwilling to inflict herself with more guilt. There's one from Marley.

"Sky! You were on fire up there, girl! We were all blown away. Joe and I were so proud of you! We're going to Wally's for a beer; you should come by. Let us know."

Joe and I. It stings like pouring vinegar into a gaping wound. The thought of actually being in a room with the two of them, seeing Joe put his hands on her, makes bile rise in Sky's aching throat. She keeps scrolling, eyes flicking over the messages from old friends, some coming in at three and four in the morning. She hears a small sigh and looks up without preparing herself. Miko's staring at her, her eyes dark and mysterious. She licks her painted lips and leans forward.

"What genre are you playing now?"

"Oh, well, it used to be alt/rock, as you know, but now I guess I'm leaning more singer-songwriter. I've been solo for three years."

"Cool. I look forward to hearing your new stuff."

"Thanks. What do you usually listen to?"

"Everything, I guess. Kinda goes with the job. But I'm a sucker for the classics. Led Zeppelin. AC/DC. The Runaways. Everything that was forbidden when I was a kid."

"Forbidden? Wow, sounds intense. Strict parents?"

"Yeah, you could say that. I grew up in Beijing. Not exactly the freedom capital of the world."

Sky has no response to this, finding herself dazed by Miko's complete fucking coolness. She wonders if she plays an instrument. She could picture her on the keys, or maybe the violin. She has no trace of an accent and Sky can't believe English is her second language. She wants to know more about her, but doesn't think she should pry. Once again, her silence is stretching out too long for social norms and becoming awkward. Luckily, Rod emerges from the hallway behind Miko's desk and saves her. He's wearing another tight suit, but he's less sweaty this time and definitely seems more professional than he did last night. She stands up.

"Sky Black. Great to see you. And cool name! I didn't mention that last night." He reaches out his hand and they shake.

"Thanks, Rod. And thanks for taking the time to see me."

"Of course! Can I get you a drink?"

Damn, she'd like a drink. A real drink. Ten real drinks.

"No, thank you. I'm good."

"Suit yourself. Come back to my office. Miko, hold my calls."

Miko glares at him. Rod walks to the back and Sky follows behind.

"Good luck," she says softly as Sky passes her desk.

She smells like jasmine or something expensive. Sky's palms prickle with sweat. Her head is swirling with nerves and the doctor's words and her new decision that might unravel at any moment. The dream she's had since she was sixteen – to sign with an actual label and record an album – might be coming true. Except she should quit singing and get treatment so she can live. But she might never sound the same again, she might sound like nothing and have nothing. At this moment she feels like she's so close to having everything. Life is fucked. She tells herself to just keep moving toward the something.

Rod Birk's office is a sharp contrast to the lobby. The walls are covered with framed gig posters and photographs of Rod with musicians and, hanging right over his desk, a long glass box housing a shiny black Fender guitar with silver writing scrawled across it. Sky can't make out the signature but she'd love to ask. *Who? When?* She wants all the details. Many of the faces in the frames look familiar and she wants to go around the room and look closer at each one, but if she doesn't sink her ass into the leather chair in front of her she might crumple to the ground. Her knees wobble and the crap in her throat builds up again. She should've asked for some water, but it's too late. Rod sits behind his cluttered desk and collapses his laptop screen.

"So, Sky, clearly I liked what I heard last night. Everyone in that crowd did. You have a lot of power, but there's also a vulnerability about you. It's rare. That's the magic. The thing people go to shows to see. Do you have any solo albums out? All I could find is the Broken Yellow Line shit. No offence. Not my taste. Let's just say you've gone in a better direction."

Birk barely separates his thoughts into sentences and Sky's mind reels trying to keep up. It stings to hear him say her band was shit.

"No. Nothing solo." Her voice is thick and hoarse. She clears it as casually as possible. "I recorded three albums with Broken Yellow Line. We toured Western Canada, some of the southern states, played a lot of bars and medium-sized venues, but nothing really happened. Eventually we put everything on hold. Our drummer wanted to go back to school and everyone needed to make some cash. Things sort of fell apart. I've been gigging on my own since then. Three years."

"Do you write all your own music?"

"I do. I write all the time."

"Cool. And you don't have any outstanding contracts? Fired managers you owe money to? Losers looking for writing credits? Anything?"

"No. I've never signed anything with a manager, only with the venues. We booked our own tours, and all the stuff I sing now, I write."

"Great, because trust me, we don't want anyone crawling out of the woodwork once the dollars start rolling in. I've seen it happen a million times. The lawyer fees won't be worth it, so you'll have to settle out of court. Pay the leeching bastards out of your own pocket. Full disclosure here: the label won't help you with that shit. You'll be on your own. It's not pretty, I can tell you that. You're sure?"

"Yes, I'm definitely sure."

"Perfect. That 'Broken Strings' song at the end of your set last night was great. The way it got the crowd. Your rasp is thick and unique. Good projection. For a woman, you can really play your guitar. And you have the look, that's for sure. Are you married?"

"Oh God, no."

"Do you have a boyfriend?"

"Uh…no."

"Girlfriend?"

"No." *Why the fuck does it matter?*

"Okay, great. I mean, it doesn't matter, but it kinda does, you know?"

He chuckles to himself and Sky has no fucking clue what he means but she wants this deal so she keeps her mouth shut.

"I'd need to hear more, before taking this any further. What I'd like to do is set you up with our main producer, Vince West. He's the guy you want for this genre. He's a big deal; I'm sure you've heard of him. Anyway, we need to get some rough recordings, maybe four of your best songs. I'm not making any promises, but from what I saw last night I think we could do something together. Does that work for you?"

"Yes." She clears her throat again. "Yeah, that works great. Thank you."

Birk stands up, signalling abruptly that the meeting is finished. Sky stands too, not sure her balance will keep her vertical. She notices one framed picture on his desk, Birk with his arm around a young boy who looks like a mini version of him. The boy stares straight into the camera, not smiling. Birk follows her gaze to the photo.

"Leave Miko all your contact info. Make sure we have a number that you'll answer right away. I'll check in with Vince and when we have a slot open in the studio, we'll contact you. And take care of that voice. You're going to need it," he laughs.

"Yeah, you got it. Thanks again."

Sky has to get out of here before this blows up in her face. It feels like a trick. The timing and the big promises, right when it was all coming to an end. She turns and walks out of the office, back down the hall and into the bright foyer. Miko is at her desk and Sky has an urge to give her a high five. Instead, she takes a wide route so she doesn't come up too closely behind her.

"How'd it go?" Her lip gloss looks fresh and shiny.

"Good, I guess. I'm supposed to give you my contact info. Rod wants me to lay down some demos in the studio when there's an opening."

"Cool. He wouldn't waste studio time unless he sees potential. What's your number?" Her fingers are poised over her keyboard, waiting. Sky feels like after years of half-heartedly trudging through her life, she just woke the fuck up. It's happening, it's *actually* happening.

11. Mr. Jones

Birk watches Sky walk out of his office. When the door clicks shut he drops back down into his chair and kicks himself into a full rotation, lifting his shoes off the ground so his feet float as he spins.

"Yes! Yes, yes, mother-fucking yesssss!!!!" The words flow out through his clenched teeth. He balls his hands into fists and pounds them on the wooden arm rests. This is it. This is the artist he's been waiting for. As soon as he saw Sky in the lobby it confirmed what he felt last night. She has the "it" factor, an energy that demands attention, and it's not just on stage. Even Miko was practically drooling as Sky walked by. Birk stops his spin and grabs for his phone. He doesn't know if his competition got to her last night, so he has to act fast, although he'd never let on to Sky that he's this desperate to sign her. That's how bad deals are done. Measured indifference is a required skill for this job, one Birk has mastered over the years.

"Siri, call Vince."

"Calling Vince West." Siri responds immediately in the clipped British accent Birk prefers her to use. If only they could all be so accommodating.

"Hey, Rod. What's up?"

"Vince, my man! Good news. I found a new artist last night. Could be the real deal. I need to get her in to record some demos, right away."

"Her? Wow, that's great, Birk. A woman. You're finally growing up. But what's the big rush?"

"I just need her in right away. Tonight, if you can. Bump somebody if you have to. I don't want anyone else digging their claws into her. She's special, Vince."

"Whoa, slow down, Roddy. I'm not bumping somebody that's already bloody here. Cool your jets. Who is this girl?"

"Sky Black. Ever heard of her?"

"Maybe, yeah. Haven't seen her play. She's that good?"

"She's unbelievable. She brought the fucking house down at the Imperial last night, completely solo. Allan was having a fit about her, and I know he didn't give me an exclusive look. Who's in today?" He can hear Vince shuffling around and erratic banging as a drummer warms up.

"Kit Wednesday is working on their album. We have them booked in all week. Pretty hard to bump them, Rod. I could try to fit Sky in end of next week?"

"No. Not fast enough. Has to be tomorrow at the latest, Vince. Put them off. They've had three fucking extensions already. They've been wasting my time for a goddamn year. Let's be honest: their new shit isn't even that good, am I right?"

"Well fuck, Rod, what the hell am I doing here if you've already written them off?"

Vince's voice is broken up, like he's cupping the phone so they can't hear him.

"Calm down. I didn't say I'm writing them off, yet, it's your job to change my mind. You think they're that good, show me the proof. All I'm saying is, I think Sky is better."

"Fine. I'll rearrange their session tomorrow, but she'll have to come in early. That's all I can do, so she better be ready."

"Yeah, for sure. She's keen, she'll be ready. And, hey, don't let on that we moved any mountains for her. Got it? You had a cancellation. That's the story."

"Fine. You're the boss. But we're both going to take some heat from the band over this. Their gear is all set up and they're in a groove. They won't like their session time being pushed. You know that, right?"

"Yeah. Well, tell them you got called in for a meeting. Tell them your cat's going to die. I don't give a shit what you tell them. Call Miko when you have a confirmed session time for Sky and she'll pass it on. And when you're finished with her, I want to hear what you've got right away. Don't fuck around with it too much. Just send it over. If she's as good as I think she is, it won't need much polish anyway."

"If she's as good as you think she is, I'm looking forward to tomorrow. I'll call you."

The line goes dead. Birk stares at his phone screen, considers calling John, but if he gets his boss all excited, and then Sky doesn't work out the way he thinks, John will be reminded that maybe Birk doesn't have the eye for talent he once did. No, he's going to sit on this one just a little longer.

He taps his restless hands on his desk, drumming out a beat to match his anxiety, then spins a few more rotations. The pictures hanging on the wall – some of the greatest moments from his career – whip past him in a blur. Contract signings and awards and platinum records. In all the pictures he looks younger and thinner and he has a stupid smile plastered on his face. He didn't know then that every next artist would be harder and harder to find, that the spotlight gets dimmer as you get older, and the glory barely lasts as long as the hangover. Sky Black might be it for him, his final great success. He starts to get dizzy from the spinning and drops his feet, settling with his back to the door. The silence in his office hurts his head. He calls out to Siri.

"Siri, play my playlist – 'When It Was Good' – 1980."

"Playing: 'When It Was Good' – 1980."

REO Speedwagon comes alive through the speakers.

Bom, bom, bom! Birk heaves his whole body into the upsurge, bending over and wailing on his air guitar, then whipping his head back against his chair. The output of energy is good, soothing. He's pent up and needs a release. He considers who he could call to come fuck him.

His eyes focus on the Fender Telecaster hanging on the wall, signed for him by Bruce Springsteen after a private event at a studio in Queens. Once a week he has Miko come in and personally dust it. He told Bruce he'd be buried with that guitar, but lately he's been wondering how much he could get for it. Sitting on the shelf below the guitar are a pair of drumsticks mounted on a polished wooden base. A plaque glued to the front says:

"Summer of '69"

Pat Steward at LIVE AID with Bryan Adams, 1985.

The sticks were a gift from Adams' manager after Birk hooked him up with a last-minute guitar tech for their North

American tour. Birk stands up from his chair and gingerly removes them from the base. He holds them in his hands, tries to tap a beat out on the shelf, but it sounds terrible. Everything is suffocating in this office, including him. Rock and roll is supposed to be about freedom, but that's just the line guys like him are selling people. He lays the sticks back on the shelf and lifts up the heavy wooden base they were displayed on, rotating it around and around in his hands. Then Birk gets an idea, and before he can consider the repercussions – like how much an act of such stupidity could potentially cost him – he extends his arm behind him like he's about to throw a football and smashes through the case housing Bruce's guitar. Shards of broken glass rain down on his Gucci loafers, scattering across the polished concrete floor. He keeps smashing, knocking away the sharp edges until the guitar is completely exposed, then he puts the wooden base back on the shelf and lifts the neglected instrument out of the rubber mounts that hold it in place. It's heavier than he anticipated, solid and smooth in his hands. He plucks a metal string and it makes an out-of-tune twang. Birk sits back down in his chair, lays the guitar on his lap, and places his hands on the fretboard, running his fingers over the strings that Springsteen touched. The strings that played "Born to Run," "I'm on Fire," and "Dancing in the Dark." He remembers that he loves this. It's a gift to be near really talented musicians, to be present where they are present, to touch what they touch, and to be a witness to what they create. To actually be there is a way to transcend the mundane. Knowing this to be true, deep down in his bones, is what brought Birk to the music industry in the first place.

Holding the guitar transports him to the first concert he ever went to. His mom took him to see the Eagles in Toronto. He remembers how dressed up she got, how she painted her nails and curled her hair. Birk had never seen her on the verge of giddy like she was that night. She played the album while she picked out her outfit, "Heartache Tonight" blasting from the newly acquired JBLs, over and over again. His job was to set the needle back after every play, cuing the *Boom, bop, pa boom bop, boom, bop, pa boom bop.*

Birk was an only child and his dad worked nights at an auto-parts factory. Music was always in the background, his mom playing records long after he went to sleep, drowning out the silence of their lonely house. Birk appreciated music, but he'd never been present when it was being made. It was November 1979, and he was thirteen years old. Standing in the back of The Danforth that night, watching everyone go crazy as Glenn Frey stood centre stage and belted it out, Birk knew this was something special. Something he wanted to be a part of. He would never be an artist – didn't have a lick of musical talent – but he would find a way to exist in their world. He could manage artists and book gigs and find talent. They would need him and he would be there, standing side stage, in the midst of it all.

"Jesus, are you trying to off yourself or something?"

Miko barges into the room, her voice bringing Birk back to the present, to the empty case and crunch of broken glass under his feet. He does a slow rotation to face her, the guitar stretched across his lap.

"What the fuck did you do?! That's signed by Springsteen, you dumbass! You're not supposed to touch it."

"It needed to breathe."

"Why are you smiling like that?"

"It's a good day, Miko baby. You and me and Sky Black, we're going to make some mother-fucking magic again. You ready?"

She laughs a soft, exhaled snicker from her nose. Birk's not sure he's ever heard her laugh before.

"I think you're finally losing your mind, but yeah, sure, count me in. I'll get a broom."

12. By and By

Sky walks the long way home, back down to the shore and along the water. The briny air is thick and cold, stinging her lungs. There's a buzz from the meeting still humming through her veins, and she likes how it feels. Near the bridge she can see the afternoon commute has begun. Cars stream past like endless snakes, honking and swerving for position. Normally their arrogance irritates her, but not today. Today she just pities them, all huffy and unfulfilled, tomorrow like tomorrow like the day after that.

Jani will be furious when Sky tells her she's thinking about not doing her cancer treatment. Yet. *Postponing.* Postponing is a better way to describe what she's doing. If she puts this opportunity off it might never come again. She lets her mind take her on a magic carpet ride of success and fame and her cheeks start to hurt. She thinks it's from the chill in the air, but when she raises her hands to warm her face, she realizes they're sore because she's smiling.

The concrete path leading to the entrance of her building is splintered with moss-filled cracks. Fat black slugs congregate in the wet spots and she steps carefully around them. She slides her key into the metal door, scraped bare of its thin grey paint and carved with names and numbers and every nasty word the human race has managed to conjure up. She pushes it open, kicking aside a crushed bottle held together by its plastic label and charred black by the fire needed to smoke whatever was in it. It looks dirty and desperate. Sky remembers when getting high was fun, not so fucking tragic. Back home when she was a teenager and the serene vibe of her small town made doing drugs feel organic. At first it was just weed and it was no big deal. They would steal it from backyard greenhouses and smoke it after school. The harder stuff started coming in with the transients who travelled through to ski and bum and congregate on the steps of the historic buildings downtown. In a quick decade Nelson changed. It became aggressive and entrepreneurial, no free love to be found, despite the promises adorned on T-shirts and Volkswagen vans. She hasn't been back since she got clean because when she thinks of home she thinks of Joe. It's impossible not to. They'd been together since they were teenagers and his house became hers, his mom like a surrogate to her. She died of pancreatic cancer two years ago. Sky didn't attend the funeral, too scared to inflict more pain on Joe. She'd already hurt him so much. The fact that he's somewhere in this city, her city, makes her heart thump erratically. She'd love to call him and tell him what's happening.

Her apartment is a simple studio and consists of an old vinyl couch, a wood-like coffee table, and a mattress on the floor. A small television sits on a red plastic milk crate in the corner. She rarely watches it. Her guitar, a 1978 Martin D-18, is on a stand in the middle of the room. Her songs are everywhere, scribbled on paper and receipts and napkins, piled on the counter and shoved in her bag, scattered all around the couch. She likes to have them close in case she gets stuck on a lyric, then she rifles back through old scraps, searching for a feeling.

She tosses her leather bag on the chipped laminate counter amid the crumbs, plugs her phone into the waiting cable, then pops her habitual four Advil into her mouth and flops on the couch. She should call the doctor back and tell the secretary about her change in schedule. Sky knows leaving that way was bad, but she can't summon the energy to deal with any of it. She wants to write songs and wait for Miko to call her about studio time. Then she'll go meet Vince the producer and record her music and blow Rod Birk and all the execs at Space Monkey Records away. She smiles again, closing her eyes, just for a second.

***

A loud vibration startles her awake. She identifies the sound as her phone but realizes it's been absorbed into the dream she was having. She was back in Nelson, going to visit her mom in the *community living* colony she joined after she left them. In the dream Sky's annoyed as she walks through a field toward a brightly coloured yurt. The grass is thigh high and deep green, the mountains painted with their evening alpine glow. She hears loud drumming and singing, her mother's angelic voice the loudest of all. She wants to get closer to her, but the mosquitos are thick and buzz loudly, right in her ear. She swats at them but they keep coming back.

Now, she jumps, wiping her face roughly with both hands, and sits up. It's somehow become dark and her mouth is pasty and foul. She gets up to go to the bathroom, avoiding the humming mosquitos that are still plugged in to the charger on the counter.

It's probably Jani calling, wanting to get together tonight, ready to discuss Sky's treatment plan and figure out what the next steps are. Jani has found a way – despite the events of their childhood – to remain kind and logical. The only pain she seems to inflict is on herself. The fact that Jani can make space for their mother in her life is astounding to Sky. She even forgave their father. At least, that's what Jani says. Before he died, Sky was haunted by conversations she needed to have with him. She wanted him to know how much he let them down, because he was good, once, when their mother was still with them. It was only a six-hour drive from Merritt to Prince George – the city where he was imprisoned – so when she was twenty-two, Sky got up the nerve to go visit him. She didn't tell Joe or Marley where she was going, just took the van and left one night after her bartending shift. She stood on the edge of the prison parking lot, watching the sun's first rays fight through thick plumes of smoke, coughed up from the adjacent pulp mill. The dirty clouds rose into the sky and laid like a blanket, choking the city with a foul stench. People lined up outside the jail, waiting to file in and visit their loved ones. Sky didn't join them. Instead, she got back in her van and drove downtown, eventually finding a guy who knew a guy so she could score some crack and lose the day. She woke up later that afternoon in an apartment she never wants to remember, and got the fuck out of there. Joe was sitting in front of their house when she drove up the driveway late that night, a guitar in his hands and an empty honey jar full of cigarette butts at his feet. It was July and the air was muggy and still. Sky can picture him like she's there now. He was wearing tattered jeans that hung from his hip bones and a Broken Social Scene T-shirt with the sleeves cut off. One of his favourites. His dirty blond hair was greasy and sticking out from under his trucker hat, his arms tanned and muscular from work. He stood up as she opened the van door.

"Where the hell were you? You can't just fucking leave like that, Sky, without telling me where you're going! I almost called the cops, but what would I tell them? I was scared they'd find you using somewhere, and throw your ass in jail."

"Jesus, calm down, Joe. I'm exhausted. I need to sleep. Do we have anything in the house?" Sky can still picture the look on his face. Pain and shock, like she'd just slapped him.

"That's all you have to say to me? Do we have any drugs? What about, sorry I disappeared. Or, you're right, Joe, I should've called you."

He leaned his guitar on the arm of the chair and stepped towards her. Her rage boiled up. It wasn't even for Joe, or about him, but that didn't matter. It never mattered.

"Fuck you! You don't own me, Joe! I can do whatever I want." She tried to push past him but he reached out and held her around her ribcage. She wanted to fall into him and tell him about trying to see her dad and what a coward she was, how lonely she felt, but her stupid pride stopped her.

"Yeah, you make that pretty obvious, Sky. Were you with someone?"

"Who cares. It's none of your business."

"What are you talking about? Of course it's my business, I'm your boyfriend, for Christ's sake!"

"Well, you don't have to be." She tore his arm from her body and walked into the house, swallowed the last two oxy she'd stashed in the bathroom drawer, and collapsed onto their bed. Joe came in at some point, smelling like cigarettes and the night. He smoothed her hair and kissed her cheek, sat her up and got her to drink some water. Then he lay down next to her, his strong body wrapped around hers, keeping her safe.

Her dad died a few months later, killed by another inmate. Sky paid to have him cremated and his ashes sent to Jani, who was only eighteen at the time and shouldn't have had to deal with it on her own. Jani tried to plan some kind of memorial, but Sky refused to attend, disappearing with her band for months. Later, Jani told Sky that she scattered their father in the river, at a spot where she remembered him fishing. Sky has no memory of her dad ever going fishing.

Now she splashes cold water on her face and tilts her head low to take a long drink from the tap. She loves the feeling of water on her skin. Ever since she was little, if there was water around, she was in it. She didn't care if she'd come out with blue, chattering lips. It soothed her somehow. She strips her clothes and turns on the shower. It's hot for once and she lets it burn. The day is gone and she knows she needs to eat. She hasn't had anything since she ate pizza with Sam the night before. She wonders if he actually made it home, and then she's hit with regret, like a hard punch, for not getting some way to contact him, a number or a last name. She might have to go looking, back down the alley of lost souls, if she doesn't hear anything from him in the next few days.

After she showers, she dries herself with a towel that smells of mildew and puts on some clean clothes. The cupboards are mostly bare, but she finds a can of tortellini. She considers eating it cold, but after the first disgusting bite she dumps it into a bowl and slides it into the microwave. While she's waiting, she turns her phone over and the screen lights up. Eleven missed calls, some texts, and endless scrolls of social media tags. She presses the voicemail icon and holds the phone to her ear as she watches the white bowl spin circles through the dirty microwave door.

"You have five new messages."

"Sky! Where are you? Come to the lobby. Everyone wants to congratulate you. Please!! Just for a minute. I went to the green room but you're not there. Wherever you are, get your ass back here. Seriously."

Jani, from last night. Too loud and a little drunk, with an edge of, *you better not leave me here to explain why you left.* Sky moves the phone from her ear and presses the number seven. Delete.

"Fine. I'm leaving now, too. I can't believe you took off. But I can, I guess. Joe and Marley hung around, waiting. Joe wanted your address, so I gave it to him and I don't care if you're mad. Stop being such a chicken and just talk to him. Anyway, you were amazing tonight. I hate you, but I love you. Asshole. I'll call you tomorrow."

Seven.

"Sky, this is Margie from Dr. Miller's office. Please return this call or come back to the office. I've contacted the Cancer Agency and they can get you in tomorrow at eleven, but you have to confirm the appointment right away or they'll let it go. Call me back. Thanks."

Seven.

"Hello, Miss Black, my name is Valerie Burris. I'm the treatment coordinator from the Cancer Agency here in Vancouver. You must call and confirm your appointment with us tomorrow, Saturday, at 11a.m. to meet your treatment team. If I don't hear from you, I'll have to give the spot away. Spots don't come up every day, especially the weekend ones. You got lucky and I can't promise I can get you another one for a few weeks. My number is 604-576-8989. Thank you."

Dammit. She skips the message, doesn't delete it. There's one more waiting for her, left twenty minutes ago.

"Hey, Sky Black. It's Miko, from Space Monkey. There was a cancellation at the studio and Vince will meet you tomorrow morning at ten, at 1045 Granville Street. Be prepared to record four songs. Be on time, warmed up, and ready to play. Good luck. I hope it works out for you."

Her voice is like a cat purring. Sky listens to the message three times before putting the phone down, then she takes a deep breath, slowly letting it go. The microwave is beeping at her and she presses the button to release the door, retrieving her sloppy, bubbling dinner. She leans against the counter, blowing on the surface and sending tangy tomato steam into her nostrils. When she can tolerate the heat, she lets the warm noodles slide down her throat, then scrapes all the sauce from the bowl. She grabs her book and phone from the counter and walks back to the couch. Margie will keep bugging her until she returns her call, but it's late so she can leave her a message without actually having to defend her decision. Just a few months. It can't hurt, at least, not more than missing this chance would. Not more than that. But first she'll call Miko and tell her she'll be there.

13. Runaway Train

Sam hears the rev of Andy's Audi as it pulls into the driveway. His mom is in the kitchen making some fancy pasta dish. She told him what it was called but now he can't remember.

"Daddy's home! Wait until he sees my brother. Yay!"

Poppy jumps up from the floor where they were playing Lego. Sam stands, too, exchanging a look with his mom that's less enthusiastic.

"Daddy! Come inside, quick! I have a surprise for you!"

Catherine dries her hands on a dish towel, wringing it into a tight curl, and reaches up to smooth her hair. Poppy has disappeared through the door to the garage, her loud voice echoing back at them. They hear Andy's bark as he gets out of the car.

"Poppy, wait! Don't get dirt on your socks; you'll track it all over the house. I'll look at your drawings after I eat."

"It's not a drawing, silly, it's WAY bigger than that."

The door slams shut and Poppy comes running around the corner, pulling Andy by the hand. He has a briefcase in one hand and a gym bag over his shoulder, some kind of racquet in a case pinned under his arm. His angled face is flushed and his slicked black hair still damp from a shower.

"See, Daddy? My brother's here! Sammy's here! Surprise!"

Andy stops, looking briefly at Sam, then focuses a hard stare on his wife.

"You're fucking kidding me, right Catherine? I knew this would happen. I knew I couldn't trust you."

"Andy, please watch your language around Poppy. Drop your stuff, and let me pour you a drink." She walks over to a long wooden cupboard and taps on the panel. It springs open, revealing several bottles of dark liquor and a row of thick crystal glasses.

"I want him out of here. Now."

Andy doesn't move. Poppy's innocent face crunches up and she drops Andy's hand, running to cling to her mother's leg. Catherine bends down and whispers in her ear, and Poppy shakes her head in protest.

"No, Mommy! I don't want to go to my room. I want Sammy to stay. Please!"

"Poppy, do as your mother says and go to your room!" Andy yells. Sam steps forward, blocking the space between Andy and where his mom and Poppy are standing.

"I'll leave, Andy. Relax. I'm going right now. I just wanted to say sorry about causing a ruckus last night. It won't happen again…"

"Do you think I'm an idiot? That's bullshit and we both know it. I'm not even talking to you. Disappear. Overdose. I don't give a shit. Catherine, get him out of my sight."

He's seething. Poppy starts to cry. Catherine picks her up and walks around the far side of the island to avoid Andy, and carries Poppy down the hall. She envelops Poppy's small body in her arms, shielding her blond curly head beneath her hand, as if she can make her invisible. Andy drops his bag and briefcase to the floor. He slides the racquet from beneath his arm and grips it in his hand.

"Look, Andy, I asked my mom to let me stay so I could talk to you. I'm going back to rehab. I'm committed this time. I want to be a musician."

"A musician? Ha! Please, I've heard all this shit before and I don't believe a word of it. What part of 'never come back' did you miss the first time?"

He walks over to the cupboard, resting the racquet on the island, and pulls out a bottle of Scotch and a glass. He pours himself a fist, then takes a heavy drink.

"And who the hell do you think is going to pay for your rehab again? Not me! Once was enough. You've wasted that chance, and eight grand of my money. Get out, punk. I'm warning you. Get the fuck out of my house."

He takes another big slug, then sets the glass back down on the polished stone. He avoids looking at Sam. Instead, he picks up the racquet again and smoothly unzips the case, unsheathing it and rotating the handle. Testing the grip. The shiny purple carbon flicks from side to side. Sam exhales, then tries again.

"Just hear me out, Andy. I met an amazing girl, a musician, who's going to help me. She'll be my sponsor. She's so talented – you should hear her play!"

Andy drains the glass, slamming it onto the island. Sam's surprised it doesn't shatter.

"This is the last time I'll say it. Get out. You're an intruder and I'll call the police. You have five seconds. 5, 4, 3…" He taps off the count with the edge of the racquet.

"Fine! Fine, I'm going. You're such a bastard. I hope my mom leaves you, and takes Poppy with her. Fuck you."

Sam turns and walks toward the door. He's not sure where he'll go. He has no money and didn't have a chance to ask his mom for some. He has Sky's phone number and address in his pocket, written on a napkin, but he lost his phone months ago. He'll have to get back downtown and find someone who can lend him one. Nag charges in, suggesting he swipe something of value on his way out so he can hawk it at the pawn shop. He doesn't need Andy or his money or his shitty fucking attitude. He puts his hand on the door handle, hesitates because he doesn't like leaving his mom and sister with this asshole. He considers calling out to them so Poppy doesn't worry. He doesn't hear Andy come up behind him. Only the crack of the racket smashing down onto the back of his head. The first blow brings him to his knees.

14. Wings

Harmony Studios is located across the bridge from downtown. Sky takes the bus to the nearest stop and then walks past the entrance three times before she finally gets the nerve to climb the steep, narrow driveway. The city is moving quickly and she's not used to the morning panic, everyone rushing to get where they need to be with pinched faces and Starbucks cups, chins tucked down, mesmerized by their screens. She's fifteen minutes early so she sits on the curb in front of the door and sings a few bars of the new lyrics for "I'm Going Down."

Her phone is vibrating and she pulls it from her pocket. Jani.

"Hey, Jani, what's up?"

"Where were you last night? I tried calling you a million times. We need to talk about your treatment. I have to figure out my life. You know I'm going to be there for you, but I'll need to take a leave from work. And there's Mom."

Before Sky can reply Jani continues.

"Everyone's been calling me to see where you are. People have stuck around Vancouver for the weekend to see you. I don't want to tell your friends you have cancer, Sky. You have to do that. They're going to find out, eventually, so you might as well tell them now."

"I'm sorry, Jani, but I've been busy. Yesterday was a wash. I was out most of the day and then I got home and I was exhausted. I fell asleep and woke up really late. Besides, they're your friends, not mine. I haven't seen most of those people in years."

"Still, they came to see your show, Sky. To support you. That's not good enough."

Sky can hear a softening in her voice. She never stays mad for long, lucky for Sky.

"I can't really talk right now. Guess where I'm about to go?" She can't help herself.

"Well, I'd love to guess, if I had any clue what was going on in your life. I'm hoping it's into the doctor's office. Something tells me it isn't. To adopt a pet? To remove that horrible Red Hot Chili Peppers tattoo? Please…don't keep me in suspense."

"Very funny. No, I'm going into a recording studio. A guy from Space Monkey Records was at the Imperial. He loved the show. They want to hear what else I've got." Sky stops to clear her throat. Stands up and spits the slimy crap into the bushes.

"What? But Sky, how can you do that right now?"

She exhales. Instantly regrets telling Jani. Her question feels like a bucket of cold water poured over Sky's excitement.

"I have to go, Jani. I don't want to be late."

"Wait!"

"What?"

"Good luck, Sky. Seriously, that's amazing, and they're going to love you. I'm sorry, I just…I need you to get better, okay? I can't do life without you. I can't. I want to have kids some day, and they need to know their cool Auntie Sky, the rock star."

Sky wants to argue but she can't. *Fuck.* Why is this happening to her? Why does it have to be so goddamn difficult?

"Go in there and show them what you can do. Blow them away. Then tell them they'll have to wait for you, until you get better."

"Yeah."

"They'll wait Sky. You're worth it."

"Let's hope they think so. Bye."

"Hey, one more thing, whatever you just did with your throat? That spitting thing? Totally disgusting. Never do that around other people. Now go. Call me later."

The studio has a vintage vibe. The floor is layered with colourful rugs and the walls are decorated with acoustic foam and hooks holding coils of black cables. Amps, guitar cases, and microphone stands are tucked neatly into the corners. There's a battered wooden desk blocking access to the open space; its turquoise paint is almost completely peeled off and it's plastered in guitar manufacturer's decals – Fender, Gibson, Yamaha, Rickenbacker. Sky wishes she could own that desk. She'd put it in her apartment and sit at it when she's writing. A dark-haired guy in his early twenties is in the seat instead, scrolling through his phone. Sky waits for him to look up, then fumbles out a greeting.

"Hey, I'm Sky. Black. Are you Vince?" He's younger than Sky expected.

"No, he's upstairs in the booth. I'm Will, his assistant. Vince will be right out."

"Cool. Is there a place I can warm up?"

"Yeah, for sure." Will stands, tearing his gaze from his screen, and leads Sky into the studio behind him.

"You can put your case by the wall and plug in. Mic's ready to go. We'll check your levels and let you know when we're ready."

Will doesn't pause for questions, just keeps walking to the back wall and disappears up a skinny staircase in the corner. Sky tries to act like this isn't a huge fucking deal. She strips off her jacket and lays it in the corner, even though her nerves are making her both sweaty and covered in goose bumps. There's a black hair tie encircling her wrist and she slides it off and stretches it around her hair in one fluid motion, perfected with years of practice. She's wearing a simple white tank top and her signature belt and jeans. Standing at the kitchen sink that morning, she'd used a wet paper towel to wipe away the mud that was caked on her boots, wishing she owned some kind of polish to shine them up. Now she removes her guitar from its case and sits on a wooden stool to tune it. There's a large square window on the front of the booth above her. She looks up and gives a wave, but with the reflection off the glass she can't see if Vince is in there. Feigning confidence, she casually picks up the guitar cable slung on a music stand in front of her and slides the long metal plug into the curved bottom of her guitar, feeling the familiar click. She starts to strum, giving her throat a few rough clears. The Advil is working at full strength right now, but she hopes it'll be enough. She starts to sing, as quietly as she can. The gravel gets smoother as she pushes, so she closes her eyes to this overwhelming place and to the pain and the fear and she goes inside, where the words come from. "I'm Going Down" flows out of her. She was planning to sing just the first few bars, but the playing is settling her nerves and she starts to feel like she's *on*. In the sweet spot. She lets her voice project. The acoustics are great and the vibration is flowing through her, sparking every cell to life. She keeps going. Finishes the song and opens her eyes to find a man who could only be Vince West standing on the staircase, watching her. He's tall, mid-sixties, his fit body layered in tailored clothes, silver chest hair springing from his half open shirt. He boldly wears a purple pompadour and wallet chain, his face adorned with a greying goatee. A perfectly aged rockabilly veteran.

"Well, fuck, Sky Black. There it is, hun. Put your headset on and let's get to work."

He turns around and heads back up the stairs before Sky can say a word. She opens her mouth and her breath catches in her throat, making a strange grunting sound. She's not sure if she feels jarred by the fact that Vince was so cool, that he seemed impressed by her playing, or that he called her hun. All three are equally overwhelming. She reaches for the black headset that's clipped on the stand. There's a small panel by her knee and she adjusts a knob as she strums, controlling how loud the guitar is in her ears, then checking the mic and adjusting the vocal level. There's a soft click and Vince's twangy voice fills her headset.

"Let's run that same one all the way through, Sky. I'll give you a piece of a click track based on the tempo you were just playing, to get you started."

Vince's voice cuts out. Sky takes a deep breath. She hears several soft clicks in her right ear, an electronic metronome counting her in. After the fourth beat, she starts to play.

15. Nose On the Grindstone

"That's it, Sky. We got it. You can pack up."

She removes the headset and unplugs her guitar, putting it back in the case. She's unsure if she's supposed to wait around or just leave, so she puts her jacket on and stands awkwardly by the doorway. Eventually the booth door opens and Vince walks down the stairs, led by his vintage leather boots.

"I'll send these cuts to Rod later today. Not much cleaning up to do on them."

Sky steps closer, hoping she can shake Vince's hand. Planning to google him as soon as she gets outside. This guy definitely has a story.

"Thanks, Vince. I really appreciate your time. You sure made that easy."

"That was you, girl. You're a great songwriter. You've really got something unique." He hands her a card. Vince West. Producer.

Sky's palm is wet with sweat and the card sticks to it. *You're a great songwriter.* Treasured words from someone she already respects so deeply, someone who knows music and musicians like Vince clearly does.

"Call me if you need anything. I'm always around."

Vince holds out his large, weathered hand. Callouses from his strings are thick and rough on the pads of his fingers. Sky slides the card into her back pocket and takes the opportunity to wipe the moisture from her skin, then reaches out to shake. They grip each other tightly, eyes locked. Vince's are light blue and knowing. One strong pump.

"See you soon. Be cool."

He winks at her. Not creepy. More like a father would.

Sky picks up her guitar and walks out the door, blindly heading down the street to the bus stop. The world swirls around her and she can't feel the weight of the guitar in her hand. She sits down on the bench, but sitting isn't working. Deep down inside her a surge of emotion is stirring. The pride for what she did and how long she worked to do it, and the satisfaction of someone like Vince thinking she's worthy. She stands and shuffles her feet. Pulls out her phone, wanting to call someone. Tell Joe. Tell him that she might've just done it. But Joe is with Marley and there's no one to call besides Jani, and she can't. Not now. Not with the buts and the questions. Sky needs to tell a stranger. Someone who doesn't know the other side of all this. Seconds pass. Minutes. The flash of happiness, maybe even hope, becomes clouded because as hard as she tries, she can't ignore the fact that she's decaying. The rage comes and she can't stop it. It mixes into her joy like ink dropped into a glass of water. The contrast of feelings and urgent frustration is impossible to conceal and Sky paces behind the bench, back and forth like a caged animal. Before she can tell herself not to, she starts to kick the fuck out of the wooden advertisement for a smiley-faced realtor. A small lady dressed in a plaid rain suit walks by and looks at her with fear, then stumbles and crosses the street. Sky grabs on to the back of the bench and squeezes tightly with both hands, her breath coming in ragged gulps.

The bus comes but it looks like a cage now, too confined for how she's feeling. She waves the driver past and picks up her guitar and starts walking, all the way across the bridge with the icy wind penetrating through her jacket and freezing her fingers. The simple pain is good, a distraction from the chaos inside her head. She needs to eat and drink and sleep. She needs Advil and she needs not to have cancer. Getting high is all she can think about. She wants to get high because she's happy and because her fucking heart is breaking. Because she's frustrated and proud. Getting high is the perfect fix for all of it. She wonders if the guy who deals behind the tattoo shop on the corner is around. She makes it across the bridge and through the streets without stopping to do something she'll regret. Her hand is cramped and raw from carrying her guitar. As she's walking toward the door of her building, she recognizes a familiar body leaning against the wall, waiting for her.

16. Crash Into Me

He's taller and leaner than Sky remembers, wearing worn leather boots and jeans and a fraying grey wool sweater she remembers from when they were together. She wants to skip the talking part and bury herself in his chest. Inhale him. Tuck her face in the space under his jaw. Let him pick her up and take her inside.

"You going to avoid me for the rest of our lives?"

Joe slides his black sunglasses onto his head and looks her in the eyes. His are blue and still kind, despite everything. Holding his gaze is agony, but she doesn't let it wander because it will stop on the jagged scar that bisects his cheek, and then the guilt will drop her to her knees.

"Joe. Hi. I…um…I was meaning to call you." She puts the guitar case down on the sidewalk and jams her frozen fingers into her pockets. It's so weak. What she's saying and how she's acting. She's such a coward, keeping a few steps away from him.

"Oh yeah? Well, it took too long, so I'm here."

He says the words but they aren't what he actually means. His eyes are saying, *get fucking real, Sky.*

"Late night?" He looks to her case on the ground, eyebrows raised.

"Ha. No. Early morning, actually. I was recording some demos. A label guy was at the show."

"Really? Wow, that's great, Sky. What label?"

"Space Monkey."

"Good. They're legit. How did it go?"

"Really well…I think? The producer was awesome." She's desperate to tell him more, give him every detail. She doesn't want this part of the conversation to stop because she knows what's coming next. Joe doesn't say anything else. He stares like he can see inside her. Waits.

"I'm sorry, Joe. I don't know how to do this. I don't want to make any excuses. All I can say is that I'm so fucking sorry."

She stops to breathe and there's still silence and it's unbearable, so she keeps talking.

"I became everything I hated. Every moment from my childhood where I felt abandoned and devalued and betrayed, I took it and I gave it all to you. I became the monster I was afraid of. I don't know how you can stand to look at me."

She never talks this much but it's all flowing out of her. A verbal barrier to stop him from saying what he came to say. Her hands are up at her chest, about to reach for him. She lowers them. Exhales and prepares for what she's going to hear. Joe stays silent.

"Please, say something."

She's flustered and humiliated by her desperate monologue and heat burns her cheeks. She wants to take it all back and run away and stop this exchange. Never have it. Die first. Finally, he speaks.

"You gave up on me. That's what really hurt. I was used to you being so fucked up you didn't know what was happening. That part I could've gotten over. I could've forgiven you. I have. But it's what came next that destroyed me. You fucking vanished! I had no way to even talk to you. It was like you died! I was trapped in the hospital, you knew I couldn't do anything to find you, and you disappeared. I don't give a shit about that guy or any of the other ones. I don't care what they did to me. It wasn't your fault. But when you left, you betrayed me and every goddamn thing I sacrificed to try to help you. How could you just throw me away like that?"

His eyes flare with anger and he's right and she can't say anything. His shoulders raise and lower with his breath. Sky remembers him coming into the dirty room and shaking her until she woke up. Pulling her naked body from another man's arms, a nasty drug-dealing piece of shit. A guy she knew was evil. But she did it anyway because she needed a hit and she didn't have any money. The dealer grabbed Sky by the hair, wouldn't let her go without a fight, so Joe jumped on top of him, landing blow after blow until he released her. Then Joe gathered her up in a blanket and carried her out to the car. He asked her why, once, but she didn't answer.

And then Sky imagines what happened next, like she always does when she wants to torture herself. Like she was there. The images that haunted her in rehab and continue to wake her up, sweating and shaking. She pictures Joe walking to his truck the next day. He'd just worked a full shift at the garage, stacking tires and fixing engines. They were waiting for him and they jumped him from behind. The guy Joe had punched, joined by three of his friends. Junkies with knives and a score to settle and no sense of what's right. They rammed Joe's body into the truck door and his face into the window, knocking two teeth out. He tried to fight back but they slammed him again and again into the metal. She can see the dealer, scabbed-up face and hate boiling in his eyes, getting really close to Joe's face, pressing him against the glass and smearing his blood in thick swaths across it. He might've said something in Joe's ear, about what Sky felt like or tasted like, about what she did to him, and then he raised the knife, drawing the sharpened point down Joe's cheek. Marking him forever and leaving him with two puncture wounds between his ribs. He had no chance to fight back. Sky wasn't there, but she remembers it like she was. She can hear Joe trying to scream and watch him fall to the ground beside his truck, his blood pouring out of the holes in his chest and forming little rivers as they travelled across the asphalt.

Jani found Sky at home, passed out on the couch where Joe had left her that morning. She shook her awake and told her that Joe was in the hospital in critical condition. They were going to fly him to Kelowna for surgery, so she better hurry if she wanted to see him. Sky went into her bathroom and shot the remnants of something in a discarded needle into her bruised arm, then packed a few of her things, grabbed her guitar, and ran like a coward. She threw her phone in the river and drove her truck to Vancouver, spiralling down so deep there was no light. There was nothing but the end.

Somehow, days or maybe weeks later, she found the will to stand up and walk. She lifted herself off the vomit-covered floor of an apartment she had no memory of entering, walked out the door and down the street and straight into a team of volunteers trying to get addicts like her off the street. She doesn't know who the woman was that walked her into treatment or what magical words she said to convince Sky to go, but something worked. Now she's here and she's sober and Joe survived and she wants to say something to make him understand, but there are no words powerful enough to do that.

"I didn't even know who I was then, Joe. I was scared and so disgusted in myself that living in my own skin was unbearable. If I hadn't run, I would've died. That's not an excuse for what I did, it's just the truth. But I got clean after that, and I've been clean ever since. It's still a struggle I deal with, every day. That's why I couldn't stick around after the show. I'm sorry."

They stand awkwardly. She's not sure what else to say. He's with Marley now and she hurt him so badly. It's been three years and he obviously needed to be away from her, too, or he could've hounded Jani to find out where she was. Nothing can fix this.

"I didn't come here to punish you, Sky. It was years ago. I've moved on."

It's like a blow to her chest.

"Yeah, I heard you and Marley are together. That's cool."

He doesn't acknowledge what she said.

"I came to your show because Jani told me you were retiring. She said you're having some health problems. I'm sorry, Sky. But whatever it is, go get treatment. Get better. And then keep playing. You were born to make music. You'd be wasting your life if you didn't. You were absolutely incredible up there."

He pauses, emotion shining in his eyes and choking his words. She feels a sob rising up from inside and bites her bottom lip to keep it in.

"I'm so fucking proud of you. You've kept at it. You've worked so hard. Don't quit now. That's all I wanted to say."

He slides the sunglasses back down but doesn't move. She wants to hold on to him and never let go. But Joe's not hers anymore.

"It's not really that simple."

"Why? What's wrong?"

"I…I can't…it's complicated."

"Well, I hope you can figure it out. I should go."

"Wait, Joe. Please. Can we talk some more? Do you want to come in? Or…get some coffee or something? I'd love to hear about your new band. Jani told me you guys signed a deal. That's awesome." Her voice is broken and squeaky and she feels panicked. He's going to be gone again and she wants him, needs him, in her life.

"I have to go, Sky. I really shouldn't be here at all, I just had to tell you that. I want you to be happy. I know you won't believe me, but you deserve it."

"Thank you. I…want to keep playing, of course, I just…I'm just not sure how much I should risk, you know? When do you decide it's never going to get you anywhere?"

"Watching you on stage, Sky, I think it's worth risking a lot. And I don't know about fame and fortune, but you seem like you've gotten somewhere to me. Last night, that was somewhere."

"Yeah, maybe you're right." She wants to keep talking to him, desperately, but he starts to walk away and she can't let him go without one more regret spoken.

"Hey…I'm so sorry about your mom, Joe. I loved her. You know I loved her. I should've gone to her funeral, I just, I didn't know if you would want me there. I didn't want to be one more thing you'd have to deal with that day."

He stops moving, drops his head down. His glasses are on and she can't see his eyes, but she knows if she could they'd be full of pain.

"Thanks. I really miss her. She…she went so fast, once she was diagnosed. It's okay, Sky, that you weren't there. I know you loved her. I'll see you."

He walks away. She watches him go, his muscular back moving beneath the thin wool. She wants to call his name, but nothing comes out.

There's a void where he stood. It's palpable in the air and inside of her, like a piece of her body was torn out. She slowly picks up her guitar, winded from being so close to him. At least now she can stop having the fake conversation in her mind. Running the scenarios like old movie clips. She'd give anything to kiss his lips and feel his hands on her body. Even for a night. Even for a minute.

17. Just Breathe

It's cold in Sky's apartment. The sun hasn't been out all day and the building's heat is shoddy at best. She feels hollow. Exhausted. From getting up so early and recording the demos and Vince's reaction but mostly from being so close to Joe, close enough to touch him. The conversation was years in the making and she should feel relieved that it's over, but all she can do is collapse on the couch and stare at the wall. Regret everything that she did to make them act like strangers.

As the afternoon wears on her phone buzzes with texts. It's Saturday and friends who stayed in town are going to a show at the Roxy, a live-music venue a short walk from her place. She should go. She owes it to them after they came all the way down here and bought tickets to watch her play. She reads their messages as they stream onto her screen.

"Sky, come on! It's going to be a great time. Come out!"

"What the fuck? Are you too big of a deal to hang with us now?"

Marley will probably be there with Joe, and after seeing him today Sky knows she couldn't stomach seeing them together. Touching. Smiling. Marley greeting her with a big hug and her exuberant questions. Her bouncy blond hair and cute dimples. It would break her. She already agreed to meet Jani and her mom tomorrow for breakfast before they head back. Jani's relentless texting forced her hand, but at least it's keeping them from coming to her apartment. She couldn't take the look of judgment on her mom's face if she saw where Sky lived. It's the first time Sky's ever had her own place – four dingy walls in a terrible neighbourhood – but her music pays the bills and that's all she's ever wanted.

One of Jani's messages includes the information about the holistic clinic in Nelson. Sky clicks on the link and a picture of a white flower floating in the water appears. She starts to read about Willa's "vision for healing," success rate, testimonials from patients, and the description of therapies provided. Acupuncture and massage, supplements and remedies, UV light treatment and something about metabolic therapy. She imagines herself going home and getting treatment that isn't cutting into her throat. Something gentler. It's not her style, but for some reason she's drawn to the idea. The wave of emotion that's been chasing her since she left the doctor's office yesterday – and maybe long before that – finally catches her. Tears pour down her cheeks. She doesn't want to die. She starts to sob and it grips her so hard she can't get a breath. She gasps, heaving animal sounds from her body, her face awash in snot and tears. She doesn't want to die. The fear is so strong it's choking her. Sky drops her phone beside her, tucking her head into the crooks of her elbows and wailing with an unfamiliar voice. She's desperate for someone to reassure her that everything will be okay. A gentle whisper in her ear. *You will survive this.* She needs Joe. No one else could soothe her in this moment. She wants to be with Joe. None of this will matter if she isn't. She wants to be healed and get this deal and live her dream. Float off the stage every night like she did on Thursday, feeling satiated and powerful. Her body curls inward on itself, exhausted. She hasn't cried since rehab and she forgot how physically consuming it is. Eventually the emotion is completely wrung out of her. She wipes her face on the bottom of her shirt and finds her phone, shoved between the cushions on the couch. Before she can talk herself out of it, she sends a text to Jani.

"Can you send me Joe's contact?"

Almost immediately, a little square with the name Joe Slater appears. Mercifully, Jani doesn't make any comment.

Sky imagines their bodies pressed together in the dark, the electricity they generate every time they're close to each other sparking as he touches her, but her thoughts are interrupted when an unknown number lights up her screen. She stares at it, then sniffs one more time, and answers.

"Hello?"

"Hey…uh, Sky? Hey, it's Sam. From the other night?" His voice is broken and hard to hear through the sounds of traffic and yelling in the background.

"Sam! Hi, how are you?" She stands up as she speaks, an instinct coming over her to start moving. She wipes at her face again. Here's something she can do that's good. Something that isn't about her and all her fucking problems.

"Um, I'm okay. I guess. I'm a little banged up, to be honest." Sky can hear the saliva pooling in Sam's mouth, causing his words to slur like he's frozen from the dentist.

"What happened? Do you need some help?" Her eyes dart around her apartment, locating her jacket and bag.

"Oh, no. I don't want to put you out." *Puh yu oww.*

"You're not putting me out. I wasn't doing anything, and I need to eat. Come over. I'll order some food. Do you still have my address?" Sky knows that even during the journey to her apartment from wherever Sam is now, things can go off the rails. She slides her arm into the sleeve of her coat.

"Yeah, 403 East Hastings, right?"

"Yes. Buzzer 331. Hey, where are you now, Sam? I can walk and meet you. I need some fresh air." There's shuffling in the mouth piece. Muffled words. Sam speaks to someone. Sky wonders if this is his phone or if he borrowed one.

"That's okay, Sky. I have the address and I'm not far away. I'll be there in about half an hour."

She feels panicky, like this call is a scream for help and if Sam gets away, he might be gone for good. She has to grab on gently so she doesn't spook him.

"Sam, I'm ordering Chinese. If you're not here to eat it in thirty minutes, I'll be pissed. Got it?" Sky confirms her keys are in her bag.

"Yes. For sure. I'm coming right now. See you soon."

The line goes dead. She glances at the time on her phone, six forty-five, then pushes her door open, jogging down the stairs and out into the damp night air. Bodies move on the darkened sidewalk. The streetlights are stretched too far apart, some broken from thrown rocks. She looks up and down the street, scanning for Sam's narrow frame. She decides to turn right, back towards the Imperial. Junkies are territorial. They usually stick to the same few blocks they're comfortable with. They know who's around and where to fix and if there's a warm grate available.

As she walks, Sky's mind wanders back to Joe. She thinks of the tattoo that lies beneath his shirt, an eagle with its wings spread, powerful feathers climbing up his chest and reaching to the spot she likes to press her face into, on his neck, just below his chin. Her name is in script beneath the bird, scrawled across his ribs. Or it was. Sky remembers the day he showed it to her, still red and angry from the needle piercing his flesh. She always loved him, but she held back, rarely letting him know how much he meant to her, always taking his devotion for granted, disappearing for nights with no contact and ignoring his calls until she could spin it to make him the bad guy. Of all her regrets, Joe is her greatest.

The smell of grease wafts through the air from a hotdog cart on the corner. Sky's stomach rumbles viciously. She has to find Sam. Save Sam. She checks her phone. Seven-ten. She should go back to her apartment in case she misses him. That prospect didn't occur to her when she fled to the street, and now it seems stupid that she left. She feels out of control. Chaotic. She's projecting her own shit onto this kid and maybe it's not even as bad as she's making it out to be. She turns on her heel and walks back to her apartment.

Sam is standing in front of the door, punching numbers into the key pad. The numbers are nothing like 331. They are long strings of digits with sloppy fingers. He has a black hoodie on that he wasn't wearing two days ago. His thick head of sandy hair is messy and flattened in the back, making him look as young as he is. Relief floods into Sky and she unclenches her jaw. Breathes deeply and feels her shoulders relax.

"Hey, Sam, it's 331. Remember?"

Sam jumps at the sound of her voice and turns abruptly. His face is mashed like hamburger. One eye is swollen closed. His bottom lip is huge and crusted with blood.

"Jesus. What the hell happened to you?" As she asks the question, Sky cringes. The shock and the questions never help. They make you want to run. She quickly covers for herself as Sam looks at the pavement.

"Never mind. Come on; let's go inside. It's fucking freezing out here."

He makes a soft grunt of agreement but keeps his head down as Sky moves around him to unlock the door. They climb the stairs in silence. She holds the apartment door open as he stops to take off his shoes, revealing dirty socks full of holes.

"Make yourself at home. You like chow mein?"

Sam stands awkwardly a few steps into the apartment. Sky wishes she could offer him a beer. Some gesture of comradery that says, *relax, you're safe here.* But that's not an option and she doesn't have anything to drink in the fridge. She takes out her phone and dials the cheap place that comes fast. She orders some ginger beef and the skinny noodles that will slide down her throat, lemon chicken, and a couple of Cokes. Sam walks over to Sky's guitar sitting in the stand and gently rubs his finger on the glossy curled wood.

"Pick it up. Play me something. I have Advil and some stuff to clean up your face in the bathroom."

Sam looks over his shoulder at Sky to make sure she's serious. His puffy eye is bloodshot and looks sore. The flesh covering his cheekbone is purple. She tries not to focus on his face, but it's difficult not to look. She wonders if he got a boot to it while he was sleeping. Made a bad deal. Ran into the wrong guy. So many scenarios that bring about the same conclusion.

"Go ahead. Play."

Sam carefully lifts the Martin from the stand and strums a G chord to see if it's tuned. He sits on the coffee table and his fingers begin to move over the strings, slowly at first, then gaining speed as they pluck and slide in a rhythmic dance. He's better than good. It's a song from Ben Harper, and as Sam plays Sky feels her skin reacting. Prickling. Her breath catches in her lungs and time slows down. The fret board is his runway and Sam's fingers fly across it, intricately picking the strings while maintaining a steady rhythm below the surface. His back is hunched and his shoulders roll steadily to the beat. He doesn't sing, but Sky wishes he would. Senses greatness. She's frozen in place and she doesn't know how long he plays, several minutes, maybe longer. When he stops she opens her mouth to say something that might just give him a reason to want more out of this life than what he's settling for now. It's hard to find the perfect words. The ones that can express how lucky she felt to be in this room. Sam looks up, his non-purple cheek flushed with embarrassment. He's barely spoken since they came inside and Sky needs to hear him. They look at each other, Sky still grappling with her reaction. Finally, Sam speaks.

"Sorry, I kind of went off there. I haven't played in months. Guess I missed it." He gets up to put the guitar back in its stand. Wobbles. Sits back down.

"Sam, I'm speechless. Seriously. I've been around guys playing guitars most of my life. I'm telling you, you're incredible. A natural. One of the best I've ever heard." She takes a step towards him.

"Come on, Sky. That's crazy. I'm not that great, I just play for fun…"

Sky cuts him off.

"No, Sam. Don't do that. I mean it. You're amazing. You can play with me anytime."

Sam's smirking now and even through the swelling Sky can see the light is back in his eyes.

"Guess that means you're not retiring after all."

He's the kid again, not a beat-up drug addict, and Sky sees everything so clearly in this instant, in this flash of a vision for the future. She tells him to shut up and keep playing, then leaves to get a wet cloth and some Polysporin and Advil from the bathroom.

They pass the guitar back and forth for hours, pausing to devour the food when it arrives. It's hot and greasy and slips easily into Sky's empty stomach, making her feel full and satisfied like she hasn't in days. They talk about music and musicians and who inspires them. Sam is young and his influences reflect it. Arkells. Wintersleep. Arcade Fire. She lets Sam riff on a melody while she writes.

Seconds tick off the clock and Sky knows they are fleeting. Sam will start twitching soon and he'll make up an excuse to leave. She hasn't asked him anything about what happened or who beat the shit out of him, but she knows what she needs to say.

Sam goes into the bathroom, when he comes out he looks to the door. Sky stands.

"Sam, I know you need to go. I get it. I just wanted to talk to you for a minute before you do." Sam looks down. Studies the floor with his good eye.

"Thanks for letting me hang, Sky, it was awesome to see you again. And thanks for the food. And the music. I haven't played like that in a long time. Too bad my stepdad wrecked my guitar. I'll have to start saving for a new one."

He says it like he's a normal kid with a job and a regular allowance. He bends over to put his shoes back on, staggers and has to grab on to the wall.

"Look. Sam. I might have some gigs coming up. I recorded a few demos today for that record label guy. I think the session went pretty well, and I think another guitar would really add to my sound. I guess what I'm saying is, I might have a spot for you. To play with me. If you're interested."

Sam's unharmed eye is wide with disbelief. The other one still looks terrible and Sky cringes studying it this close.

"Holy shit. Are you serious? I mean. Of course, I'm interested. I'd love that, but you know my situation. I don't have a guitar. I don't even have a fucking change of clothes."

Sam looks down at what he's wearing and pulls at the edges of his hoodie.

"I went home after your show. I really wanted to see if I could make a change, you know? Talk to my mom about getting back into rehab. At least have a shower and get some clothes. It didn't exactly work out." Sam gestures to his swollen face.

"What do you mean? Someone at your house did that to you?"

"My stepdad. He hates me. I promised I wouldn't show up late at night, or…under the influence, but I kinda screwed up."

"Shit, Sam. I'm sorry." Sky feels responsible. She's the one who told him to go home. She walked him right into this.

"I just wanted to talk to the guy. Tell him I was sorry, and that I was going to try again, to get clean. He wouldn't listen to a word I said. The asshole went ballistic. Grabbed his pansy-ass squash racket and smashed my face in."

Sky feels hot with rage.

"That's fucked up, Sam. But we can't let that be the reason you don't play with me. He doesn't get to win. There has to be a way to make this work. I'm willing to help any way I can, but first you've got to get clean. It isn't easy. I'm not going to pretend it is. But it's worth it. You're so talented, and I think we could do something cool. I'm sick of playing by myself. We could have some fun together, before…well…I don't want to do this much longer. I can't. But maybe one more little run at it. I could call the clinic I went to, and see if we could get you in. They reserve spots for young people who…can't really wait. It's free, but it's only a four-week program, then you're on your own. You have to want it. Bad."

Sam is standing a little straighter and Sky instantly feels pangs of regret for what she's promising this kid. What if she can't make good on what she's saying?

"I'm not sure if this record thing will happen, Sam. I won't know until they listen to the demos. But if it does happen, it'll be fast. If you want to come for the ride, you have to be ready."

Sam leans his head against the wall and closes his eyes. Sky knows exactly how he feels in this moment. When you know you're at the bottom. A place you never thought you'd end up. A place where you have to own your weakness and admit that you can't get back up without help, even when you told everyone around you that you had control of the situation. All this time, you believed your lies. But everyone could see it except for you, and you finally have to admit it. It's a soul-stripping, pride-swallowing state to find yourself in.

A single tear escapes from Sam's swollen eye and runs down his cheek. He quickly brushes it away and seems to gather himself.

"Okay, Sky. If you believe in me, I'll do it. If I can get in, I'll go. I just hope I don't let you down."

Sky's so relieved she almost lets out a whoop, but keeps it in at the last second.

"You won't let me down. You've got this. You can do it." She pats him on the shoulder, then backs up to let him come back to the couch.

"I didn't have a reason before. Now I do." He smiles through his broken, puffy face and Sky knows she's doing the right thing. Sam has his whole life in front of him and she's going to save him.

18. Sleeping Sickness

It's after two in the morning when Birk's phone finally rings.

"Hey, it's me. Check your email."

"Are they good?"

"Have a listen. I'm exhausted. As soon as she left, Kit Wednesday showed up and they've been at it until now. I think they did it to prove a point. Can't say I blame them after they had their shit moved all over the place. They weren't happy, Roddy. Consider that a heads up."

Birk leans forward and heaves his lumpy body up from the supple leather recliner he was inhabiting, then hurries down the hall to his office, flipping light switches on as he goes. His screen saver is a picture of him with his arms draped over two of the Pussycat Dolls. He appreciates it for a second – their perfect skin and voluptuous tits – then hits the spacebar as he slides into his office chair.

"I don't care, whatever. I'll deal with it. Tell me about Sky. She's fucking fantastic, am I right? And sexy as hell, obviously."

Vince exhales. Long and drawn out, like he's smoking.

"Yeah, Roddy. You're right. She's special, no question about it. Her sound is unique, for today's standards. Real old soul stuff."

"Yes! I told you! Fuck yeah! This is it, Vince. I know it. Hang on tight, 'cause we're going on a wild ride my friend!"

Vince releases a deep chuckle on the other end of the line.

"Well, maybe so, Roddy. Just don't fuck it up. From what I can tell, she's been through some shit. Go easy on her. Don't push too hard. She'll disappear. I promise you, she'll be gone."

Birk isn't listening, he's clicking on the link to his Dropbox. Sky Black – Demos. His finger tremors with excitement, and probably from the few lines of coke he did while he was watching *Timber Kings*.

"Of course. I got it. I know this type, Vince. Don't worry. Just get ready to clear your schedule, 'cause we're making a record that's going to blow everyone's minds. Start thinking musicians. I want the best for this. And not that shitty drummer we used for the Riot Dogs."

"Yeah, I got it. Sign her first, okay? Give me some dates and then we'll get it sorted out on our end."

"Done. I gotta go. I want to do this right. I'll be in touch. Are you going to be up for a while?"

"No, Rod. I'm going to bed. Call me tomorrow. And we need to talk about a voice coach for her. She's shredding pretty harshly. Might need to see a doctor."

"Don't jinx it, Vince. She's fine. A doctor will put that bullshit about *nodes* into her head and she'll be obsessed. That shit is all mental. All the greats had nodes. Her shred is the fucking magic. It's what makes her so unique. The shred and her hot ass. You can't take your eyes off her, am I right? No way in hell we're messing with any of it."

"Well, if she loses her voice halfway through the tour, she won't be so magic anymore."

"Go to bed, gramps. I'll talk to you tomorrow."

Birk ends the call. He doesn't want Vince's lack of enthusiasm bringing him down right now. The first track, "I'm Going Down," is cued up and he opens his desk drawer, removing a small wooden pipe and a lighter. It's already packed with Donegal, his favourite type of weed for happy occasions like this. He flicks the flame to life and draws in a long, sweet breath, holding it in his lungs and closing his eyes. He doesn't say a prayer, exactly; it's more of a wish. Then he hits play.

19. Midnight Regulations

Sky passed out on her bed for a few hours, periodically awoken by the music. Sam went back to the guitar and played. Intricate picking and soulful songs that Sky struggled to stay awake just to listen to. Now it's morning and Sam's asleep on the couch, her guitar laying across his lap. She stands up and gingerly lifts it from his body, places it back in the stand, then goes straight to her phone and googles the website for the rehab clinic. She dials the number and speaks with the coordinator, Peggy, the same woman who'd run the place when Sky was there three years prior. Miraculously, there's a spot for Sam. Someone bowed out the day before and vacated one of the reserved spots for patients who are currently *without residence*. Peggy tells her Sam has to be on site to claim the spot and start the intake procedures in one hour, and he has to be sober. Sky assures her he will be, then takes a quick shower, afraid to let Sam out of her sight, even for a minute. She wakes him up and, without many words, they walk to the clinic. Sam's shaky, chewing his already decimated fingernails, but he marches through the doorway and fills out the paperwork, even calls his mom to let her know.

Sky says a quick goodbye and takes off, the chemical odour and visceral memories of the place making her gag. On her way home she walks by a pawn shop on Granville, stopping to check out a sweet little Yamaha guitar in the window. She steps inside and speaks to the bored guy behind the counter, wrangling the price down to three hundred bucks. It comes with a beat-up case, which she fills with several packages of new strings. Sam can't have visitors for three weeks, but Sky will drop the guitar off at reception for him in a few days. He'll have to survive withdrawal first. She shudders at the memory, like the worst flu and food poising and acid trip, all combined into a soul-crushing reconciliation where you relive every bad decision you've ever made. The rage is so intense it can send you through the wall.

Sky walks home, moving slowly, lifting her face to feel the sun's rays when they break through the clouds. She can't ignore the fire of excitement in her belly. What if it could all mean something? Everything she's been through. All the shit she's done and mistakes she's made. What if it's brought her to this place and given her an ounce of power and she can actually help somebody?

She ambles up her stairs and lets herself into her apartment. Her entire body throbs with pain. It starts on her tongue and travels through every available pathway, leaving shards of glass in her veins all the way down her legs and to her toes. She wants to lie down so badly, but she can't. She's late.

20. Poets

Birk can't wait another minute. He picks up his phone and dials.

"Hey, I've got big news."

Miko lets out an irritated sigh, then tells whoever's lying next to her that she'll be a minute.

"Rod, we've been through this. It's Sunday morning! I don't give a fuck who you hooked up with last night. I'm going back to sleep. Tell me tomorrow, at work, although I still won't care."

"Wait! This isn't about a chick. It's Sky Black. Vince sent the demos over late last night."

A pause.

"And?"

"And…they're fucking incredible! Amazing! Huge range. Gut-wrenching lyrics. Melodies that hook. The whole package. I'm telling you, Miko, we've got ourselves a star. I knew it! I told you! Didn't I tell you??"

"Yes, Rod, you told me. Jesus, calm down."

"See? I've still got it. But listen, I need your help, and we have to be fast."

"I knew there was a catch. What do you need?"

"I need the full package. Her sound is perfect, but her image needs work. She's got way too much of that boho-hippie vibe going. I want her tighter. Edgier. No more big belt buckles and twenty-dollar T-shirts. Ditch that bulky leather jacket. I want skin. Sex."

"Yeah, okay. I can see that for her. I'll call Leon and book something with his team."

"Arrange it for tomorrow night. I'm inviting John and the execs in for a showcase on Tuesday. I'll call Sky and let her know. But let's play it cool. Quiet. I don't want her to think it's a done deal. She might be harder to sway on the image piece if we give her any power. And I want to sign her for the bare bones. She was about to quit music when I found her. She'd sign for free, so that's basically what we're going to offer. It'll be legendary. Westlake is going to worship me when this is over."

"Oh my God. Stop. You're giving me a headache."

"Miko, I really need you to grease her wheels before you bring her to Leon. Woo her. Take her out for drinks and work your magic. That's what we pay you so much for, isn't it?"

"Fuck you, Rod. Be careful. I'm not the Space Monkey prostitute."

"Oh, right. So, you don't want to fuck her?"

"Well, I didn't say that."

21. Fire and Rain

The restaurant Jani chose for breakfast isn't far from Sky's apartment. She makes a hard left and wanders up into the fancier part of downtown. Robson Street is a tourist beehive, people swarming in and out of the high-end shops, arms full of bags, and purses fat with cash. They don't smile or seem like they're having fun and Sky never envies them. Not their Roots sweatshirts or shiny pinched shoes or their big hurry. She always wonders why they all seem to be in such a rush when they're supposed to be on vacation.

She used to busk on the corner of Robson and Thurlow when she was short on rent, but for every person who actually stopped to listen, there'd be twenty pushing past her with annoyed expressions, dropping cigarette butts at her feet. It wasn't worth the damage to her soul.

With the sunshine comes the smell of the ocean. It's often masked by other smells this far into the city, but not today. She breathes deeply to take it in, hoping it will clear her mind and give her the energy she needs to have this conversation. A striking man in a grey wool jacket is walking towards her on the sidewalk. He slows as they get closer to each other, looking at her like he might say something. Like he wants to. Their eyes meet. She smiles, and he stops, says "Hey, hi," but she keeps walking. Bad timing, but she's tempted. She hasn't been with a guy in months and seeing Joe brought that fact clearly to her attention. She misses being touched. The feeling of a man's weight on top of her. Skin touching skin. Joe's probably driving back home today. Marley next to him, her legs tucked under her, a steaming cup of tea in her hands. Sky gnashes her teeth together, then shoves the image out of her mind.

The sidewalk is getting busier as she turns the corner. The sunshine brings people out of the woodwork and it seems like they all came downtown. She steps to the side to let a crowd walk past her, all bunched together and speaking loudly in a foreign language. She remembers why she doesn't meet people for brunch. The signs from the shops are lit up and she scans them, knowing the restaurant is somewhere close to her. She pulls out her phone to look at the map. The small blue dot that is her is standing where the directions tell her to go. She finds a text from Jani.

"We have a table. Hurry up. You're late."

Finally, she finds the window painted with the name she's been looking for: Baked.

I wish, Sky thinks, as she pulls open the door and runs smack into a long lineup of people jammed into the entrance. She slips to the side and edges past them, avoiding their dirty glares, finding Jani and her mom at a table by the window.

"Hey. Sorry; crazy morning."

Jani jumps up and wraps her skinny arms around Sky's neck, speaking in her ear so their mother can't hear.

"Could you be later? Be nice, please, for me."

She pulls back to look Sky in the eye. Her smile is fake. Sky knows her real one, when her nose gets crinkly and her eyes shine. This isn't it. Her curly hair is pulled back in a high knot on her head and she wears no makeup. Freckles dot the smooth skin under her eyes.

Sky clears her throat, looking down to address her mom.

"Sorry I'm late. I had something to deal with this morning."

Her mom smiles up at her. Stands slowly. She's wearing another robe-like garment, similar to the one she wore to the concert. It looks weird and religious and Sky wants her to sit back down before people notice.

"Sky. It's so good to see you, love. Your spirit is so bright today. Your aura is much lighter than it was at your show. I'm happy you've found some peace, honey." She leans in like she might hug her. Sky pulls out her chair and sits in it as quickly as possible. There's a steaming cup of black coffee waiting for her.

"Yeah, well, thanks, I guess. I'm starving. Jani, what are you getting?"

Sky looks at her sister and rolls her eyes, but can't escape the little buzz in her mind that what her mom just said was right. Jani bites her bottom lip to hold in her giggle.

"Eggs."

Sky feels a small surge of relief that Jani said eggs, plural. She smiles at her but doesn't dare make a comment.

The waitress comes and they order. Her mom questions the poor girl for five excruciating minutes about what's organic and where it was grown. Eventually she settles on sliced avocado, despite her disapproval that it was shipped from Mexico. Sky takes a sip of her coffee and it burns but in a good way compared to the usual burning. They sit in painful silence for several seconds that feel like hours, her mom looking at her with an awkward half-smile. Sky starts to squirm.

"Look, Mom, it was nice of you to come all this way to see my show, but I'm not sure what you want from me. Nothing's different, for me at least."

Jani flinches. Sky didn't mean to sound like an asshole. Her mom takes a long breath in. Sky hates how patient she is, wishes she'd just tell her to fuck off. That's something Sky can deal with. Instead, she reaches out and puts her hands on Sky's. She pulls away and her mom's face drops.

"I'm deeply sorry that our relationship is so damaged, Sky. That was never my intention. I never wanted to hurt you the way I did. At the time, my escape was a means of survival. I'm regretful that I didn't take you kids with me, but my path wasn't yours."

Here's the bullshit she likes to spout as justification for everything she did. She hasn't changed a bit and Sky is so sick of her excuses.

"Mom, that's such bullshit." Her voice is too loud and she stops to get control of herself. She knew this was a bad idea and now she's wondering why the hell she let Jani talk her into it.

"You're our mother. Why did you have us if we weren't supposed to be on your path? Please. The truth is, you abandoned us. No. It was worse than that. You left us with an alcoholic, abusive asshole so you could go get high and have orgies in a tent. Then you used all your philosophical crap to make excuses for yourself. To make us feel like it was our fault. You couldn't hack it as a parent, I get it, I'm over it, but at least admit it. Don't come here with expectations of me. You don't deserve a second of my time, and honestly, I'm not interested in anything you have to say."

Sky sits back in her chair. Jani's eyes are fixed in her lap where she's frantically tearing a napkin to shreds. Their mother stares. Blinks. She might have tears building in her eyes, Sky can't stick around to find out. She has to leave. She stands up.

"Sky." Her voice cracks. "Please, don't go yet. Let me speak. Let me try to explain."

"No, Mom. I don't need you. Not now. Where were you when I was just a kid making a fucking mess of my life? When I was in rehab? When I got out?"

Heads turn to look. It's not brunch conversation, but Sky doesn't give a shit. She feels a release with every truthful word she speaks. She continues, despite the pain on her mother's face.

"Look, I don't want to leave this any worse than it was. I hope you're happy. I hope you and Jani can have some sort of relationship, if that's what Jani wants."

Sky looks at her sister. Tears roll over Jani's cheeks and off her chin. She feels bad for being so harsh, but she can't find the energy to be fake. She's hungry and exhausted and fucking pissed. She didn't even realize how much anger she was holding inside until this moment. She has to get out of this tiny restaurant and away from her mom.

"Please leave me alone, Mom. Don't come here again. I'll deal with everything in my life, just like I always have." She turns to her sister. "Jani, drive safe and I'll call you in a couple of days. I love you." She speaks softly to her, then leans down and kisses her head. She smells like trees. Sky hates to leave her crying, but this is too much. As she walks out, she passes the waitress carrying two plates of steaming eggs and buttered toast and the fucking Mexican avocado. Her hunger is temporarily gone but her nerves are on edge and she sure could use a hit.

Outside it's still busy and the sun is still shining. She needs something to keep her occupied while she waits for the call from Birk. It could be weeks, or it could be never. She walks a few blocks, then stops to buy a falafel from the cart on the corner, not because her hunger has returned, but because she knows she needs food.

When she gets home her apartment is too empty. Too quiet. She plugs in her phone to make sure it's charged. There are two texts from Jani that she scans, trying not to read all the words and have to process them.

"I'm sorry. That was shitty and I know I forced you into it. Maybe you'll never forgive her. That's okay. You don't have to. I love you. I'll talk to you in a few days."

And then: "oh, and talk to Joe. You still love each other. Stop being so stupid."

Sky picks up her guitar, but she's too antsy to play it. It's two o'clock on a Sunday. She should get some sleep, but she has to relax first. She flips on the TV and watches a show about fly fishing because the river reminds her of home. Eventually, she sleeps. Her dreams are urgent and scary. She's trapped in a forest. The trees circle her and she spins and spins but doesn't know the way out. She can't breathe. Her throat closes off and black, sooty drool pours onto her hands. Then she sees Joe. He's walking in front of her and he turns and says "come on" with a soft smile. She feels safe. He turns his face again and the cut on his cheek is fresh and bleeding and there's a zipper. She reaches up to close it, pulling hard until the edges of the wound join together. When it's all the way to the top he smiles and thanks her, then takes her hand and leads her to a path she hadn't noticed before. They break through the trees and onto the beach where Joe lives now, in his mom's old cabin. Sky pulls off her clothes and follows him down the colourful rocks, pearly pinks, grey-blues, and sparkly whites. They reach the water's edge and he presses his hands to the sides of her face, kissing her lips. His size dwarfs hers and she closes the space between them and melts into his body, laying her face on his chest. They stand that way, his arms wrapped around her bare skin like they're one thing, then he steps back and strips off his clothes and they hold hands and walk together into the calm liquid. Joe stops when the water reaches his chest, but Sky lets go of him and keeps moving, the water inching up her body until her head dips below the surface.

22. She Talks To Angels

Her phone reads 11:04 a.m. She's been sleeping since yesterday afternoon and the taste in her mouth is coppery burnt death. She imagines cutting a hole into the soft indentation where her chest meets her neck and ripping out what's gone rotten, how great it would be if she could solve this problem that easily.

The shower squeaks to life and she lets the hot water burn her skin, enjoying the pain being somewhere other than her throat. She swallows a handful of pills and doesn't feel like eating or playing her guitar or writing. This waiting will kill her. She's too in her head right now and she knows a really quick way out and it's all she can focus on. Just the thought of getting high makes her hands shake. She considers calling Gary, but he'll give her a sponsor pep talk and hound her to come to a meeting. Sky's not up for it.

A brochure sits on her counter titled *Financial Assistance for Patients Undergoing Cancer Treatment.* She checks the balance in her bank account from the app on her phone. $1,767.06. Fuck. She'd agreed to $1,500.00 for her gig at the Imperial, after they'd insisted that was the most they could offer since she's not exactly "well-known" and the increasing costs of liquor licences and sound techs and blah, blah, blah. Sky wishes she'd known that Jani would sell the place out with people from Nelson who know how to have a good time. The Imperial must've raked in thousands on beer sales alone. Ramen. She'll have to eat a shitload of ramen this week.

She grabs a hoodie from the closet and shrugs it on, leaving her apartment. She has to walk. It's her therapy, maybe her meditation, and right now she needs to be in a crowd even though she has no desire to interact with anyone. She steps outside and the sunshine hits her, warm on her shoulders, promising spring. It smells like rotting leaves, moist and mouldy. The small green shoots will pop up through the gaps in the concrete soon, bringing freshness. Forgotten tulips will appear in random patches of grass along the sidewalk.

She turns down towards the path along the seawall. It'll be less crowded on a Monday so she won't have to fear being run over by the fitness fanatics. She walks. Thinks of potential lyrics and melodies. A story that you have to hear the end of, combined with a rhythm you can't stop humming. The phone buzzing in her pocket yanks her back to the cold, saturated ground, and her soggy feet. She looks at the screen and it says Space Monkey Records. She stops. Takes a breath. She wants to lean on something, but there's nothing. She might collapse if she doesn't keep moving. It's no big deal, just her life. Just her dream.

"Hey, this is Sky." *Why the fuck did she say that?*

"Sky. It's Miko, from Space Monkey. Hold for Rod, please."

Sky turns around and starts walking back to where she came from. Stops. Turns. Walks. The air feels stuck inside of her. Her stomach twists into tight knots.

"Sky Black! Rod Birk here. How are you doing?"

"Hi, Mr. Birk. I mean, Rod. Good, thanks. Yeah. All good." *Get it together, Sky, for fuck's sake!*

"Great. I'm calling because I got a chance to hear your demos."

Did he like them? Sky can't tell from his voice. She's speechless. Swallows.

"Vince said you did a really great job at the studio. Said you were very professional and he was impressed. Take that as a huge compliment; he's not one to blow sunshine up anyone's ass, that's for sure."

"Thank you." Sky chokes it out. "He was really incredible to work with. It was an honour." She can barely hold the phone in her shaking hand. Her voice doesn't sound like her own and she wants to clear her throat desperately.

"So, Sky. I liked what I heard. Really impressive. I'd like you to come in to the office tomorrow. Bring your guitar. I want my partners to have a look at you. Hear you play live. We need to see how you connect with your audience. I know it's not the packed Imperial, but it's just to get a taste of what you can do. Be ready for a thirty-minute set. Let's say four o'clock. Does that work for you?"

"Yes. Absolutely, Rod. Thank you.*" What songs will she play? What songs? Holy shit. What songs?*

"Great. We'll look forward to seeing you tomorrow. Rest up. Don't go out partying too hard yet. Got it?" He pauses to laugh to himself. "That's happened before – didn't end well for the artist. Nothing's in the bag. Understand?"

"Yes. For sure. I'll be ready."

"Great. See you tomorrow."

Sky hangs up the phone, looking around her, completely bewildered as to where she is. She was pacing back and forth like a caged lion while Birk was speaking, her brain exploding with emotion and adrenalin. Somehow, she's wandered off the cement walkway and through the wet grass, into the thick patches of goose shit. She turns a full circle. A few walkers are going by. A lady pushing a stroller. She can't hold it in and she doesn't know if she's ever felt quite like this before and with no power to stop herself, she raises her arms and tilts her head to the sky and lets out a giant "YEAH!!" Then jumps into the air. Just like in the movies. The walkers all stop and look up to where she's standing, then lower their heads and hurry on. Probably assuming she's crazy. She doesn't care. Thoughts spray through her mind like machine-gun fire.

I should call Jani and tell her. But she'll ask about treatment. Sing "Caged Bird," maybe. Pick up more Advil. Eat something. Call Joe. What? NO. Maybe. He'd want to know. It's not in the bag. Yet. Not yet. What does a good recording contract look like? Google that. At this point I'd sign my life away. I just want to sing. Shit, is that what I'm actually doing – am I signing my life away? No. It's just a pause. I'll go to treatment after I record this album. Just one album for a lifetime of hard work. A legacy. What kind of advance will I get if I sign a deal? Maybe enough to not worry about rent every goddamn month. Sam! I can't wait to tell Sam. This is unbelievable.

Her phone buzzes again and she grabs it from her pocket, exhaling sharply. Looks at the screen. It's Birk's office calling back. *Shit.* He changed his mind.

"Hello?"

"Sky, it's Miko. Congratulations, rock star. You're on your way."

"Hey, Miko. Thanks. It's just an audition, so we'll see what happens. But, thanks." She doesn't want to sound ungrateful, but also wants to keep her cool. She sucks at this.

"So, hey, can you meet me downtown tonight at six?"

"Uh, yeah?"

"Great. There's a champagne lounge called Ice on Hamilton Street, a few blocks from the office. You know it?"

"I'll find it. Should I be ready for...anything specific?"

"I just wanted to chat before your audition tomorrow. The label has strong ideas about image...I mean, don't get me wrong, I think you look fantastic...but a little polish might go a long way. We'll talk. See you there."

She hangs up. Sky glances down at her rumpled sweatshirt and muddy boots. The jeans she's worn for countless days straight. Yes, she could use some polish. But polish costs money, and she's hanging by a thread. And there's another problem. Going to a bar, watching people swill champagne all around her, will be challenging in her current state.

The pain in her throat is becoming unbearable from all the talking, and the scream of joy didn't help. She has to protect it for the show tomorrow, and if she's in a bar talking all night, she might be mute tomorrow. But she has to go. She can't cancel now, and what Miko has to tell her might seal the deal with Birk. She needs help. Something to soothe her pain, just for the next couple of days. Just until she signs the contract. She clears her throat and spits a slimy wad of cancer death into the gutter. It's bloody and disgusting. She stands and stares at it for a sccond. She can't leave it there for anyone else to see so she gets her boot under the decaying leaves and flicks a few on top, covering it up. There. Gone.

The drugstore is bright and busy. Sky walks to the aisle for pain relievers and picks up two large bottles, one Advil and one Tylenol, hoping that mixing the two will help with the stomach pain she's been having. She starts to walk to the front to pay. Stops. Remembers that her doctor told her she could buy cough syrup that contains codeine without a prescription, but only from behind the counter. She has to ask for it, if she wants it. Her hands start to shake again. She can't imagine having more than a five-minute conversation with Miko in this state before the pain will be too much. It's medicine, she reminds herself. Why shouldn't she be allowed to take medicine for her sickness? She's not doing it to get high. It's only to manage the pain. Only to manage. She's walking towards the pharmacy counter before she's even decided if she's doing this and then she's there and the small blond lady with diamond studded glasses asks how she can help.

"Hi. So, I'm having a lot of throat pain. I have cancer, actually. Laryngeal. My doctor, my oncologist…" *Think…what is it? Margie at…Dr…Miller!* "Dr. Miller from Vancouver General Hospital said I should get cough syrup with codeine to help with the pain while I wait for my surgery. Do you have something you could recommend?" She holds her gaze and stares at the woman calmly, hands gripping the two large bottles of pills. The lady smiles and stands up, bumping into her desk and knocking papers to the floor. She blushes while she stoops to pick them up.

"Yes, Robitussin is probably the best. The concentrations of codeine have been lowered for over-the-counter versions recently; people were buying them for recreational purposes." She rolls her eyes at Sky, who tries to mimic the expression. "Unless you have a prescription, then I could give you something with a higher concentration. Do you have a prescription?"

"You know, I did, but I lost it. The milder one is fine, though. I just need something a little stronger than these." She holds up the bottles and shakes them so they rattle like candy.

"Hang on, I'll be right back." She dashes away. Sky has the urge to run. She should run away. Go out the door and down the street and find a meeting. But she hates those fucking meetings. Before she can change anything that's happening, the blond lady is back with the bottle and Sky just wants to stop this pain. Just for the night. Just until she plays tomorrow.

"So recommended dosage is thirty to fifty milligrams every six to eight hours. I have to ask if you've had any issue with opioid addiction in the past?"

"No." Her breath catches. "Thanks," Sky mumbles, giving her a weak smile as she turns and walks to the front to pay, then out to the street and to her apartment building and up the staircase, feeling like there's a spotlight on her. She places the bag on the counter and stares at it. Her breath is coming too quickly and her throat is pure fire. Burning, burning fire. She opens the bag and takes out the Tylenol. Rips into it and puts four bitter pills onto her tongue. She can feel each one travel over the raw patch at the back. It's agonizing and she grunts like an animal. Drinks water. Leans her full weight on the counter, dizzy from the pain. Waits. Minutes tick off. Eventually she makes herself leave the kitchen. She feels disconnected from her body. The glass bottle is still covered by the white plastic of the bag. She walks into the main room and picks up her guitar from the stand. Puts it back down. Goes to the bathroom and takes another shower. Tries to focus her thoughts on Miko and her audition and everything that's happening but it's all clouded by what she could do. Might do. Shouldn't do. She gets dressed, finding a fresh pair of jeans and a short black tank top. Her belt. Puts on an old pair of black heels then immediately switches them for her boots. Lines her eyes with a thick black smudge and an extra coat of mascara. Not sure if that's the polish Miko has in mind, but it's all Sky's got.

It's 4:30 and she has to leave and get some food before the meeting. She lingers at her counter. Puts on her jacket and grabs her bag and phone. She's missed a call from Margie but she doesn't listen to the message because she can't handle any more guilt right now. Even though she hasn't done anything wrong, yet. She knows even having a drug in her house is wrong. She knows. Stares at the bottle. Pictures Joe's face. The sadness in his eyes when he told her how much she hurt him.

The deep, long scar on his cheek. She leaves the bottle and walks out.

"Sky, so nice to hear from you. What's up?"

"Hey, Gary. Is it a good time?" Part of the deal you strike with your sponsor is asking for permission before you spill your guts. The boundaries are important and Sky always makes a point of respecting them.

"Yes. You craving?"

"Yes. And I bought something. It's cough syrup with codeine. The pharmacist said it was low dose. But I bought it and I knew I shouldn't but I did it anyway. My throat is killing me and I want to down the whole bottle."

"But you haven't. You called me instead. You still have control. Where are you now?"

"I'm walking. I left my apartment. I'm meeting someone at six and I need some food. But I'm scared to go back there, Gary. I'm not sure I can hold on."

"I hear you, Sky. But you can do this. When you get back you have to walk in and dump it down the sink. Right away. Picture yourself doing it as you walk back, and then don't hesitate when you go in. Can you go back and do it now? Blow off your appointment, and I'll meet you for the six o'clock meeting in Mission. Can you meet me there?"

"I can't. This is really important. It's with a girl from a record label. If they sign me, I'll get to record an album. A legit album with a producer I respect. I have to be there. It's my shot."

"I get that. But what about your cancer treatments? Have you asked the doctor if its okay to hold off? Sounds like you're in a lot of pain."

Ah shit. Here we go.

"No. I haven't really talked to the doctor yet. This all happened so quickly, and it's not a sure thing."

"Don't you need to put the music on hold and get your treatment? Wasn't that the whole point of the 'last show' thing?"

She regrets calling Gary. Needs to get off the phone.

"Yeah, that was the point, I'm just stalling it for a few weeks, maybe months. It's not a big deal. I've worked my whole life for this. How can a few more weeks matter?" There's silence on the other end. Then she hears Gary sigh.

"You know how this relationship works, Sky. I'm not your parent and I'm not your parole officer. I'm definitely not your doctor. I'm your friend. I'm going to try to guide you to make the right decisions, but I can't force you to do anything."

"I know, Gary. I'm sorry to put you in this position."

"I'm not going to lie to you, Sky. I think you're on dangerous ground right now. You need a meeting. Will you go to one after you meet this record girl?"

"Yes. I promise. And I'll dump that shit out as soon as I get home. Thank you, for being there for me. It means a lot."

"You're welcome. Where are you meeting her?"

Sky hesitates, knows she shouldn't lie, but she wants to end this conversation as soon as possible.

"Coffee shop."

"Cool. Okay, well good luck. Call me if you need anything. I'll have my phone with me all night. And don't break that promise. Got it?"

"Yeah, I got it. Thanks Gary."

Fuck. Lying to your sponsor is an indication that you're not well. Sky isn't well. She knows this, but it's not the right time to unpack it any further than that. She has to keep moving. Be strong. Meet Miko and let herself enjoy this moment and this night and everything that might happen tomorrow. After all, life is short.

23. Falling

Sky pulls open the frosted glass door of the bar. The interior is supposed to look like it's made of ice, she imagines, with its blue walls and white marble tables. It's not a place she'd ever walk into if she wasn't meeting someone. She's not surprised it's the place Miko chose. It suits her cool perfection. She's greeted by a gorgeous brunette wearing a white mini skirt and fur-lined silver bra.

"Hey. Welcome to Ice. Table for one?"

"Hi. No, for two. I'm meeting someone. Nice uniform."

She can't help herself. The girl smiles mischievously and takes her to a table at the back of the room. Sky feels underdressed as she manoeuvres through the delicate furniture. There are only a dozen people in the small space but that's enough to make it crowded. Most of them are well-dressed women. Balanced in their manicured hands are skinny glasses of gold and pale-pink liquid. Sky sits down where the waitress has pulled out her chair. She's handed a single sheet of drink options clipped to a sterling silver board. She scans the options quickly, trying not to laugh out loud at the ridiculous prices. She could easily spend a week's worth of food money on a single round of drinks. She didn't prepare for this moment – assuming Miko would already be here. Now she's alone in a bar and she starts to panic. The words on the page swirl in front of her eyes. The waitress points one long red fingernail near the bottom of the menu and leans down towards her. She smells like strawberries.

"Besides champagne, we do have a few vodka options, distilled here in Vancouver. If you want something a little stronger."

Sky looks up, wondering why she seems like someone who needs something stronger. The waitress is batting her long eyelashes at her and she's not sure if she's getting hit on or baited for a big tip. Confusion clouds her brain and she forgets how to think. All she can do is repeat what was said to her.

"Yeah. Sure. Um…vodka. Sure. I'll try the vodka. And a glass of water, please. Thanks."

What else could she do? She has to order something besides water or she might get kicked out of a place like this. Soda! She should've asked for soda water. She knows better. Gary would've told her to have her order ready in her mind, on the tip of her tongue, before stepping inside. But she didn't tell Gary she was going to a bar, so she failed to be reminded of this advice. Now it's too late. Sky considers signalling the girl to change her order, but she's already walked away and she has to play it cool. She doesn't have to drink it. She'll drink the water instead.

The door opens and Miko walks in. She's striking. Dressed in all black, again, sculpted, and tight. Everything fitting her like a second skin. A skirt that stops just above her knees, black wool trench coat. Spiky boots. She scans the room and finds Sky, starts walking over with the waitress trailing behind, her greeting ignored. A woman at another table looks up and squeals when she sees Miko. Miko offers a cool greeting, leaning down to speak in her ear, then kisses her on the mouth. She comes towards Sky's table.

"Sky. Thanks for meeting me. Sorry I'm late." She reaches out her hand to shake. Sky takes it. It's thin and bony. Cold. Miko's eyes are drawn with a thick black line that extends past the fringe of her lashes in a swoosh.

"Hi. No problem, it's nice to see you again."

Miko holds onto Sky's hand for an extra beat, her eyes making their way around Sky's face. She's intimidating as hell and Sky pulls her hand back. Miko slinks out of her coat, handing it to the waitress who's been hovering a few steps away from the table. She folds it gently over her arm and offers Miko a menu, but she already knows what she wants.

"A bottle of the Krug Rosé and two very chilled glasses."

"Yes. Of course." The waitress spins on her heel and hurries off, holding Miko's jacket out and away from the white fur of her bra. Miko's structured black top cuts in sharply over her small breasts and fastens behind her neck, highlighting her pencil thin collar bones.

"I actually already ordered something. Sorry, Miko, I'm not much of a champagne drinker."

"I think this bottle might change your mind."

Fuck. She's screwed. This is the part where she cops to the fact that she's a recovering addict. *I don't drink*, she should say. Except she already ordered a vodka she's planning to not drink. Miko's going to think she's a complete nut job. The pain in her throat had been at bay, but as her body clenches with the embarrassment of this moment she gets a surge of it. Miko smooths her already smooth hair, staring Sky down again for a few long seconds before she speaks.

"So, you have an audition tomorrow."

"Yes..." Was it a question, or a statement? *Shit!*

"I shouldn't tell you this, but Rod is freaking out about your demos. He loves you. Don't screw up tomorrow and you'll be the newest Space Monkey artist."

Miko's leaning into the table like she might pounce on her at any second. Sky lets what she said about Rod loving her ricochet off her consciousness. She can't focus on that right now or she might lose what little composure she has left. She's still trying to figure out the motive for this meeting. The waitress is returning with a tray holding the bottle of champagne in a silver bucket, two very frosty glasses, and a single tumbler with clear liquid and one giant ice cube. She puts everything on the table, showing the bottle to Miko for her nod of approval, then pops the cork very subtly and pours the pink bubbles into the glasses. They rise exactly to the rim and then settle. Before she leaves, the waitress turns to address Sky.

"I hope you like the vodka. I'll be back with your water in a minute."

Miko raises her glass and Sky starts to sweat. She has three years of sobriety and this is all so fucked. It's just a tiny glass of champagne. It's like syrup, really. She also has cancer and she's supposed to be in treatment taking handfuls of drugs so this isn't a big deal and she might die and she might be a rock star first and what the hell is the point of any of it? People in recovery return to being casual drinkers all the time. Sam crosses her mind. Sam struggling through detox, trying to get sober. Sweating and vomiting and wishing he was dead. But if she doesn't sign this deal, she'll have nothing to offer Sam when he gets out. That's worse, Sky thinks. That would be worse than her having one little drink. Unfortunately, the schmoozing is all part of getting the deal. She lifts the glass, taps it to Miko's, and pours some of the fuzzy sweet goodness down her throat. It feels natural. Like nothing. Like the same thing everyone else is doing. She instantly regrets it and wants more, simultaneously. Three years of hard work, gone in a few seconds.

"I wanted you to meet me because I have a surprise for you. For your big debut tomorrow." Miko fills Sky's glass as she's speaking. Sky watches the fizz rise and cling to the sides.

"Oh yeah? What's the surprise?" There are so many thoughts swirling around in her head, just like the bubbles in the glass. She feels like she might be dreaming. But she isn't. Her sobriety is gone, and she can't take it back now. Miko's excited and wants to tell her something and she has to get out of her head and come back to this moment. It's happening and she might as well enjoy herself. Sky smiles at Miko and reaches for the vodka. The ice cube has the logo of the restaurant branded into it. She's never seen such a fancy ice cube before. She raises the glass and sips the vodka and it's so smooth and it fixes everything. Makes her feel warm. Calm.

"Rod wants to make sure everything goes really well tomorrow. It has to be perfect. He thinks you could be a star. I have to admit, I heard a few of your demos today and I agree. You're really talented, but – and don't take this the wrong way – your image needs a little tweak. Not much." As she speaks, she reaches out a long red fingernail and flicks the necklace dangling between Sky's breasts.

"The style you've got is…sexy…but these guys tomorrow, they look at everything. It's not just about the music – that can be shaped – it's about marketability. Followers. Streams. They need the teenagers to go crazy for you. That means your image has to be cutting edge."

Sky's not sure if she should be insulted. She thinks probably, but she doesn't really have any ammunition to fight this. It's not like she has other options. She's more alarmed with how casually Miko remarked that her music could be shaped. What the hell does that mean?

"What do you have in mind?"

"Like I said, not much." She leans in further, inches from Sky's face.

"We have a stylist, Leon. He's on retainer for the label and works with the artists Rod deems worthy of investing in. He's a genius, Sky. I promise. We're booked in to his studio for seven, so drink up. He's pulled some looks for you. He'll clean up your hair, maybe a facial and a manicure. Tiny details."

Sky stares at her, trying to process everything that's happening and sipping the delicious vodka that's already giving her a buzz. A facial and a manicure. Just five days ago she was planning for her life as a bald, lonely cancer patient with a hole cut in her throat. She can't help but laugh to herself.

"I'm happy to go meet this guy, but I'm not wearing any crazy shit I don't like, nothing with my ass or boobs hanging out. And no stilettos. I'll fall on my face."

"Of course. Like I said, I think your look is sexy, and your body is insane. I don't know why you don't show it off more." She puts her hand on Sky's arm and gives it a squeeze. "We're just going to smooth the edges. A little."

Miko signals to the waitress, who was standing at the bar watching them. Sky downs the last of the vodka, then finishes the champagne in her glass and picks up the bottle to fill both the glasses one more time, even though it tastes like perfume after the vodka. It would be a shame to waste it. The waitress brings a sleek iPad concealed in a glass case and hovers with it, wondering who to give it to. Luckily, Miko reaches up and takes it.

"This is on Space Monkey, Sky." She opens the glass cover, glances at the amount, then pulls a black credit card from her purse.

"Thank you. I could get used to this."

"That's the idea."

The waitress thanks Miko quietly and retreats to retrieve her coat. *What the hell is going on?* Sky thinks, draining her glass before following Miko out into the night.

24. Kiwi

Leon's studio is located in a beautiful heritage building converted to shops that Sky would never dream of entering if she wasn't with Miko. She wants to call Jani and tell her what's going on, but she'd have to colour it with so many lies – *no, I wasn't drinking – yes, I'm going to my treatment – yes, I've told them I have cancer* – that she can't manage it right now. Later. Tomorrow. For now, she follows Miko around the side of the building, amazed at how quickly she moves in her pin-thin heels.

There's a well-lit glass door with a small red carpet out front. Inside the shop Sky can see several people milling around a large white desk. The whole place is white and Sky looks down at her scruffy leather boots, hoping they're clean enough to wear into a place like this. Oversized chandeliers hang from the ceiling and sparse racks displaying crisp-looking clothes are placed around the shop. There's a wall of mirrors on one side. In the back she can see sinks and large white leather chairs and tables overflowing with bottles and tubes. She looks to Miko for some kind of reassurance. She's applying lipstick. She must've pulled the tube from somewhere unseen, like a magic trick, because Sky didn't see her move. She presses her perfect red lips together.

"Ready for the new you?"

"Yes. But remember, we're just tweaking, right?"

"Yes, of course. You'll hardly notice a difference."

Miko pulls the door open and steps back to let Sky walk in first. All heads turn. Three men and one woman come towards her in a wave of comments and greetings, sporting streaks of wildly coloured hair and bold prints and pants that seem too short, in Sky's uneducated opinion. A large, very fit black man wearing skintight leather pants and a plaid shirt unbuttoned halfway down his chest steps forward. The others part to give him the floor. His nipples are pierced and both have large glittery rings with dangling feathers. He leans forward and brings Miko in for a triple kiss ooh-ahh hug-like thing that Sky really hopes he doesn't try on her.

"Sky Black! So nice to meet you, sweetheart. I'm Leon. I'll be styling you for the showcase tomorrow."

They shake hands, then Leon grabs her other hand and holds her out in front of him as he looks her up and down, slowly, not trying to disguise the fact that he's doing it. He spins her and she laughs loudly, then bites her lip, the vodka making her feel warm and uninhibited.

"Nice to meet you, Leon. And thanks for doing this. Miko just told me about this a few minutes ago. I'm sure you can tell from looking at me, but I'm not really up on the latest fashion. I really like more of a casual look."

"Oh darling, you're a stunner. You scream sex. We won't have any problems here. Don't worry, just trust. I'm reading your vibe, but sweet Christ on a cracker, do you ever have potential. The kids will go crazy for you. Crazy!"

He raises his hands in the air and waves them around, ordering people to places. One young boy holds a blank notepad, pen poised in the air, eager to capture whatever Leon might say that requires writing down. After all the hellos Sky is speechless and feels way out of her element.

"Please come in and make yourself comfortable. You're taller than Miko estimated, but I know what I'd like to see you in. I know exactly what I want to SEE YOU IN!"

He screams the last part. It's so loud that everyone jumps to attention and there's no more chatter. It was half thrilled, half manic. Sky looks to Miko, wide-eyed, with a smirk she's trying to hide because this is all so absurd and she wishes Joe was here. It's a sudden and desperate longing for him. He'd never believe this. Miko doesn't seem to get the joke. Her expression stays neutral, almost bored, which seems impossible in this crazy atmosphere. The boy with the pen is shaking and Sky can see he's made indecipherable ink marks on the paper. Now that Leon has everyone's attention, he speaks sweetly and calmly again.

"We'll start with esthetics. I'll *personally* cut your hair. I have a jacket in mind, but it's in another part of the city; I'll send a runner." The kid is writing furiously and everyone else is standing at attention, waiting for their orders.

"Come. Sit. Drinks are on the table and if there's anything you need, Wynzel is here strictly for that reason. I'll just consult with my team. Let's have some fun, shall we?"

Leon claps twice and the team huddles around him. Loud pop music starts blaring through the speakers. He's throwing out words Sky has only read in magazines, Dolce and Prada and Givenchy, and Miko comes over and ushers her away from the crazy. She must sense that Sky's way out of her comfort zone because she softens as soon as they're alone.

"Hey, I know Leon can be a little much, but like I said, he's a genius. I promise everything that happens tonight will be reversible. If you don't like it, wear whatever you want tomorrow."

She laces her arm through Skys and brings her to a glass table laden with gourmet food and steel vats full of ice, jammed with bottles of beer, wine, and vodka.

"I know image should be unimportant compared to the music, but in this industry it isn't. Everyone has a screen and everything is visual. It matters, Sky. You have to be the full package, and that's what you are, but the execs need to see that they can sell you that way. If they buy in to you, you can have everything you want."

She pours vodka into a thick crystal tumbler full of ice and hands it to Sky with a wink. Her head is swimming and she really shouldn't accept the drink, but the night's already a write-off. She already broke three years of sobriety. Tomorrow, she has to start over. Day one. She takes a long sip.

"The only thing I want is a record deal. It's all I've ever wanted. Paying the bills would be nice, but mostly I want to make a record that people want to listen to. I want to leave a legacy. You know?"

"Yeah. I get it." Miko speaks like a robot, pouring champagne into a tall flute.

"Right." Sky knows she doesn't get it, but it's not worth explaining further.

The next few hours are filled with experiences she's only seen in movies. Warm towels on her face, hand and scalp massages, people putting nice-smelling creams and gels on every part of her. Sky closes her eyes and lets it all happen. Her buzz is strong and her glass is never empty. Her throat is pain free for the first time in months, and every time the poison threatens to choke her, she washes it down with more icy vodka. After her hair has been washed, she's brought to the chair for Leon to work his magic.

"Honey, now don't worry. You look nervous. I promise I won't mess up this edgy, rock-and-roll-goddess vibe you've got going. I'm just going to give you a few extra angles. But first, please, let me do the honours."

He reaches to the back of Sky's neck and releases the clasp on her necklace, the metal pieces clanging together as he lifts it off her body and drops it on the side table like he pulled it out of the drain.

"There. Now, we begin."

He focuses on Sky's face and lifts strands of her hair up, then spins her so she can't see the mirror, and starts cutting from the bottom. His nipple piercings dangle near Sky's eyes, so she closes them again. When she looks down pieces of her hair litter the floor. She thinks she should protest, but she's edging closer to drunk and it feels so goddamn good and everyone's standing behind Leon watching. She thinks she should write a song about this, but there are no words right now. Just the buzz and the warmth and everyone's eyes on her. When Leon finishes with the blow dryer, the team pulls her out of the chair and whisks her into a change room. It's almost as large as Sky's apartment. The mirror has been covered up with black fabric and a long metal rack placed in front of it. Sky runs her fingers over the clothes hanging from it. Slim black dresses and buttery leather jackets, swaths of lace that look like napkins but must be shirts. A row of shiny black pants that all look identical. Belts with studs and some that are shiny and some that are like snakes. The part that actually gets Sky really excited is the boots. They're leather art and Sky can't believe she gets to try them on, much less walk out with a pair. Then she wonders if she has to give the outfit back, after she wears it tomorrow. Especially if she doesn't get the deal. If she screws it up, they might strip her in the lobby. She laughs to herself, again, at the absurdity of all this.

They're all talking outside the curtain. It sounds like a party until Leon's voice rises briefly above the rest and they shut up instantly.

"Start with the midnight leather Dolce bomber, the black Givenchy trousers, and the coral Prada bralette. And the studded Choos. Let's see the Choos."

"Um… okay?" Sky isn't even sure those instructions were in English. She drains her glass and puts it on the wooden chair in the corner, strips to her underwear, then stares at the rack wondering which pair the "Givenchy trousers" are. Before she can figure out how to ask this without seeming like an absolute idiot, the curtain opens roughly and Leon bursts into the room.

"I'm sorry, darling, I forgot. You don't speak fashion."

He starts to pull things off the rack at lightning speed and piles them into Sky's arms, seemingly not noticing that she's practically naked. She's glad she chose a cute black thong. Unfortunately, her bra is old and the lace is torn on the side. Leon pauses to put his hand on Sky's collarbone.

"Oh, honey, yes." Then he looks down at the clothes he's given to Sky. "These. Start with these." He turns to his crowd of staff gathered outside the change room, who can all see Sky standing in her underwear also, and shouts at them, "Who the fuck said she was a two!? She's a zero, people, and we better have the fucking sizes we need. If you can't tell a zero from a two, leave immediately and go get a job at Abercrombie and Fuck."

They bow their heads in shame. Sky bites her lip so she won't burst out laughing. Leon slides the curtain shut behind him and calls out, "Hurry hurry!" in a sing-song voice.

She slides on the black pants he gave her. Even before she's done them up, she knows she's never worn a pair of pants like this. They fit like a second skin and feel like velvet. She had no idea clothes could fit this perfectly. Nothing has price tags attached, but she'd love to know what they sell for. The top he gave her is a bright pink lace bra. It's so intricate and beautiful she's afraid she might tear it as she slides it over her head. Her hair is much shorter, just grazing her breasts. It feels like silk and she can't wait to see it. She straps on the black studded boots. They're alarmingly high, but somehow feel comfortable when she stands up. The pants stop just below her belly button and there's about three inches of her flesh exposed before the lacey trim of the bra starts. The jacket waits on the chair, smoky black with thick stitching, shapes carved all over it that remind her of vintage tattoos. Arrows and skulls, hearts and wings, all tooled into the supple leather. She slides her arms into it and it becomes part of her. They meld together and she never, ever, wants to take it off. She looks down at the stranger who is her and wishes she had a mirror, but the only measure of her image available to her is the staff's reaction, so she steps out from behind the curtain.

They go wild. There's cheering and gasping and even Miko is wearing a giant smile. Leon is the most critical, his fist clutched to his mouth as he ponders his creation. Sky wants to crawl into a corner. This kind of attention is nothing she's comfortable with. Not without a guitar and a mic. She watches for Leon's approval, hoping he's satisfied.

"I'd like to see the Gucci boots and the top in emerald…but yes, Sky Black, I think we've gotten there."

The group cheers again and then Leon lifts his arm and they all move aside, allowing Sky a clear view at the large mirror behind them. Her mouth drops open before she remembers to be cool and closes it. Her hair shines like oil, pieces frame her face and end bluntly, some at her chin and then just past her nipples. It's lighter at the bottom, like caramel, and perfectly messy, like beach waves and bed head combined. The shorter length makes her eyes look huge. Her skin is glowing and the makeup she barely noticed them applying is subtle, but edgy. The magical pants fit her perfectly, and the boots – studded leather rock-and-roll perfection – make her legs go on forever. She looks so thin, almost sick, but no one seems to think it's a problem. The jacket. The jacket has a wide collar that sticks up and frames her face. The rest of it is so tight, as if it's sewn to her body. Sky never thought she could look like this woman she finds in front of her. The clothes make her feel powerful, like she's only the best parts of herself.

"Thank you, so much. All of you." She has to stop and clear her throat. The pain is so much less than it usually is and she knows it's the alcohol and that's bad, but it just feels numb and great.

"As you can tell, I'm speechless. Leon, Miko was right; you really are a fucking genius. I hope I can sound as good as I look." She smiles into the mirror and the team claps again. She needs to get out of here.

She walks back to the change room, away from all the eyes, then peels the clothes from her body and starts to carefully hang them back on the rack.

"Knock. Knock."

"Come in. I'm almost finished."

The curtain pulls back and Miko sneaks through, letting it close behind her. She laughs when she sees Sky, a wooden hanger clutched in her teeth, attempting to drape the pants over it with the perfect crease they had when she put them on.

"You don't have to do that. There are people for that."

She leans against the wall of the dressing room and gives Sky a look she hasn't seen in a long time. Especially from a woman.

"You look good, Sky."

"Yeah?"

"Oh, yeah. Are you happy you trusted me?"

"I have to admit, that was fun." Sky smiles and Miko steps closer to her. Sky's mind goes to the kiss Miko gave the woman in the restaurant. She's never been hit on by a woman before, not really, and she doesn't want to do anything that changes Miko's opinion of her. She needs her as an ally.

"Do you want to come to my place for a drink? I think we need to celebrate, don't you?" Miko's puts her hands on Sky's shoulders and Sky realizes people are very touchy in this new world and maybe she just needs to relax. Miko has booze at her house. All Sky has is the cough syrup. She might as well keep this party going a little longer, before reality crashes back down on her.

"Sure. Just one, though. Big day tomorrow."

Miko leans into Sky until their lips are an inch apart, her gaze travelling over Sky's face before stopping at her eyes.

"Sure. Just one."

"Um, hello! You can fuck in the change room if you want but NOT on the clothes! I don't want to be scrubbing anything out of those trousers. Thank you!"

Sky starts laughing and Miko looks a little thrown until she realizes it's funny, then smiles. She steps back and smooths her skirt. Sky puts her old jacket back on and it doesn't feel like skin but it does feel like home.

The crew packs up the clothes Sky will wear tomorrow and offers to have them sent to her apartment, but she insists on taking them with her. She doesn't think Leon's ever had Gucci delivered to East Hastings. They say their goodbyes and she walks out after too many cheek kisses. She has two large bags filled with thousands of dollars' worth of clothing. The ropey loops rest in her calloused palm where the handle of her guitar case usually grinds and she wonders what the hell just happened, and if this is all part of having a record deal, and if it's something she could ever actually get used to. Right now, she's buzzed and Miko's leading the way to a car that Leon called for them and she'll worry about her guilty conscience tomorrow. Or maybe her life has sucked for so long that she'll just let this roll for a while.

25. She Ain't Coming Back

Just off the water in Coal Harbour, with floor-to-ceiling glass, Miko's apartment doesn't disappoint. Sky wonders how much Space Monkey pays her to be a not-that-glorified secretary. By the looks of this place, it's a lot.

It's dark outside and the lights flicker in the marina as they exit the car. Boats that are homes are tethered to long wooden docks. Sky imagines that's a nice way to live. It must feel like you have an advantage over all the schmucks rooted to the ground. Cut the rope and you're free to drift away, bringing all the comforts of home with you.

They didn't speak much on the drive, casual chit-chat about Leon and what a trip that whole experience was. Mostly Sky, trying to fill the empty space. They have next to nothing in common except music and the fact that they both want her to be successful, for their own personal reasons. Miko tipped the driver and they entered the fancy building and took the elevator to the seventh floor. She pulled her keys from her studded purse and let Sky in, using all her weight to push open her oversized door. She said something Sky couldn't decipher over her shoulder and disappeared down the hallway.

Now Sky is waiting, but she's not exactly sure what for. The numbing of the booze is slowly wearing off. She should've stuck a handful of Advil in her pocket before she left her apartment, but she was too distracted by the cough syrup. If she'd known she was going to ruin her three years of sobriety anyway, she would've stopped torturing herself and just chugged it down. She needs water, but doesn't want to rummage through Miko's cupboards searching for a glass, so she leans into the sink and takes a chug from the tap. She's just bringing her head up when Miko appears from the hallway, wearing tiny black shorts and a short grey sweater that looks soft and expensive. She's the most perfect looking woman Sky's ever seen. She wonders if she ever isn't perfect.

"You don't have to drink from the tap like a degenerate."

Sky laughs awkwardly, wishing she turned this invitation down and went home instead. Miko steps around her and opens the fridge door, the light illuminating the white tile floor. Not a crumb that Sky can see. The fridge shelves are lined with clear containers of designer food and green and black drinks in thick glass bottles. It looks like a magazine and Sky can't believe people actually live this way. Miko takes out a bottle of champagne and reaches up to get two glasses from the cupboard, brushing against Sky's arm. The sweater is as soft as it looks and Miko smells like flowers.

"So, just one, you're sure?"

She pours Sky a glass, staring at her like she's looking through her clothes. Heat burns up to Sky's face from deep inside and the only thing she can do to quench it seems to be to keep drinking. She drains her glass, the bubbles burning in her nose. Miko holds the bottle up to her, like a question.

"Maybe, two," Sky responds.

They drink the champagne and she wishes it was vodka but pours it down her throat anyway. It eases the pain again and she knows she has to get straight tomorrow but it's not tomorrow. Or maybe it is, but ignorance is fucking bliss. Miko walks across the room and Sky's grateful for the distance between them. She's never been with a woman, but right now she can't quite remember why. Miko pushes a button on the wall. Mechanical blinds whir to life and descend slowly, blacking out the pretty boats with their twinkling lights. She turns on a speaker. Tom Petty is playing and Sky remembers Miko has great taste in music and considers the fact that maybe they could be friends after all.

Miko sits down on the leather sofa, curling her sleek bare legs beneath her in a choreographed movement.

"So, Sky Black, you're going to be a star. Everyone who met you tonight said so. Are you ready for everything to change?"

Sky wonders how the people who gave her clothes and cut her hair could know she was going to be a star. They've never heard her music.

"Well, thank you for saying that, but I'm not sure how much is going to change. If everything works out, I'm going to have an album out. Lots of people have albums out. I just hope it sells so I can make enough money to buy myself more fancy pants. I could get used to those." She smirks at Miko, trying to lighten the mood.

"Everything will change, Sky. Including you. Just wait."

Sky's thinking that Miko doesn't know everything, and she definitely doesn't know her. As if Miko can read her mind, she adds, "Fame changes everyone."

Sky finishes her drink, trying not to choke on the bubbles or the word. Fame. Who said anything about fame? She just wants to make music, and get paid for it. Maybe have people know her enough to buy a ticket to her shows. She's not sure Miko would understand that, and it doesn't seem worth trying to explain, so she shifts the focus to Miko.

"This apartment is incredible. You've done really well for yourself. Congratulations."

"Thanks, but I didn't buy this place. My parents own it. They still live in China. They bought it when they shipped me over here to go to school. It's an investment. We both were, actually. Although one of us isn't paying off." She laughs to herself, her lip curling up in a disgusted snarl.

"What do mean, both?"

"The condo and me. My parents wanted to get into the Vancouver real estate market, and they wanted me to become a surgeon, so they sent me here, to go to university. I live in their condo, and they get a huge tax break. Some 'foreign buyers' thing. They're going to flip it and make lots of money." She stops talking to take a drink. Sky is suddenly seeing Miko in a different light. She's not the steely, powerful woman Sky thought she was.

"That sucks, Miko. I'm sorry."

"Oh, don't worry about it. I'm fine. I showed them. They wanted me to be a doctor, so they could brag to their friends about it, but when I got here, I switched all my classes, and didn't tell them until I graduated. They showed up for the ceremony, all stiff and arrogant, and I introduced them to my girlfriend – who was living with me at the time – then told them that I actually got my degree in music appreciation, with a minor in women's studies. Needless to say, we don't talk much anymore."

A silence hangs in the room and Sky doesn't know what to say next. She knows how it feels to be abandoned by your parents, too, but she sure the hell doesn't want to get into that tonight. She's had more than enough vulnerability for one day. She finishes her second glass of champagne and excuses herself to use the bathroom. Miko points her down the hall. It didn't go unnoticed to Sky that Miko said she was living with a woman. Sky doesn't want the fact that she's here this late, drinking on Miko's fancy couch, to give her the wrong impression. But maybe she isn't, exactly.

She continues down the hall. Everything is white, including framed pictures of nothing that look like they may be someone's brilliant idea of a joke. Sell blank paper to the rich people and tell them it's art, like the emperor's new clothes. Sky peeks into Miko's bedroom and the clock by the giant bed reads 2:15. The sun will be up in a few hours and she has to get home and get her head on straight. Figure out her set list and re-string her guitar and warm up her voice. Be the best she's ever been. It's hard to connect to a bunch of stiff guys in suits who care as much about her outfit as they do about her lyrics, but she has to find a way.

She flicks on the light and the image in the bathroom mirror is shocking. A girl with shiny hair and huge eyes, glowing skin and glossy lips, stares back. She's gorgeous, Sky can't deny it. She laughs, and the girl laughing sounds foreign and distant and she isn't her, she's someone else. This is the girl who got her in all the trouble. Who ruined her band and broke Joe's heart. Sky has to get the fuck away from her. She backs up quickly, startling the ghost in the mirror, and opens the bathroom door.

Miko is waiting for her in the hall. She's leaning against the entrance to her bedroom, a coy smile playing on her lips. She sips from a short glass of clear liquid, then holds it out between them. Sky wants to take it, but she's not sure where that would lead, and suddenly this all feels wrong. She's losing control and she has to get it back before this whole thing blows up in her face.

"I'm sorry, Miko, I should go. Thanks. For everything."

"You're leaving now?"

"Yeah. I'll see you tomorrow."

Sky doesn't wait for her to respond. She walks down the hall, collects her bags, and gets herself into the elevator. As she descends to the street, Miko's words stick in her mind, heavy like the deflating bubbles from the champagne. *Fame changes everyone.*

26. One Night in Bangkok

Birk stands behind his desk, reefing on the legs of his stretchy underwear that have crept up too high on his hairy thighs, encroaching on his balls. The light is streaming in through the cracks in his closed blinds. They're usually open when he arrives, but today he was first into the building. He had to unlock the door and without Miko there to take his coat and hand him his coffee and hangover medication, he was forced to go to the staff room and get everything himself. He spilled water all over his pants trying to fill the coffee pot, then dried them with a crunchy brown paper towel, which was a huge mistake. Crumbly bits of fibres smeared all over his perfectly pressed jet-black Tom Ford chinos, a special pair Leon couriered over to his condo yesterday. He had to take them off and rinse them in the sink. Now they're hanging on his door knob drying, and he's stuck in his office with no pants.

He paces a few more laps around his desk. He's been up most of the night drafting Sky's contract. It's one of the best he's ever created. Clauses are inserted for extra tour dates and fractioned merch payouts and upfront recoup of her piddly advance. It's a work of art, if he does say so himself. He imagines the bonus he'll receive and his steps get faster. He spins on his heel and unwinds himself by walking the other direction. This circling definitely qualifies as cardio.

He has a sudden thought and reaches for his phone in his back pocket, grabbing his own squishy ass instead.

"Fuck! Siri, call Vince West."

He yells the command into the empty air, hoping he brought his phone out of the coffee room.

"Calling."

Beautiful. After several rings, Vince answers with a groggy, pissed-off voice.

"Jesus, Rod. Are you kidding me? It's six-thirty in the goddamn morning. Have you even been to bed yet?"

"Yes. Well, sort of. I'm at the office. The work day has begun, my friend. I need to ask you a favour."

"Yeah, what's new. What the fuck do you need this early in the morning?"

"I need you to come to Sky's showcase today. And…I want you to do the sound."

"Rod, come on. She's gonna be great. You don't need me there to run the goddamn PA. I'll send Will over, and I'll make sure he has the premium gear."

"No Vince, that's not good enough. She worships you. I'm afraid she might spook, and I need her to be her best."

"You know I hate those starchy motherfuckers, Rod. It's just not my scene."

"I wouldn't ask if I didn't think it was necessary. I have her contract ready. If it goes well, I'm going to sign her today. I know it would mean a lot to her if you were here. She might get nervous in close quarters, with the pressure really on, you know? And you know girls. All I need is for her to start crying or something."

"Come on, Rod. Really?"

"Do it for Sky. She needs you. And I'll pay you twice your hourly rate."

Birk can hear Vince huff out an irritated sigh in the background. He waits. He knows how to manipulate Vince, and going for the heart strings gets him every time.

"I'll do it for her. But I want triple, and don't ask me to do Mickey Mouse shit like this again. This is why you have sound techs on retainer."

"Fine, triple. But bill me for overtime in the studio, and don't tell John about this. Don't be late."

"Fuck off. And I'm not mingling around, chatting with Westlake. I hate that douche."

"Yeah, yeah. Leave that to me."

Vince hangs up. Birk pulls out his chair, plunging himself into it, then jumps up with a howl when the cold leather hits his bare skin. He really needs his pants.

27. Knocking at the Door

Sky runs her hands through her wet hair, trying to reproduce the look Leon gave her last night. Wrapping strands around her fingers to form waves like he told her to. Her head aches along with her throat, but this pain she deserves. It matches the guilt that's formed a dark mass, sitting on her chest. She wants to feel it. Punish herself with it. She's wearing the black pants and the studded boots, but she threw a white tank top over the pink bra. It seemed garish in the light of day, just like the empty bags and tissue paper that litter her floor.

Sky passed out for a few hours when she got home, but she was too wound up to relax for long. Gary has called, but she hasn't picked up. She can't lie to Gary today. She feels terrible and she'll have to tell him the truth, just not today. After a long shower and a lot of throat clearing, she's warmed up enough to sing. The blood she's spitting up is red. Fresh. She'll have to swallow it during the audition. Her set list is ready. She takes the four Advil she laid out on the counter with a glass of water. Waits. She feels nothing but the throbbing pain and after twenty minutes she retrieves the cough syrup and without analysing her actions, takes a long swig, Then another. She has to start on day one anyway, so why not let it be tomorrow.

Miko left a slightly awkward message, asking if she needed a car to pick her up, saying she had a good time last night. Sky texted back that she was fine, and yeah, it was fun. Now she ambles down to the street in her tight pants, hails a cab, and slides in beside her guitar. As the car moves through the traffic the cough syrup starts to warm her from the inside. She tells herself she can do this. They loved her at the Imperial and these people will love her, too. She will get this deal and make the record she's always dreamed of. She'll keep control. Make the decisions. Stay ahead of these suits and their expectations.

The cab pulls up in front of Space Monkey and Sky takes one last deep breath. She pays the driver with her dwindling money and steps out. It's a warm, sunny day and she squints against the glare of the glass wall, reflecting the rays into her eyes. Miko pushes though the large front door.

"Hello, stranger. You look fucking great."

"Hey. Thanks. Nice to see you."

Sky's not sure what the proper greeting should be, but the way Miko's lingering at the door says she's expecting more than a *hey*, so Sky leans in and half-hugs her, holding her guitar out to the side so she doesn't hit her with it.

"You're right on time. I heard them listening to your demos a few minutes ago. Have a seat; you need anything?

"Water would be great."

She won't make that mistake twice. Miko's wearing her signature black again, this time a buttoned-up suit jacket with no shirt underneath. Just her bony chest and shiny skin and a single silver chain hanging between her breasts. Leather pants and studded black shoes like Sky's, but with heels so high and so thin she can't believe Miko can walk in them. She clicks off and Sky exhales, trying to stay calm. It was just a few days ago that she sat here wondering if she should leave. Now there are people in a room somewhere listening to her sing and considering giving her a deal. What a fucking roller coaster ride.

Miko comes back with her water and Birk is right behind her.

"Sky! Wow. You look fantastic! Sexy as hell. Isn't Leon the best? How're you feeling? Voice good?"

He comes at Sky like a wave of energy, crashing into her with a handshake and a weird low-handed hug around her hips and all the words and questions. He seems high. Coke, probably.

"Thanks, Rod. Yeah, I'm feeling good. Leon was incredible. He really worked magic on me." She holds out her arms to show him what she's talking about it, instantly regretting the gesture.

"Great. Perfect. Our team is assembled and they've just heard a sample of your demos. Vince has a PA set up for you. Should be everything you need. Just show them what you've already shown us, and things look good."

Sky smiles, feeling grateful that Vince is here. A wave of nerves roll through her, exacerbated by the frantic energy from Birk. Miko steps around him and hands Sky the water. She thanks her and chugs it down. The cough medicine is like magic and she feels little pain, just a slight buzz in her head.

"Let's do this," Birk says.

At the end of the hallway there's an open door. He steps aside and lets Sky walk through first. The room is a theatre with thick leather chairs arranged in rows, stadium style. There are steps that lead down the side of the room to a stage at the front where a lone mic stand is waiting, a guitar cable hanging freely from it. Vince is standing behind a table at the back. He's fiddling with the board and Sky waits until he looks up. She catches his eye and gets a much-needed smile.

The room is only half full, mostly men in suits. Two women sit together on the far side. A good-looking man in his early fifties with slicked black hair stands up.

"Hi, Sky. I'm John Westlake, CEO of Space Monkey Records. Thank you for taking the time to play for us today."

"You're welcome, Mr. Westlake. It's my pleasure."

"Please, call me John. Feel free to set up, I think Vince has you all ready to plug in. We've heard your demos, and we like your vibe, but as you know with music, the show is everything. We're looking forward to seeing your performance."

He sits back down. All the other people are staring at Sky, blatantly commenting to each other in whispers. Rod steps in and ushers her down the stairs and to the stage. She steps up and sets her case down near the back, then takes her guitar out and tunes it, keeping her back to the group, giving herself a few precious seconds to get grounded. She'll start with "I'm Going Down," then "Caged Bird," "Devil Girl," and "White Lies." She scribbled the order on a piece of paper with a few more at the bottom in case she doesn't feel like those songs are hitting. She shrugs out of the leather jacket and drapes it over the back of a chair on the stage. As she unrolls her guitar strap, she repeats the mantra that was burned there all those years ago. *Only this.* It has to go well or she'll have to go back to nothing and she doesn't know how she'll do that, after she came this close. How would she tell Sam it's not going to happen?

She turns to face the people with her stage smile and her desperation and a little cough syrup buzz. Rod jumps up from the front row and speaks too loudly into the mic.

"Alright, so as I mentioned in the pre-screen, this is Sky Black. No solo recordings, small following, about three thousand on Twitter and Facebook. No IG. The advantage of her invisibility is there's nothing scandalous to manage besides a few bad clips and some hater comments we could get wiped.

No copyrights or song writing credits, currently. Used to be a member of a small indie band called Broken Yellow Line. Amateur recordings, some YouTube content. Solo writer, at this point."

He looks to Sky to see if he should add anything, but Sky has no idea what to say after that. Based on Rod's criteria she sounds like an amateur hack with nothing to offer. Rod moves aside and Sky steps to the mic. She has to get these stiff, sober people in this bright room at four o'clock on a Tuesday to love her. How the fuck is she going to do that?

"Hi, everyone. As Rod said, I'm Sky Black, from Nelson, B.C. Thank you for having me. Vince, can I please get a little more vocal in my monitor." She strums her guitar as Vince adjusts the sound.

"Check one. Check mic. Perfect, thanks."

It's clear and loud and Sky gets the feeling she always gets before she's about to play. Excitement. A whisper of fear. And this time, something new. Something like – *watch this, you motherfuckers. Watch. This.*

I had to get high, without you I never was

I didn't care what kind of damage was done

If only I'd stayed when you needed me most

If only I'd told you how broken I was

I think you knew

I think we knew

I was going down

Maybe I should've stopped before I hurt you

I know it's too late now

The golden ring is slipping past me

It's not coming back around

I'm going down, just when my feet might touch the ground

I'm going down, and I can't make a sound

I'm broken, I'm lost, and I'll never be found

I'm going down

Heaven won't help me now

She stares into the eyes of every person in that room. Right into their fucking souls. One after another. She fills her lungs with air and she reaches and pushes for each note. Her voice is gravel and velvet and every word is from her heart and her gut. Miko is up in the top corner of the room, watching her. She closes her eyes and she pictures Joe's face. His body and his back when he walked away. It hurts but she pictures it all and then the pain swells up in her and she pours it through the microphone and out to the strangers in this room. She thinks of the secret poison that lives inside her, right where the music comes from. What if it kills her? What if? What if this doesn't happen and she got so close, but she never quite got the dream? What if she never sees Joe again? That fear comes out in every beautiful sound she makes and Vince blasts it into the room.

When the song is over, she steps back off the mic. Rod stands up and starts to clap, a huge smile on his face. The rest join in, eyes wide, thoughts on their lips as they whisper to each other. Vince tips his brown felt fedora to Sky, a moment only they share, and then he raises both arms wide in the air, as if to say, it's yours. It's all yours.

28. Silver Lining

Joe's long day is finally over. His boss was grinding him incessantly about finishing a repair on a Jeep engine that was overdue, then made him call the pissed-off owner personally to tell him it was finally ready. Now he manoeuvres his Chevy half-ton through the slushy ruts on Main Street and pulls up in front of the Co-op, dreading the fact that he has to go buy groceries. He's tired and starving and might run into someone he has to talk to. Unfortunately, his cupboards are bare and the only person who can fix that problem is him. He watches through his windshield as people shuffle along the sidewalk in parkas and clompy boots. Nelson usually gets an earlier spring than most mountain towns — the snow turning to a dirty soup-like consistency in March — but locals know winter isn't over yet. Just when the sun starts to carry a little warmth in it and you dare to consider putting your heavy down jacket in the closet, the snow will come back with a vengeance, walloping the mountains with another coating of white. Joe tugs the zipper of his oil-stained hoodie up to his throat and is just opening his truck door when his phone rings. He pulls it from his pocket hesitantly, afraid it might be Marley wanting to scream at him some more. It's a number he doesn't recognize. He considers screening it, but his curiosity gets the better of him, or maybe he feels like telling off a telemarketer who definitely dialled the wrong guy today. He answers with a tight, annoyed tone.

"Hello?"

"Hi…Joe?"

"Yeah?"

"It's Sky."

"Hey! Sky! I, uh…are you okay?"

"Yeah," she laughs, "I'm good. Sort of. I have a…kind of a music question. Do you have a minute to talk?"

"Of course! Absolutely. I just got off work. What's up?" Joe's heart is racing at the sound of her voice, his mind swirling with nerves and excitement, his hunger instantly forgotten. He reaches out and closes the door so he's free from any distractions.

"I just played a showcase at Space Monkey Records, and…it went really well, so… they're offering me a contract!"

"What?! No way! Sky, that's amazing!"

"Thanks. I'm kind of freaking out. They put the contract in front of me to sign, and started talking about the numbers and percentages, and there's all these people standing around waiting to celebrate, and I kind of ran out of there. I just want to make sure I'm protecting myself, you know? And since you guys recently signed a deal, and I trust you, I was hoping you could walk me through it a little?"

"Of course, yeah. I'm not an expert but I can tell you everything I know to watch out for. Where are you now?"

"Um…hiding in the bathroom."

Joe starts to laugh, picturing her in the stall.

"Are you laughing at me?"

He can hear the smile in her voice.

"No, not *at* you, exactly. Well, yeah, maybe I am. I don't know many artists who hide in the bathroom when they finally get offered a deal. I'm glad you called. Okay, get down to the main clauses and tell me what the splits are, and I can compare them to ours."

Sky starts reading off numbers and he's trying to focus but all he can think about is starting his truck and driving to Vancouver. He could have her in his arms in eight hours. He struggles to stay with her as she reads everything through. It's a much bigger contract than the Dirt Junkies signed, with a longer tour and the possibility for a multi-album deal. Sky's about to hit the big time, and as excited as he is for her, a nagging in his gut says her career might make her very unavailable to him.

"Wow, Sky. This is a huge contract, tour-wise. The numbers sound similar to ours, which I think is industry standard. And if your first album sells – and of course it will – you have the possibility of recording two more. That's very cool. You obviously have them excited. I guess you could ask about future commitments and tour dates? Make sure they don't try to overschedule you when your career really starts to take off. Make sure you have time to take care of yourself."

"Yeah, I…I know. I need to do that."

Her voice trails off and Joe wants to ask her what's really going on, and with her health, but she's not offering up the details, and he doesn't want to pry.

"Make sure you do. But for now – sign! I'm so excited for you. You worked so hard to get there. You did it, and now you're going to be a star, Sky, just like you always wanted." He's trying to keep his cool, but he can't help himself. His enthusiasm might make her hang up and never call him again.

He bites his lip so he won't say anything else. Starts picking at the loose threads of his jeans where a small hole is forming.

"Thanks. That means a lot, Joe. I knew you were the right person to talk to. I…I've really missed you. I mean, missed talking to you. About music. And sorry for taking so much of your time. Please tell Marley I said hi."

"It's no trouble, Sky. I'm glad I was here. Call me anytime you want. And, you might have to say hi to Marley yourself. I don't think she's speaking to me anymore. We broke up."

"You did? When?"

"Right after we got back."

"Oh, crap…well, sorry?"

"No. Nothing to be sorry about. It was never anything real." He takes a deep breath, figures, what the hell? "Sky, I miss you. Not just talking to you. I miss being with you. I want to see you." There it is. What he's wanted to say to her every day since she left, three years ago. What he felt so strongly in every cell of his body when he went to her apartment. He can hear her exhale. Long and slow. He waits.

"Me too."

"Yeah?"

"Yeah."

Joe feels like his heart is going break through his ribs. He's so glad she can't see him right now because he has the stupidest smile on his face.

"Should I leave now?" he asks.

She laughs.

"What do you mean leave? Drive back to Vancouver?"

"Why not?"

"Joe, I have a lot going on right now. My career, of course, and other stuff. I…well, we'll have to talk, sometime…"

It's too much. He knew it. Although he can't help but wonder what else she wants to talk to him about. Is it about her health, or is she seeing someone? He's dying to know, but he can't ask.

"Sky, I'm kidding. Sort of. Stop hiding in the bathroom and go sign your deal! Celebrate!" He has an urge to say something protective, like be careful or be good, but he's not her boyfriend, and she told him she's been sober for years, so instead he ends with, "Have a great night and I'll talk to you tomorrow. Or whatever. No rush."

She sighs, laughs again. He exhales with relief, like he's been holding his breath since she left him. His thread picking has been relentless and he's split the hole in his pants all the way to the seams on either side, his bare knee exposed to the elements. He'll have to scrounge up a different pair for work tomorrow or his boss will have another reason to razz him all day.

"Thanks, Joe. Seriously, you really saved me. I'll call you. Soon."

He shakes his head, smiling at the fact that she doesn't commit to *when* she'll actually call. Classic Sky. Thank God he loves her so fucking much he can put up with all her quirks.

29. Mockingbird

The pen hovers over the paper, clutched in her hand like a knife about to pierce skin. After she came out of the bathroom and announced she was ready they all crowded into Rod's office, then waited as Rod gave a ridiculous speech, going on and on about the agency and his long and storied history as an A&R representative, blah, blah, blah. Sky could barely concentrate on what he was saying. He put the papers down on his desk and abruptly shoved a fancy silver pen at her, placing his fat finger on the line where Sky's supposed to sign. They've reviewed the major points, briefly, but when he told Sky about the fifteen-thousand-dollar advance, the rest of the details were hard to focus on. She's so glad she got up the nerve to excuse herself and call Joe. Her fingers were shaking when she pressed the contact Jani had sent her, but as soon as she heard his voice she was reassured. The rest of the conversation – the fact that he'd broken up with Marley, and that he wants to come to Vancouver to see her – are making her even more anxious than she already is. She wants Joe back in her life more than anything, but she'd have to tell him about her cancer. And then what? He'd try to talk her out of recording this album and going on tour, just like Jani. She can't fight with someone else about all that right now.

There are glasses of champagne sitting on trays made from glossy slabs of wood. It looks delicious and Sky's thirsty.

What do I have to lose?

The voice is loud in her head, cutting through all the other thoughts vying for her attention. She scans the room and finds Vince leaning on the wall. Sky waits for a nod that says she's doing the right thing. Vince isn't that generous. He raises his eyebrows, more like a question. *What are you going to do?*

Exhaling all her doubts, Sky leans down and signs her name, letting the black ink soak into the paper. She is officially a recording artist with a record deal. The room erupts into cheers. Strangers come forward to kiss her cheeks and pat her on the back. She lets them. Rod and John shake her hand too hard and pull her in to awkward hugs, her breasts squished against their chests. They pose for pictures that will be posted on all the sites and shared and now everybody will know. Their smiles are huge and Sky feels like she's the most special person in the room and she never wants this moment to end.

"Congratulations, Sky." Miko is smiling, carrying a tray full of glasses that she offers to Sky. She reaches out to take one, the thought of Joe causing her hand to hover in mid-air, but her throat and maybe other parts of her are screaming – take a glass. Just one. Just to soothe her. This is a big moment in her life and she should be able to enjoy it.

"Thanks, Miko."

Miko winks, her tongue flashing between her slightly parted lips, then continues to pass out the glasses to waiting hands. Sky weaves her way through the room, dodging pointed elbows as people try to manage holding their glass while typing into their phones. Finally, she makes her way to the one person she'd like to talk to.

"Hey. Thank you for doing sound, Vince. I appreciated having a familiar face up there."

"You're welcome. You really delivered today. Not an easy room to bring all that emotion. You walk that line like a pro."

"Thanks. I can't believe this is all happening. I can't wait to work with you."

He reaches out and puts his hand on her shoulder. Sky feels a sob welling up from deep inside her. She's not sure why and she's embarrassed, turning her face away from him, biting down on her bottom lip. Heat stings her eyes. Vince gives her shoulder a squeeze.

"I gotta take off. These things are a bit much for me, but I'll see you around soon. Have fun tonight."

Before he steps away, he leans in close to her, his leathery skin smelling of soap and cigarettes. The cold glass is slick in her clammy hand.

"They're never your friends, Sky. Remember that. Even when they act like it, they never are. Watch your back."

His warning hangs in the air between them as he backs up and walks out, her shoulder still warm where his hand rested. The champagne churns in her stomach like acid.

Sky is called back into the room and brought into conversation after conversation. She's lost count of the drinks she's consumed, but the buzz feels good. It makes the barrage of questions people keep asking her more bearable. *What inspires your lyrics? What genre are you hoping to be categorized in? It's like you're singing just to me; how do you do that?*

Eventually people filter out and Miko comes over to her.

"Hey, do you have plans, or can I buy you dinner?"

She's smiling like she's up to something and Sky's pretty sure the offer isn't just for food, which makes her feel cornered. She can hear Joe's voice in her head, proud and excited, all the anger she imagined he held for her seemingly erased.

"Uh…I'm not sure, Miko. Let me just say goodbye to Rod first. I'll meet you in the lobby?"

Sky scans the room for Birk. He's in the corner by his desk, chatting up the girl who was helping to serve the drinks. He's all hands and loudness and Sky realizes with a pang of alarm that she's just chained herself to this guy.

The waitress has managed to get a very timely phone call and is backing away from Birk as Sky approaches. He mumbles something foul and yanks violently at the crotch of his pants, a thick roll of blubber bursting out above his stretched waist band.

"I'm going to head out, Rod," she pauses to clear her throat, her voice barely more than a whisper. "I wanted to thank you, again, for putting your faith in me. It was a really great day. I can't wait to get in the studio and record."

Birk turns around and grabs a coffee cup from his desk, which contains something that definitely isn't coffee. Sky can smell the hard liquor. Rum maybe?

"You're welcome. You were on fire up there. John was blown away with you."

He pauses to take a big swig from his cup, then reaches over to a shelf behind his desk and grabs another coffee mug from it. He opens his desk drawer and pulls out a bottle of dark liquor that looks expensive and pours a heavy amount into each mug, presenting it to Sky like an award she's just won.

"That's Crown Royal Northern Harvest, flown in from Gimli, Manitoba. Impossible to get. John doesn't know I expense this, but it's for special occasions. Today I deserve it. Look what I did?"

He gestures at Sky like she's some kind of object.

The whisky smells spicy and she takes a drink so she doesn't have to respond. She can be quiet. If that's what it takes to record an album and line her pockets with enough cash to get out of her shitty apartment and maybe take Sam with her, she can put up with Birk and his ridiculous pants. She swallows the rest in one smooth pull, surprised at how easy it is to be a regular person who drinks at parties. Too easy.

"So…what's next? Do we get together to talk about songs for the album?"

Birk lets out a big laugh and leans back against his desk, but it's more of a stumble and he's drunk and Sky regrets asking him anything important.

"Oh, Sky, you eager beaver. So many steps before then. We have to start with some marketing and promotion. A couple photo shoots right away. Get social media buzzing. *Who's Sky Black?* After that we'll record a single so we can get you doing radio interviews. A few podcasts, where you can really get personal. You have to tell your story and why your lyrics are sad and what bad things happened to you in your childhood, or whatever. We'll run it all through your publicist, of course, and make sure the stories are effective, you know, that they'll play well with listeners. Lots to do. But for now, just go out and enjoy yourself! Hey, do you want to grab a bite together?"

Sky feels stuck to the ground. All she wants to do is make music and get paid for it. Everything Birk just spewed out of his mouth sounds way too personal and kind of like hell and she needs to get away from him.

"Sorry, Rod. It's been a big day. I better rest my voice. I'll catch up with you later?" She holds out her hand and he takes it, although his slumping posture says he's not happy with her response.

"Yeah, sounds good. Get some rest. Oh, and I almost forgot…" He releases his grip on Sky's hand, opens the middle drawer of his desk, and pulls out an envelope with Sky's name scrawled across it. Beneath the envelope is the picture of Birk with the little boy. He pauses for a second to look at it.

"Is that your son?"

"Uh…oh, yeah, yes. Charlie. That's an old picture." Birk quickly closes the drawer.

"Cool. How old is he now?"

"Thirteen."

"Wow, a teenager! He must think his dad's got a pretty cool job."

"I wouldn't say that, exactly. He's in one of those teen mood-swing phases right now, unfortunately. I'm sure he'll come around. His mom's a real bitch, so that's not helping."

"I'm sorry to hear that, Rod. I'm sure you're right. He'll come around."

Birk stares blankly at her for a second, then seems to remember what he was doing before she asked about his son.

"Anyway, here's your cheque. Fifteen thousand. Don't spend it all on shopping and spa treatments, got it?"

Sky pulls open the flap of the envelope. Her name is typed in black ink on the top line.

"Thank you, Rod. Wow. This is incredible. Thank you. Bye." It takes everything in her to walk, not sprint, out of the office. She has a velvety buzz, fifteen grand in her pocket, and a record deal. Joe is back in her life. Then she gets an idea and it makes her feel warm all over and she can't stop herself from smiling. She walks around the corner and Miko is waiting in the lobby, staring into a compact with a tube of lipstick pressed to her lips.

"Well, you sure look pleased with yourself. Ready to go?"

"Sorry. I can't, Miko. I'm exhausted. I better get some rest." Sky keeps walking towards the exit. Miko puts the lipstick away and follows her out the door.

"What are you going to do, just go home alone?" she asks, barbs clinging to every word. Luckily, a cab whizzes by and Sky throws up her arm. It screeches out of the lane and pulls in front of her.

"Yes. I have somewhere to go tomorrow. Early. But thanks for the offer, and have a good night!"

Sky opens the door of the cab and puts her guitar in the back seat, throwing a smile back at Miko, whose freshly painted lips are slightly agape, her brow furrowed with irritation.

The driver pulls away from the curb as Sky takes her phone out of her purse and googles where the closest car rental company is located.

30. Hold On

Rain pelts the windshield of the small silver car Sky's rented. The guy who worked for the rental company promised she would be fine if she ran into snow on her drive – the car has all-season tires and handles great – he promised. She really hopes he knows what he's talking about. She has to drive through two mountain passes on her way to Nelson, and even with the rugged tires, she feels unsure. She wishes she was in her old truck. Cars make her feel vulnerable, like her butt is dragging on the highway.

Her coffee steams in a large paper cup, filling the interior with its comforting smell. Sky's purse is open on the seat next to her and she reaches over to fish out the bottle of Advil, working the top off and shaking a few pills onto her tongue. She chases them with the hot coffee. The two-lane highway stretches out in front of her, visible in the distance every time the wipers complete an arc. Taillights grow scarce as she gets farther from the city. The mountains loom ominously through the rain and fog, capped in brilliant white. She hopes the pills will kick in soon, soothing both her throat and the pounding in her head. She's hungover and disappointed in herself, but she's been working the program long enough to know that dwelling on the shame of a slip is the worst thing she can do. Today's a fresh start and she's taking it. She's back to sober and she's going to stay that way.

Sky's phone is streaming through the speakers of the car, selecting songs at random. Currently Tom Waits urges her to *hold on* with his scratchy vibrato. She hasn't been to Nelson in three years, but once she got the idea in her head it was impossible to ignore. She just needs to breathe, for a second. The last week of her life has been absolutely wild. She knows that being a successful musician is what she wants – it's what she's always wanted – but last night it occurred to her that she also wants to be alive to enjoy it. She's scared, and she doesn't want to make all these decisions by herself. She's so tired of being alone and trying to be strong. She lifts the steaming cup to her lips, takes another sip of coffee, then speaks over Tom's crooning, asking Siri to call Jani.

"Sky…oh God…are you okay?"

"I'm fine! Why does everyone ask me that when I call them?"

"Because you never call anybody! And especially not at…" Sky hears Jani rustling around at her desk, "nine-thirty in the morning! Seriously, what's going on?"

"Nothing's going on. I'm fine. I'm actually on a little road trip."

"A road trip? You haven't left that god-awful city in three years. Where the hell are you going?"

"I'm coming to see you." Sky waits for the wild reaction, but Jani is silent for a few seconds.

"Sky, seriously, what's going on? I mean. I'm happy, of course. Yay… But you'd never come to Nelson if something wasn't really bad. Not to mention I just saw you a few days ago. Just tell me. What is it? Is the cancer worse than you told me? Are you dying?" As she speaks her voice escalates from worried to frantic.

"Jani! Jesus. Calm down. No. I just need a break, for a minute. I signed the deal with the label last night, and I got an advance, so I figured – why not? I'm going to make an album, Jani! A real, legit album."

"Sky! Holy shit…You did it!" Jani cheers, shifting instantly back to happiness like only she can.

"Yeah, I'm pretty excited. So, I thought I'd come home for a couple of days – celebrate with you, of course – and maybe go check out Willa's clinic. Just to hear her out, see if she can do anything…a little gentler. Instead of jumping right into the surgery."

"Really? Oh, that makes me so happy! But…did the doctor say it was okay if you wait? Would it be better if you did both treatments together?"

Sky sighs loudly.

"Jani, let me handle this. I'm not a child. You're the one who told me to check out all my options. That's what I'm doing." Sky hates trying to navigate these conversations. Even when she's trying to meet Jani in the middle, it's not enough. She squirms in her chair. The windows have started to fog up so she reaches out, adjusting the vents and turning up the fan, blowing the warm air directly at the glass.

"I just…I just want you to get better. But thank you, for listening to me and going to see Willa. I'll call her right after we hang up and make you an appointment for tomorrow. I'm proud of you, Sky."

Tom Waits finishes his song and Joni Mitchell picks up right where he left off. "Anyway…when will you get here? Should I organize a little get-together?"

Sky laughs, not surprised at the request. Jani loves a crowd.

"Can't it just be us?"

"You, me, and Dave? Celebrating your record deal? Come on, Sky. Let's just invite a few friends. The people who came down to the show, at least. You can apologize for not seeing them in Vancouver."

Jani's teasing her, but Sky knows she should explain, or at least say sorry. Even though they're really Jani's friends, not hers.

"Sure, Jani. Whatever you want. If the roads are good, I should be there around six."

"I'll set it up at the Dockside at eight."

Sky's about to hang up when Jani jumps back in.

"Oh! One more thing…should I invite Joe? I heard him and Marley broke up…" She's practically singing the words.

"Um, no. I'll take care of that. See ya." Sky hangs up before Jani can ask anything further.

The hours of Sky's drive pass in a blur of songs and what ifs and wondering how everything got so crazy. The faces that have become part of her life over the last week all pass through her mind. New ones like Sam, Vince, Birk, and Miko. Old ones, who carry so much emotion with them. Her mom. Joe. She feels everything, excited and confident one minute, terrified and desperately sad the next. A deep longing for something she can't name. Maybe because she wants such conflicting things. It all comes in waves and after three years of living so carefully and quietly – afraid to slip in her sobriety and consumed by guilt – she is now awakening to the fact that she really wasn't living at all. The only thing that made her heart pump was performing. What kind of life was that? She might not be making all the best choices, but at least she feels alive now. She smiles at herself in the rearview mirror, her shiny hair tied back in an elastic, pieces falling across her cheekbones, her eyes bright with tears that might be from joy. Real joy. She thinks of the party Jani's planning, and who will bother to show up after she ghosted them all in Vancouver. But there's really only one person she wants to see.

She should call him. Once Jani starts spreading the word, he'll find out she's coming to town. She'd like him to hear it from her. She'd also like to pick up where they left their conversation yesterday– when he said he missed her. Now she's picturing his body and how he holds her and moves her when they're naked together, making her feel small and powerful at the same time. His skin on hers. His arms wrapped around her, strong hands touching her exactly how she likes. She starts to sweat, then laughs at herself, turning down the heat and cracking the window to breathe some fresh air.

When she stops for gas she picks up her phone, and after typing out, then deleting, several attempts at sounding casual, she sends him a text.

"Hey. I'm coming to town tonight, last minute. I think we're going to Dockside around eight. If you're free."

Within seconds the dots appear, circling, while he types.

"See you there."

She's glad she brought her new outfit.

***

Sky pulls up in front of Jani's house and kills the engine. The car treated her well and she gives the steering wheel a pat of thanks, then pulls the emergency brake because Nelson is built on a steep hill and no matter where you park you're either pointed up or down. She lets her hair loose from the elastic and gives it a fluff, then gathers her purse off the seat and grabs the small duffle she packed from the back. When she steps out of the car the evening air is cool and laced with the smell of cedar. The sun is just setting and the final rays reflect off the lake in the valley below her. Joe lives in one of the houses that sit at the water's edge, but she can't see it from where she stands now. She stretches her legs and walks the stone path to Jani's front door. It flies open when Sky is still several strides from knocking. Jani's eyes turn to saucers and her mouth gapes open at the sight of her sister.

"Oh my God! Sky! You look gorgeous!" She grabs Sky's shoulders, pivoting her roughly from side to side. "Jesus! You look like a supermodel! What did you do to your eyebrows? And the colour of your hair?"

"I had a little makeover, before my showcase yesterday. Not bad, hey?"

"Not bad! I'd say it's a little better than that. I barely recognized you! Joe's going to DIE! I mean…if you invited him." Jani tries to cover, but Sky has a feeling she already knows that Joe is coming.

"Get out of the doorway and let me in, for God's sake. I need a shower; that was a long drive."

Pineapple the dog comes ripping down the hallway and launches at Sky's legs, all licks and fuzzy wriggling. Dave follows behind her, his round face and soft chin giving him a lazy teenager vibe. The large grey sweatpants he's wearing complete the look perfectly.

"Pineapple, get down! Down! Hey, Sky, wow. Looking good!" He moves Jani out of the way and gathers Sky up in a big hug.

"How was your drive? Did you run into any snow?"

"Hey, Dave. No, it was wet, but the roads were clear. Sorry I didn't see you last week in Vancouver…it got pretty crazy." She backs out of his arms and lets him take her bag.

"Don't be silly! We were so proud of you. Your show was really good…and I heard the people who know their stuff thought so too – congratulations on the album!" He pats her on the shoulder, a wide grin beaming on his face, his straight brown hair flattened in the back like he just got off the couch.

"Thanks! I can't wait to start recording."

"Awesome. I'll let you guys catch up, because no matter how long I leave you two alone, Jani says it's never enough time. I'll put your bag in the VIP suite." He walks down the hall to the spare bedroom, turning back before he goes inside.

"Sky, do you care if I come to the party thing tonight? I just saw all those people, I don't really like most of them, and there's a hockey game on that I wanted to watch…"

"Dave, I told you not to ask her that – you're coming!" Jani pipes up before Sky gets a chance.

Sky grabs Jani and puts a hand over her mouth. Jani tries to squirm out of it but Sky holds her tight.

"Dave, of course you don't have to come. Watch your game. We'll be just fine on our own."

"Sweet. Thanks, Sky. You guys have fun."

He looks at Jani, pressing his lips together and raising his eyebrows as if to say, *see?* and also *don't kill me.* Sky lets go of Jani's mouth and ushers her to the kitchen before she can say anything else to Dave.

Their house was built in the sixties, the same vintage as most of the houses in this neighbourhood. It's small but cute, always spotless, the shelves and surfaces covered with delicate plants and all sorts of pottery and knickknacks that would drive Sky crazy, if they were hers. But they work here. Sort of like visiting your grandma. Jani has a crockpot full of soup bubbling on the counter and a pot of tea steeping. She pours two cups, although Sky is sure Jani'd rather have a glass of wine. So would Sky, but she takes the tea gratefully. Jani doesn't waste any time jumping into the questions.

"Alright, spill it. Tell me why you're here. Really. Is it honestly just to see Willa?" Jani pauses for a second, then seems to remember Sky's annoyance at her from their conversation in the car, and quickly adds, "If it is – I think that's fantastic. But it's not your style to take my advice so quickly. You usually get mad at me for suggesting anything you *should* do, wait for months, and then pretend it was your idea the whole time."

Sky laughs. She'd argue, but Jani has a point.

"Jani, can't you just stop prying for a second and let me have some secrets?"

"Are you kidding me? All you are is secrets!"

They stare at each other, both cupping their mugs of un-sipped tea. Sky realizes she's not going to get out of this conversation without giving up a little bit of truth.

"Okay, but don't start freaking out. I just…I have a lot on my mind, obviously, with the contract and my treatment and…I want to record this album, Jani, so badly. I can't risk getting my throat cut open and maybe losing my voice. I just can't. So yeah, I think that seeing Willa – finding out if there's some treatment, or something I can take that might help me bridge the gap until I can get the album recorded – is a good idea. So, thank you."

"You're welcome…" Jani says suspiciously. "And…"

"And…I talked to Joe yesterday. And also last week when he was in Vancouver. He came to see me. We finally talked about everything. I got to apologize. It went really well, I guess, but I didn't think he was going to break up with Marley. I…feel bad about that."

A smile is growing across Jani's face as Sky talks.

"Bullshit, Sky. They were never meant for each other. So…are you getting back together?"

Jani's puts her cup down on the island. Sky senses she's about to start jumping around the room or something.

"See? This is what I mean, Jani. Calm down. I don't know. I have no idea what's happening. I called him yesterday, just to help me go through the contract. That's it. He was very helpful."

"I'm sure he was."

"Shut up. I don't know, seriously. He lives here. I live there. I have to be in the studio, he has a job and a band and a house. And also…I haven't told him, Jani."

"About your cancer?"

"Yeah."

"Oh…Wow. I think you should, Sky. You know he'll be so incredible. He loves you so much, he'll want to be there for you."

"I know, Jani, but that's just it. Think about the impact on his life. If I dump all my shit on him, like I always have, he'll have to make all the sacrifices again. He'll probably want to move to Vancouver, and hold my hand through all the treatments, and I just…I wish I could take care of *him* for a change. You know? I wish I could just float in all easy-breezy and be the one to help him, not be such a goddamn burden all the time." Sky finally takes a sip of her tea. It's comforting and tastes like cinnamon, soothing her raw throat.

"I hear you, Sky, but that's not your decision to make. Joe's an adult. He can decide what's right for him. And it's not like you asked to get cancer. It's not your fault. You should give him a chance to be there for you, if he wants to be. And besides, you're going to get through this and get better, and your life will be amazing. Joe wants to share that with you. You guys have always been magic together. You know that."

"I know. That's what makes it so hard. I miss him…so much. But what if we get back together, and he's with me through everything, and then…I don't make it?"

Sky's voice breaks. She doesn't want to cry. She hates crying. But ever since she let go the other day, she feels like she opened the flood gates. Years of bottled-up emotion has collected inside of her and now it's sitting so close to the surface, waiting to release. Jani wells up, too. She stands and wraps her arms around her sister.

"You're going to make it, Sky. I know it. You have to."

***

Sky pushes open the door of the bar, nerves whirling in her empty stomach. She tried to eat Jani's soup but could only force a few bites down. They both promised Dave they'd eat full bowls when they got back. Instead of eating they sat in the bathroom, Jani perched on the counter and Sky doing her best Leon impression, laughing hysterically at their lack of skills when it comes to girly things like hair and makeup.

The Dockside is a nautical-themed pub located at the public docks on the water, a few blocks from downtown. In the summer it's packed with both tourists and locals who pull up in fancy boats, coming for cold beer and greasy fish and chips. Tonight, it's half empty, but as Sky glances around the room she sees a gathering of about twenty people at a long table by the window. They wave and call the sisters over. Sky scans the faces, barely recognizing any of them. Joe isn't here. When she gets to the group everyone greets her and yells congratulations and tells her how good she looks. She tries to remember when she last saw these people – it would've been at least three years and she was probably so high she wouldn't have known their names then, either. But they know her, and they showed up, twice. One of the people she does recognize is a girl named Diane, who's been one of Jani's best friends since they were in middle school. She was the other bridesmaid at Jani's wedding, and ended up doing everything, including helping get Sky into her dress a few minutes before the ceremony. She seems to notice that Sky is disoriented because she stands up and lifts her glass.

"Cheers to Sky! She's going to be famous and we can all say we know her!"

Sky looks to Jani, smiling with an edge behind it that only she will interpret – *you know I hate this shit. I'm going to kill you later.*

One of the guys yells "Speech!"

On the table are several pitchers of beer and one of water. Sky wishes so badly that she could fill a glass with beer and chug it down. She salivates at the thought, but picks up the water instead and fills a glass, holding it up and hoping words will come to her.

"Thanks, guys." Her voice is hoarse, her words broken. She clears her throat and tries to speak louder. "Thank you for coming down here tonight. Jani can be very bossy, as you all know, so I'm not sure what choice you had, but it's really nice to see you. I'm so sorry I didn't get a chance to visit with you last week. I really appreciated you being there. I heard you all cheering for me. It meant a lot." She pauses, looks around at the faces. "Yeah…so, I signed the contract yesterday. I'm going to be recording the album soon. I'll let you guys know when it's going to come out." She can't think of anything else to say but they're all still looking at her so she adds, "It sure is nice to be home." She reaches her glass into the crowd and there's clinking and more cheering and she smiles at everyone and looks in their eyes. They're genuinely happy for her and probably happy to be out and be together. It makes Sky feel warm inside, like she's a part of something or belongs somewhere that she'd forgotten about. The girls start to fawn about her hair and her clothes. She wore the pants and the boots, and the lacey pink bra/shirt is covered with a Johnny

Cash T-shirt. Before she can answer anyone about her new look, she hears a deep voice behind her.

"It sure is nice to have you home."

She spins around to see Joe standing right behind her.

The glasses of beer are downed and people start to fill them again. They say hi to Joe and pass a full glass to Jani. They seem to take note of the fact that Sky is drinking water and no one offers her beer. Diane goes over to hug Jani and whisper in her ear. They both laugh – looking from Sky to Joe. A few of the girls at the far end of the table call out to Sky, wanting her to come over and tell them about the music business and her jacket and where she got it and *how much?* and there are sounds and talking and bodies moving and none of it even registers to Sky. She and Joe have locked eyes and they don't need to say anything because the electricity between them is doing all the talking. Joe's wearing jeans and a black jacket that Sky's never seen before. He's just shaved and his skin is fresh and shiny and the scar makes him even hotter. She can smell shaving cream or something else sexy wafting off of him and he looks a little different or older but still like him and just *so good.* He has the mischievous half-grin she knows so well on his lips and the spark in his eye that means he's undressing her in his mind and probably doing other things, too. She wants to be alone with him so badly she can't breathe.

"How was your drive?"

"Good. Quiet."

"You look fucking great."

"Thanks. So do you."

"Thanks."

He bites the edge of his bottom lip. She should say something else now. It's her turn.

"Do you want me to pour you a beer or something?" Sky drags her eyes from his to look over her shoulder for an empty glass. The table is cluttered with glasses but they all have liquid in them. When she turns back he's moved even closer to her, inches from her face.

"No, thanks. I don't want beer. I want you. I can wait, if I have to. I'll wait all night. But just so you know, I want you to come to my place, and I'm ready to go whenever you are." His voice is husky and low and he's leaning down near her ear and if she turned her face slightly his lips would touch her temple. She looks around her and everyone's talking and they seem to be having fun and she doesn't want to ditch them all again and especially Jani, but Jani can get a ride with someone. She doesn't have her bag, but she doesn't think she'll be needing any clothes. She looks up into Joe's eyes.

"I'm ready."

He takes her hand and squeezes it, then turns and pulls her gently with him towards the door. His fingers mesh with hers like they were never apart and a rush of tingling runs up her arm and down into her belly. Sky finds Jani in the crowd. She's watching them leave and smiling so big her cheeks are wrinkled like tissue paper. Sky should go over and say thank you and goodbye and tell her to get a ride from someone sober and make sure she eats the soup when she gets home, but she's incapable of doing anything but following Joe out the door. Jani will know all those things. Sisters know.

Joe's truck is parked right out front. It's a black Chevy he's had since they lived in Merritt. He's taken good care of it and it still looks new. That's the thing about Joe. He works hard to get what he wants, and then he cherishes it. He walks her to the passenger side and opens the door. The smell of his truck – mint and grease and freshly chopped wood – hits her nose and the nostalgia of it makes her knees wobble. She throws her purse up on the bench seat and turns into him, their bodies finally pressed together. His hands circle her waist and reach up her back. She grabs his jacket and pulls his face to hers and their lips come together like an explosion. They kiss for minutes or hours and then Joe lifts her onto the seat, his grin returning.

"Let's get home. You have way too many clothes on."

She laughs as he closes her door gently and then walks around the front of the truck. When he gets in he fires up the engine and takes her hand again. They drive along the dark shoreline and over the orange bridge that Sky and Jani used to walk across when they were kids. They lived in several different houses, scattered on the hillside and back in town, moving when they couldn't pay the rent. Sky has no desire to ever see those houses again. They aren't happy memories. The road bends with the contours of the lake and she knows this drive so well. She thinks of her mom; the commune where she lives is another thirty minutes down the lake from here. She feels a pang of guilt at how she ended things the last time she saw her, but she has no intention of dealing with that now. Joe might sense her mind has wandered, he knows all her connections to this area. He squeezes her hand and she comes back to him. Remembers the countless times they drove this road together as teenagers, melded together on his motorbike. Joe's mom would smile when they came in, seemingly always in the kitchen, happy to see Sky, even though she probably knew Sky was high or drunk or both.

"I haven't been here since your mom passed away."

"I know. She'd be so happy to see you," Joe says, emotion thick in his voice.

They look at each other, so much going unsaid between them. He pulls off the road and down the dark gravel driveway. The kitchen light is on and it makes the small cabin glow. Joe gets out of the truck and Sky grabs her purse and opens her door. He's there to meet her, pulling her off the seat and into his arms. He kisses her again, sweetly, brushing the hair from her face, then closes the door. They walk into the cabin.

Joe has kept it almost exactly as his mom had it. It's a simple open space, sparsely furnished, one window above the sink in the kitchen that faces the driveway, and larger windows on the far side of the room that look out to the water. Two bedrooms and a bathroom down a short hallway. Joe's guitars are on stands next to the worn leather couch. He flicks on the light and drops his keys on the wooden table by the door, right where his mom kept hers. It smells the same as it always did, like cedar and smoke from the fire. Something faintly floral, like a ghost of his Mom's lotion. Sky remembers the sound of her coming in the door after work, her keys hitting with a loud thud, probably harder than she needed to. Sky and Joe racing to get out of his bed and dressed. She smiles, feeling like she's come home. The wooden floor creaks the same as she walks toward the windows. It's too dark to see the water, but the lights from the houses shine on it and flicker with its movement. She lets her purse slink off her shoulder and fall to the floor. Her phone buzzes from inside, but she doesn't care who it is or what they want. Joe has taken his jacket off and he comes up behind her and wraps his powerful arms around her small body. His forearms are inked with shapes and words. *You're already there* written in script. His mom's initials. The silhouette of a guitar and musical notes she hasn't seen before. She wants to freeze time and just be here – with all the anticipation of what's about to happen, when everything's so perfect, and Joe doesn't know about her cancer – but that's not how it works. He starts to kiss her neck and she bends her head to the side to expose as much of her flesh as she can. His skin and lips move across hers and he turns her around and time keeps moving and even though she wanted it to stop she doesn't anymore because it's the best thing she's ever felt in her life. She realizes that they've probably never been together when they were both sober. Every nerve ending she has is responding to his touch and for the first time in as long as she can remember, it's the only thing she wants.

31. Something in the Orange

Joe startles awake to the sound of gravel crunching on his driveway. Sky's naked body is curled into his and he doesn't want to move a muscle and risk waking her. She's lying so peacefully on his chest, softly breathing, her silky hair fanned across his shoulder. The vehicle stops and the driver turns off the engine. It sounds like a small car, and he can't imagine who it could be. The clock reads eight-fifteen. The door of the car slams closed and he hears footsteps making their way to his front door. He puts his lips to Sky's forehead.

"Don't move, baby. I'll be right back." He gingerly slides out from underneath her and she moans softly, turning away from him and on to her side. She's so striking to look at, lying in his bed, her tiny body wrapped in his blankets. The black trees tattooed on her back. He remembers sitting with her and holding her hand for hours when she had it done, her fingernails drawing blood in his palm. The footsteps outside reach his front porch and there's a soft knock on his door. Whoever it is better have a good fucking reason for being here. He grabs his jeans from the floor and pulls them on, squinting as he goes out of the bedroom. For a second he considers it could be Marley, and he freezes. He has no doubt she heard

Sky was in town and her absence at the bar says she knew he would be there, too. But whoever it is knocks again and he just wants them to go away so he can get back to Sky. He doesn't give a shit about anything else. He pulls the door open slowly, deeply relieved to find a mop of wild curls on the other side.

"Hi, Joe! Oh no, I woke you up! I'm so sorry to bug you guys." Jani's smile is huge and she covers her mouth with her hand. She's trying to whisper but she might as well be using her regular voice. She's holding a duffle bag and the keys to a silver Honda parked behind her. Her energy is so jacked up Joe wonders how many pots of coffee she's consumed. He looks back at the car and shudders at the thought of Sky driving through the mountains in that shitbox.

"Hey, no worries, Jani."

He rakes his hand through his hair. Jani's staring at the tattoos on his shirtless chest, her eyes coming to rest on Sky's name. She shakes her head, smirking, then hands him the keys and the bag.

"Yeah, so, here's her stuff. I was trying to call her last night to tell her I'd come by this morning. Dave and I have to get to work and I didn't know if you'd be working today, but she needs her clothes and her car. She has an appointment at one. Tell her to check her damn phone and she'll see the details. Is she up? Maybe I should just talk to her myself."

She's about to walk past him and into his house and as much as he loves Jani, there's no way he's letting her mess up this morning.

"Jani, I got it. No problem. Go to work. She's sleeping, and honestly, I think she could use the rest. I took today off. I'll make sure she gets to her appointment. Who's it with?"

He asks before realizing it's none of his business. Jani looks at him cautiously, sucking in her lower lip like she wants to say something, but she holds back.

"You should ask her, Joe. Ask her."

"Yeah, okay." He doesn't like how she said it or the expression on her face. The air is cold and his bed is warm and Sky is in it and he can't get back there fast enough. Luckily Dave's truck pulls up behind the car. He lifts his hand to Joe – a simple guy salute – and Joe does the same back. "Hey, thanks for helping me out, giving me her address and everything. I think…well, who knows, but maybe…things might work out." They smile at each other and it should be a happy smile, but now Jani has something else in her eyes and it makes him uneasy.

"I really hope so, Joe. You guys are so good together. She looked really happy when you left last night."

"Yeah. That makes two of us. Do you think I should hold off on the proposal for today – or just go for it?"

Jani's eyes expand to the size of tennis balls.

"Oh my God, you're joking, right? Tell me you're joking! You know her, Joe. You have to go slow or she'll…"

Joe laughs, cutting her off mid freak-out. "Jani, I'm kidding. I'm kidding."

"Well, don't. You just about gave me a heart attack."

"One day at a time. I promise."

"Good. Not never, just not yet."

"See ya, Jani."

"Bye. Make sure she checks her damn phone, and tell her to call me later."

They share a look of understanding. No one can *make sure* Sky does anything, the two of them know this better than anyone. Jani walks away and Joe shuts the door on the cold and the rest of the world and whatever Jani left unsaid. He gently lays Sky's keys on the table and brings her bag into his room, closing the door behind him. Sky hasn't moved since he left her. He peels off his jeans and crawls back under the blankets, wrapping his body around her. She sighs contently and snuggles into him and he knows that he actually wasn't kidding about proposing. He wants to marry Sky. There's no doubt in his mind, but he'll have to keep that quiet, for now. He needs to be supportive and encouraging and make sure she gets everything she wants. He's waited for three years and he'll wait as long as it takes. When they finally get to be together, they won't have any regrets.

32. All Again

"Hey, sleepyhead. Time to get up. Your sister's going to kill me if you miss your appointment."

Sky slowly opens her eyes and finds Joe sitting on the bed next to her. His hair is still wet from a shower. He's wearing jeans and a wrinkled black T-shirt, holding two mugs of coffee. He's pulled the bottom of the blind up to let some light in and as her eyes adjust, she can see gentle waves stirring the lake. She stretches her arms above her head, then buries her face under a pillow.

"No…what time is it? Come back to bed…," she mumbles, breathing in the smell of him from the pillow and reaching out to snake her hand over his thigh.

"Sky, I wish I could – believe me – but Jani has me on strict instructions, and I already let you sleep longer than I should have. She dropped off your car and your stuff this morning. You have to be out the door in forty-five minutes."

Sky keeps her head under the pillow, processing what Joe just said. Jani was here and she has to go see Willa. She can't do that without telling Joe why. She wants to stay curled up in his bed and not deal with any of this – not have the conversation she knows she's about to – but that isn't an option. He deserves to know. She eases the pillow off her face, then sits up and bunches it behind her, gathering her hair in one hand and taking the mug Joe passes her with the other.

"Jesus, Sky. You're so beautiful."

He's looking at her the same way he did last night and it makes her feel sexy and coveted. Their night together was so fucking amazing. So much better than it had ever been before. They couldn't get enough of each other and she realized she'd forgotten what real passion felt like. How everything else in the world can disappear except the sound of two people breathing together.

"Thank you," she says, taking a sip of the hot coffee. She wants to say more but her voice is hoarse and her throat raw like she swallowed glass. She hasn't taken anything for her pain since yesterday.

"Your throat doesn't sound so good. Have you been sick?"

"No, I mean…not a cold or anything like that."

"So…overuse? Are you resting it between gigs?"

She's squirming inside. Doesn't want to tell him, especially after everything he's been through with his mom. But she has to. *Get it over with. Tell him.*

"Um…it's kind of…more than that. I guess. A little."

"What do you mean?"

"Well…I…It's kind of the reason I'm here. My appointment today, it's with Willa Phillips. At her clinic."

Joe's forehead wrinkles with confusion. "I heard she's good, but, I'm surprised, Sky. With your mom and how much you hate her hippie stuff, I didn't think that a naturopath would be your thing."

"I'm not sure it is my thing. Jani suggested it. Remember how she told you I was having some trouble with my health?"

"Yeah, but after your show – how good you were – I assumed it wasn't anything serious. Honestly, I thought it might be something you were saying so you could get out of music without all the questions. Not that I blame you. I can't imagine how hard it's been, doing it all on your own. But now that you've signed your contract…" he pauses, then smirks at her, running his hand up her arm. "But hey, if you want to quit and come live with me, I think we could arrange that."

She wants to stay like this, smiling and flirting, not destroy it with what she's about to tell him.

"Well, thanks for the offer," she says, and puts her hand on his, "but unfortunately, I really do have something wrong. My doctor in Vancouver said I might need to have throat surgery, so I thought I'd come and see Willa, ask her if there was an alternative, at least until I've recorded my album."

"But then you'll be on tour. Your contract was pretty specific about that first year of touring. If it's nodes, I think the recovery for surgery can be as short as six weeks. Jason May from Bloodline had surgery last fall and he's already back performing. It'll be okay, Sky, but you should get them taken care of before you do some permanent damage."

He's so sweet and concerned and she wishes so badly that it was that simple.

"It's more than nodes, Joe."

"What is it?"

She exhales, has to tell him. *Say it. Just say it.*

"It's…cancer. Throat cancer." She stops talking, tries to clear the lump of poison choking her. It burns on cue. She hates that word. Hates that fucking word. Joe's eyes grow huge.

"Cancer? How bad is it?"

"It's fine," she lies, already hating how this is changing everything. "It's really not that big of a deal. I need to have some treatment for it, but it'll be fine. I can put it off, for a bit, I just wanted to see if there was anything else I could do in the meantime."

He's quiet for a minute, his face draining of colour.

"Fuck. Sky, I'm so sorry. I'm…damn. Are you sure you should wait? Did your doctor say that would be okay?"

"Yes. I'm sure." She can't tell him the whole truth. She can't. She needs his support, for whatever she decides, and she won't have it if she tells him everything the doctor said. Besides, doctors have to be overly cautious. It's their job.

"It's cool that the label is so behind you, that they're scheduling a tour even though…wait…do they know?"

She pauses before answering, trying to come up with something that makes sense, but he's putting it all together faster than she can come up with the lies and now it's too late.

"Holy shit, Sky. They don't know?" He takes his hand away from hers and rubs his forehead with it.

"I didn't think it was any of their business. I haven't told anyone! Jani, and now you. That's it. My mom knows, but Jani told her. It's all so new, Joe. That was the whole point of doing the show last week. I found out a month ago, and Jani insisted on the show, and then I was retiring, just like I said. Who would've thought I'd get signed at my last fucking show!? What would you have done? If a big label is offering you the chance to make an album, and holding out this amazing contract and a cheque for fifteen grand, what would you have done!?" She feels tears coming, but more than feeling sad, now she's fucking angry. Not at him, but he might be in the way of it if he makes her explain this anymore. It's a loop of outcomes that goes around and around in her mind and it keeps changing. There's still so much to process and she has to do it on her own. Especially after last night. Now she has to consider the possibility that she still has a life with Joe. A good life. Something she didn't have a few days ago.

She can tell he wants to ask her more questions, his eyes searching hers, but he knows her, and how this will go, so he doesn't. He takes the mug of coffee from her hand and puts it on the bedside table, then pulls her into his chest and wraps his arms tightly around her.

"You're not going to do this alone, Sky. I'm here and I'm not going anywhere."

She wants to tell him that she's fine, it'll all be fine, she's recording her album, and everything is great, and this isn't sad, but those words won't come out. Instead, the tears that she can't chase away anymore spill down her cheeks and soak into his shirt. She doesn't want to need him this badly but she does.

Eventually the tears run dry and she realizes she's running late and she should probably have a shower and take something to soothe the fire in her throat. She pulls herself away from him and takes her bag and purse to the bathroom, swallows some Advil, and steps into the shower. Joe still uses green Irish Spring soap. She lifts up the partially disintegrated bar and smells it, the strong chemicals burning her nostrils. There are at least four other slimy wedges just like it on the shelf, and she remembers she used to call him soap hoarder because he never threw them out, just let them pile up until they became one nasty green blob she'd have to scrape off the ledge with her fingernail. Her phone buzzes incessantly from inside her purse and when she's dressed and ready to leave, she dares to check it. The first three messages are Jani from last night.

"Willa confirmed your appointment tomorrow at 1:00. Don't be late. The address is 12527 Lakeside Drive. It's just past the ferry terminal."

Sky scrolls to the next one.

"I'm watching you talk to Joe and you look so happy, and also like you might fuck him in the bathroom any minute now. Go home with him! I'll get a ride with Diane. You look skinny: eat something."

She smiles, flashes of last night dancing in her mind, as she reads the final message.

"You left without saying goodbye, but I get it. Have fun. I'll drop off your car and your stuff tomorrow morning. Don't forget your appointment. You guys are so good together."

Sky sends her a quick reply: "I got ALL your messages. I'm leaving now. Thanks for bringing my stuff this morning. I'll call you later."

Seconds after she presses send, Jani replies:

"Hurry up; you're late. When did Joe get your name tattooed on his body??? I'm surprised Marley didn't claw it off. (Laughing emoji). CALL ME IMMEDIATELY AFTER YOUR APPOINTMENT."

There are two more messages, both from Miko.

"Hey, Sky, I hope you got some rest. Dinner?"

"?"

Sky hates the single question mark. She deletes both of the messages, then gathers up her stuff and comes out of the bathroom. Joe is sitting on the couch in the living room, picking a melody on his acoustic guitar. It's intricate and haunting. She forgot how good he was. She'd love to sit down and play with him, not go to this appointment and listen to someone give her another doom-and-gloom speech. She drops her bag by the door and picks up her keys, then walks over to Joe. He lays the guitar on the couch and stands, his face serious.

"Do you want me to come with you?"

"No, it'll be boring. I won't be long."

"Will you eat something before you go?"

"I don't have time, but I have some food in the car."

"When you get back, I'll make you dinner."

She nods. Doesn't know what else to say to him. They stand awkwardly for a second, and then Joe steps through the space between them and takes her in his arms, kissing her temple. She buries her face in his shoulder.

"I love you, Sky."

"I love you, too." It comes out so easily, like she never stopped saying it.

***

Sky drives back along the lakeshore road on autopilot, her mind swirling with everything Willa said to her. Beside her on the seat is a large white shopping bag filled with remedies and supplements with pages of instructions about how and when to take them all. They are a short-term Band-Aid, a fact Willa reinforced profusely. They will not fix her, only keep her cortisol levels down and her immunity strong enough to fight. Once Willa saw the results of Sky's biopsy and scans – begrudgingly emailed over from Margie – she was adamant. Sky needs treatment. Soon. Her cancer is aggressive, just like Dr. Miller told her. Willa is one of the few naturopaths in Canada licensed to perform targeted chemotherapy and she thinks Sky would be a great candidate for it, considering her circumstances and the fact that – as far as they can tell – the cancer hasn't spread. It definitely sounded like a better option than getting a hole cut in her throat, but the odds that it will work as effectively, and that it will get all the cancer out of her, aren't as high. Also, Sky would have to be at the clinic every day for three months for the treatment. Besides the time commitment, it would be really expensive. Willa estimated about fifty thousand. There's no way Sky could record her album at the same time. Touring would be out of the question. Her phone rings and she checks the number, expecting Jani or Joe, but it's Birk. *Shit.*

"Hi Rod, how are you?"

"Sky! How's my star? You resting? How's the voice?"

Oh God. Birk and his strings of questions.

"I'm good, thanks. Yeah, just…visiting some friends." She leaves out where, exactly, the friends are. She doesn't think he'd like her taking long road trips without his knowledge.

"Well, visit quietly, and make sure you have an early night. We have a big day tomorrow."

"Tomorrow?"

"Yes! We've booked a photo shoot for your socials and profile shots at eleven. Leon needs to start your hair and makeup by nine. Then Vince wants you to drop by the studio at four. He has another band in there, but he thought it might be good for you to come in and watch the process, so you have an idea of what it'll be like for you. He figures he can get you in as soon as next week, so we've got to get a list of song possibilities figured out, and I want you to sit with your PR people and hand over all your social passwords so they can get your feeds cleaned up. Busy times!"

Tomorrow. She has to be in Vancouver by tomorrow. She'll have to leave right now and drive through the night to make it home for a few hours of sleep. *Fuck.*

"Um…okay, that all sounds good, Rod."

"Yeah, it should!" He exaggerates the word *should* with extra volume and a thick layer of sarcasm. "We never move this quickly with new artists. John wants to push your single for a May release. Get it on the summer playlists. This is going to happen fast, Sky. I told you to be ready, right?"

"Yes. Of course, I'm ready. It's very exciting."

"All right, that sounds better. I'll get Miko to arrange a car to pick you up tomorrow morning. She'll text you an itinerary. Like I said, get home soon and get your beauty rest!"

He chuckles to himself and then cuts out. Sky feels nauseous. Her hands are shaking. She pulls off the road and leans her head against the back of the seat, trying to force some deep breaths into her lungs and slow her racing heart. She has to go. As much as she wanted to spend another night with Joe, she's signed a contract, and this is her dream, and it's happening right now. It might never happen again.

She looks out at the lake, watching the large ferry power across the channel, carrying cars and people from one shore to the other. It's such a beautiful place – she couldn't see that when she was a teenager – but she can see it now. A place to settle down in, one day. These domestic thoughts are so foreign to her and she laughs at how one night of fantastic sex can turn her toughness to goo. Of course, it's tempting to stick around and spend time with Joe, after she finally has him back. They have years to catch up on, and being with him makes her feel safe and supported, like she can share this heavy burden, instead of letting it sink her. But then what? She'd end up being a cancer patient he'd have to take care of, physically and financially. She knows he would generously volunteer, but she doesn't want that. She just needs some time – to decide which treatment she's going to do, then make the money she needs to cover it. Even if she goes with the surgery option that's covered by basic medical, the time off work and all the trips to the hospital will cost thousands. Sky rubs her face with her hands, trying to wipe away the memory of the alarm she saw in Willa's eyes as she read Sky's lab reports.

Sky finally has her breathing under control. She roots around in her purse and finds an elastic, twisting her hair into a messy knot on her head, then pulls back onto the road. It's a beautiful day for March, the trees drip with a slow melt, and the sky is a soft blue. She'll pass Joe's house in a few minutes and she considers that she could just keep going. Call him once she's left Nelson and explain she had to rush back. It would be easier that way. Instead of spinning lies again or having to admit that both Willa and Dr. Miller agree she should get treatment now. She passes the odd car, but it's mostly quiet. She'll need to get gas before she starts the long drive home. And food. She hasn't eaten today – despite telling Joe she had snacks in the car. His house is coming up on the left and she has to decide right now what she's doing and if she's finally matured enough to stop running away from him every time things get hard. At the last second, she decides that she has, and swerves off the road and down his driveway. She puts the car in park and turns off the engine.

Joe steps out onto the porch as she's opening her door.

"I was afraid you forgot to come back. How did it go?" He leans against a wooden post, a gentle smile on his face. Sky has a sudden rush of love for him wash over her, weakening her resolve to leave. But she has to. He's wearing the grey sweater that she loves, his hair sticking up like he's been running his hand through it, a habit he's had since she's known him. She walks across the driveway and stands below him.

"It was okay. Fine. Lots of stuff to read and figure out. But…I just got a call from Rod, at the label. I have to go back to Vancouver tonight. I should leave in an hour. So…we could talk about the appointment, or we could…do other stuff." She smiles up at him.

He jumps down from the porch, hitting the cold gravel with a crunch under his bare feet, and picks her up like she weighs nothing, wrapping her legs around his body and carrying her inside.

"Other stuff," he mumbles into her neck.

Sky leaves for Vancouver two hours later with a peanut butter sandwich wrapped in tinfoil and a smile on her face that lasts long after the lights of Nelson fade behind her.

33. Crooked Old World

There's a pencil hanging from a string, attached to the calendar in Sam's small room. He uses it every day to make a large X in the square. He does it in the quiet hour before dinner, but as he makes the mark, he knows he's tempting fate a little. The day isn't over yet. He walks out of his room and down the too-bright hallway to the general congregation room where he gets his assigned task, written on the white board in orange Sharpie. Today he has "empty recycling." It's a sweet gig, one saved for the long-term, more trustworthy residents. Sam claps his hands together, sliding his feet back and forth in his step-together-step shuffle. No bathroom, no nasty smells or puke or chewed up food. No one moaning or telling him to get the fuck out. He gets to stroll around the building, dumping empty cans into a bag.

He scans the board to see where the other twenty-six patients will be. Lacey – the new brunette with the nose ring and the sweet eyes – has "dish bin." Not fun. Sam remembers his dish-bin days, just after he'd survived detox, when the last thing you want to do is smell and touch strangers' partially eaten food. It was only a few weeks ago. A short amount of time by real-life standards, but not here. In here, time trudges with such imperceptible forward momentum you swear to God it's going backwards.

After completing detox, jobs like "dish bin," "kitchen scrub," and "table clear" are the only assignments you get. These are the duties that leave you entrenched in the main hub of activity. There's always eyes on you, offering no opportunity for *funny business*. That's what the thick-bearded detox counsellor, Marcus, likes to call it. *Funny business*. He means trying to make a run for it. Everybody in the facility has thought about it – Marcus likes to make sure all the new residents know he's aware of this – but once you're out, you're out. And most of the people here are on their very last chance. *In* sucks, but out isn't good, either.

Bad Breath Billie comes in and stands next to Sam, too close for Sam's liking. His head hangs consistently low and he smells like garlic and Sam can't figure out where he's getting all the garlic from. The food here is bland at best, but somehow Billie always manages to obliterate the air around him with his foul breath.

"Hey Sam. Ah – you lucky bastard – recycling. You must be getting out soon."

"Yup. One more week."

"Nice. I've had vacuum duty for three days now. It's disgusting. These floors are covered with chewed off fingernails, especially in the group session rooms. The *click click click* sound they make when they're shooting up the tube makes me want to puke. It's nasty." As he speaks, Billie chews on his thumbnail, using his tongue and a sharp spitting sound to release the slice he's managed to free. It drops to the ground at his feet, suspended in a slimy, garlicky wad of spit.

"Ah, vacuuming isn't so bad. Just put on some tunes and groove to it, man. Catch ya later." Sam steps back and into some less pungent air. He's got seven days to go and he doesn't want anyone bringing down his mood. He'll keep busy and keep Nag quiet and he'll participate in tonight's group sessions and maybe he'll catch Lacey's eye at dinner when he drops his plate in the dish bin. He'll earn that X he made in no time.

He grabs a clear blue bag and a pair of white plastic gloves off the duties table and starts his walk, moving from room to room to empty the overflowing bins, piled with cans from the energy drinks and Coke no one can get enough of. Most of the residents take a nap at this time of day, so it's peaceful. As Sam walks the halls, he can hear low murmurs coming from some of the rooms. His roommates will be leaving their room to get their duties soon and if he times it right, they'll just be starting as he's finishing. Then he'll have the room to himself for forty-five minutes before dinner. His guitar calls to him all hours of the day and night, but he's been warned multiple times by the staff and his roommates about playing it too often. So he strategizes, and when he gets the opportunity, he plays. Then this place and all the pain it's filled with, his mom and Andy and the fear that he might fail again, all drop away. It's just him and the music.

There's a phone station in a closet-sized room near the front entrance. A couple of square beige phones with raised squishy buttons are plugged into the wall, spiral cords attached to their handsets. They look strangely huge and hilarious to Sam, like a display from a phone museum. The lady staffing the front desk – either Carol (nice) or Lenore (grumpy) – can hear everything you say. He's been avoiding the phone room since he got here, besides a quick call to tell his mom he survived detox, but he can't avoid it any longer. His counsellor has been bugging him to secure a sponsor. He hates to ask Sky for more, but there's no one else. Sam stands in the entrance to the room, holding his fat bag of cans, and stares at the phones, terrified that Sky might have changed her mind, or maybe she's too busy now. His stomach clenches with the fear that if this call doesn't go well, he might have to go back to who he was before he got here. The cans crush against the doorframe as he steps in. He has Sky's number memorized and he dials it quickly, then puts a fingernail in his mouth and starts to chew.

34. Dark Angel

"Hello?"

"Hi…Sky?"

"Yeah?"

"It's Sam."

"Sam! Hi, how are you?" Sky pushes herself to a sitting position on the couch, covering the phone with her hand so she can clear her throat.

"Hanging in there. Better," he says, taking a breath before continuing. "You know, some days are harder than others."

"It'll get easier." She stares at the empty bottle of cough medicine on her counter as she lets the lie fall off her tongue.

"Yeah. That's what the counsellors say. I've got one more week to go here. Then I'll be out on my own."

His voice is shaky and Sky remembers the fear of the release date. If it doesn't work – then what?

"Hold on, Sam."

She stands up and walks to her kitchen, letting the silence on the line hang heavy as she opens the cupboard under her sink and drops the empty bottle into the garbage. Three weeks have passed since Sam started rehab, and a few days after that she found herself in Nelson. It feels like a lifetime ago. Her drive home was filled with a deep ache to turn around and go back to Joe, an instinct she was barely able to fight off. But since that night it's all a blur of studio sessions and photo shoots and too many empty bottles of cough medicine. And other things, too. Whatever it takes to keep her singing. The shame of abandoning her sobriety again was eating her up at first, but she knows it's the only way she can do this, and it's only temporary. She has a sip of water that smooths the gravel so she can talk.

"I'm back. Sorry about that, Sam. When you get out, I'll catch you up on everything that's been going on. I signed the deal, and I've been working my ass off in the studio. I asked the producer, Vince, if you could play on the album, and he said he'd hold a spot for you, but you'll have to do a little audition. Don't worry; he's going to love you."

"Wow. That's awesome Sky! Congratulations! And, hey…thanks for the guitar and the help and, everything. I don't know what would've happened to me that night without you."

Sky can hear all the emotion in Sam's voice and it makes her uncomfortable. She needs to clean her shit up before Sam gets out. She's got a week. She's not sure how she'll go back to dealing with her pain using only Advil, but she'll have to.

"I gotta go here, Sam, I'm supposed to be at the studio in an hour. But good luck on your last week. I'll come by for your release, okay? Text me the details."

"Sure, Sky. I just have one other thing, really quick. They told me I need to secure a sponsor, for when I'm out. I was wondering…if you would do it?"

Oh shit.

"Sure, Sam. Of course. I just…I hope I can do a good job. I'm definitely a little distracted, but yeah. I can do it. For sure."

"Thanks Sky. It means a lot." Sam releases a long breath. "I'll see you next week." His voice has relaxed and Sky can tell he's smiling. "I've been playing every day, as long as they let me. I got my old calluses back! I'm working on that riff you gave me for "Going Down," and some new stuff, too. I'll be ready to play. I can't wait."

"Great, Sam. Keep working. I'll talk to you soon."

Sky hangs up before he says goodbye, then drops the phone, leaning over to put her forehead on the cold counter. She's not sure how she got back here. When did she stop trying to stay sober? It's hard to remember. She came back from Nelson to the craziness, Birk and Leon and Miko all telling her how fabulous she was, while gradually changing everything about her. The non-stop flow of booze and the vocal-cord relaxants Birk was passing her felt so necessary. Unavoidable, really.

Sky pushes herself off the counter and opens her fridge. Inside is a neat row of bottled health drinks, next to all the supplements Willa gave her. Miko had cases of healthy stuff sent to her apartment because she said her diet was "worse than a college student's." *Yeah, because I was as poor as one,* she thought, but kept it to herself. She selects a green drink from the row and cracks the top. It tastes like mowed grass. but she manages to chug it down, swallowing handfuls of capsules and drops along with it.

***

"Sky, can you come up to the booth for a minute?"

"Sure Vince, I'll be right up."

Vince doesn't ask her to come up in the middle of a session. Not when they're flowing, like they just were. She takes off her headset and puts her guitar in the stand beside her chair. The studio musicians put their instruments down, too. On any given day there are four or five of them. They know each other well and speak in a short hand Sky doesn't always understand. They showed up on the first day of rehearsals with all her songs charted out and in folders. Vince had given them the demos and they converted the riffs and progressions Sky made up in her head to a numbering system developed in Nashville. When Sky walks past their music stands she can see the titles of her songs and a page of numbers and notes about lyrics and timing in the margins. It feels like her music has already grown legs.

Sky climbs the steep wooden stairs slowly, feeling guilty, even though she doesn't know what she did wrong. The fear of disappointing Vince is enough. She keeps her body out of the room and pokes her head through the open door.

"Hey, Vince, something wrong? I rushed the tempo on the third verse. I'm happy to do it again." Sky knows this isn't the problem. Vince would've told her in her headset.

"No, you were great. We'll patch in another take if we have to. Come in and sit."

He motions to an empty chair by the wall. The small room is dominated by the large mixing board. Hundreds of dials and knobs adorn it and Sky has no idea what most of them do. There are posters and pictures of album covers pinned up on the walls. Vince has a headset slung around his neck. His face is weathered, but his blue eyes shine with life. She perches on the plastic seat, waiting for him to start.

"I was talking to Rod yesterday. He's got some plans coming down the pipe for you. Soon."

"Oh yeah? Did he like the cut of 'Caged Bird' with Scott on pedal steel?"

"Yes, and I think I convinced him to go with the more acoustic sounding one. Take that jangly bit out and really focus on your vocal."

"Great. So, we're good?"

"Yeah, we're good. He said he wants to release it next week as a single, have a big party and get you doing the radio circuit and the whole bit. I just wanted to have a word, make sure you're as ready as you can be."

Sky feels like Vince is talking around what he's actually trying to say. It's not his normal style of communication and it makes her jumpy.

"Don't worry, Vince. I'm ready."

Vince just smiles, staring at Sky a little too long before he responds.

"You can't be ready, Sky. Not for this. It's a shit show. Don't let them push you too hard, and watch what you're using to balance yourself out, substance wise. I know Birk likes to hand out pills like they're treats, to keep everybody feeling good and ready to work, but you have to protect that throat. Seems like it's fraying a little…"

"I can do more takes, if it's not sounding great. I'm only taking some throat relaxers. Birk says everyone takes them…"

Vince rolls his eyes, cutting her off mid-sentence.

"Your voice is sounding great, but with the hours we've been putting in, you have to take care of it, going forward. Especially with press stuff. Interviews. Parties. Remember your singing is the most important thing. Got it?"

"Yeah, I hear you. I'll rest it. I promise."

Vince nods, a singular motion that indicates he said what he needed to.

"We're good for the day, Sky. Will and I will clean a few of these tracks up, but we've got solid vocals on everything. I'll have the boys hang around in case I need them to add anything. Let us put it all together and we'll send it over to the office. Give the suits a listen. In the meantime, take a few days off. Rest that voice. We'll catch you next week. Cool?"

She nods, but she doesn't want to be done here. It's her safe place. She's afraid what she might get up to with nowhere to go for a few days. Sam's face pops into her mind.

"I talked to my friend, the one I was telling you about, Sam? He'll be available to come in next week. Does that work for you?"

"Yeah, for sure. We'll have a listen to him. If he's as good as you say, we'll get him playing on a few of the tracks."

"Thanks, Vince. See you in a few days." Sky stands and leaves the room, the throb of guilt in her belly refusing to subside.

She packs up her guitar and says goodbye to the musicians, then steps outside and into the bright afternoon light. They've finished earlier than usual and the car that picks her up isn't here yet. She takes her phone out of her pocket and looks at the screen. Vince insists on no phones on the floor. "Don't even look at the fucking things!" Sky's given up on trying to stay caught up with messages. She lets them roll in and out like the tide now, except the ones form Joe. She always answers those. He's out on tour right now so they come in less frequently than when she first got back. They still try to talk every night, but that promise has been hard to keep with their erratic schedules. There are a few messages from Jani that she scrolls through.

"Hey rock star. How's the throat? Any decision on your treatment yet? I know you said don't ask, but I'm going to keep asking until you give me an answer."

And then,

"Your social media is going crazy, are you posting all that? The picture barely looks like you."

Birk hired a girl named Anna to do her PR. She posts all kinds of stuff on Sky's behalf, reporting back that her accounts are picking up traction. Sky stopped looking because she finds the whole thing so cringey, but it's part of her contract.

"When's the launch? Oh wait, it says here on your Facebook page. Saturday, April sixteenth. Should I be dressed up?"

Jani follows this question with emojis of fire and a dancing girl.

Sky considers starting to walk. Spring is in full bloom and she can smell the fluffy pink blossoms on the cherry trees that line the street. She decides to respond to Jani first, so she'll leave her alone for the night.

"Hey, loser. I don't write those posts, it's Anna. Yeah, the launch is next Saturday. Buy a new dress, my treat! I'll send you and Dave plane tickets. Someone from the label will call with details tomorrow. Love you."

Within seconds Jani texts her back.

"Who the hell is Anna?"

"My PR person."

"You have *people* now? Holy crap. Thank you, big sister. My dress will be very expensive. Just warning you."

There's a string of laughing faces and hearts and airplanes and dresses. Sky's not sure how Jani could possibly compose and send the text back so quickly.

35. Cast Iron Skillet

The clinic smells like disinfectant and soup. The lady at the front doesn't know Sky from her stay there, so Sky has to show her ID before they buzz her through.

Sam is standing at the desk, signing papers. He looks great. He's gained weight and his blond hair is styled with some kind of product. He's such a good-looking kid, the girls in here must love him. His skin is clear and he's wearing a black button-up shirt and jeans. Both look brand new. The guitar case Sky bought for him rests at his feet. His shoelaces are long and untied and definitely a tripping hazard. He's so young. Sky had forgotten how young he was.

"Hey, Sam, you look great! All spiffed up I see."

"Sky! You're here!"

Sky reaches out to shake but Sam comes right in for the hug. Grabs on tight. She stumbles backwards. Starts to feel like this was a bad idea, like it's too much responsibility for her to take on. Before rehab, Sam was a junkie, a few steps from the edge. Now he's this shiny kid full of promise and excitement. He should be in school or something.

Sam steps back and his cheeks are flushed. He lowers his head and turns to the papers on the counter, embarrassed by his own enthusiasm.

"Sorry, Sky. It's been a long month. You know how it is."

He slides into a more subtle demeanour and Sky wishes she wasn't grateful, but she is.

"Yeah, of course. No problem. Are you ready?"

"Yes, I just need you to sign here, saying you're my sponsor. Then I think that's it."

She steps in and looks at the blank line where her name is supposed to go. Where she will commit to being a role model and twenty-four-hour support person for Sam. She thinks of the life she's about to bring Sam into and how impossible it was for her to stay sober. There's another skinny, angry girl being brought through the door as Sam's about to walk out. Sky grabs the pen and signs because she has no other choice in this moment. Sam beams at her and picks up the guitar.

"Thanks, Sky. I can't wait to show you what I've been working on." He walks over to the row of chairs against the wall. There's a woman sitting in one with a blue duffle bag on her lap. Her knees bump up and down and she fidgets with the strap of the bag. Her clothing and hair are perfect, her face tight, ready to jump or react.

"Sky, this is my mom, Catherine. Mom, this is her. This is Sky Black. Soon-to-be world-famous musician."

"Oh hi. Hi, Sky. It's so nice to meet you. You're all Sam talks about."

She's pretty and she smiles cautiously at Sky. They both know more than strangers should know about each other.

"Hi, Catherine. I didn't realize you were here. It's nice to meet you."

Catherine stands to shake Sky's hand, but Sam steps in front of her.

"She just came to drop off some stuff for me."

"Yeah. Of course. I just…are you sure you don't want to spend some time…"

Sky trails off because she remembers Sam's face the night he came to her place. His eye swollen shut. The asshole who picked up the racquet and beat him. She can't send him back into that situation. She has to follow through on this promise.

Sam reaches out and takes the bag from his mom.

"We better get going. Thanks, Mom. I'll call you, sometime soon. Say hi to Poppy for me. Tell her I'm doing great."

"Sure, Sam. Don't forget to call me. I'll tell Poppy. Good luck."

Catherine looks like she wants to say more, but Sam turns and pushes through the door. Sky steps out behind him, squinting into the bright sunlight. She pulls the black hat she's wearing lower and slides on the pair of sunglasses that Leon gave her. Sam falls in stride with her.

"Cool shades."

"Thanks."

"So, what's the studio like? How are the recordings coming?"

He's practically bouncing as he walks, oozing the energy of a Jack Russell terrier. Sky takes a deep breath. Smiles, wishing she could swallow a few of the pills that rest in her jacket pocket.

"Yeah, everything's going really well. Vince is fantastic as a producer, the studio musicians are super talented. The single is ready to roll out tomorrow, so it's going to be a bit crazy for the next few days, Sam. You're walking into a tornado."

Sky feels itchy, her skin crawling under her clothes.

"No problem. I'm up for anything, just happy to be along for the ride."

"I'm glad you're here. I miss normal people. Some of this stuff – the stylists and photographers and PR people – have been a real trip. You hungry?"

They duck into a popular restaurant that Sky wouldn't have dreamed of going into before she got her signing bonus. Thirty-five-dollar burgers and trendy teenagers everywhere, but she needs some kind of distraction right now, and this place was the closest. A beautiful girl who looks younger than Sam comes to take their order. Her cheeks are glowing pink. The other waitresses gather near the kitchen and giggle, staring over at their table and, Sky assumes, at Sam. Sky smiles over at them. She wants to order a double vodka on the rocks, but that's impossible. She's with Sam and she's supposed to be the model of sobriety. She orders a Diet Coke instead, then waits until Sam goes to the washroom before she swallows a few pills.

Birk has gigs lined up in Vancouver next week. Samplers, he calls them. Just a few songs, part of a larger lineup of musicians, so he can test out the crowd's reaction without an official show. Something about managing first reviews. Sky doesn't listen much when Birk drones on about the business of it all. The way she sees it, the music is either good or it isn't. But according to Birk, that's not how the game is played.

Sam comes back to the table and they talk about the future. What they'll play in the studio and when. Vince hasn't signed off on a final cut of "Going Down" yet, and Sky would like Sam to play lead guitar on that track. It'll be up to Sam to show Vince he's got the chops to do it. As Sky goes over the details,

Sam is wide-eyed. She hopes this isn't too much to throw at the kid. She offers to give him the keys to her place, because the itinerary locked into her phone says she has to report to Leon in half an hour. Sam hesitates, and Sky clues in that leaving him alone isn't the right thing, either. She calls the car service to come pick them up and deal with Sam's bag and guitar. Sky pays the cheque and leaves a huge tip, because for the first time, she can. The waitress stumbles out a thank-you as she leads them to the door and holds it open, batting her eyes at Sam. Out front, the shiny black car is waiting at the curb, the driver standing at the ready to let them inside. Sky hears the waitress yell back to the pack of jealous girls behind her, "I TOLD you they were somebody!"

36. Wish I Knew You

"Sky! And, fucking hell, who is this gorgeous little man? My loins can't take this people!"

Leon is in fine form. He squeals this absurd greeting from the back of the salon. All the staff and clients freeze. Sam stumbles backwards into the door. Sky shakes her head, laughing. Leon throws some long strands of fake hair he was holding into the air behind him and does a part run, part skip to bridge the distance to the entrance as quickly as possible. Sky steps aside and lets him get his hands on Sam first.

"Sam, meet Leon."

Sam is still backed into the door and is now cornered. Leon spreads his giant arms wide, taking up all the space. He wears a brilliant blue silk vest, no shirt, black leather tights and – obvious to anyone who glances in the area – no underwear. Black leather boots with a two-inch heel, and a squared off goatee that he's dyed purple.

"Sam. Sammy. Samuel. Your innocence is intoxicating. I want to devour you and wash you down with a mug of chardonnay. Absolutely delicious." He kisses Sam on each cheek, then steps back for a breath, and repeats the process. Sam looks to Sky for some kind of assistance. Sky shrugs.

"You'll get used to it. Hey, Leon. How are you?"

Sky lets Leon bring her in for the kisses as well. It's just easier this way. Leon rips the hat off Sky's head and puts his hands into her unwashed hair. He looks her up and down, clicking his tongue with a *tsk tsk* against the roof of his mouth.

"Sky, seriously. You look like a streel. You know that treating your beautiful self this way is insulting to me, personally, yes? All the work I've done, the hours, the sacrifice." He pauses his reprimand to throw Sky's hat against the wall. "Come on people, we've got work to do!"

He spins around and claps his hands, taking giant steps back through the room, waving his arms and barking orders. Bodies scatter. Sam looks like he might fall over. Sky remembers how she felt the first time she stepped through these doors. She should've called ahead and warned Leon not to serve alcohol, or any other substances, but now it's too late and she can see the bottles of champagne chilling on the table. She feels a pang of guilt for dragging Sam from rehab directly into this world full of temptation.

"Don't worry, Sam. Leon's a little wild, but he's also a genius. Just let it happen. I promise you'll walk out of here looking like a new man."

"What's he going to do to *me*? I thought I was just here to hang out."

"I don't think you're going to get away with watching."

Sam leans in closer to Sky and lowers his voice.

"It's going to be pretty tight for me, financially, until I can get some work. My mom gave me a hundred bucks. That's all I've got."

"Don't worry about it. This stuff is all on the label. The clothes, the food, Leon, all the staff – it's all covered. Just enjoy."

Sam smiles. A smirk that slowly grows on his face until it stretches from ear to ear. An "I could get used to this" kind of smile. Leon screams at them from across the salon.

"Beauties! Get your hot, rumpled assess over here! We don't have much time before Birk swoops you away."

They follow his orders. The other clients stare as they walk by. Sam smiles at them. He has a natural ease, an innocence that makes his skinny frame and broad, coat-hanger shoulders even more enduring. Sky watches as he surveys the chilling bottles on the table when they pass it. He looks away. Leon sits them down and asks one of his assistants to run off and get them a refreshment. Sky jumps in.

"We have to stay sharp. Big days ahead. I'd love a Coke. Sam, do you want a Coke, too?"

"Yes, please."

Sam sounds relieved. Sky looks in the mirror and catches Leon's eyes, questions looming in his slightly raised browns. Sky holds his stare.

"Okay, then. Clean and sober it is. Just like angels. Let's get to work."

Sky nods to Leon gratefully, then sits back and lets him take over. The clock is ticking and everything is lining up for this moment she's wanted for her entire life. A song on the radio. An album coming out. Radio interviews where they ask her about her music.

Birk and Miko arrive at the salon just as Leon is finishing with her. Birk goes straight for the booze on the table and pours himself a stiff drink.

"Sky! You look exactly like the star you are. I love it. How're you feeling? How're the pipes?"

"Hey, Rod. Good. Ready to go."

Sky stands up and gives them both the obligatory kiss on the cheek. Sam comes out of the change room, the same expression of uncertainty on his face that Sky wore after her transformation. He's in new dark jeans and a tailored plaid shirt that accentuates his green eyes. His hair is cut and styled up, standing on end in some parts with a messy perfection Leon knows how to get just right. Sky feels a surge of gratitude that Sam is along for her ride. It's nice to have the company. He gets a look at himself in the mirror and his big smile comes back.

"Whoa. Is that me?"

"Looking good, Sam! I told you Leon knows what he's doing."

Leon's head snaps up from a conversation he was having with one of his assistants.

"Were you questioning my abilities? Puh-leeze."

He waves his big hand at them in dramatic fashion. Birk slides over to Sam. Sky has the urge to push him back a few steps. She doesn't want Sam to smell the booze wafting from Birk's stale breath.

"So, you're the famous Sam. Sky tells us you're quite the musician. We're looking forward to seeing you play. What's your last name, Sam?"

"Hi, Mr. Birk. It's Prince. Sam Prince."

"That has a nice ring to it. Call me Rod."

They shake hands and Sky doesn't like it. Sam is so young and innocent. Birk is the opposite.

"Well, you look great, Sam. I'm glad the label could do something for you, our gift. Sky's friends are our friends. Can I steal her for a few minutes?"

"Yeah, of course."

Sam looks to Sky for direction. Miko comes over, gives Sam a cool greeting, and puts her hand on Sky's arm, leading her to Leon's office. Sky glances back at Sam, who's watching Miko's ass walk away in her signature skintight skirt. He mouths the words *holy shit* to Sky, who laughs and shakes her head.

In the office, Miko lets her hand slide down Sky's arm. Birk didn't follow them. He probably made a U-turn to refill his always-empty glass.

"Do you want to get dinner tonight?"

"I can't, Miko, sorry. I've got Sam now. He's staying with me and it's his first night, so I can't ditch him." She feels relief as she tells Miko this. Birk bursts in before Miko can get pissy about being rejected.

"Stop eye-fucking each other and let's get these papers signed. Sky, Miko has some new contracts we need your signature on, now that we have most of the tracks complete."

He clears a place on Leon's large wooden desk, lifting up a red snow globe with a giant white penis in it. He gives it a shake and a flurry of silver penis-shaped confetti floats across the liquid sky. They all watch it fall. Birk smiles and puts the globe on a cabinet, sloshing his drink onto the ground. Miko opens the large case she's carrying and lays the papers on the desk. Sky wants to get away from both of them as soon as possible. She swallows and can't help but grimace at the taste and the burn. Birk notices her reaction.

"Fuck. That seems bad. Do you need more medication?"

"Yeah, I could use more, I guess. Lots of talking today."

"I think I have another bottle in the car; we'll top you up when we leave."

"Thanks. It was a big month."

"They're only getting bigger, Sky. I'm investing a lot of money, a lot of Space Monkey's money, on that throat. Make sure you protect it."

Sky ignores him.

"What am I signing?"

Miko still looks annoyed as she points to the colorful little sticker indicating where Sky's name goes. The pages are thick with print and the words are small. Birk hands her a pen.

"Standard stuff, Sky. Similar to what you've already signed, but we had to add in the new dates, which tweaked the numbers. You know, catalogue rights, here, and this line is for your touring financials. Ticket dollars go to pay for the venue, staff, security, opener, transportation, etc. All your needs. Any extra dollars go to the label to fund production of your album. That's it. All standard, no surprises."

He speaks so quickly Sky can barely make out what he's saying. Her instincts scream at her to take more time before she signs.

"Should I have a lawyer look this over?"

"Only if you want to make this complicated, and possibly delay your tour dates, which would be a nightmare for the label, and your reputation. Once the single gets radio play tomorrow, we'll follow it up with another, then announce the tour and drop the full album a few days before your debut show here in Vancouver. We booked The Vogue, by the way. Who gets to start their career by playing a show at The Vogue?"

Sky thinks this is hardly the start of her career, but Birk doesn't like to be corrected, so she stays quiet.

"We're starting you out with medium-level shows across Western Canada. Major cities, of course. Two nights in Vancouver, then Victoria, Calgary, Edmonton, Saskatoon, Regina, Winnipeg. After that we'll go east. St. John's, Halifax, Montreal, Toronto. Sound good?"

"Yeah, it sounds amazing." She swallows hard again, knowing she needs to put the brakes on, but she has no idea how to do that now. "And Sam will be a part of my band?"

"Sure. If Vince thinks he's good enough, he's in."

She hesitates. Birk is looking at her expectantly. She thinks of the paycheck that she needs to get her treatment. If Birk knew, if the label knew, about her cancer, this would all disappear. In less than a year the tour will be over and she'll have more than enough money to take a break and get well. In the meantime, she gets to release her album and go on the road with Sam and play her music. She's rationalizing it all in her head, exactly how she'll explain it to Jani and Joe. She's already down the road this far, how could she say no now?

Sky scribbles her name in the spaces Miko indicated with the stickers. Birk smiles and pats her on the back.

"Let's go have a drink. Celebrate!"

"Sorry, Rod, but Sam and I are going to take off so I can rest my voice. The car is coming at seven tomorrow morning, right?"

"Oh, come on, Sky. You just signed your tour contract! Don't be a tight-ass. One drink, and then home."

Sky will be glad when she's out on tour and Birk will be nowhere in sight. Just her and the band.

"Fine. One drink. Sam doesn't drink, though. He's in recovery, so can we have it in here?" Sky can't let Sam see her drinking, but she could really use one after dealing with Birk's slick talking and Miko's attitude.

"Oh Jesus. Recovering. Everyone's *recovering* these days. Wet fucking blankets. It better not be a problem out on the road. I don't want him killing your vibe, Sky. Fans want to see you having fun up there. You need to sell the dream and they need to buy into it. That's when they spend their money on merch and start bidding wars for tickets to your next show. Because they want a piece of what you have. Wearing a Sky Black T-shirt will mean you've been to a party. That T-shirt will say something about the person wearing it. It'll be a symbol of cool. But it starts with you, Sky, and its way more than the music. The music is just your way onto the stage."

Birk turns to Miko for her acknowledgement that everything he just said was the absolute truth. Sky can see through his greasy locks of hair to the prickly scalp beneath. It provokes a sudden urge to vomit.

"Miko, run and fetch Sky a secret drink. And fill this one while you're at it." He drains the last swallow, his magnified teeth pressed grotesquely against the glass, then he holds it up and shakes it at her.

"I'm not your fucking dog, Rod. I don't fetch," she quips, lifting her elegant middle finger to both of them. Then she leaves to get the drinks.

37. Just Fear

"Get ready Z95 listeners. I'm Jazzy B., it's the morning show, and we're back with a treat for you. As promised, new artist Sky Black is live in the studio to bring you her debut single, "Caged Bird." This is radio, so you have to take my word for it, but you will be VERY excited to check her out. I mean the song. Check the *song* out. Ha ha. Sorry Sky, I don't want to embarrass you but, well, you're hot! Let's just put it out there. She's hot, guys. Pics loading on my reels soon. Welcome Sky!"

"Uh, thanks, Jazzy. That was quite an introduction. I hope I can live up to the praise."

Jazzy's rambling on again and Sky has to pay attention. She can't believe this woman has the number one radio show in the morning.

"Oh, no worries there, Sky. Trust me. Even if your song sucks, you *definitely* won't disappoint in the looks department. So, seriously now, you're a new artist here in Vancouver and you just signed a deal with Space Monkey Records! Congratulations! You're a lucky girl!"

"Thanks. It's been exciting, although I'm definitely not a new artist. I've been playing for over a decade, in Vancouver, and all across Western Canada."

"Oh. Right. Sorry, I haven't heard of you before today, but I'm old and I'd rather Netflix it up with a burrito, you know? You feeling me out there, listeners? Going out to bars to hear a band? Forget it! I'd have to wear makeup and Spanx and talk to people. Screw that!"

She's laughing. Really cracking herself up. Sky can barely maintain a half-smile. She looks through the glass to Sam, who's cringing, but tries a hopeful expression when he meets Sky's glance, gives her a thumbs up like she's actually doing well. Birk's chatting with the twenty-year-old coffee-fetcher, not even listening.

"Okay, so maybe Sky doesn't agree…. Anyway, tell us about your song."

Sky clears her throat. She wants to make up a story that is nothing like the truth, but unfortunately, she's a little foggy and not that quick on her feet. Her mind has gone blank from the sheer torture of this conversation and this woman.

"Sure, well, it's the story of my childhood, I guess."

Jazzy moves her finger in a quick circle, signalling she wants Sky to say more.

"My sister and I kinda raised ourselves, after my mom left. I guess it's about that. My mom always seemed like a caged bird. One day she just flew away."

Jazzy B. looks up from her note card, wearing an irritated expression, panic flashing in her eyes. There's a silence, then she seems to realize she's not saying anything, either. She slips her radio personality mask back on, and springs back to life.

"Ooh. So sorry for you, Sky. And stay with us here, listeners! That's a bit of a downer for a Z95 morning, isn't it? Don't cry in your coffee, and please don't change that station. I've listened to the song, and I can vouch for my new friend Sky here, it's great. A little slow, but get out the tissues, it's a heartbreaker. Was it fun to record?"

Sky wants to crawl out of her skin.

"Well, it was very rewarding to work with Vince West, the producer. All the musicians who played on the track, on the whole album, were incredibly talented. So yes, it was a great experience."

Jazzy pays no attention to Sky's answer, looking over her shoulder and gesturing to the producer in the window.

"Well, let's give this a listen! And next time you come in, Sky, promise you'll bring us something a little more upbeat, would ya? Ha ha, kidding! Here it is, the exclusive world premiere for Z95 listeners, 'Caged Bird' by the finger-licking-good Sky Black!"

The guitar intro to "Caged Bird" fills Sky's ears. Her song is on the radio. It's in people's kitchens and their cars and in their headsets as they walk. But the way it was delivered to them, like she's some cliché Spears-like Barbie doll who's "new" to music, is making every muscle in her body clench. She can't take the fucking headset off fast enough. She has six more interviews just like this to get through and she can't imagine doing another one sober.

Sam is standing, his hands jammed into his pockets, face void of its regular shiny gratitude. Birk is turned to the side, smiling, as he hands his card to the coffee girl. Sky gets up from the desk. Jazzy B. is looking down at her notes for the next segment. Sky mumbles a thanks.

"Hey! You can't leave yet. We'll do a post-mortem when the song ends, and then I need a few intros for my show. The station would've put that in your contract. You know 'I'm Sky Black and you're getting Jazzy in the morning.' That kind of stuff. Just sit tight."

"No. Sorry, I have to go."

Jazzy's mouth drops open, like a sagging black hole, but Sky walks out of the booth anyway, past Sam and Birk, and out the door. She'll let Birk deal with the *post-mortem*.

After hours of conversations similar to the painful one with Jazzy-the-stunned, they arrive at the hotel where the launch party is being hosted. There's a giant lobby full of people waiting to speak to her. Sky walks directly to the private washroom next to the check-in desk, careful not to make eye contact with anyone, and locks the door. She avoids looking into the mirror as she leans over and fishes the mint container out of her bag. The one that's been screaming at her for most of the day. She pops open the metal top and dumps two of Birk's pills on the granite bathroom countertop, smashing them into a powder with the corner of her credit card, then she cuts two thin lines and without an ounce of hesitation sniffs one up each nostril. It burns so good. Like she never stopped doing this. Rubbing her nose roughly, Sky stands up straight and stares at herself in the mirror. Her hair and makeup are perfect, due to the ongoing touch-ups from one of Leon's cronies. If only people could see inside, where everything's a mess. The day has been endless and exhausting, causing her to strain her voice so hard she could feel blood trickle down the back of her throat. She didn't have a minute alone. People were always there and now her pain has gone past where she can manage it with anything but this. A direct hit.

Her thoughts become less frantic as the chemicals enter her bloodstream and she can hear sounds from the party. It's at a fancy hotel right on the water with wheat growing on the roof and rooms that cost a few months' rent for a single night. Birks's been bragging all day about the fact that Sky has a suite on the top floor. She doesn't care so much about the room, but she knows it has a full minibar and privacy and she'd love to go straight there and skip this whole thing, but she has obligations and responsibilities. She has to make a speech. Jani and Dave will be here, Jani with her new dress and unbridled excitement. She wishes desperately that Joe was here, but he's playing a show in Winnipeg. He offered to get a replacement, but Sky knows it's not that easy. Besides, he's coming to her first show next week. That's more important to her. Her lungs burn as she breathes and she wonders if she's having a panic attack. There's a knock at the door. She turns on the water full blast. Grips the counter. Swallows some water and another pill. Here it comes. Here it comes.

The relief is sweet and she closes her eyes to it, letting it wash over her like a hot shower. Her throat starts to feel fuzzy, or gel-coated, or not at all, and her lungs are open and it will be okay. She repeats this to herself, willing it to be true. *It will be okay.* Her fingers and toes tingle. She'll get through this night and pretend she doesn't have cancer so she can live the dream. Enjoy it. Except this isn't what she imagined. She wants the studio and the stage. The money, of course. She thought she wanted the attention, or at least the admiration. So quickly she's learning she was wrong.

There's another knock on the door. More persistent. Sky puts the mint container that doesn't contain mints back in her bag and unlocks the door. Jani.

"There you are! Sky, it's crazy out here! How are you? Oh my God, look at you! You look like a movie star! You're so tiny, Sky. Wow."

They both look down at Sky's barely covered body. She's wearing a black leather mini skirt, lace-up leather boots that curve over her knees and end halfway up her thighs, and a sparkly piece of gold fabric slung across her bony chest. Her skin is tanned and shiny, her thin arms and angled shoulders dusted with glitter.

"Hey, Jani! I'm good. Great. I just needed a minute. Of course, it's you who has to go and ruin it."

She brings Jani in for a hug and lets her sister grab on to her like she'll never let go, her fuzzy head resting just below Sky's ear. Her high is coming in warm waves and the hug is nice but tight and she needs a drink.

"Where's Dave?"

"He's out there, mixing it up with the industry folk. I think he's on his third beer. That might be helping. You know how shy he is around city people."

"Yeah, he's not exactly an extrovert. It's amazing he got the courage to ask you out. Hey, you look gorgeous, by the way."

Jani turns and they stand side by side in the mirror. She fluffs the skirt of her new dress. It's short and deep green. Strapless. She's so thin, but as they stand side by side, Sky can't help but notice they're the same size. An alarming observation, since she's been worried about her sister's diminishing body most of their lives. Jani stands a bit straighter and bends her elbows slightly, so her already bony arms look even smaller.

"Well look at us. Aren't we something."

"Yeah. I'm starving. Let's go find some food."

Sky turns abruptly from their disturbing image. She can't worry about her weight, or Jani's, right now. She has enough on her mind. She starts to leave the bathroom, but Jani holds her back.

"Sky, wait. I heard your song on the radio, like, ten times. I just, I'm so freaking proud of you." She gushes, the emotions making Sky squirm.

"Jani, please don't start crying. Thank you. Yeah, it's cool, right? Now come on, let's go."

Sky lets her sister trail behind her as she strides into the room, full of chemical confidence. People turn to look at her. Faces she doesn't recognize are smiling. The room breaks into applause and Birk is already on the small stage near the back with a microphone, calling Sky forward. She hands her purse to Jani. The people separate to make a path and now they're cheering and she thinks she might be dreaming. The drugs are making her okay with it all. She walks slowly, making eye contact and nodding hello. Smiling. She's soaking in the applause and it feels fucking great.

"Ladies and gentleman, here she is! Space Monkey Records is proud to present Canada's next rising star, Sky Black!"

They love her and she loves them all back. She loves everything. Birk hands her the mic and a small bottle of champagne, plunged from an icy vat, the condensation dripping from the smooth glass. Sky smiles and pops the cork. Everyone cheers. She brings it to her lips and takes a healthy swig. More cheering. It's icy delicious and it soothes her throat and she completely forgot for a second who she is. As her head comes down and she puts the mic to her lips to greet her new fans she finds the shocked faces of Sam and Jani, standing next to each other near the back of the crowd.

"Wow, thank you. I'm not sure what to say. Thank you." She holds the bottle by the neck and puts her arm behind her back. Knows it doesn't matter now. It's too late. Everyone's looking up to her for more.

"It's so nice to see everyone. I just want to give a huge thanks to Rod and John, and everyone at Space Monkey, for taking a chance on me. And to Vince West, and all the musicians at Harmony Studios, for helping me make a record I'm really proud of. I really didn't think this day would come, although I've dreamed about it for most of my life." Her voice breaks and she has to pause. "Enjoy yourselves tonight. Thank you!"

They cheer again. She hands the mic and the half-empty bottle back to Birk, who looks at her with a puzzled expression. She makes her way through the people, all wanting to talk to her. They pat her on the back as she passes. Touch her arms. Sam is trying to smile, but Jani isn't. She won't pretend. Sky goes to her first and hugs her. Whispers in her ear.

"It was one sip. I wasn't thinking. It's not a big deal. Relax."

Jani pushes her back and looks into her face.

"Be careful, Sky. You've worked so hard. Don't screw it up now. Promise?"

"Yes, I promise. Now go have some fun." She moves on to hug Dave, who's clearly oblivious to what's happening.

"Congratulations, Sky! The song sounds great. When it came on the radio your sister lost her mind!"

"Yeah, I can imagine. Have a good time tonight, Dave. I really appreciate you being here, and being so good to my sister." She pats him on the arm, moves on to Sam.

"Hey, Sam. How are you doing? It's a little wild in here."

"It's incredible! How are you?"

"I'm good. Don't worry about that…what happened on stage, No big deal. I barely tasted it."

"Of course. Totally."

Behind Sam all the big execs are standing in the corner and Birk is waving her over and she doesn't want to feel bad anymore.

"I better go talk to the suits. You guys have fun. Check out the table of seafood at the buffet. I spotted it from the stage – it's insane! I'll catch you later." She doesn't wait for permission.

The night is long and everyone wants to talk to her. Miko slides her a few vodkas that look like water and they make her feel loose and charming. She can talk to anyone. Eventually the people fade away and she starts thinking about her room again. About being alone. She walks around the edges of the dwindling party, avoiding Miko, who's chatting cozily with one of the suits. He's standing an inch from her face with his hand on her ass. Sky chuckles to herself. She hasn't seen Birk in a while and assumes he left with one of the waitresses he'd been talking to. Sam left, too, exhausted and thrilled to have a room all to himself. Sky takes the elevator to the top floor. As she turns the corner she sees a small figure on the floor, slumped against her door.

38. Dirty Paws

"Jani, wake up. What the hell are you doing? Are you lost?"

Jani's eyes jolt open and she stands clumsily, pulling her dress down so it covers her butt.

"No! I'm waiting for you, big shot. We need to talk."

Oh my God, not more talking. Sky can't do it. Every fibre in her body is exhausted. All she can think about is lying on the silky hotel sheets with a glass full of whisky.

"Jani, I'm all talked out. You have no idea. Tomorrow, okay? Go to bed. Where's your room? Where the hell is Dave?" She clears her throat loudly.

"I'm going, Sky, but I had to say this." She reaches out and grabs Sky's arms to steady herself.

"I'm worried about you. I don't like this whole scene. And I hate that Birk guy. He's a sleaze bag. This is too hard for your recovery. And what about your surgery? Did you forget you have *cancer*? Do I have to remind you of that little fact?"

She's loud and drunk and Sky wants nothing to do with this conversation.

"Shhh! Jani, quiet. This isn't the time. I told you, I'm tired."

"I know. I'm going, but not before I say this, because I know you'll have some excuse tomorrow and you'll ditch me and I don't know when I'll see you next." Her words are slurring into each other. Sky wants to put her hand on Jani's mouth before she says anything else. She knows what's coming.

"Sky, you made your album. Now you have to stop. You promised me that after you made the album, you'd get your treatment. You have to, Sky. Your cancer will spread and you could die! You're all I have and you could die."

She starts sobbing and stumbles. Sky links her arms around Jani's back and pulls her into a hug, partly to console her and partly to stop her from saying anything else. Especially that fucking word that makes her head scream. She lets Jani cry into her shoulder. She's right and Sky knows it, but she doesn't want to hear it.

"Okay, Jani, you said what you needed to say. I'm fine. I'm a big girl and you have to back off. You need to go to sleep. We'll talk about this later." Sky turns her by the shoulders and walks her down the hallway to the elevator. When the door opens, she shuffles her inside and takes her down to the lobby, because Jani can't remember her room number. They get the number and a new key card from the desk and go back up to the third floor, wrestle the door open, and find Dave passed out on the bed. Sky takes her little sister into the bathroom and helps her get her dress off, makes her drink two glasses of water, then puts her in the bed next to Dave, who moans about what an awesome time he had. Sky kisses Jani's forehead, wishing the night didn't have to end like this.

39. Roll the Bones

Birk can't believe what he just heard. He had to shush the coffee girl, who was nattering on about nothing. He'd invited her from one of the radio stations that day but he can't remember which one and he's not sure he ever got her name. He was fumbling for his key when he heard the elevator door open, and was trying to hurry her inside before anyone came by. There are only three suites on the top floor and Space Monkey booked them all, so the chances he was about to get busted were high. He assumed the girl was twenty, but he's been wrong before.

He was just slipping the key across the sensor when he heard Sky's voice from around the corner, trying to get her drunk sister off the floor. He held his finger to Coffee Girl's lips as the sister went off, slurring a scolding at Sky. Birk heard his name. She called him a sleaze bag. How dare she. She doesn't even know him. Then things got interesting. Recovery? Birk's been handing Sky pills like they're fucking Tic Tacs. But he's not surprised. Every musician he knows is in some state of failed recovery. Then he heard the word cancer. Treatment. That could be a real problem. If Sky quits before she tours, the label won't get the return on investment they expect from her.

The live shows are when they make the real dough. When they get the artist out of the cozy studio and make them grind a little. After a few months on tour they all call Birk up, crying about how exhausted they are, and pleading to take a break because they need some *self-care*. He pretends he cares. As long as the tickets and T-shirts keep selling, the label wants them on the road. But if Sky is too sick to tour it will look bad on Birk, and he doesn't need any more fuck ups right now. #SkyBlack is trending online and the single is already getting a huge buzz. Birk has to make sure he gets her on tour before her throat gives out. He just needs a year. He'll book more shows for her. Push her harder while he can. That's what happens when you keep secrets. When you try to pull something over on him.

He hears the sisters get into the elevator. His mind is spinning with phone calls he needs to make first thing tomorrow, but for now they'll have to wait. He pushes open the door to his room and takes Coffee Girl inside.

40. Hey Joe

"Sky, you're on in ten!"

She stares into the mirror. It's circled with bright lights that emit a scorching heat, like looking directly at the sun. In this light nothing can hide. The drops Miko gave her work like liquid eraser and the whites of her eyes are crystal clear. Her lips are painted with a dark pink matte lipstick. They feel dry and she wishes she had a tube of gloss, but she left it at the hotel. Someone would get her one if she asked, but she's savouring this rare moment of privacy. She can deal with dry lips.

She's been staying at the hotel since the launch party. Birk suggested the idea, saying it would be more convenient if they knew where she was whenever they needed her. She couldn't think of a reason to say no. The room is her sanctuary and she only has to pick up the phone to get anything she wants. The minibar keeps her in booze and Miko and Birk supply the rest. All the days bleed into each other and the only one she's been anticipating is today. Her first show of the tour.

Her full album, titled *Ghost Stories*, was released today. They did a photo shoot for the cover at the beach near Squamish.

Sky sat in front of a raging fire with her guitar and stared through the flames and into the camera. The smell reminded her of Joe, an intense ache for him forcing tears into her eyes.

Leon's team has outdone themselves tonight. She's wearing a heather-grey dress that looks like denim but is actually velvet. It clings to her body and stops well above her knees. The back is a series of criss-crossing straps, highlighting her tattoo. Her skin is its new shade of always-tanned and she wears delicate red and turquoise necklaces and bracelets. They gave her dangly earrings, but she's already removed them. They rattle when she plays. After much discussion she's been allowed to wear a pair of chunky black boots that fit under the "motorcycle boot" description. Not that you'd ever get them near anything with grease. At least they're comfortable and she can move around the stage in them, something she's been told she has to do much more of. "Give them a show!" is one of Birk's new mantras. "Let them see that body!" Her face is perfectly made up and she understands now why the people who are trained to apply makeup are called artists. Her cheekbones jump from her face and her lips are bold and pouty – although Birk has commented a few times that she should consider having them permanently plumped. Her eyes are like their own solar systems. Even Sky can't stop staring at them.

The band will be heading to the stage now and Sam is among them. He's been rehearsing at the studio with the boys and Vince is impressed with his raw talent. He's also taken Sam under his wing, and Sky's glad the pressure isn't all on her. She has enough to worry about, and it's hard to medicate herself appropriately with Sam always by her side.

Birk arranged to put Sam up at a crappy hotel near Vince's studio until the tour started. Then he had someone go over to Sky's apartment and clear it out, since she'll be on the road for the next nine months. Sky wanted to do it herself, but couldn't find the time. Now her old clothes and furniture are in long-term storage somewhere in the Vancouver suburbs. She has no idea where, or who has the key. She wishes she would've asked someone to pull out her old jacket and bring it to her, the one Jani bought her from the thrift store in Nelson. But it's too late now.

There's a knock on her dressing room door. She jumps from her chair, hoping it's one specific person and not any of the others.

"Yeah?" she asks from behind the still-closed door. If it's Birk there's no way she's letting him inside.

"It's me."

Sky flings the door open. Joe is standing in front of her. The sight of him, the sweet smile and comfort of his presence fills her with emotion. Tears well in her eyes and she doesn't dare try to speak.

"Hey, baby. Sorry, my flight was delayed, but I made it. Damn, you look incredible." He reaches out to her and she throws her body at his, burying her face in the cool leather of his jacket that smells like home. There are people milling in the hallway and she pulls him into the room and closes the door before anyone comes over to them.

"I missed you." Her words are muffled against his shoulder and she knows she's ruining her makeup but she doesn't care.

"I missed you, too."

He holds her until she lets him go. She looks up into his eyes and finds concern. She's not acting like herself and he'll know something's wrong. She wonders what lie is worse, that she's using again or that her cancer is worse than she told him, and she's scared. She wipes at her eyes, trying to collect herself because now is not the time for confessions.

"Sorry, I think it's the nerves."

"It's okay, I get it. You're going to be incredible out there. You know how you get before the show. You just need your guitar in your hands, and you'll calm down."

She has the urge to grab onto him and just run, down the hall and out the door, which is crazy, because this is the first show of her tour and she's worked so hard to get here. This is the fun part. She forces a smile.

"You're right. I know you're right." Before she can say anything else there's a knock at the door, then it opens, and Miko barges in.

"Hey, I…Oh, hi. You're obviously Joe." She says it with an edge of disgust, then holds out her hand to shake his like she's being forced to. "I'm Miko. I'm with the label."

"Hey, Miko. I'm Joe. I'm with Sky." He smirks at Sky as he says it and Miko scrunches up her face like she ate a lemon. Sky laughs.

"Hmm. Anyway," she turns to Sky, "they said five minutes and…what the hell happened to your face?" She doesn't wait for Sky to respond, just turns and yells into the hall. "Leon! Send someone for touch-ups, fast! She's a mess!"

There's a flurry of yelling in the hallway. Leon charges in with two of his assistants trailing behind, expressions of terror on their faces. Joe's eyes go wide at the sight of this giant man in a brightly coloured silk kimono and knee-high red-leather platforms. He ushers Sky back under the lights and they all gather around and talk about her like she isn't there. Joe moves to the side, bumping into the arm of a couch that makes a screech as it slides on the glossy floor. Leon screams, "Oh dear fucking God can we have quiet please people! The artist needs quiet!"

Sky isn't sure if he means himself or if he's referring to her. She catches Joe's eye in the mirror, who's trying not to laugh but also looks horror-struck by the whole scene. They're just dusting her with powder when the stage manager comes in to say it's time. Sky stands as everyone clears the room. She moves over to Joe and whispers to him.

"Here I go."

"You're amazing. I'll be side stage the whole time if you need me."

"See you out there." She moves towards the door, nerves prickling her skin like fire.

"Hey, Sky?"

"Yeah?"

"Have fun."

People line the narrow hall that leads to the stage. A few faces she recognizes but most she doesn't.

"Go kill it, Sky!" someone from the opening band says. Sky forgets their name but will have Birk remind her before she walks out, so she can thank them. Birk is waiting at the end of the hall. There's a flight of red painted stairs. The smell of cigarettes.

"Sky, this is it! First show of the tour. Are you ready?"

"What was the opener's name again?"

"Kit Wednesday."

"Got it. Thanks."

"Go be your amazing self. You deserve it."

"Sure. Thanks." She should say more to him, but she's not in the mood to be fake. The crowd is cheering and the band is playing and she reaches the top of the stairs and comes out to the side of the stage. She can see the people in their seats but they can't see her. There's a table of water bottles and she takes one and chugs half of it, watching as her talented band plays her music. She might throw up and she might fuck the whole thing up and in this moment she's so goddamn alive. She can't be dying when she's this alive. It's impossible. She puts the bottle down and walks across the stage to the mic.

"Hello, Vancouver!"

The crowd she's pictured in her mind for so long is right there and she soaks in their smiles and anticipation and energy.

"How are you guys doing tonight?" Sky lifts her guitar from the stand behind her and slings it over her head as they cheer again. She starts to play the intro to "White Lies," a cue to the band that they'll start the song in eight bars. She can hear Sam's guitar, clear and loud. She looks over her right shoulder to where he's standing, dressed in jeans and a fitted black leather vest over a white T-shirt, a wallet chain slung from his hip, black boots, and the most vibrant, shit-eating grin Sky's ever seen. He's having the time of his life and it's all worth it. Whatever happens from here, it's worth it. They nod to each other, artists-in-arms, about to go to battle. Sky looks to all the guys on the stage and they nod. Ready.

41. Stone

Birk watches Sky's show from side stage. They love her. They want to devour her like a piece of meat, and he can't blame them. She looks sexy as hell, her cordy muscles straining as she moves. He stands near her boyfriend, a big dude who's been standoffish with Birk so far. Miko said he's a musician, and Birk wonders if the guy understands who he is. How much power he has. As soon as he finds out, he'll be kissing Birk's ass, desperate to get his B-level band a deal, too. Fat chance. Birk doesn't like the arrogance of this guy. The way he made Sky cry right before her show, ruining her face. But he just nods and smiles, because he knows he doesn't need to worry. This guy will disappear, just like all the old relationships do when an artist goes on tour. Happens every time.

Since his recent discovery about Sky's cancer, Birk has renewed his resolve to get the big bonus he deserves this year, and when he does, he'll buy a house on the water with it. A nice place to retire. To do that, he has to turn Sky Black into a household name in six months. That means TV appearances. Awards shows. The Junos will be an easy get, but he wants to go bigger. American. The Billboards. AMAs. The Grammys. That's when he'll get the big dollars.

He's left a dozen messages with Walter Jones, the head of the biggest PR firm in LA. Walter represents everyone who's anything in music. He's a cutthroat asshole and his artists hate him because he tells it to them straight. He doesn't blow smoke up their assess, and they do what he wants, when he wants.

Walter has ins with everyone in the business and he makes people very rich. It's all about exposure and timing and getting four solid minutes on a major network production. Then being controversial. Like Janet Jackson and her perfect nipple at the Super Bowl. Miley Cyrus riding that foam finger and giving every man alive a craving for illegal ass. Give them something to talk about the next day. Be the headline, then let the tweens start buzzing about you. No one at Space Monkey can deliver that kind of maximum exposure. But Walter hasn't responded to the video of Sky that Birk sent him last week, so Birk needs to come up with something a little more dramatic to get his attention, and he better figure it out fast.

Then an idea hits him like a kick to the balls. He remembers some slurred wisdom whispered to him by a label exec he met in Nashville who was trying to save Jet Walker's career after he cheated on his wife. *When faced with bad press, use your weakness as a strength.* That's it. That's the way Birk can save this situation. It's so obvious he can't believe he hadn't thought of it before. He pulls his phone from his pocket and walks further backstage. Walter's assistant answers and he tells her it's absolutely urgent he speak with Walter immediately. Life and death. After a few minutes of shameless begging, she reluctantly patches him through.

"This is Walter; who the fuck is this?"

"Walter, it's Rod Birk, again. Space Monkey Records in Vancouver. Can I have sixty seconds?"

"Rod, are you fucking serious? My secretary said it was urgent. Urgent, Rod? You're lucky I'm stuck in traffic. I'm late for a dinner reservation and I'm fucking starving, and I've had an absolute shitpile of a day. Literally. My office parking lot has sewage backing up into it, and D-Rage is being a real bitch about his new album cover. This better be fucking good."

"Did you watch the video I sent you?"

"Jesus Christ. Yes, Rod, I watched the video. And I told you the last time you sent me a video of a hot chick dripping tears on her acoustic guitar, we have our own girls like that. A million of the them! I could hit an open mic on Sunset and find a clone of your girl in ten minutes. They don't sell."

"I know what you said, Walter, but Sky's different."

"I didn't see different. I saw a good-looking girl with a great vocal and a sad song. See it every day. Unless she happens to sing a fucking duet with Bradley Cooper, she's the same. Trust me. And the same doesn't sell concert tickets. The same doesn't make me money. Folk artists are boring to watch. They don't get people excited. I need to be excited. I need a show. Swift. Dua Lipa. Even Twain! Those girls know what's what. They stand out. Try Jake Boyd in Nashville. Maybe he'll look at her."

"Walter! Shut up for a fucking second and listen. I have a team working on her stage presence. She's strutting the stage in a dress the size of a fucking napkin as we speak, and she looks incredible. The crowd is going crazy for her. Her tour is selling out at a record pace. But there's an angle here. She's sick."

"Sick?"

"Cancer."

"Is it terminal?"

"Looks that way." Birk has to make this good. Dramatic. He pauses to glance around him. Makes sure no one's listening.

"She wants to go out with a bang, Walter. Wants people to know who she is, or was, I guess. She wants to die famous."

"Well fuck, Roddy! You should've led with that! THAT I can sell. Social media will eat this shit up. She wants to die famous! I fucking love it. How soon can you get her here?"

Birk organizes the details with Walter and hangs up the phone. He can hear Sky finishing "Caged Bird." The crowd roars in adoration.

42. Highway Boys

"This is fucking amazing!!" Sam yells into the theatre. He's playing his guitar like a man possessed, absolutely shredding. No one can hear him yell over the music booming from the amps. He can't even hear himself, but that doesn't matter. He just had to let it out. He looks around at the other guys on the stage. They all appear calm to the point of being unimpressed. The drummer is casually biting his lower lip, flipping his sticks between beats like they're on swivels attached to his palms. The bass and acoustic guitar players groove to their rhythm, each tapping a foot effortlessly. Sam tries to pull the corners of his mouth down into a concentrated artist's face, or at least some expression resembling cool, but he can't stop the smile that shows all his teeth, stretching to his ears like a giddy child. He's never had so much fun in his entire life.

Sky ends the song with a flourish, letting her guitar ring out to the crowd and jumping with two feet to emphasize the final word. She's so brilliant. Intoxicating. Sam always wants to be as close to her as possible. He loves it when he has her all to himself. When they're in the studio or go out to eat, just the two of them, she relaxes and lets her guard down more than with anyone else, except her sister. Those two seem to have their own language. But Sam's happy with second place and he'll do anything to keep it.

Sky picks up her water and takes a drink, turning to look at him as she does. When she sees his face, she laughs, spitting water onto the stage. From her reaction, Sam can tell he was unable to make himself look cool. Sky's eyes are shiny, sweat making her skin glow. She mouths the word *loser* at him, but she's smiling just as big as he is now. Sam can't believe how meeting one special person can cause your life to do a complete one-eighty. She turns to address the crowd and he looks out into it, too, trying to find Poppy and his mom. They're out there, somewhere, but it's a full house, which means more than a thousand faces to sort through. He gets stuck on one pretty blond in the second row who's looking up at him like he's God or something. She licks her lips and waves. Sam waves back at her, another uncool thing the other guys will bug him about later, but he doesn't care. They don't have cute blonds waving at them. He takes a step closer to the edge of the stage, as far as the cable attached to his guitar will reach. He hears the guys laughing behind him, but he just wants to soak in every second of this. He wonders if it's an even better view from where Sky gets to stand. She starts to play the next song and he joins her. She glances over and finds him almost beside her so she steps over and leans her back against Sam's shoulder. He was right. It's fucking beautiful up here.

43. Supernatural

Sky wakes up the morning after her first show to her phone beeping and ringing, overriding her *Do Not Disturb* setting. She checks the screen and finds multiple texts from Miko.

"There's a car downstairs waiting for you. Come to the office immediately. Birk is pissed about something."

Shit. What the hell could Birk be pissed about? The show was a huge success. The fans loved it. Sky was grooving with the band and especially Sam, who went completely nuts with his solo and got a standing ovation when Sky announced his name. Even from the back row they could tell he was special. Maybe it's good news and Miko's fucking with her, or it's nothing and she's just trying to disturb her morning with Joe, who's sleeping next to her, his body half-covered by the crisp white sheet.

Sky kisses him gently on the forehead, whispering that she'll be back in an hour. He mumbles something about coming with her, but she tells him no, she's just running to the office and she'll be back with breakfast. He kisses her and rolls over.

She has a quick shower, throws on some clothes, then finds her pill bottle in her purse and takes a few. She needs twice as many now to get where she needs to be. Not to be high, just to get out from under the pain. She grabs a coffee in the lobby. The girls behind the desk watch her, ready to deal with any request she might have. Laundry, food, toothpaste. They'd have her room filled with whisky and Sour Patch Kids, if she wanted.

"Good morning, Miss Black. Your car is waiting. Is there anything we can do for you while you're gone?"

"Hi. Yes, please. I'll be back in an hour. Could I get breakfast for two sent up when I'm back?"

"Of course. We'll have it ready. And…if you don't mind me adding, wonderful show last night. You were incredible."

"Oh, thank you."

Miko is standing in the lobby when she walks in to Space Monkey. She greets Sky like the frost queen she can be, sending air kisses to the area near her cheeks, without actually touching her. Sky walks to Birk's office without waiting for him to come out. Joe's waiting in her bed and she wants to spend every second she can with him. He has to fly out later this afternoon and she has another show tonight. She doesn't appreciate being summoned like this. She knocks once then enters the room. Birk's head is down, and Sky can see the oily balding patch on top, staring at her like an empty eyeball. Sky doesn't wait for an invitation, just steps forward and sits down in the same chair she sat in the day this all started. The picture of his son is back out on his desk. Birk looks up at her, he doesn't mince words.

"I know what's been going on."

"What do you mean?"

Her voice is thick and scratchy from the night before. The pills haven't worked and she should've taken more. Always more. She has to clear her throat and she tries to do it subtly, but it's impossible. Birk watches, a tiny curl raising his ugly lip.

"That. That's what I mean. You've been lying to me. To all of us. It's time to come clean. You're in breach of your contract, Sky. You signed on to play a full tour, stating nothing that you are aware of would prevent you from doing that. Are you going to be able to hold up your end of our deal, considering what's happening with your throat?"

Sky starts sweating. Panicking. *Fuck! How the hell did he find out?*

"Rod, I'm sorry. Yes, I have a bit of a throat problem."

"A *bit* of a throat problem?"

"I'm sorry I didn't tell you when we first met. I was still deciding what to do. I need to get some treatment, surgery, maybe, but it can wait until after the tour. That's why I didn't mention it. I'm here. I'm giving everything, at the studio, and now on stage. This won't affect our deal or the contract. After the tour I'll get treatment, and then we can record the next album."

"After surgery? Let's not get ahead of ourselves, Sky. What if it isn't that easy? What if your voice completely blows out on you?"

"Rod, I'm taking care of it. I haven't been out at night since the launch party. I'm taking a bunch of stuff from a naturopath. I can handle it."

"Handle what? What, exactly, is wrong with your throat? I need to know everything now, Sky, so I can try to spin this to the label. To John. We could both be out of a job if I can't."

Sky stares at him. Takes a deep breath.

"Cancer." She clears her throat again. She hasn't said the word out loud since she told Joe. "It's laryngeal cancer."

"How bad is it?"

"How did you find out?"

"It doesn't matter how I found out. I did. And we've just spent thousands investing in you and your album and booking venues and promotion for your tour. How will we recoup those costs if you're getting treatment?"

Sky wants to stand up and punch him square on the jaw. Send him flying off his fancy leather chair.

"It's not that bad, Rod. The doctor said I was fine to do the tour and get treatment afterwards," she lies. Can't help it. Always lying.

"This is why you consume a super-size bottle of oxy every week? Because it's fine?"

"It hurts, a bit. Yes, I'll admit that. But my voice sounds great, once I manage the pain. You can't deny that. And I've never wasted studio time. Ask Vince. I'm always ready and I'll be the same way for the tour. Don't worry about it. It's my problem, not yours."

"That's where you're wrong, Sky. All your problems are my problems. Because I own you. We own you. You signed a contract and committed to us and you were lying. That's my problem. What are we going to do about it?"

"Nothing. Just let me do the tour. When it's over, I'll take a short break and get treatment. No big deal."

"What if it gets worse?"

Sky hesitates. She doesn't have an answer, just a blazing headache. If Space Monkey drops her, after everything she's done to get here, she'll never get another label. Plus, she might have to pay back the advance, and probably get sued for the rest. She waits for Birk to offer up a solution.

"I have a plan, Sky. If you're sure you can make it through the tour, I think we could…"

"I can." She cuts him off.

"Fine. I'm glad you're so confident. But you don't know that for sure. We have to cover our bets. You chose to lie, now we need you to tell the truth. To everyone."

"What the fuck does that mean?"

"It means I want to make this information public. I want everyone to know you have cancer. That it's serious. I don't want the tabloids jumping to conclusions after you have a bad night and stumble on stage or something. Then we have to play catch up, try to convince everyone it's not just a run-of-the-mill drug problem. No, I want to take control of the information and deliver it our own way. I've called Walter Jones. He's the head of the largest PR firm in LA. He's going to handle the American side of this. Get the right message out. You know, something like, 'musician with cancer fighting for her one shot at fame.' Then we'll have you do a few exclusive interviews. Who knows, it might actually be good for your career! The eighteen-to-thirty demographic loves an underdog story."

Sky stares at the weirdly optimistic smile on Birk's face. He's enjoying this. He planned this whole conversation. A silence passes between them, a revelation of what their relationship really is. Sky is dollar signs and Birk wants to suck her dry. Sky is owned and she has no choice here. She's completely fucked. She stands up, like she always does when she's done with whatever shit life is throwing at her. She stands up and walks to the door.

"When will you release this? I need to talk to some people first."

"It's already done."

"It's done?"

"We released a statement an hour ago. Like I said. I have to get in front of it. Who knows when someone else might leak it? We had to be first. We didn't want ticket buyers getting antsy, either. They have to know you're going to be there. That the situation is tragic, of course, but also that we have it under control."

"Fine, Rod. Do what you want. Tell the world. I'll do the interviews. I'll tell the truth because I want to play music. But let's never pretend that our relationship is anything more than this moment."

Sky tears open the door and Miko is standing against it, listening. She stumbles backwards, eyes wide with this new information and how it might affect her. Maybe Sky won't look as shiny, to Miko or anyone else, when they find out she's sick. Maybe this is how it will end, despite Birk's efforts to spin it differently.

Sky rushes through the lobby, pushes open the stupidly large door, and stands on the sidewalk. It's a warm and beautiful spring day. People are carrying jackets over their arms. She breathes. It hurts. Her lungs feel heavy and little spasms of electric pain ignite in them when she inhales deeply.

Everything's about to change again. The secret she's tried so desperately to keep is about to be announced on every radio station as an introduction to her music. Posted on social media for people to comment on. The phone rings in her pocket. She starts walking in case Miko follows her. She doesn't want to see her face or any fake pity she might be wearing on it. Sky looks to see who's calling. Jani. Her timing impeccable, as always.

"Sky! I'm so glad you picked up! I thought you'd still be sleeping."

"No, wide awake. But if you thought I was sleeping, why the hell are you calling me?"

"Ha ha. I was going to leave you a message, asshole. You're such a jerk sometimes. Is that street noise I hear? Are you actually out in the world before noon?"

"I don't go to bed at nine like you, Jani." Before Sky can say anything else Jani cuts her off.

"I'm calling because I read the reviews from your show last night! They're so good! The *Vancouver Sun* called you 'the next hometown hero' or something crazy like that. Was it fun?"

"Yeah. It really was. I wish you were there."

"Me too! I was thinking I could get some time off and come to Calgary or Edmonton."

"Perfect. Let me know and I'll get you tickets." Sky pauses, dodging a crowd of businessmen and crossing the street.

"Jani, I need to give you a heads up about something."

"Uh-oh. What?"

"Well, I'm not sure how he did it, but Birk found out. About me…being sick."

"What!? How? I hate that guy!"

"I know. I hate him, too. But if it wasn't for him, I wouldn't have an album or this tour. So, we have to put up with him."

Sky steps around a few twenty-something girls grouped on the corner. When they notice her, they elbow each other. It's possible they recognize her – her face is plastered on billboards all over the city – but maybe she's just being self-conscious. She turns up the street and notices the girls start following behind her, pointing their phones in her direction. Jani is raging about Birk and doctor-patient confidentiality. Sky's not responding because it doesn't matter. It's too late.

She turns down the next street and walks back towards the water and her hotel. The girls keep coming and people are turning to see what they're fussing about. She hates this. It's dehumanizing. She feels rage. Injustice. She wants to melt through the storm drain. Wash away.

"Jani, I gotta go. I think people are following me. It's weird."

"What do you mean? Like paparazzi?"

"No, just people. They're recording me on their phones. I'll call you later, okay?"

"Fine, but I'm not done with this. We could sue that guy, for something. You should be able to keep this private. It should be your choice what information about your health is released to the public."

"I'm not sure I have choices anymore, Jani. I think I signed those away."

"Sky. Really, who cares what people know. You're starting your treatment soon, right? Just tell people that."

"Yeah, well, after the tour."

"Yeah, but Willa and your doctor both agreed that was okay, right?"

"Ummm…yes?"

"Sky! Did they?"

"Sort of, yes. I mean, I think they both would've preferred I start now, but a few more months isn't a big deal."

"Sky, if you're lying to me…"

"I'm not, Jani. I better go. Joe's back at the hotel."

"Does he know any of this? Or did you keep him in the dark, too?"

"Jani, I didn't keep you in the dark. You knew I had cancer. I told you, *both* of you, I'm getting treatment. Soon. That's all true."

Sky hears her sigh on the other end.

"I love you, Sky. Please take care of yourself."

"I love you, too, Jani. I will. Stop worrying, okay? Good chat."

She hangs up the phone and picks up her pace. The girls are wearing heels and they're struggling to keep up. Her hotel is up ahead and she can't wait to get back inside.

Sky reaches the lobby when her phone blows up. She sits in one of the large leather chairs near the wall so she can read what people are saying before she goes upstairs. People tag her with the headlines, asking if the rumours are true. "Sky Black Has Deadly Cancer," "Sky Black Has Terminal Disease," "Sky Black Chooses Career Over Treatment." They make it sound like she's about to drop dead at any minute – exactly how Birk scripted them, she's sure – because he loves the drama. And it's working. If people hadn't heard of her before, they will now. Texts start to come in from Sam and Vince and the band and people from high school and everyone at the label. She should explain, especially to Sam, but she has a show in a few hours and there's only one person she needs to talk to. She stands up and takes the elevator to her floor.

When she walks in, Joe is sitting on a chair by the window. He's wearing jeans and no shirt. There's a towel crumpled on the floor beside him. He looks up and she doesn't have to ask if he's seen it. His face is ashen, his eyes swimming with confusion and anger.

"Do you know about this?"

"Yes. I just came from Birk's office. Somehow…they found out. I have no idea how. He released it intentionally, to get people talking. It's for publicity, he said."

"For publicity? They're using the fact that you have cancer for fucking *publicity*? And they're completely exaggerating how bad it is!" He stands up, starts pacing in front of the window. "This is bullshit, Sky. They can't just release your medical information like this. It's private. You have rights."

"Not anymore."

"Yeah, no shit. What did you say to him?"

"I mean, I was angry, of course. But so was he. He said I'm in breach of my contract for not disclosing this up front. Since I didn't tell them, he said they can handle it however they want to."

"Fuck that. Even if you didn't tell them, it doesn't give them the right to just tell the world about your medical details." He's still holding the phone in one hand and Sky worries he might throw it at the window.

"I think it does, Joe. The alternative is they sue me. I'd have to give back my advance, which is already half gone, and maybe the money they've invested in me? I can't even imagine how much that is. Besides, I need my paycheck, so I can pay for all this treatment. It's not cheap."

"Why didn't you tell me you were worried about money? I can help you, Sky. You don't need these guys."

"Joe, come on. That's sweet, thank you, but Willa said her bill could be fifty grand. Do you have fifty grand?"

"Let me worry about that. Yes, I can get fifty grand if you need it."

"How the hell would you do that?"

"Sell the house."

"You're not selling your house for me, Joe. You love that house. I'll figure this out. I feel fine. I'm taking handfuls of supplements and stuff from Willa. She said it would build my immunity and make my body stronger to fight when I do the chemo. And honestly, I don't care who knows. In a way, it's a relief. I'll just go and play my music. It's only nine months. Then I'll take a break and do the treatment. Now that the label knows they won't try to extend the tour or put me in the studio right away. It's all going to be fine." She realizes she's used the word fine twice already. Joe looks skeptical, but he stops pacing.

"Sky, just tell me one thing, and be honest. Is your cancer as bad as these articles are saying? One has a quote from an oncologist saying throat cancer can be very aggressive, that it spreads easily. Did the doctor really say it was okay to wait? By the time your tour is over, it'll be almost a year from your show at the Imperial. That seems like a long time."

She exhales. They look at each other and even in those brief seconds he knows. She can see it on his face.

"How could you fucking lie about that?" He collapses back into the chair, dropping the phone to the floor, and putting his face in his hands. She walks over to him and kneels at his feet.

"It'll be okay. I promise."

"You can't promise that, Sky. Look at my mom. She promised, too."

"Joe…"

"Do you want to die, Sky? Because if you keep denying what's actually going on, you're going to. Is being on stage, and going on tour, and having all of this shit," he throws his hands up, gesturing to the fancy hotel room, "is it worth your life?" He's breathing heavily, his face softening as his anger shifts to sadness. Tears pool in his deep blue eyes. She looks up at him, her stubborn resolve weakening with every word he says.

"I love you, Sky. I want to marry you, and have kids, and teach them to play guitar, and catch fish, and ski, and…don't you want that, too?"

They're both crying now and she probably knew all of this but hearing him say it shatters her.

"Yes. Yes, I want that, too." Her voice is a broken whisper.

"Then quit. We'll both quit. Get your surgery and get all the treatment you need and get better. Please. Please." He picks her up off the floor and cradles her in his lap. Her tears fall on his chest and roll over the tattoo of her name.

"Joe…I can't. They'll sue me. We'll be bankrupt, and I can't get the treatment without money, and no – you're not selling the house. It was your mom's house and it'll be our home. This is months. That's it. Then we can do everything you just said." They hold each other and she presses her lips to his shoulder. He's silent for several minutes. When he speaks again his tone has changed.

"No, Sky. It has to be now. I'm not kidding. Now, or I'm walking away. I mean it."

She lifts her head from his shoulder.

"Seriously? You won't wait?"

"I'd wait for you to do anything, except kill yourself. I did it for years, it's a miracle you weren't successful, and I swore I'd never do it again. I love you too much, Sky. And you love me. Fuck all this. Come home. Be with me. Get better."

"Joe, I can't. Not yet."

He stands up with her in his arms, then sits her on the bed. She watches him collect his clothes off the floor, still lying where he threw them last night. He walks into the bathroom just as someone knocks at the door, startling both of them.

"Room service!"

Breakfast. Sky had forgotten she'd ordered it. It feels like that was a different life from this one. She wipes her face and goes to open the door, lets the young guy in a crisp uniform wheel in the table. He sneaks glances at her as she signs the bill.

"Thank you."

"You're welcome, Miss Black."

He leaves and Sky hears the water stop running in the bathroom. Joe comes out with his jacket on and his bag slung over his shoulder.

"Joe. Stop. Let's take a breath, for a second. Eat something."

"I can't. My flight leaves in a few hours. Good luck at your show tonight."

"You're really leaving? Like this?"

"I have to. Think about what I said, okay? If you change your mind, I'll grab a flight back and we'll go straight to your doctor's office. Or we'll call Willa. Whichever route you want to go. I'll be there with you. Every minute, every decision. I'll be there."

He comes over and takes her face in his hands, kissing her deeply. She can't breathe. The room is swirling around in her periphery and she has another show at the Vogue in a few hours and one in Victoria tomorrow night. People have bought tickets and the album just came out. She has commitments and promises to uphold. He has no idea what he's asking her to do, how irresponsible it would be to just disappear. People are counting on her. Sam. Sam needs this or he might end up back on the street. How can Joe make this so hard for her? How can he be so selfish?

"You don't understand, Joe. You just…you haven't been where I am. You don't get it."

He laughs sharply, hurt, like she intended.

"I get it, Sky. I might not have a big solo deal like you do, or PR people and stylists fawning all over me, but I understand what you'd be turning your back on. I know you'd be letting people down. But I also know what life is really all about. Trust me. You'll never be happy trying to satisfy this world full of fake people. No matter how good you are, or what an amazing show you put on, it'll never be enough. If your ego wasn't blinding you, you'd be able to see that, too."

"Fuck you, Joe. That was mean."

"It was mean. I agree. But I need to say something to wake you the fuck up!"

"I told you, I'm fine! It's not that bad!"

"Yeah, I've heard enough of that story. I gotta go. I love you. I'll wait for your call."

He turns and walks out the door. Sky stands frozen, the smell of warm bacon wafting through the air around her. This exchange has left her stunned, and pissed off, and so, so sad.

44. Younger Days

Nine Months Later

Sky rolls over and clutches a pillow around her head, trying to block out the screaming. Her thoughts are scrambled and her ears ring. It could be Saturday or Tuesday, it doesn't really matter because in this make-believe world she now inhabits everyone always acts the same.

And then it comes. A rush of terror or cortisol or something else vicious but invisible. It shocks her heart and creates beads of sweat in a rash across her skin. It's been arriving more frequently, lately. Unprovoked. She avoids the word "attack." It comes in a hard wave. Crashes on her. She has to move when it starts to flow so she jolts up into a sitting position. The threat feels real, like she might die. She wants to cower or scream, but the therapist said not to do that. Breathe slowly, he said. Just breathe. Like it's so easy. Sky sucks at the air, gulping, then remembers he said in through her nose, out her mouth. He said breathing through your nose sends a signal to your brain that you're safe. Nothing is threatening you. Sky wishes that were true.

She scans the tables on either side of the huge bed. They are littered with glasses and liquor bottles. A clear plastic cup with red lipstick left on the rim. A shade she doesn't own and a memory she doesn't have. She leans across the expanse of the bed and scrambles through the garbage, knocking it all to the floor until she hears the *thunk* of something heavier. Her phone. She reaches down for it and her throat screams in agony, parched and poisonous. In the rawness of the morning the death creeps further up, living closer to the surface of her. She wants to release a long stream of curses directed at her pain and her desperation but she can't. They fire off in her head because she doesn't speak now, unless she has to. Every ounce of voice she has is already earmarked for interviews and the stage. It's a very strange thing, not owning your voice. Makes you feel like you've gone insane.

As difficult as the last nine months have been, every time Sky walks on the stage and the ever-growing crowd starts to cheer for her, she feels weightless. Unburdened. She looks in their faces and watches their lips sing her words and it's so damn satisfying that for that blissful slice of the day, she gains the strength to persevere through everything else. It's a high she can't get anywhere else and even though Jani and Joe don't understand why she's doing it, it's worth it to her. One day she'll show her kids the videos of what she did, of who she was, and they'll be so proud of their mom. But she can't deny nursing her voice through a whole show is becoming more challenging. Last month the production team had to cut three songs from her set and increase her opener to an hour, and when she goes on there's always a backing track ready to be amplified, if she falters. A vocal therapist named Huey makes her sit in a hyperbaric chamber for thirty minutes before she begins to warm up. It looks like a little blue tent with a window in the front and Sky isn't sure it does anything, but at least no one can get to her in there. She watches the people enter and leave her dressing room, making her decisions for her. After the treatment she takes her meds. Some are refills of the remedies Willa gave her and some aren't. She doesn't even ask what they all are anymore, just swallows them with an icy Corona. Sky hasn't been to a doctor since she last saw Dr. Miller in Vancouver, so she doesn't know if the cancer is getting worse, or possibly spreading. She didn't want to know because it wouldn't make any difference. She said she'd finish the tour and that's what she's done. Jani gave up asking her to go get checked out again because she's sick of Sky getting angry as she gives her perpetual excuse, she's too busy and never in one place long enough to get the tests done. After the tour. After.

Sky brings her phone to life and scans through her texts from last night. Dozens of them. Many have the same message, "Good luck at the Grammys tomorrow!" That's what today is. Grammy day. She's performing a song. Birk and Walter are freaking out about every detail. "Caged Bird" is currently third on the Billboard Charts. It's been top ten for forty-two consecutive weeks, bringing the whole album with it. They released "I'm Going Down" as the second single, but "Caged Bird" has stuck. People can relate, they tell her. They post their sad stories on social media, linked to #cagedbird. So many souls feeling caged, or abandoned, or betrayed. Caught behind the wire. There's an epidemic and it starts with the person in the mirror and suddenly Sky needs a pen. Lyrics. Finally. Except she can't find one in all the garbage and it would make her head pound to get up and look around and then her eyes drift back to her screen.

She's been tagged in thousands of posts, her notifications say. She starts to scroll. People wishing her luck. A picture of her name carved into the frost on a store window. A tattoo on a female hip bone that says Caged Bird. She lays her head back down on the pillow.

Tonight, she's getting her four minutes on network TV, performing "Caged Bird" live. Millions will be watching and streaming the feed online. She's nominated for Best New Artist and Birk thinks the viewership could break records. Because of her circumstances. Because she might never be back to the Grammys again. Sky wonders if Birk hopes she keels over after she finishes the song and dies right there on the stage. What an ending that would be.

She flicks through the fake garbage texts, names that don't conjure the faces they belong to, looking for only two. Joe, always Joe, but she's barely heard from him since she called him last week and asked him to be here. Even though they're not on the best of terms, she can't imagine winning a Grammy and him not being there with her.

Sam is the other name missing from her texts. No word in two days. He wasn't at sound check yesterday, which is completely out of character, but Birk – in town for the big show – explained it away, saying security was so tight and maybe he lost his phone or ID. Sky had seven interviews and three pre-Grammy parties and Birk insisted she attend all of them, even though she couldn't speak after the interviews.

They played their last show of the tour in LA two nights ago. Sky wanted to disappear with Sam, but she got tied up with Birk and a shrill woman interviewing her and she was exhausted and thirsty and she watched Sam across the room talking to some guys from the crew. Then he was gone. Sky jumped in the limo with Birk and the PR people from LA even though she needed to get away from everyone who wanted something from her.

Sam usually checks in every morning, making sure he's up on the plan for the day and to weigh in on the always crucial choice of what food they should get delivered. Mostly to see if Sky is okay, because all the secrets are out now. Sam knows that Sky's using again. He's witnessed it all and he doesn't judge, despite Sky's broken promise to be his sponsor. With the medicine and the upcoming treatment, being sober doesn't seem worth it. She can't sing without the drugs and she's too wired to sleep without the whisky. Sam understands and few words were spoken about it. Slowly, Sky watched him fall, too. She warned Sam that if he got back into the hard stuff, Sky couldn't keep him on the tour. No track marks and no heroin. No meth. Sam shows up every night, ready to play. He's had offers from other bands, once Sky's tour is finished. Good bands. But he's also been writing and singing and he's great. Maybe not the vocal power that Sky has, but he's got the truth. That's worth everything.

There's a spot reserved for her at the Mayo Clinic in Arizona next week. Birk is spouting off about the best care money can buy. The catch – and of course there is one – is that he wants to let some American film crew make a documentary about the whole ugly ordeal. She lets Birk think it's happening to avoid his incessant talking. She told Joe about it, and even though he thinks it's fantastic that she could get such great treatment for free, he thinks the idea of filming it all is crazy.

As she got closer to LA and her Grammy date, the screamers started to come. They stand outside of her hotel room so she can't sleep and they hold up signs when she drives by in the limo that say things like Don't Die Yet; Get Well Sky; God Loves You, and on, and on. That's why they're so fascinated with her. Because she's fleeting. She's a shooting star and she's burning out.

She finishes scrolling through the last two days' worth of messages. Nothing from Sam. She types "Hey, buddy. Where are you? Call me," then throws the phone on the bed and steps over to the window. She peaks through the heavy black curtains, designed to hide the fact that the day started long ago.

In the courtyard below her room is a large pool. It's brilliant blue and looks like a piece of the sky. Three men work around its edges, sweeping and picking up errant leaves from the surrounding trees. On the other side of the legendary gates of the Chateau Marmont she can see a slice of the cars streaming along Sunset Boulevard. Could Joe be in one of them? Sam? An empty hotel room has to be the loneliest place on earth, Sky thinks, letting the curtain fall closed and flopping back onto the bed.

Jani and Dave are arriving sometime today, but Sky won't see them until after the show. She's looking forward to being with people who make her feel normal, even if her sister is furious with her and Sky will have to hear all about it. She's restless and she picks up the phone again. Her mind refuses to be still, it's always looking for a distraction. She's startled from the screen by loud knocking, punctuated in the gaps by the sing-song voice she's grown to enjoy.

"Sky!! Wake up you gorgeous human, I need to get my hands on you immediately! We have soo much to do my dahling! Grammy DAY!"

Sky considers grabbing a sheet to cover herself up, but they've seen it all before. She crosses the room in her panties and opens the door to the massive travelling entourage Leon brought to LA. She's tired of being alone and in her head.

45. Angela

Birk grabs another glass of champagne from an overflowing tray. Even for him, the energy in Sky's room is too much. He told Leon not to hold back today, give it everything he's got. She needs it. Lately, Sky looks like a corpse after her shows. That won't work for tonight, not with twenty-six cameras and angles so close they can see a fallen eyelash. All Birk has to do is limp her through this night. One more performance. It's network TV for Christ's sake. It's everything. Sky can drop dead after this, if she must, and Birk will still come out a winner. He wants to send a giant bouquet of flowers to Walter's office with a card that says, I TOLD YOU SO, MOTHERFUCKER! Not very professional, but who gives a shit. He chugs the champagne as he steps out of Sky's room, raising his eyes to see Vince staring at him. Startled, he backs up into the door.

"Hey, Vince, you scared me, man! Why are you lurking out here? How are you? Nervous? You've got it in the bag, baby. Trust me"

Vince doesn't respond, his expression reeking with judgment, making Birk feel like he's talking too much or too fast. What the hell does he expect? The guy never says a word.

Birk has to carry the whole conversation. He wants to tell Vince to just fuck off, but he can't risk it. Not yet. Vince is nominated for Producer of the Year and Birk's hoping that if he wins, he'll mention him in his acceptance speech.

"I'm waiting to talk to Sky. Do you know when she's going to be ready?"

Birk's mind fires through excuses, reasons Vince can't see Sky now. He doesn't want any thoughts going into Sky's head today that he doesn't pre-approve. He's having people stationed by her side right until the second she steps on stage, just in case.

"I'm not sure, Vince. She has a lot going on. And you know women, so obsessed with every little thing. Can I get a message to her? Something you want me to tell her for you?"

Vince stares him down. Unflinching.

"No. I'm worried about Sam, but I'll speak to her myself when she has a minute."

They keep eye contact until Birk weakens and breaks it off. Vince has had this attitude since he found out that Birk leaked the news of Sky's cancer on purpose. Birk doesn't know who told him, but it doesn't matter. It was the right call for Sky's career and no one can deny it. Fuck Vince and his high-and-mighty attitude.

Birk needs to make calls and take a shit and maybe have a puff to calm himself down. It's already two o'clock. They completed sound check yesterday but they have to leave soon. Traffic. Walter used his vast network of connections to get Sky on the red carpet thirty minutes before show time. It's a coveted spot. Enough time to do a few interviews with the major networks and personalities, but still have to be rushed in right before the show starts. Only the biggest stars have to be rushed in. Birk needs to confirm everything else is ready to go. Deal with this annoying Sam problem. Sam being MIA isn't the worst thing to happen today, in Birk's opinion. He can be a distraction. He's a little too good looking and goes too far with his solos. Birk doesn't want anything on that stage that steals the attention from Sky. She's the star. The only problem is, Sky loves the kid. He's like her little sidekick. Sky won't be able to focus tonight if she thinks something's wrong with Sam. He probably just went on a little bender. It happens. But if he's not here and ready to play then Birk needs to find a way to spin it to Sky. At least until the performance is over. He doesn't care what happens after that.

He makes himself take a step. He'll text Leon as soon as he gets to his room and tell him not to let Vince see Sky.

"Sure, Vince, that's fine. Wait all you want. You should probably get yourself to the Staples Center soon, though. The traffic will be a nightmare and they want all non-performers off the carpet by four." He made a point of stressing "non-performers." Hopes it stung a little. If Vince is going to give him attitude, he can dish it right back. You never made it, Vince. You're just a producer. No one gives a fuck about producers.

Birk smirks to himself as he turns and walks down the hall. He feels like he got one up on that self-righteous bastard, but then he hears Vince chuckling behind him. Birk digs his manicured fingernails into the palms of his hands and starts plotting. He doesn't need Vince. He'll have every producer in the business wanting to work with his artists after tonight. He won't be disrespected in this business ever again.

46. Find My Footing

"Seriously, Leon, give me my fucking phone. Now."

Sky's not supposed to be speaking but she doesn't give a shit. Her voice is a pitchy whine, a new version of broken that would be alarming if she really thought about it. Right now, she's focused on Leon, who's been playing a game of keep-away with her phone. It was fine, for a while, a nice break even, but it's almost time to leave and she doesn't know if Sam's texted or what she'll do if he doesn't show up. Where the hell could he be? There's no way he'd miss this if he was okay. It might be the last time they play together. How will Sky even begin to find him? Leon recognizes now that Sky's quickly losing her patience. He signals to one of his ever-changing assistants. The frightened millennial pulls the phone from an iPad case he was carrying and hands it to Leon.

"Alright, sweetie. Don't get too excited. I don't want you sweating. You'll get all shiny. Birk is completely savage today; he doesn't want you distracted, so if he finds out I gave it to you tell him you found it on your own and I spazzed out but you didn't care. Something like that."

Sky grabs the phone from his outstretched fingers and wobbles slightly as she scrolls through the texts. Jani wishing her luck. Freaking out about her giant hotel room. Her mom, sending "love and light." No Sam. Leon tells her she should sit down, asks if she's eaten anything today, but Sky doesn't acknowledge what he said. She messages the rest of the band on the group text they use for their daily itinerary.

"Hey, have you guys heard from Sam? Is he with you?"

She waits. Watches the three little dots circle.

"No. Nothing. We're backstage at the venue. If we see him or hear anything, we'll text you. Scott can take the solo in case he doesn't show."

"Okay. Thanks."

Should she call Sam's mom? Sam will be choked if he shows up and Sky got his mom worried for nothing. He hasn't spoken about her lately and Sky doesn't think they communicate much. There's a loud pounding on the door and Birk charges in. His suit is navy and classically too tight and Sky's sure it cost thousands of dollars. Leon and the team circle around him, brushing non-existent lint from his shoulders and pulling the fabric, searching for a spare inch that doesn't exist. He waves his hands at them like they're a swarm of bees and steps past, walking over to where Sky is standing, her contraband phone in her hand. He gets close to her and holds on to her arms, forcing her to look up. Sky has an urge to thrust forward and drive the top of her skull into his face. Break his nose. She shrugs off his hands and steps backwards, putting as much space between their bodies as possible.

"Sky, this is it. This is your moment. Everything we've worked so hard for is here. You'll be one of the biggest stars in the world after tonight. You ready? I know you're ready. Don't answer. I'm saving you."

"Have you heard from Sam?" She hates wasting words on Birk, but no one seems to be worried except her and it's really starting to piss her off. Birk's eyes dart to the side. Searching.

"No. But this sort of thing happens, Sky. It's LA. Guys get with a girl and maybe take something too strong and they go radio silent. We have contingency plans for this. Scott's ready to play Sam's solo and we'll have a studio guy stand in for Scott. No one will notice. It's all good. Just focus on yourself."

Sky pushes her hands into Birk's chest, sending him stumbling backward. The room goes silent.

"Fuck you, Rod. It's not all good. Sam is missing. Something might be wrong. He might be dead or lying in a ditch and I have no way to find him. He's my responsibility. This is bullshit! I'm about to call the cops, and I might not have time to get to the stupid show tonight, so you better start taking this seriously. Get some people looking for him. Call the crew and find out who he left with Friday night. Now!"

Spit explodes off her words. Birk says nothing, seemingly shocked that she pushed him. He pulls his phone out of his pocket and dials. Starts speaking to someone, asking the questions he should've been asking yesterday. Leon and the team are quietly gathering all their products and racks of clothing and scurrying out the door. Birk gets off the phone. His tone and demeanour are drastically different. Sky knows it's not that he actually started caring about Sam, but if Sky doesn't show up tonight, Birk would be laughed out of the business. Walter would probably consider having him killed. Sky holds all the cards here and they both know it.

"Miko is on it. She'll call the crew manager immediately and follow the trail. We'll find him, Sky. I can't promise it will be before you go on, but we will find him. She said she'll text us with updates as soon as she has them. The car is waiting downstairs. Let's get moving. If he's going to show up anywhere, it'll be at the venue. I have extra passes set aside for him with security, in case he's lost his. Leon is bringing his clothes. It'll be okay."

"Fine. But I want to know everything you know. Immediately. If I find out you filtered any information from me, I'm done. Got it?"

"Of course, Sky. I would never. He's my friend, too. Let's go."

47. Ho Hey

The Grammy red carpet reminds Sky of the annual Winter Carnival parade that used to thunder down Nelson's Main Street when she was a kid. Jani and Sky would walk for an hour, leaning into the bitter wind, across the orange metal bridge and up to town, with holes in their boots and fingers freezing, to watch the floats go by. And get candy. Candy was the primary mission and it wasn't a casual one. The parade was at night and the adults would spend the afternoon drinking in the beer garden. When the first bars of "You Shook Me All Night Long" wailed into the crowd, they roared with appreciation and pushed out of the wooden fence that kept them corralled. Local people rode the floats dressed as furry animals and ice fairies, sports mascots, and Sasquatches. Kids would line the slushy edges of the road, pushing in closer to the pylons, jostling for the best position to receive the handfuls of lollipops and wrapped toffee that were tossed into the air. Sky and Jani would stand together and scream in unison when anyone on a float even glanced in their direction. *Over here! This way!*

This is the scene that lays before her now. The voices of photographers and autograph seekers yelling those same taunts

– over here! this way! – seep through the darkened windows of the limo. Sky waits in the car until the organizers with radios decide it's her turn to step out. The security is like nothing she's ever encountered. They stand two deep, shoulder to shoulder, lining the street and the entrance to the mayhem. The air conditioning is cranked in the car, but she's sweating in the cobalt blue backless dress Leon finally decided on. Birk natters to the two assistants he's scooped from Leon's team about EXACTLY where and how they should stand, the interviews Sky should accept, and which ones to avoid. Sky ignores the conversation. Her mind is lost at home. At the parade. The photographers on the carpet shove each other and then scowl and swear if they're bumped by their equally desperate colleagues. The artists are lost in the mob. The crowd breaks from time to time and Sky recognizes faces. Shawn Mendes. Katy Perry. Anthony Kiedis. They face the festering throng of reporters with waxy smiles, taking the one or two steps afforded to them when the carpet clears. It's absolute madness. Their assistants hold phones and water bottles, necks strung with lanyards clipped to laminated passes, trying to make space for the lavish outfits they wear. Fluffing skirts and straightening ties, their faces are creased in concentration. Sky watches a frantic guy with a pincushion on his wrist reach in and snag the gum from Carrie Underwood's mouth. She's a pro and doesn't even flinch.

Sky's managed to avoid walking a red carpet until now, too busy with her tour to attend the movie premieres and charity events she gets invited to. As bad as she imagined it would be, this looks worse. It's not about the music or the artists. No one cares what answer she'll give to the questions. It's about what she's wearing and who she might step out of the car with.

Security knocks twice on the window. Sky exhales sharply, then swigs the last of the Corona she'd been drinking. She's taken enough medication to numb her throat but not her mind. She hopes. It's a fine line.

Birk is so fired up he's vibrating. Dark-coloured sweat drips from beneath his slicked hair.

"It's time, Sky. Show the world how a rock star owns a carpet. Make them go crazy."

The assistants, a boy and a girl who both look twenty and terrified, slide down the long leather seat and knock twice back. The door opens and the crowd starts to scream, even though they have no idea who's about to exit the car. It's close to show time so it must be someone big. The assistants are adorned with their passes and water bottles. They smile at Sky uneasily. The girl stops moving and puts her hand tentatively on Sky's arm.

"If you need me to interrupt an interview that isn't going well, put your hand behind your back. I'll be watching you and I'll pull you away. Good luck."

She's sweet and seems genuine. Sky is embarrassed that she doesn't know her name. They rode for an hour in the car. She was six feet away from her the whole time. Why didn't she care enough to ask?

The crowd is in an absolute frenzy now. The anticipation killing them.

"Wait until they announce you," Birk commands.

He's moved right next to Sky, peering out the window over her shoulder. He smells of weed and nerves.

"Back off, Rod."

Sky clears her throat. She wants to slide under the car and run. She promises herself she'll never do this again. She will never put herself on display like a goddamn peacock, ever, ever, again. An unseen announcer's voice booms over the screaming. Her head spins and she remembers she didn't eat anything and maybe that's why she feels so detached from reality.

Get ready for the artist you've all been waiting for! Nominated for Best New Artist, and a performer tonight, it's SKY BLACK!!!!!

The chorus from "Caged Bird" blasts through the speakers. Sky feels like she might pass out. Birk shoves her from behind and says something ignorant. Sky feels like she's underwater. She's moving in slow motion and the air is thick. She can't get a full breath into her lungs. She stands. The crowd is screaming. Always screaming. It sounds like terror, not love. She raises her hand to wave and finds the Corona bottle still there. She didn't even feel it. She takes a swig but the bottle is empty. Pretends it isn't. Throws it back into the open car door where it might've hit Birk. Hopefully. She forgets what the assistants look like. Feels disoriented. Everyone's smiling and yelling. She wants someone to take her hand and lead her through this. Verbal instructions aren't enough. Not for this. Security is moving the bodies that are in her way and touching her exposed back with their powerful hands and she keeps smiling but she can't walk and all her instincts want her to run. Just get the fuck out of here. Instead, she smiles and pretends. The assistant girl's face appears from the mass and she screams at her.

"Sky, step this way! We have to get to NBC in thirty seconds. They're live."

She makes a small space with the boy and Sky slides through it. The people go wild again. Because she's moving? There's no reason. No rational thinking. Only chaos. She makes her way through the bodies. Strangers reach out their hands and touch her like they're old friends. She keeps smiling. Reaches the bright lights of a small raised platform. The host is familiar. She looks like wax and has two people brushing her hair and dusting her powdery forehead with more powder. Sky steps up and the lady spins to face her and her lips go from neutral to a strange, pinched grin.

"Sky Black, right?"

"Uh, yes."

"Great. We're live in seven seconds. I'm Marcy Mathers. I'm sure you know that, but make sure you use my name in the interview."

She's all business. Rude, even. The lights get brighter and the large camera focuses directly on Sky's face. She tries not to squint into it. The tiny woman steps beside her. Their shoulders touch. Even through the multiple layers of perfume and hairspray Sky can smell the woman's sweat.

"And we're back! I might be the envy of every man in the stands right now. I'm here chatting with my gorgeous new friend, Sky Black!"

Roaring. Screaming. She looks at Sky with a giant, warm smile. Completely transformed.

"Sky, it's so wonderful to see you here, looking so healthy and up for Best New Artist! I hear you're walking away from your tour to begin treatment for your well-publicized battle with throat cancer, treatment that may leave you without a voice. How are you feeling about that?"

The question winds her. Her skin prickles with a cold chill. Over the woman's shoulder she can see Birk, his fingers pushing at his cheeks, gesturing wildly for her to smile. His actions are so exaggerated it reminds Sky of the Joker. She needs space. She steps back, making a larger gap between them, then looks over at the lady's big fake smile and glaring white teeth. The clock is ticking and she can see everyone behind the camera starting to panic. She forces herself to speak.

"Uh, well, yes. I completed the tour, and now I'm going for treatment. I feel great, thanks." She forgets the woman's name and the sign she's supposed to use so the assistant girl will rescue her from this little platform. A flash of irritation crosses through the interviewer's tightly pulled eyes. That wasn't enough. Sky's not playing along. She wanted emotion and a sound bite about her pain.

"Well, that's fantastic to hear, Sky. You'll have the thoughts and prayers of a nation with you, as you go into treatment. Your country loves you, clearly." She raises her hand to the crowd and addresses them, hoping to find her emotion somewhere else. Already writing Sky off.

"Don't you love her? Let's show Sky Black some love!" The camera pans over as the people get their cue and call out her name. Hold their Get Well Soon signs higher. The camera comes back and the woman's face has transformed again. Sympathy. She glances at the card a producer holds up.

SKY BLACK.

BEST NEW ARTIST.

CANCER.

SONG: CAGE BIRD

ALBUM: GHOST STORIES

"Do the doctors think you'll be able to perform again, Sky? It would be an absolute tragedy if you couldn't. We're all waiting for you to follow up your hit, 'Cage Bird.'"

She holds the microphone an inch from Sky's mouth, waiting for some pitiful reply. Sky's entire body is reacting to this bullshit. Something snaps inside. Sam is missing and no one cares and this lady is trying to corner her to get a scoop. She doesn't give a shit if Sky ever sings again. She's never heard her music and she doesn't even have the right name for her song. Sky's brain swims in thick confusion, struggling to remember how she ended up here. She knows it was her choice – she wanted this – but she can't figure out why. She can see Joe's face, and all the agony he felt, when he said he wanted to marry her. That he didn't want her to die. But she let him walk out the door and it might've been the biggest mistake of her life. In this chaotic moment she knows all the rush and joy she gets from the stage isn't enough to make this worth it. It's just not enough. The fake lady is waiting for an answer.

"I don't know if I'll be able to sing again. I'm not sure if I want to. I'm kind of over it, to be honest."

Marcy's famous mouth hangs open for a second, then she collects herself enough to ask the follow-up.

"You're *over* it? Over what, exactly?"

"All of it. This fake bullshit and rude questions from reporters like you about my private life. People who call themselves my fans screaming at me all the time. Wanting more. If people like my music, that's great. But that's all I'm offering. I don't owe you anything else, and I'm sick of the expectation that I do. You don't get to ask me about my life. Ask about my music, and I'll answer. Come to my show and maybe I'll tell you why I wrote a certain song. It stops there."

Sky turns away from her shocked face and looks right into the camera.

"Sam, if you're out there, call me."

It feels so good to speak her mind. Sky turns to step off the platform. The assistants are standing behind her, eyes wide and all colour drained from their faces. They're probably terrified about what Birk will do to them. Sky has to get out of here. She's disgusted by these arrogant people and all the cameras and frenzied worshipping and the vile hierarchy of human worth she is a part of. But she forgot something. She'll never forgive herself if she doesn't say it. She turns back and grabs the microphone out of Marcy's shaking hand. The producer has jumped up from his knees and is waving frantically for her to cut.

"One more thing. This isn't my country. Canada is my country."

She shoves the mic back and steps off the platform, but there's only air. The people are moving in a brightly coloured heap, all fuzzy and connected to each other like they're one thing, and then the red carpet reaches up and clobbers her.

48. So Long, Honey

Joe's seat is at the far left of the stage, fifteen rows back. He's been sitting in it for more than an hour, watching as musicians he recognizes from magazines and album covers file in. Most of them look miserable. Uncomfortable in their own skin. Wearing ridiculous outfits and adorned with jewels and tattoos, eyes darting around the room to make sure people are watching. Or not watching. It's hard to tell which and it seems either option makes them uneasy.

His ticket arrived in a glossy FedEx envelope last week. Sky said she was sending it, and even though they fight almost every time they talk these days, he promised her he'd be here. How could he miss her big moment? The stage is massive and people run back and forth across it, testing lighting and microphones. Large screens scroll through all the nominees for the evening. In her photo, Sky's face is steely serious, her chin raised slightly. She's so gorgeous it stings.

Two skeletal women in glittery dresses and orange skin stumble down the aisle and sit in Joe's row. Their perfume and energy form a toxic cloud and he puts his head down, trying to breathe through the offensive fog. They chat loudly and rudely about other people, pulling their phones from tiny purses and scrolling, commenting on the comments. The section they are sitting in required showing a backstage pass, and for a brief second he wonders which artist they're connected to, then just as quickly decides he doesn't care.

"Oh my fucking God, look what Sky Black just did on the carpet!"

Joe can't help himself. He looks over, but the image on the screen is too small.

"Holy shit, it's already going viral! You know I've always hated that fake bitch Marcy Mathers; she asks the most boring questions. But still, Sky really gave it to her! She'll get destroyed over this! Hilarious!"

They begin typing at a frenzied pace and Joe can't help but stare at them. He wants to rip the phones from their hands. What did Sky do? He manoeuvres his own phone out of the pocket of the suit he borrowed from his bandmate, and googles her. The story comes up after he types the S and the k.

"Sky Black goes ballistic on the Grammy red carpet, tells Marcy Mathers to screw off, and declares the US is NOT her country!"

"Sky Black loses her mind, and her American fans, at the Grammys."

"Sky Black collapses at the Grammys, taken away in ambulance."

Joe jumps up from his seat. He has to find Sky. He turns to the girls, who are hunched forward, blocking his way.

"Excuse me; can I get through?"

They look up from their screens, annoyed that they've been interrupted from their feverish texting, then lean back slightly so Joe has to step over their purple, swelling feet. He dials Jani's number as he walks out of the giant theatre.

"Jani, did you hear?"

"Yes, we're outside now but we can't get a cab. Dave's on the street trying to get killed, by the look of it." She lowers the phone and yells at Dave, *They won't stop there! What are you doing?!* then brings it back up to her mouth. "The parking lot attendant said to go to Cedars Sinai. That's where they're taking her. We'll meet you there. I'll text you if I get any more details. I'm trying to get a hold of that idiot, Birk, but he won't pick up. She'll be okay."

"Of course she will. Thanks, Jani. I'll see you there."

Joe exhales sharply as he pushes through the crowded lobby. He considers saying a prayer, but it's never helped him before. He pictures Sky's face, holding the image in his mind, until he can get to the real thing.

49. And If Venice Is Sinking

Birk locks himself in Sky's dressing room and opens the chilled bottle of celebrity-endorsed tequila. He promised the company that Sky would be photographed drinking it after she won her Grammy, for a large kickback, of course. He takes long swigs. They loaded Sky onto a stretcher and carted her away in the ambulance that the Grammy producers pay to have idling in the parking lot, in case anyone ODs. Despite his frantic request that they give her an IV and try to revive her first, she's on her way to the hospital. It's over. In the space of a two-minute interview, Sky ruined what Birk had worked his whole life for. Walter and John call and text him relentlessly, making demands he's incapable of delivering.

Walter Jones: "Just get fluids in her and get her on the stage! We'll release a statement saying she has a brain tumour. Marcy Mathers is such a wrinkled old cunt. She's through. She'll never get a table in this town again. I hear her kid's nanny will sell dirt about the husband. I've got people on it right now."

John Westlake: "Where the fuck are you, Rod? Call me back! If she doesn't go on, Walter is already threatening to sue! She'll be fine; she probably just overheated. Stall. Tell the producers she's on her way back to the venue."

John Westlake: "Your assistant has informed me Sky's been replaced by Kiesza. FUCK. How could you get her this close and then drop the ball? We'll talk when you return; don't count on having a job."

Chaos is unfolding in the hallway. People scrambling. Swearing. The band is knocking on the door, demanding to speak to him. Asking if Sky is okay. If he's heard anything. Birk ignores it all. Sweat drips from his brow and when he wipes at it dark streaks of hair dye mark his hand. He checks his email. Charlie said he'd be watching the show, and Birk promised that after the craziness let up a little, he would take Charlie and a few of his buddies to a Canucks game. Box seats. That got Charlie's attention, but there's no new email wishing him luck tonight. Birk has to find a way out of this building. Maybe he'll get a flight to somewhere tropical. Thailand or Fiji. Where the girls are young and the drinks are cheap.

The band yells obscenities at him, calling him a coward, then everything gets quiet. On the monitor in the dressing room, he watches Kiesza flawlessly execute her performance. Birk takes the half-empty bottle of tequila, opens the door, and slinks down the hall unnoticed.

50. Hurt

She hears his voice first. He's talking to someone across her body or over her head. His words sound far away and she can't make out what he's saying. She fights with her eyelids, desperate to lift them, but they're so heavy, almost like they've been taped closed. She wants to scratch at her eyes until they open, but her hands won't move, either. She starts to struggle, moaning, but no sounds will come out, like a nightmare. *Is it a nightmare?* Panic burns through her. Then she feels him, so close to her, whispering in her ear, his face touching hers.

"It's okay, Sky. Shhh. It's okay. Lie still. It's me. It's Joe. I'm here. Jani and Dave are here, too. You're in the hospital. There's a tube down your throat, helping you breathe. You won't be able to talk. Can you open your eyes?"

She tries again and after a few seconds the light starts to flutter in. Objects slowly define themselves. A chair in the corner. Bodies. The metal rails of the bed. There's a large window. The sun is shining and it's very bright. Burning bright. Joe is above her, leaning over her body. He smiles down at her and she tries to smile back but she feels crunchy plastic against her lips. She looks into his eyes. Tries to relax. Joe's here.

"Hi, beautiful. It's nice to see you. You scared me." He moves to the side and Jani's curly head appears from behind him.

"Hi, Sky! I'm so glad you woke up. You're going to be just fine. They have amazing doctors here and they're going to make you better."

Tears are running down Jani's cheeks as she talks, her eyes wide like a child. She wipes her face and Dave steps to the end of the bed, jostling for a spot in Sky's field of vision.

"Hey, Sky. We love you." He chokes it out and then disappears again. Jani reaches out and touches Sky's cheek.

"Sky, the doctor said we shouldn't overwhelm you, so Dave and I are going to get some coffee, then we'll trade off with Joe. Okay? Oh wait – don't try to answer! He said not to speak with the tube in. They're going to take it out in a few days, when you're strong enough. Then they're going to do your surgery, but we can tell you all about that later. You just rest now. We love you. You're so brave. We're so freaking proud of you! The whole country is proud of you, Sky. You really told that lady off. You're a meme!"

Dave whispers something to Jani like *not so loud* or *calm down* and she snaps back at him. They leave the room, and Sky feels a wave of exhaustion settle on her. Fragments of what Jani said flash in her mind, but she can't remember exactly what happened. She remembers she was at the Grammys. Almost. She doesn't know how she got here from there, but she doesn't care. Joe pulls up a chair beside the bed. He lifts her hand, something she couldn't seem to do herself, and holds it to his face. Kisses it. She wants to tell him she was wrong and that she loves him and she can't wait to start their life together, but by the look on his face she thinks he already knows.

"I'm so sorry I was a stubborn asshole all year. I'll never forgive myself. You needed me, and I wasn't there. I won't make that mistake again." He rests his head on her hand. He seems exhausted, too. Just as she's about to drift off he squeezes her hand and speaks again.

"Hey, I talked to Vince. He came by, but they wouldn't let him visit until you're stable. He told me to make sure you knew that they found Sam. He's in this hospital, too. Just a few floors down. He ODd, but he's going to make it. I'll go check on him when I leave here. I'll tell him you're awake."

Sky tries to smile. Tears slip from the sides of her eyes. Sam's okay. He's okay. Her eyelids flutter, the room flashing from light to dark.

"One other piece of good news, baby, then I'll let you sleep. You won a Grammy! Best New Artist. You won, Sky. You did it."

She drifts off, wondering if she even cares.

51. Feels Like Home

Joe pulls the navy-blue robe from the chair it was draped over. He looks through the large window of his cabin, along the path of stones laid flat to protect her feet, and out to the calm water. Night comes earlier now and he can see the first star taking its place over the darkened mountains across the lake. It's the end of August, and when the sun dips low there's a cool bite to the air. The promise of a change coming. It nudges you, a reminder to soak in all your favourite parts of summer before they disappear. August days bake the lake in the hot sun. The water becomes pond-still and the top few inches are warm. The spaces between your fingers glow white as you glide out towards the darkness on the other side, where nothing lights the shore but the odd passing train. The stillness broken only by the loons flapping their wings and diving down for their supper.

He crosses through the kitchen to collect her hot tea from the counter, steaming the smell of cinnamon into the soft light. A long row of orange bottles stretches out beside it, each wearing a bright white label with thick black letters directing dosage and side effects. Behind the row are several vials containing homeopathic tinctures, the labels scrawled with

Willa's bubbly cursive. Joe looks at the clock then checks the chart secured with a magnet to the fridge. Thirty minutes. He picks up the tea and walks out through the sliding glass door to the beach.

Joe is now well-schooled in cancer drugs and their side effects and the pain killers that addicts must avoid. Once a week, Willa delivers the natural tinctures that are supposed to help build Sky's immunity and alleviate her discomfort. After speaking with the oncology teams in LA, and Vancouver, Jani, Dave, and Joe decided that doing Sky's treatment in Canada would make more sense, physically and financially. When she was ready to be moved, they medevacked her to Vancouver. Joe rented an apartment and sat by her bedside through multiple surgeries to remove the tumours from her vocal cords and several that had metastasized in her lungs. There are more, but her body was frail and the doctors are hoping the chemotherapy and radiation might shrink them. Joe tries not to think about the numbers. The odds and the counts and the levels. There are so many and they mean different things and he can't ride the roller coaster up and down all the time. What he knows for sure is that he loves her, despite the fact that right now he's more nurse than lover. Sky's voice is reduced to a whisper and she barely eats. Her hair is gone. The doctor isn't sure if her full voice will come back. There's a lot of damage and scar tissue. When she's naked in the bathtub she looks like a ghost. He wraps her with the soft, thick towels he bought when she agreed to come and live with him so he could take care of her.

After five long months in Vancouver, they drove home with the few items Sky wanted to salvage from the storage room, stacked in the back of his truck. Mostly books and folders filled with songs. Her guitar. She sat next to him wearing her old leather jacket, knees pressed against the glove box. He carried her inside and she sunk into one of the leather chairs in the living room, then looked around with a gentle smile on her face. His worn hardwood floors, marked with the familiar trails of his mother's feet, were layered in dust.

Now he makes his way to the edge of the dock and sits, letting his feet dangle an inch from the water. He places her tea beside him and watches as Sky's head dips below the surface of the water, then re-emerges. She's moving towards the darkness. She swims every night since they arrived, a month of reprieve before another round of treatment. She struggles to get down to the shore, but she won't let him help her. At night they sleep side by side. The medications cause her to thrash and sweat. Joe lays his hand solidly on the small of her back. When the sweating turns to shivering, he moulds his body to hers, absorbing what cold he can.

He has the urge to call out to her, but she slides back under the water. He wants to scream, loud enough so she startles and turns back. It's time to take her meds. Time to warm up. He whistles instead, but she lies flat. Still. The stars grow thicker, their glow reflecting off the water. Her head disappears beneath the silky black surface and he waits, holding his breath and counting off the seconds, until she reappears.

52. Do It All Again

Two Years Later

He's not the headliner. For tonight, he's just the opener, but he has to start somewhere. The Key City Theatre in Cranbrook seats about six hundred, and the place is full. The show starts in three minutes and they've already flashed the lights. The excitement of the fans, many wearing City and Colour T-shirts, is palpable.

He leans forward and peeks out from behind the side-stage curtain, looking to the three seats he'd placed on hold at will-call. Fifth row, right, on the aisle. From his vantage point he can't see if they're occupied. Sky's guitar is waiting on the stage. A guy from the theatre asks if he's ready and he can only nod, a flurry of nerves temporarily silencing him.

Inhale.

Exhale.

Again.

It's okay.

Most of them aren't here to see you, anyway.

He's played for crowds ten times the size of this one, but not from centre stage. His set list is short, just six songs. The guy that's supposed to introduce him is on the mic talking about the new renovations the theatre has just completed. He lands on a plea for donations, which gets crickets, then circles back around to his introduction and the fact that he used to play with Sky Black. The crowd erupts into cheers. Show time. The house lights drop.

He steps on to the stage and they get louder. It feels so good to be here again and he lets it soak in as he walks to her guitar, throwing the familiar strap over his head and moving up to the mic, swallowing the surge of longing that threatens to break him anytime he touches the smooth leather. He smiles. They cheer. It's a great relationship to be a part of and he wants to play his very best for them.

His tuning pedal is lit up red, indicating the guitar is muted to the audience. He plugs in and looks down at the display on the small screen as he plucks each string, turning the pegs until the note rests right in the middle. The seconds feel like hours and he wishes he could come up with some casual banter as he goes through this process, but he's way too sober to attempt it. He completes the ritual and stomps the skinny metal button with his sneaker, bringing the guitar to life.

Even though he can't see their faces, he looks in their direction and finds bodies filling the seats he'd reserved: two large and one small. They're all here.

"How's everybody doing tonight?"

The crowd whoops and whistles. He starts to strum, gliding his pick over the metal strings as he plays the intro progression to his newest song, "She Let Go."

"Thanks for coming out. It's gonna be a great show."

The guitar resonates throughout the theatre with a full, woody tone that hushes the lingering voices.

"I want to thank Dallas Green and the band for asking me to join them for this tour, and all the nice people at the Key City Theatre for their hospitality. I'm going to play some new music for you, songs I've been working on over the last couple of years. It's been quite a journey, and I need to shout out my mom and little sister, Poppy, for being such a support for me." He can hear Poppy giggle at the sound of her name.

"And thanks to my good friend, Joe Slater, for coming up from Nelson to see the show. You've been like a brother to me, man. I wouldn't have made it through all this without you."

He backs off the mic, his throat clenching with emotion.

Breathe.

He continues playing her guitar, feeling her presence all around him.

"This performance is dedicated to the most extraordinary person I've ever met. She picked me up when no one else would. She gave me hope and inspiration, and I loved her so much." His voice breaks and he wants to stop talking, but he has to say her name.

"Sky Black, I miss you every day."

The crowd claps respectfully. He can't see Joe's face and he's glad because they've cried so many tears together and he can't do that now. He has a show to do and if Sky were still alive, she'd tell him to take all the pain he's feeling and channel it into the songs, just like she did. He leans back into the mic.

"I'm Sam Prince."

THE END

Acknowledgements

I have a picture of a colourful bird on my office wall with the words "Trust the Journey" scrawled beneath it. I've looked at it more times than I can tell you. Sometimes it motivates me, other times I swear at it. Loudly. This journey has had moments that were difficult to trust, taking me places I never dreamed possible, both joyous and painful. As this novel is about to leave the nest, I can only continue to trust that this final reinvention of a story that's lived with me for so long is the one meant for you.

Thank you to the wonderful people in the communities of Fernie and Cranbrook for the support you've given me as a writer, and a musician with Wild Honey. You continue to show up and encourage local artists and we thrive because of you. The people I surround myself with, my family and close friends, are absolute gold. I love you all fiercely, would defend you to the end, and appreciate your long hours of listening, laughs, advice, and encouragement through it all. You never gave up on me, so I never gave up on this dream. A special shout out to the Newfies, The Bombers, and my parents – Don and Sally Cain – who found a way to instill me with the absurd amount of confidence I require to keep pursuing my crazy dreams, and a soft place to land every time I fail.

My agent, Hilary McMahon, with Westwood Creative Artists. You believed in Sky before she even existed, but more importantly, you believed in me. Thank you for your pep-talks and suggestions that made One Night Only truly sing. I can't wait for the next one.

I want to thank Mark Kusnir. Fuck, I wish you were here to celebrate this in person. I have your notes in all the margins and endless emails of encouragement that I will never stop reading. Your belief in this book, making sure I got the tough stuff right, your vulnerability and honesty when I needed it, and your passion for music made this story what it is. I miss you all the time. Your wicked sense of humour and horrible language and your deep, desperate love of writing is legendary. Just like you.

Fernie Mountain Writers Group – Nic Milligan, Gord Ohm, Denine Milner, and Shane Bryson – you've read all the versions of this book over the last few years, standing with me through the victories and defeats. We're an unorthodox group of ruffian-poets, all tethered together with the same desire – to inspire, to challenge, to be better. Always better. To your point, I love you all.

When I struggled to write this novel, it always came back to the music. This story is a celebration of music and musicians and the beautiful process of watching it all come together. Of how much it means to us all to be able to create it. If I mentioned you in the large collection of artists highlighted in this novel, you've inspired me. You are a part of the soundtrack of my life and your art means something to me. Thank you.

Barney and Kath Bentall, thank you for listening. For sharing. For making us all feel like we can do anything we set our minds to, and for the stage to do it on. Barn, your generosity and trust made all the music possible.

Wild Honey. My chosen sisters. Over a decade, and we continue on for one simple reason: we love to be together. I've had some of the best moments of my life with you two flanking me. It was never easy, but always thrilling. What we did?! My deepest gratitude for always having my back and believing in me way more than I ever believed in myself.

Sloan and Riley. My girls. There aren't enough words. I'm so proud of the young women you've become. I literally burst with it every time I see you. I love spending time with you. I love our laughing fits and lake days and all the subtle ways that you are. I can't wait to see what the future holds for you both. Thank you for always giving me five more minutes, listening, and for all the wishes you used up hoping we'd get here. We made it, and we did it our way. My heart explodes with love for you two.

Steve. Thank God for bars and last call and one last dance. For locking eyes. For knowing. My journey was always leading straight to you. You stand back and let all the light shine on me. There's so much of you in this book I wouldn't know where to start. We got the dream and I don't know why we were so lucky but it makes everything else seem like it's worth the risk, because I always get to come home to you and the girls when the day's over. Love you.

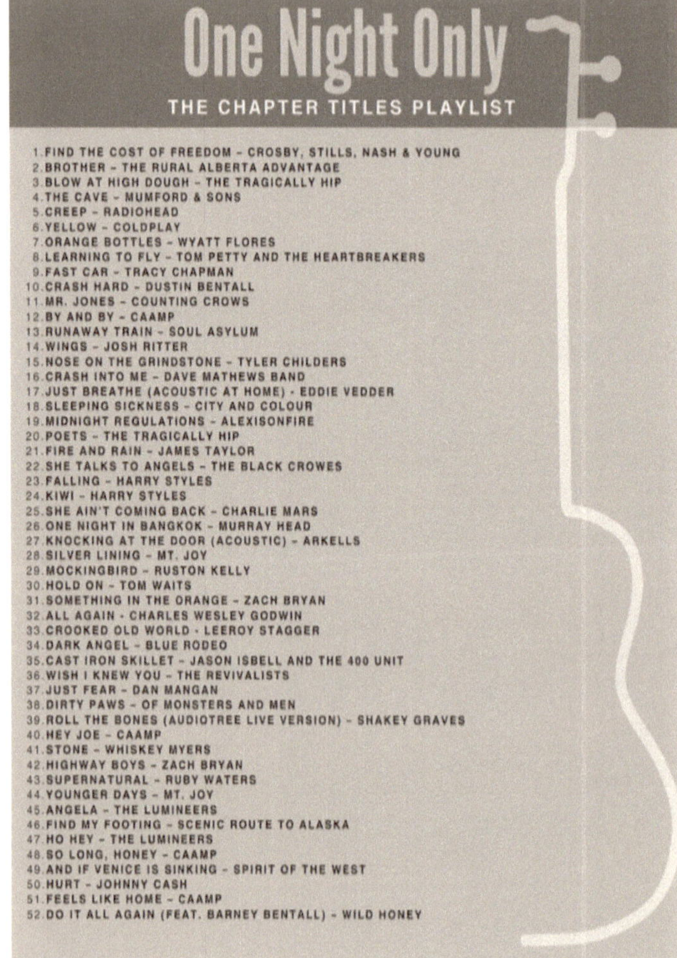
One Night Only
THE CHAPTER TITLES PLAYLIST

1. FIND THE COST OF FREEDOM - CROSBY, STILLS, NASH & YOUNG
2. BROTHER - THE RURAL ALBERTA ADVANTAGE
3. BLOW AT HIGH DOUGH - THE TRAGICALLY HIP
4. THE CAVE - MUMFORD & SONS
5. CREEP - RADIOHEAD
6. YELLOW - COLDPLAY
7. ORANGE BOTTLES - WYATT FLORES
8. LEARNING TO FLY - TOM PETTY AND THE HEARTBREAKERS
9. FAST CAR - TRACY CHAPMAN
10. CRASH HARD - DUSTIN BENTALL
11. MR. JONES - COUNTING CROWS
12. BY AND BY - CAAMP
13. RUNAWAY TRAIN - SOUL ASYLUM
14. WINGS - JOSH RITTER
15. NOSE ON THE GRINDSTONE - TYLER CHILDERS
16. CRASH INTO ME - DAVE MATHEWS BAND
17. JUST BREATHE (ACOUSTIC AT HOME) - EDDIE VEDDER
18. SLEEPING SICKNESS - CITY AND COLOUR
19. MIDNIGHT REGULATIONS - ALEXISONFIRE
20. POETS - THE TRAGICALLY HIP
21. FIRE AND RAIN - JAMES TAYLOR
22. SHE TALKS TO ANGELS - THE BLACK CROWES
23. FALLING - HARRY STYLES
24. KIWI - HARRY STYLES
25. SHE AIN'T COMING BACK - CHARLIE MARS
26. ONE NIGHT IN BANGKOK - MURRAY HEAD
27. KNOCKING AT THE DOOR (ACOUSTIC) - ARKELLS
28. SILVER LINING - MT. JOY
29. MOCKINGBIRD - RUSTON KELLY
30. HOLD ON - TOM WAITS
31. SOMETHING IN THE ORANGE - ZACH BRYAN
32. ALL AGAIN - CHARLES WESLEY GODWIN
33. CROOKED OLD WORLD - LEEROY STAGGER
34. DARK ANGEL - BLUE RODEO
35. CAST IRON SKILLET - JASON ISBELL AND THE 400 UNIT
36. WISH I KNEW YOU - THE REVIVALISTS
37. JUST FEAR - DAN MANGAN
38. DIRTY PAWS - OF MONSTERS AND MEN
39. ROLL THE BONES (AUDIOTREE LIVE VERSION) - SHAKEY GRAVES
40. HEY JOE - CAAMP
41. STONE - WHISKEY MYERS
42. HIGHWAY BOYS - ZACH BRYAN
43. SUPERNATURAL - RUBY WATERS
44. YOUNGER DAYS - MT. JOY
45. ANGELA - THE LUMINEERS
46. FIND MY FOOTING - SCENIC ROUTE TO ALASKA
47. HO HEY - THE LUMINEERS
48. SO LONG, HONEY - CAAMP
49. AND IF VENICE IS SINKING - SPIRIT OF THE WEST
50. HURT - JOHNNY CASH
51. FEELS LIKE HOME - CAAMP
52. DO IT ALL AGAIN (FEAT. BARNEY BENTALL) - WILD HONEY

SHELBY KNUDSEN has been a member of the all-female band Wild Honey for more than a decade. Her first novel, Mountain Girl, was an intense thriller about forbidden love and captivity. She lives in Fernie, B.C. with her husband and daughters.

Contact: www.shelbyknudsenauthor.com